Sharon Kendrick once won a national writing competition by describing her ideal date: being flown to an exotic island by a gorgeous and powerful man. Little did she realise that she'd just wandered into her dream job! Today she writes for Mills & Boon, and her books feature often stubborn but always *to die for* heroes and the women who bring them to their knees. She believes that the best books are those you never want to end. Just like life…

Cathy Williams can remember reading Mills & Boon books as a teenager, and now that she is writing them she remains an avid fan. For her, there is nothing like creating romantic stories and engaging plots, and each and every book is a new adventure. Cathy lives in London. Her three daughters—Charlotte, Olivia and Emma—have always been, and continue to be, the greatest inspirations in her life.

THE SHEIKH'S SECRET BABY

SHARON KENDRICK

CONTRACTED FOR THE SPANIARD'S HEIR

CATHY WILLIAMS

MILLS & BOON

First Published in Great Britain 2019
by Mills & Boon, an imprint of HarperCollins*Publishers*
1 London Bridge Street, London, SE1 9GF

The Sheikh's Secret Baby © 2019 by Sharon Kendrick

Contracted for the Spaniard's Heir © 2019 by Cathy Williams

ISBN: 978-0-263-27331-1

MIX
Paper from
responsible sources
FSC™ C007454

This book is produced from independently certified FSC™ paper
to ensure responsible forest management.
For more information visit www.harpercollins.co.uk/green.

Printed and bound in Spain
by CPI, Barcelona

THE SHEIKH'S
SECRET BABY

SHARON KENDRICK

This book is for Elaine 'Lainey' Glasspool,
who not only has the sunniest smile,
the most Rapunzel-like hair and a spirit of *joie-de-vivre*
which is positively inspirational, she also knows
a wagonload of facts about horses.

So thanks for all the equine help, Lainey!

CHAPTER ONE

IT WAS THE LAST place he'd imagined her living.

Zuhal frowned. Jasmine? *Here?* In a tiny cottage in the middle of the English countryside, down a lane so narrow it had challenged the progress of his wide limousine? The woman who had loved the sparkle and buzz of the city, hiding herself away in some remote spot. There had to be some kind of mistake.

His frown became a flickering smile of anticipation. Not that he had given a lot of thought to her accommodation. If ever he'd stopped to think about his lusciously proportioned ex-lover—something he tried not to do, for obvious reasons—then it had usually been a predictable flashback to her soft skin. Or the tempting pertness of her breasts. Or the way she used to rain kisses all over his face so that his heart used to punch with pleasure. His groin, too.

He swallowed.

And that, of course, was the reason for his unexpected appearance today. The reason he'd decided to drop in and surprise her.

His throat dried. Why not? He liked sex and so did

Jasmine. Of all his lovers, she had been the one who had really lit his fire. Sparks had flown between them from the start and it seemed a pity not to capitalise on that explosive chemistry with a little trip down memory lane. After all, it wasn't as if either of them had entertained any unrealistic expectations. There had been no dreams to be shattered. They hadn't asked for the impossible and had known exactly where the boundaries lay. They had conducted their affair like adults. What possible harm could it do to revisit the past and revel in a little uncomplicated bliss at a time in his life when he needed some light relief like never before?

He felt the smile die on his lips as part of him questioned the sanity of revisiting the past—and a woman— like this. Because he never went back. If you reignited an old relationship, then a woman could almost be excused for thinking it meant more to you than it really did…and no relationship ever meant more than sex to Zuhal Al Haidar.

And since Jazz was realistic enough to accept that, maybe this one time he could be excused for breaking one of his own rules, because destiny was leading him down an unwanted path—a path which had altered his whole future. Silently, he simultaneously cursed and mourned his foolish brother, but all the wishing in the world wasn't going to bring him back, or rewrite the pages of history which had changed his own destiny. He wasn't going to think about that. He was going to concentrate on Jasmine Jones and her soft body. To have her obliterate everything except desire and fulfilment. He was growing hard just thinking about it, because she was the sweetest lover he had ever known.

He stepped over a cracked flagstone, through which a healthy-looking weed was pushing through. It had crossed his mind that she might have replaced him in her affections during the eighteen months they'd been apart, but deep down Zuhal refused to countenance such a scenario—mainly because his ego would not allow him to.

And if she had?

If that were the case, then he would graciously bow out. He was, after all, a desert king, not a savage— even if at times Jazz Jones had possessed the ability to make him feel as primitive as it was possible for a man to feel. He would wish her well and take his pleasure elsewhere, although he couldn't deny he would be disappointed not to revisit her enchanting curves and seeking mouth.

He pushed open the little gate, which even his untrained eye could tell needed a coat of paint, and made a mental note as he walked up the narrow path. Perhaps he would send someone out here to do just that. He lifted the loose door-knocker, which clearly had a screw missing, and frowned. Maybe even get someone to fix that for her, too.

Afterwards.

After he had enjoyed some badly needed solace.

He lifted the knocker, and as it fell heavily against the peeling paintwork he could hear the sound echoing through the tiny house.

* * *

Bringing the whirring drone of the sewing machine to a halt, Jasmine lifted her head to hear the sound of loud knocking, and she narrowed her eyes. Eyes which were tired and gritty from sewing until late last night. She rubbed them with the back of her fist, and yawned. Who was disturbing her during this quiet time when she'd got a rare opportunity to do some work? For a moment she was tempted to ignore it and stay there, neatly hemming the velvet curtains which needed to be delivered to her demanding client by next Wednesday, at the latest.

But she chided herself as she got up from her work spot in the corner of the sitting room and went to answer the unexpected summons. Surely she wasn't being suspicious just because someone was knocking at the door? If she wasn't careful she would become one of those sad people who became nervous at the thought of an unplanned caller. Who twitched whenever they heard a loud noise and were too scared to face the world outside. Just because she'd recently completed a radical lifestyle change and moved out of the city lock, stock and barrel didn't mean she had to start acting like some kind of hermit! Especially since she had discovered nothing but friendliness from the locals since arriving in this quiet hamlet—a factor which had helped cushion her sudden and dramatic change in circumstances. It was probably somebody selling raffle tickets for the local spring fayre.

She pulled open the door.

It wasn't.

It most definitely wasn't.

Shock coursed through her like a tidal wave. She could feel the physical effects of it and fleetingly thought how much they resembled desire. The rapid increase in her pulse and the rush of blood to her face. The wobbly knees, which made her glad she was gripping the door handle for support. And most of all, that slightly out-of-body sensation, which made her think this couldn't be happening.

It couldn't.

Heart still pounding, she studied the man who was standing on her doorstep—as if he might disappear in a puff of smoke if she stared at him long enough. But he stayed exactly where he was, as solid as dark marble and as vital as the mighty oak tree which towered over the nearby village green. She wanted to somehow be immune to him but how could she, when just seeing him again made her heart clench with longing and her body quiver with long-suppressed lust?

His face was angled—slashed with hard planes and contours which spoke of an aristocratic lineage, even if his proud bearing hadn't confirmed it. With hair as black as coal and eyes a gleaming shade almost as dark, his rich gold complexion was dominated by a hawk-like nose and the most sensual lips she'd ever seen. Yet the suit he wore contradicted his identity for it was urbane and modern, as was the crisp white shirt and silken tie. But Jasmine had seen photos of him in flowing robes, which made him look as if he'd stepped straight from the pages of a fairy tale. Pale robes which had emphasised his burnished skin and hinted at a hard body which had been honed on the saddle of a horse, in one of the world's most unforgiving desert landscapes.

Zuhal Al Haidar—sheikh and royal prince. Second son of an ancient dynasty which ruled the oil-rich country of Razrastan, where diamonds had been discovered close to its immense mountains and world-class racing horses were bred. The man to whom she had given her body and heart—although he had wanted only her body and she had pretended to be okay with that because there hadn't been an alternative. Well, the alternative would have been to have spurned his unexpected advances and that had been something she'd found herself unable to do. There hadn't been a day since they'd parted that she hadn't thought about him but she'd never thought she'd see him again because he had cut her out of his life completely.

And that was the thing she needed to remember. That he hadn't wanted her. He'd cast her aside like yesterday's newspaper. She bit her lip as questions flooded through her mind.

Why was he here?

And then, much more crucial…

She mustn't let him stay here.

But Jasmine wasn't stupid. At least, not any more. She might once have acted like a complete idiot where Zuhal was concerned, but not now. She had grown up since splitting with him. She'd had to. She'd learned that you sometimes had to stop and think about what was the best thing to do in the long term, rather than what you really wanted to do. So she resisted the urge to close the door firmly in his face and instead forced a polite smile to her lips.

'Good heavens, Zuhal,' she said, in a voice which sounded strangely calm. 'This is a...surprise.'

Zuhal frowned, irritation dwarfing the anticipation which was shafting through him. It wasn't the greeting he had been expecting. Surely she should have been rapturously hurling herself into his arms by now? Even if she had decided to act out a little game-playing resistance for the sake of her pride, he still would have expected to see her eyes darkening with desire, or the parting of those rosy lips in unconscious invitation.

But no. Instead of desire he saw wariness and something else. Something he didn't recognise. Just as he didn't recognise the woman who stood before him. He remembered Jazz Jones as being a bit of a fashion queen. Someone who was always beautifully turned out—even if she'd made most of her clothes herself because her budget had been tight. But she had always had a definite *style* about her—it had been one of the things which had first drawn him to her, and presumably why the Granchester Hotel had employed her as manager in its sleek London boutique.

He remembered her honey-coloured hair swinging to her chin, not grown out and tied back into a functional plait, which hung down the back of a plain jumper, which inexplicably had some unidentifiable stain on the shoulder. Her legs weren't on show either; their shapely curves were covered by a pair of very ugly jeans—a garment she'd never worn in his company after he'd explained his intense dislike of them.

But he told himself that her clothes didn't matter, because he didn't intend her to be wearing them for much longer. Nothing mattered—other than the yearning which was already heating his blood like a fever. And wasn't it ironic that Zuhal found himself resenting this sensual power she'd always had over him, even while his body hungrily responded to it? He let his voice dip into a velvety caress as it had done so often in the past, adopting the intimate tone of two people who had once been lovers. *And who would soon be lovers again.* 'Hello, Jazz.'

But there was no lessening of her wary expression. No answering smile or impulsive opening of the door to admit him to her home and her arms. No ecstatic acknowledgement that he was here, after nearly two years of not seeing each other. Instead, she nodded in recognition and once again there was a flash of something he didn't recognise in her eyes.

'How did you find me?'

He raised his eyebrows, because her unwelcoming attitude was something he wasn't familiar with—and neither was her bald question, which was bordering on the insolent. Was she really planning to interrogate him as if he were a passing salesman? Did she think it acceptable to leave the future King of Razrastan standing on her doorstep?

His words became tinged with a distinct note of reprimand, which had been known to make grown men shudder. 'Isn't this a conversation we should be having in the comfort of your home, Jazz, even if it doesn't strike me as very *comfortable*?'

She flinched. She actually flinched—before seeming to pull herself together. She was smiling now, but he could sense it was forced, as if she were pushing her mouth against the soft resistance of slowly setting concrete. He was confused. Hadn't they parted on good terms—or as good as they could be when a man was terminating what had been a very satisfying relationship? Although Jazz had been that little bit different from his other lovers, he recalled. She alone had refused to accept the keepsake piece of jewellery he always offered his ex-lovers as a memento. To his surprise—and, yes, his annoyance too—she had carefully repackaged the emerald and diamond pendant, along with a polite note telling him she couldn't possibly accept such a generous gift.

His mouth hardened as he looked at the peeling paint on the front door. She above all people could have done with an injection of cash.

'I'm afraid you can't come in,' she was saying. 'I'm sorry, Zuhal. It isn't…well, it isn't really convenient right now. Perhaps if you'd given me some warning.'

And then he understood. Of course. It was exactly as he had anticipated. Outwardly, she had accepted their break-up with dignity and a remarkable absence of begging, or tantrums. As he recalled, she hadn't even shed a single tear when he'd ended their affair—at least, not in his presence. But Jasmine Jones wasn't made of stone. She was the sexiest woman he'd ever met and had thrived under his expert tuition. Having awoken her body, surely he wouldn't have expected her to return to her celibate lifestyle after he'd introduced her to the joys of sex?

He felt the slow and heavy beat of a pulse to his temple. It was hard to believe—but why wouldn't she have replaced him in her bed with someone more suitable? Someone of her own class who might be willing or able to marry her. Perhaps he should have rung first. Or written. Given her time to prepare herself—to rid herself of her current squeeze and pretty herself up for his arrival. But since when did Zuhal Al Haidar ever have to ring ahead to make some sort of appointment?

He attempted to sound reasonable but could do nothing about the sudden dark clench of jealousy in his gut. 'You have another man in your life, Jazz?'

She looked genuinely taken aback—as if he had said something shocking and contemptible. 'Of course not!'

Zuhal expelled a breath he hadn't even realised he was holding. And wasn't it crazy how swiftly jealousy could become an overwhelming sense of triumph and then hot anticipation? 'Well, then. I have come a long way to see you.' He smiled. 'As I recall, when we went our separate ways we did it in the most civilised way possible. Which makes me wonder why you are so reluctant to let me in. Isn't that the modern way, for lovers to remain friends? To sit and talk of old times, with affection.'

Jasmine felt her body stiffen, grateful her left hand was still hidden behind the partially open door. Glancing over the Sheikh's burly shoulder, she could see the black gleam of his limousine sitting in the narrow lane, easily visible through the still-bare bushes. She supposed his driver was sitting there waiting, as people always waited for Zuhal. His bodyguards would be there, too, and there would probably be another carload of security people a little further along the lane, hidden from sight.

Hidden from sight.

Her heart contracted painfully but she tried to keep her face serene, even though the fear inside her was growing. She'd been so certain that the course she had taken had been the right one but now, as she looked into the carved perfection of Zuhal's dark features, she felt the disconcerting flurry of doubt—along with the far more worrying pang of recognition. What should she do?

If she refused to let him in it would arouse his suspicions—she knew it would. It would arouse his interest too, because he was alpha enough to always want what was denied him. And she still had at least an hour of freedom before the matter became more urgent than academic. So why not ask him inside? Find out what he had come for and politely listen before sending him on his way, no harm done. She felt the prick of conscience as she opened the door wider and saw him register the gold ring she wore on her wedding finger, and she saw his face darken as he bent his head to accommodate the low ceiling.

'I thought you said there wasn't a man in your life,' he accused as the door swung squeakily shut behind him.

'There isn't.'

'So why the wedding ring?' he demanded. 'Are you back with your husband?'

She flushed. 'Of course I'm not. That was never going to happen. We're divorced, Zuhal. You knew that. I was divorced when I met you.'

'So why the ring?' he demanded again.

Jasmine told herself he had no right to ask her questions about her personal life and maybe she should tell him so—but that would be pointless because Zuhal had never been brought up to conform to the rules of normal behaviour. And wasn't the truth that he *did* have the right to ask, even if he was unaware of it? She felt another painful twist of conscience before realising he was appraising her with a look she recognised only too well. The look which said he was hungry for her body. And that was all he ever wanted you for, she reminded herself bitterly. When the chips were down he wasn't offering you any kind of future. He took without giving anything back and she needed to protect herself to make sure that never happened again.

He was probably married by now—married to the suitable royal bride he had always told her he would one day marry.

She needed to get rid of him.

'I wear the ring as a deterrent,' she said.

He raised his dark eyebrows. 'Because men are regularly beating down your door with lustful intention?'

Ignoring the sardonic tone of his query, she shook her head. 'Hardly.'

'It's true that your appearance is a little drab,' he

conceded. 'But we both know how magnificent you can look when you try.'

Jasmine gritted her teeth, telling herself not to rise to the backhanded compliment. 'I realised I hadn't made the best relationship choices in the past and that I needed some time on my own,' she explained. 'Time to get my career up and running.'

'And what career might that be, Jazz?' he questioned softly. 'What made you stop working at the hotel boutique—I thought it paid reasonably well?'

Jasmine shrugged. She wasn't going to tell him about her soft furnishings business, which was still in an embryo stage but gaining in popularity all the time. Or her plans for designing baby clothes, which she hoped would one day provide her with a modest living. Because none of that was any of his business. 'London was getting too expensive and I wanted a change,' she said. 'And you still haven't told me why you're here.'

With genuine surprise, Zuhal realised that maybe he had misjudged his impact on her. Was it possible she hadn't been as besotted by him as he'd thought—and that she wouldn't take him into her bed without forethought or ceremony, as she'd done so often in the past? He remembered how her soft and undemanding nature had always acted like a balm on his troubled senses. How she had always been eager and hungry to see him. But now her distinct lack of interest punctured his erotic thoughts and instead he was filled with the unusual urge to confide in her. He sighed as he walked to the window and looked out at the yellow flash of the few straggly daffodils which were poking out from the overgrown grass in the tiny garden.

'You know my brother is missing?' he questioned, without preamble. 'Presumed dead.'

She gasped and when he turned round her fingers were lying against her throat, as if she were starved of air. '*Dead?*' she managed eventually. 'No, I didn't know that. Oh, Zuhal, I'm so sorry. I mean, I never met him—obviously—but I remember he was your only sibling.'

He narrowed his eyes. 'We kept it quiet for as long as possible, but now it's out there in the public domain. You hadn't heard?'

She shook her head. 'I don't... I don't get much chance to read the papers these days. World news is so depressing—and my TV isn't actually working at the moment,' she added, before biting down on the lushness of her lower lip and fixing him with a wary look. 'What happened, or would you rather not talk about it?'

He'd thought she might take him in her arms and comfort him and wasn't that what he wanted more than anything else? To feel the warmth of another body—the soft squeeze of flesh reminding him that he was very much alive instead of lying prone and cold somewhere in a merciless desert, while vultures hovered overhead. But she didn't. She just stood on the other side of the small room, her green-gold eyes dark with distress, though her body language remained stiff and awkward—as if she didn't know how to be around him.

But still he found himself talking about it, in a way he might not have done so freely with anyone else. Almost imperceptibly, his voice grew harsh. 'Although

Kamal was King of Razrastan, with all the responsibilities which came with that exalted role, my brother never lost his love of recklessness.'

'I do remember you saying he was a bit of a daredevil,' she offered cautiously.

He gave another heavy sigh as he nodded. 'He was. All through his youth he embraced the most dangerous of sports and nobody could do a thing to stop him. Our father tried often enough, but our mother actively encouraged his daring behaviour. Which was why he piloted his own plane and heli-skied whenever possible. Why he deep-sea-dived and climbed the world's most challenging mountains—and nobody could deny that he excelled at everything he put his mind to.' He paused. 'His coronation as King inevitably curtailed most of these activities, but he was still prone to taking off on his horse, often alone. He said it gave him time to think. To be away from the hurly-burly of palace life. And that's what happened last year…'

'What did?' she prompted uneasily as his words tailed off.

Zuhal felt the inevitable sense of sorrow mounting inside him but there was bitterness, too. Because hadn't Kamal's actions impacted on so many people—and on him more than anyone? 'One morning he mounted his beloved Akhal-Teke horse and rode off into the desert as the sun was rising, or so one of the stable boys told us later. By the time we realised he had ridden off unaccompanied, a fierce storm was blasting its way through the desert. Even from within the protection of the palace walls we could see the sky growing as red as blood and the wind whipping itself up into a wild frenzy.'

His voice grew unsteady for a moment before he continued. 'They say there is no escape from the blanket of sand which results from those storms, that it infiltrates everything. You can't see, or hear, or breathe. For a while it feels as if hell has unleashed all its demons and set them free upon the world.' He swallowed. 'We never found either of them—neither man nor horse—during one of the biggest search operations our country has ever mounted. Not a trace. It is inconceivable that he could have survived such an onslaught.' There was a pause as his mouth twisted. 'And the desert is very efficient at disposing of bodies.'

'Oh, Zuhal,' she whispered. 'That's awful. I'm so sorry for your loss.'

He gave a brief nod of his head, dismissing her soft words of sympathy because he hadn't come here for *words*. 'We're all sorry,' he said matter-of-factly.

'So what will happen?'

'Kamal cannot be officially pronounced dead for seven years, but the law states that the country cannot be without a king during that time.' Like a boxer in the ring, Zuhal clenched his fists so that the knuckles cracked and turned deathly white beneath the olive skin. 'And so, I have agreed to rule in his absence.'

She blinked at him as if the significance of what he had told her had only just sunk in. 'What exactly does that…mean?'

'It means that in seven years' time, if Kamal has still not returned, then I will be crowned, since I am the sole surviving heir. Until that time I will be King in everything but name, and I will be known as the Sheikh Regent.'

It was the mention of the word *heir* which set Jasmine's senses jangling with renewed fear. A trickle of sweat whispered down her back and settled at the base of her spine, soaking into the waistband of her jeans. Did he *know*? Was that why he was here today?

But no, of course he didn't know. He wouldn't be standing there with that bleak look on his face talking about his powerful new role if he had any inkling of the momentous thing which had happened in *her* life. And there were reasons he didn't know, she reminded herself painfully. Reasons which had helped spur her desire to stop reading the papers and listening to the news.

'And is your *wife*...' Somehow her voice didn't tremble on the word. 'Is she happy about her position as the new ruler's consort?'

'My wife?' he echoed, frowning at her uncomprehendingly. 'I don't have a wife, Jazz.'

'But I thought...' Jasmine swallowed as her perceived view of the world did a dramatic shift. 'I thought you were seeing a princess from a neighbouring desert region, soon after we split. Zara, I think her name was.'

Zuhal nodded. 'I was.' His eyes narrowed as they swept over her. 'Yes, Zara was the latest in a long line of mooted royal brides, with a pedigree almost equal to my own.' He shrugged. 'But she had a laugh which used to set my teeth on edge and I could not contemplate a life-long partnership with her. And back then, there was no sense of urgency. Now it is different, of course. Now I must rule my country and for that I will need a wife by my side.'

Jasmine's heart flooded with heat and began to pound loudly with something which felt like hope, even though afterwards she would ask herself how she could have been so stupid. But for a few seconds she actually allowed herself to believe in the fantasy which still haunted her some nights when sleep stubbornly refused to come—of her desert prince returning to sweep her off her feet. 'I still don't understand,' she said cautiously, 'why you're here.'

He lifted up the palms of his hands like a man on the point of surrender. 'I'll tell you exactly why I'm here, Jazz,' he said, a hard smile flattening the edges of his sensual lips. 'Next month my life will change beyond recognition, when I sign the papers which are currently being drawn up to officially recognise me as the Sheikh Regent. But beneath all the inevitable celebrations that the line will continue my people are grieving and uncertain, for my brother's disappearance has unsettled them. The country needs stability and they are looking to me to provide it, for while Kamal had many commendable character traits, steadfastness was not one of them. I need a bride,' he said, not seeming to notice that she had gasped again, or that her hands had started trembling. 'But this time I cannot afford to be picky. I must marry someone suitable—and quickly.'

She gulped the words out breathlessly. She just couldn't help herself. 'Someone l-like?'

'Someone of royal blood. Obviously.' His black eyes crinkled with that rare flash of mischief which used to tie her up in knots. 'Not a divorced girl from England, I'm afraid, Jazz—just in case you were getting your hopes up.'

'I wasn't,' she said, furious with him, but even more furious with herself—for allowing herself that stupid little daydream which had made her heart begin to race. Hadn't she learnt *anything* during the time she'd been his secret mistress? That she was as disposable as an empty baked-beans can? 'Is that why you're here, Zuhal?' she demanded. 'To talk about your marriage prospects? What were you hoping for—my advice? Perhaps you'd like me to help you vet your future bride for you?'

'No, that's not why I'm here. Do you want me to show you why I'm here, my beautiful Jazz?' He had started moving across the small room until he was standing right in front of her. Until he had pulled her without warning into his powerful arms, his black eyes glittering with pain and desire and something else, as he stared down into her face. 'I'm here because I'm empty and aching and because I know you can take that ache away.'

She should have given him a piece of her mind. Should have told him she wasn't just something he could put down and then pick up again, as the whim took him. So why didn't she? Was it his touch which made common sense fly out of the window, or just the yearning inside her which had never gone away? She should have realised that by *aching* he meant sex, but for one crazy moment Jasmine thought he was talking about his heart. So she let him tilt her chin with those strong, olive-dark fingers, just as she let his mouth travel towards hers in what felt like a slow extension of time. She had to urge herself not to rise up on tiptoe to make the kiss come sooner, but somehow she retained enough restraint to hold back. But perhaps that wasn't such a good idea because by the time their lips touched, she felt a flash of connection so intense that she gave a little moan of joy.

And Jazz forgot everything. Forgot why he shouldn't be there and why she shouldn't be reacting to him like this. Why it was wrong to allow his strong hands to burrow beneath the thick-knit sweater she was wearing and to cup her breasts with luxuriant familiarity. It felt like the best place she'd been for a very long time as his mouth explored hers with a thoroughness which left her reeling, his tongue licking at her with intimate familiarity. The blood pumped through her veins like honey as she felt the drift of his fingers over her nipples—briefly flicking over the engorged buds before creeping down to her torso.

And this was heaven. Jasmine's throat dried as he reacquainted himself with the curve of her belly and she wriggled accommodatingly as he slipped his thumb beneath the waistband of her jeans and began to tease the warm, bare skin. Did she suck her stomach in, hoping that he would move his hands further inside the thick denim to caress her where she was hot and wet and longing to be caressed, and didn't she want that more than anything else? She could feel the hard press of his erection and instinctively her thighs parted by a fraction and she could hear his low murmur of appreciation.

He drew his lips away. 'You've changed shape,' he observed unevenly.

'Y-yes.' She nearly asked him whether or not he liked it—and how crazy was *that*?—when a sudden thought hit her like a squirt of icy water and fear began to whisper over her. Drawing in a deep breath, she looked directly into his eyes as comprehension began to dawn on her. 'Are you here just because…because you want to have sex with me, Zuhal?'

He seemed momentarily taken aback by her question but she knew the moment she saw him shrug that her worst fear was true. Well, maybe not her *worst* fear…

'You…you want some kind of physical release, is that it?' she continued unsteadily. 'Some easy, uncomplicated sex, before you return home in search of your suitable royal bride?'

At least he had the grace to look abashed but the look was quickly replaced by one of defiance. 'What did you expect, Jazz?' he murmured. 'That I would present to my very conservative people a foreign divorcee as the woman I had chosen?' His black gaze burned into her. 'We both know that was always going to be a non-starter. Just as we both know that the chemistry which has always sparked between us is still there. Nothing about that has changed. I still want you so much that I could explode with it—and so do you. You come alive whenever I touch you, don't you? Your body cries out for mine, the same way it always did. So why waste it?' His voice dipped into a sensual caress. 'Why not give into what we both want—and make love one last and beautiful time?'

Dazedly, Jasmine listened to his arrogant statement—and didn't his attitude justify some of the tough decisions she'd been forced to make? She was about to tell him that it was a mistake to call what he had in mind *making love* and wondering if he would attempt to persuade her otherwise, when a distant sound changed everything. She moved away from him—not so quickly as to arouse suspicion—praying that Darius was only whimpering in some kind of happy little infant dream and would shortly go back to sleep.

But her prayers went unanswered. The whimper became louder. It morphed into a cry and then a protesting yell and she saw Zuhal's face change. Watched the black eyes narrow as his gaze swept questioningly over her and she quickly stared down at the threadbare rug for fear that he might see the sudden tears welling up in her eyes. She thought about all the things she *could* say.

She could pretend that it was a peacock, because weren't they supposed to sound like young babies? Or maybe that was babies younger than Darius which sounded like those squawking birds. And anyway, peacocks lived in the grounds of stately homes, didn't they? They promenaded elegantly over manicured lawns—their magnificent blue-green plumage wouldn't dream of gracing the scruffy little garden of a rented cottage just outside Oxford.

'What was that, Jazz?' Zuhal questioned ominously.

She knew then that the game was up. That she could attempt evasion to try to deflect his attention and send him on his way by pretending that the baby belonged to someone else and she was just childminding. But she couldn't. Not really—and not just because the time frame would prove her a liar. No. No matter what had happened in the past or how little Zuhal thought of her now, she was going to have to come clean. And hadn't she always wanted that anyway, on some subliminal level?

'What was that, Jazz?' he repeated, only now a note of something dangerous had been added into the mix to make his voice grow even darker.

Slowly she lifted her gaze to meet the accusation in his eyes and prepared for her whole world to change in the telling of a single sentence. 'It's my child. Or rather, our child,' she said, sucking in a breath of air. 'You have a son, Zuhal, and his name is Darius.'

CHAPTER TWO

AND THEN, AS IF by magic, Darius went back to sleep. Jasmine could hear it quite plainly in the sounds which were issuing from his baby monitor. The lessening of his cry into a gulping sob which gradually became a little coo, which was so much a feature of his daily nap. She knew he would now be peacefully asleep again and that if only her son's timing had been a little better, Zuhal would have been none the wiser.

But Jasmine knew there was no point wishing that Darius had delayed his cry until the Sheikh had been hurried away from the premises. If Zuhal hadn't been kissing her, then he would already have left. If she hadn't been stupidly *letting* him kiss her and wanting the kind of things she should be ashamed of wanting…

And anyway—wasn't this what she had always wanted to happen? Had tried to make happen, if she hadn't been blocked along the way by his position and power. *So don't let guilt beat you up*, she told herself fiercely, even though it was difficult not to flinch as she met the naked accusation in his black eyes. You've tried to do your best.

'My son?' he repeated incredulously.

She nodded. 'Yes, he—'

'Don't you dare say another word. Just take me to see him,' he cut over her words, his voice laced with a layer of ice she'd heard him use before—though never with her.

'You will see him. I promise—just not yet. Let him sleep, Zuhal. Please,' she said, with the confidence of someone who'd been bringing up a baby on her own for the last nine months and knew how cranky they could get if they were woken prematurely.

'I won't waken him but I want to see him.' His autocratic command hissed through the air. 'Take me to him, Jazz. Now.'

Her lips dry, Jasmine nodded. How had she ever thought she could oppose his wishes? She'd never managed it in the past—so why should now be any different? He had dumped her without warning—and, even though he had told her from the start that she could never have any future with him, it had still seemed to come out of the blue. But she had held it together then, just as she must hold it together now. 'Come with me,' she said in a low voice, the hairs on the back of her neck prickling with unease as she led the way from the room.

Feeling like a participant in some bizarre dream, Zuhal followed Jazz up the narrow staircase, his mind spinning with disbelief as she reached the top and gestured towards the open door of a nursery painted in sunny shades of yellow. He wanted to convince himself that she'd been lying and that it was no child of his who lay sleeping in a cot beneath the window. But as he silently crossed the room to gaze down at the infant, he knew there was absolutely no question that this was his baby. It was more than the shock of ebony hair so like his own. More than the olive skin, which was a paler version of his. It was something fundamental and almost *primitive* which activated a powerful surge of recognition deep within him as he gazed down at the gently parted lips of the baby boy. He saw Jazz tense as he reached down and briefly laid his forefinger against the baby's soft cheek, before withdrawing it and turning abruptly on his heel, to walk out the way he had come. He didn't say a word until they were back downstairs— he didn't trust himself to speak—and even though he wanted to rage and rail at her, he kept his voice low.

'Do you realise the constitutional significance of what you've done?' he hissed.

Jasmine flinched and a part of her wished she could have given into the luxury of tears if she hadn't recognised the need to stay strong. *Constitutional significance?* Was that the only thing he cared about in the light of his discovery? Of course it was. It was why he'd ended their relationship and why he had turned up here today, to use her body as he might use a stone vessel filled with water to quench his thirst. For him nothing mattered other than the needs and demands of his beloved country and everything else came second to that.

'Did you not think to tell me, Jazz?' he continued, still in that icy undertone of suppressed fury. 'That the seed of my loins had borne fruit?'

Jasmine shivered as his words created a powerful image in her mind which made her heart clench with impotent longing until she forced herself to push it away and focus on what was important. 'I did try to tell you.'

His cold expression suggested he didn't believe her. 'When?'

'After we…split up.' *When he'd sweetly informed her that she was the kind of woman who made a perfect mistress, but not the kind of woman he could ever marry.* 'Not for many weeks, it's true. I… I didn't realise I was pregnant. At least, not straight away.'

'Why not?' he bit out witheringly. 'You may have been a virgin when we met but please don't make out you were born yesterday, Jazz. What do you mean, you *didn't realise* you were pregnant? What, were you waiting for the stork to fly in through the window and surprise you?'

His words were cruel. Sarcastic. Deliberately so, it seemed. Jasmine tried to convince herself that his anger was understandable. Wouldn't she have felt just as angry if the situation were reversed—to have discovered that she'd become a parent and have been kept in the dark about it? 'I was all over the place,' she admitted. 'I was operating in a bit of a fog—on autopilot, if you like. Just getting through the day took all my energy and I felt disorientated because…well, it was *weird* getting used to life without you.'

Zuhal's lips tightened but to his surprise he found he couldn't disagree with her because he too had been disconcerted by the discovery that Jazz had left a peculiar hole in his life. He had explained it away by reminding himself that it had all been about sex—the best sex he'd ever had. Against all the odds she had captivated him—

for he had never been with someone as low-born as her before. She'd been working in the boutique attached to London's famous Granchester Hotel where he'd been staying, and on a primitive level he had initially been drawn to her pert breasts and curvy hips. By the buttery swing of her blonde hair and the way her lips curved into a sweet smile whenever she was serving customers. But although many women caught his eye and made it clear they were his for the taking, Zuhal rarely gave into his most base desires. Sometimes he took pleasure in denying himself sexual gratification because deprivation was good for the spirit and what was easily gained was easily discarded. Plus, he liked a challenge—and a challenge had certainly been presented to him when the humble shop girl had blushed as he'd spoken to her and had had difficulty meeting his gaze.

His hunger ignited, he had been pleased to discover she was divorced because divorced women were often cynical about marriage, with few of the marital ambitions of single women, which bored the hell out of him. They also possessed an earthy expertise which made them the best lovers.

But Jazz hadn't been experienced.

He remembered his shock—and then his pleasure—when he had discovered her innocence. When she had opened those soft thighs and he had broken through the tight hymen, which had flagged up the gratifying knowledge that he was her first ever lover. He remembered the orgasm which had followed. Which had rocked him to the core of his being. And the one after, and the one after that...

With an effort he dragged his mind back to the present because none of that was relevant now. Not in the light of his discovery that she was a secretive little manipulator.

'Talk me through what happened, Jazz,' he bit out and could see her trying to compose herself, rubbing her hands up and down over the arms of her sweater, as if she were cold.

She swallowed. 'When you went back to Razrastan I just carried on as normal, terrified someone at the hotel was going to discover I'd been having intimate relations with a guest.'

'But nobody did?' he probed.

Jasmine shook her head. 'No. Not a soul. But then, we were very discreet, weren't we, Zuhal? You made sure of that. I was never even permitted to stay with you in your fancy penthouse suite and we only ever went to the borrowed house of one of your rich friends, under cover of darkness.'

'I have always tried to be discreet about my relationships—and the newspapers would have had a field day if they'd discovered I was sleeping with someone like you,' he said coldly.

'Someone like me?' she echoed.

'You know what I'm talking about. It was almost a cliché—the prince and the shop girl. In a way, I was protecting you.'

Jasmine bit her lip, because it had been much more likely he had been protecting his own precious reputation. Should she tell him how difficult it had felt to carry on serving behind the till with that bright smile pinned to her lips, when she had been missing him so much? Maybe it was the effort of that—of trying to appear normal—which had meant her first missed period had passed by without her noticing. And then when she *had* noticed something was amiss, she'd been unable to confide in anyone. Her parents were dead and she hadn't dared place her trust in friends and colleagues, terrified someone might run to the press with the story. She had a cousin she was close to, but Emily lived miles away and Jasmine had never felt quite so lonely.

Even now, as she looked up into Zuhal's flinty features, she could still remember the scary sense of isolation she'd felt as she'd realised she was pretty much on her own, with a tiny life to support. Factor in the fact that she'd been missing him so badly and you ended up with someone who had found herself in a precarious situation. 'I tried to ring you but your number came up as unobtainable.'

He met the question in her eyes. 'I make a point of regularly changing my phone number,' he informed her coolly. 'My security people tell me it's safer that way.'

'And, of course, it keeps troublesome ex-girlfriends at bay?' she guessed, forcing herself to confront the bitter truth.

He shrugged. 'Something like that,' he conceded. 'When did you try to contact me?'

Accurately, she was able to relay the exact month—because at that stage her pregnancy had been well established. She'd been determined to show Zuhal that she intended going ahead with the birth, with or without his approval. That she didn't need a man—or a husband—

in order to survive, because experience had taught her that marriage was by no means the magic bullet which so many women imagined it was.

Feeling on firmer footing now, she sucked in a steadying breath. 'Eventually, I managed to get through to one of your aides. Adham, I think his name was. I told him I needed to speak to you urgently and he promised he would pass on the message to you.'

'But I never got it,' he said, his voice hardening.

'So blame him.'

'Adham is a loyal servant who would have been acting in my best interests. The palace was in uproar because of my brother's disappearance and, of course, that impacted profoundly on my future. And not just that.' His black eyes bored into her. 'Do you have any idea of the amount of women who are eager to speak to me, who try to phone the palace switchboard?'

'Strangely enough no, I don't,' she answered, colour rising in her cheeks so that suddenly she felt hot and uncomfortable. 'Tallying up the numbers of your ex-lovers isn't a pastime which has ever appealed to me.'

'You could have told him you were pregnant!' he accused. 'You knew that would have ensured you got through to me straight away. Why didn't you do that, Jazz?'

Jasmine licked her lips. Because she'd been scared. Scared of Zuhal's influence and of the reality of confronting it for the first time. He'd always left his sheikh status at the door of the bedroom, but during that brief and fruitless phone call, she'd got an inkling of the real man behind the very sexy facade. It had taken her ages to get through to his office and during the long wait she'd realised just how powerful her former lover really was. She remembered the way his aide had spoken to her—as if she were a piece of dirt he'd found on the bottom of his shoe. And she'd been fearful that, although Zuhal obviously didn't want her any more, he might want to claim sole custody of their baby—and he'd have the wherewithal to make it happen.

And that was something she could never allow.

'You told me you were planning to marry a royal princess,' she reminded him. 'I thought that was another reason why your aide was so *off* with me. There were reports about your burgeoning romance in all the papers. About how two desert kingdoms were going to be united and it was going to be the greatest thing to happen in the region for decades. The Dream Desert ticket, I think the tabloids called it.' Which had been another reason why she'd stopped reading them. 'Wouldn't it have completely ruined everything if some casual lover had come forward with the news that you were to become a father?'

Zuhal's eyes narrowed as he forced himself to dismiss her persuasive words. Because weren't these accusations and counter-accusations diverting his attention from the monumental discovery he had just made?

He had a son.

A ready-made heir.

Perhaps fate was showing him a little benevolence for once.

He looked at the woman standing in front of him. A few minutes ago he'd been kissing her and her response had indicated that if it hadn't been for the baby's cry, she would have allowed him to be deep inside her by now. *Would* she, he found himself wondering, with a brand-new disdain which had blossomed as a result of his unbelievable discovery? Had she become one of those women who would cast aside the needs of her baby in pursuit of her own carnal pleasures? And if that were the case, then wouldn't that be easy to prove in a court of law—thereby putting him in a morally superior position and demonstrating his own suitability to bring up the child, instead of her? Surely that would be simpler all round.

He noted the trepidation flickering in the depths of her green-gold eyes as she returned his gaze, just as he noted the sudden tension which was stiffening her narrow shoulders. The silence between them was growing into something immense and uncomfortable but, unlike most people would be, Zuhal was unperturbed by it. Indeed, he often *orchestrated* silence when necessary, for it was a powerful tool in negotiation and never had negotiation been more vital than now.

'How are you managing for money?' he questioned casually.

He could see a look of faint confusion criss-cross her brow and wondered if she was disorientated by his sudden change of subject.

'I manage,' she said defensively.

'I said "how", Jazz?'

She shrugged. 'I sew.'

He frowned. 'You sew?'

'Yes. You remember. I always liked sewing. I was

planning to go to fashion college when my mother got sick and I had to defer my place to look after her.'

He thought back. Had she told him that? Even if she *had*, he suspected it would have gone in one ear and straight out of the other. He hadn't really been interested in her past, just as he hadn't been interested in her future, because he'd known there could never be one—not for them. The only thing which had interested him, and for a time had obsessed him, had been the magnificence of her body and the sheer sexual dynamite of their coming together.

'That's right,' he prevaricated as some long-buried fact swam up from the depths of his subconscious. 'You wanted to be a fashion designer. Is that what you're doing now?'

She gave him the kind of look which suggested he had no idea how normal mortals lived. 'I wish,' she said. 'You can't just set yourself up as a fashion designer, Zuhal, especially when you've got no real qualifications. For one thing, the overheads would be prohibitive, and for another, there's a whole heap of competition out there. You see that sewing machine over there?' Her finger trembled a little as she pointed to it. 'That's what I was doing when you arrived. Mostly, I specialise in soft furnishings—cushions and curtains, that sort of thing. People always need those and Oxford isn't far away. There are plenty of folk with deep pockets who change their decor all the time, even if there's nothing wrong with it. Probably because they're rich and bored and can't think of anything better to do,' she added.

She seemed eager to deflect his attention from

the life-changing news with her mundane chatter, he thought grimly. And she would be, wouldn't she? But her words made him consider both her income and her environment and for the first time Zuhal took proper notice of his surroundings, his lips curving with ill-concealed contempt. The furniture was of the cheapest variety, the rug threadbare and the paint on the window frames peeling. Only the curtains and cushions redeemed the place, their brightness adding an unexpected touch of jollity to the small room. Presumably her own handiwork.

His disdain turned into anger. And she was bringing up his son in a place like this! The heir to the Al Haidar dynasty was growing up in some scruffy little house on the outskirts of Oxford, with no security at the door and barely enough warmth inside. He wanted to berate her. To tell her she was unfit to care for his child, but something made him bite back his words as he sensed that hostility would be counterproductive to his cause. He looked at her faded jeans and the sweater with that ugly stain on the shoulder. Wouldn't it be sensible to offer her an easy way out? To leave her free to live the kind of life she had been destined to live before their paths had unpredictably crossed in an upmarket London hotel.

'We need to discuss the future,' he said.

She looked at him warily. 'What do you mean?'

He took a step closer and then wished he hadn't because her unsophisticated soapy scent suddenly made his senses become keen and raw. And wasn't it crazy that, despite his anger, he could still feel the powerful jerk of his erection pressing uncomfortably hard against the zipper of his trousers? Hadn't she always had that power over him—and hadn't it been that power which had made him terminate their relationship sooner than he'd intended?

'What do you think I mean, Jazz?' he demanded. 'Did you think I would be content to be granted a brief look at my son before shrugging my shoulders and walking away? That I would be prepared to say good-bye to a child who has been kept a stranger to me until now?'

She swallowed. 'Of course I didn't.'

'You say that with remarkably little conviction!' he accused.

'Because it's all happened so quickly! I wasn't expecting you to just turn up like this, Zuhal. It's difficult to know what to think.'

'At least we are agreed on something,' he said. 'Though I think that, of the two of us, I have received by far the greater surprise today. I need a little time to assess the situation properly and work out where we must go from here. Decisions made in the heat of the moment will benefit no one, least of all my son.'

'You mean…' Her green-gold eyes looked hopeful. 'You mean you'll go back to Razrastan and contact me when you've had a chance to mull it over?'

He gave a short laugh. 'Go back to Razrastan? Are you really that naïve, Jazz? Do you think that, having found my child, I will now exit myself from his life?' Ruthlessly, he found himself taking pleasure from her lip-biting response to his words. And why *shouldn't* he enjoy her distress? She hadn't given *his* feelings a second thought when she'd kept his progeny hidden from him, had she? 'I will return later to take you to dinner. Somewhere neutral away from here, where we can consider our options. I will have one of my people book somewhere suitable.'

'No. I can't. That isn't going to work,' she protested. 'I'm not leaving Darius while I go out for dinner with you!'

'Why not?' he demanded. 'Do you think I'm going to have him spirited away while you're out?'

She met his gaze with a fierce challenge on her face—a look he had never seen her use before. 'I wouldn't put it past you.'

He inclined his head in unwilling admiration. 'You are wise indeed not to underestimate my determination,' he conceded. 'But you still haven't explained your refusal to dine with me.'

'Because I don't have a local babysitter, not yet,' she babbled. 'And I'm not leaving Darius with a stranger!'

His lips twisted. 'You think I would compromise childcare, Jazz? He is a royal Prince of Razrastan—and he will be cared for by the finest professional money can buy.'

'No.'

'*No?*' he verified incredulously.

'I'm not leaving him with a stranger,' she repeated stubbornly.

A pulse flickered at his temple as he trained his gaze on the minuscule kitchen which could just be glimpsed over her shoulder. 'You expect me to eat dinner here?'

'I don't particularly care whether you eat or not, since food is the last thing on my mind,' she returned. 'But since you are determined to have this meeting, I dare say I can rustle up something for supper.'

There was a moment of tense silence before, slowly, he nodded his head. 'Very well. I will return at eight.' He paused. 'In the meantime, my bodyguards will be stationed around the property, so if you're contemplating making some dramatic break for freedom, I urge you think again.'

Jasmine stared at him, feeling as if she was being backed into a corner. Was that how he intended her to feel? As if he had all the power and she had none? *Because that was true, wasn't it?* She looked at him. 'Bodyguards?' she echoed. 'Are you out of your mind? We've been living here perfectly safely for the last six months. This is rural Oxfordshire. We don't need bodyguards.'

'On the contrary, you most certainly do. You may have lived that way in the past, Jazz, but those days are over. This child has pure Al Haidar blood pulsing through his veins and will be treated accordingly.' He slanted her a warning look. 'I will see you later. Just make sure you are ready to receive me.'

His final request was like a throwback to the past and she wondered how she was supposed to do that. Was he hinting that he'd like her to be waiting for him wearing some tiny scrap of silk-satin lingerie the way she'd done in the past—showing as much flesh as possible without actually being naked? She studied his hard face. Unlikely. At this precise moment, his expression betrayed nothing but contempt. His bearing was both regal and imperious as he turned and walked out of the front door, closing it softly behind him. Jasmine could hear the purr of a powerful car engine as it started to move and now that the shock of seeing him again had begun to wear off, she began to tremble.

Unwanted tears stung her eyes, but she brushed them away as she tried to centre herself and make sense of what had just happened and to wonder how it had all come to this.

She heard Darius beginning to wake again and determination flooded through her in a hot rush as she recognised that she needed to have her wits about her when dealing with a man as powerful as Zuhal.

But most of all she needed to be strong.

CHAPTER THREE

SHE SHOULD NEVER have fallen for the royal Sheikh—
that was the thought which plagued Jasmine for the rest
of the afternoon, even while she was playing peep-oh
with Darius then splashing him in the bath and making
him giggle in that heartbreakingly innocent way of his.

But Zuhal had been determined to seduce her, despite the fact that she had been a shop girl and he a
royal prince of noble descent. Her marriage had ended
and she'd been feeling a failure when the Sheikh had
waltzed into the Granchester boutique and subjected
her to a highly effective charm offensive. She remembered his dark gaze licking over her skin and it had felt
like being bathed in sweet black molasses. Sensing an
unknown danger, she had let the other, rather pushy
assistant deal with him, but her reluctance to engage
had only seemed to increase his desire. Had she been
surprised when he had turned up the following day to
subject her to some more of that lazy charm? Not really. And she would have challenged any woman with
a pulse to have resisted him for long. The strict rules of
the hotel concerning relationships between guests and

staff meant their resulting flirtation had been conducted amid great secrecy, and afterwards she'd realised that had probably added an extra layer of piquancy.

But the tumultuous ending of her marriage had left her feeling undesirable and Zuhal had changed all that so, of course, she'd agreed to have dinner with him. The restaurant had been small and badly lit—chosen mainly for discretion, she'd suspected—and even though the implied secrecy of that had been a little disappointing, already she'd been in too deep to care. To her astonishment—but not his—she had ended up in bed with him.

It had been…bliss. No other word for it. The soft plunder of his lips. His slow undressing as he had peeled off her cheap clothes. Her first sight of him naked—all that honed and burnished flesh and the unmistakable evidence of just how much he'd wanted her. She should have been shy, or even daunted—but she had been neither. In fact, she had been wet and ready, uttering nameless pleas as he'd stroked erotic pathways over her heated skin. Even the brief pain of losing her virginity hadn't marred her mounting enjoyment and Zuhal had confessed afterwards that it had added an extra layer of excitement to his. Orgasm had followed orgasm and he hadn't said anything until afterwards, when she'd been lying gazing up at the ceiling in dazed disbelief as he'd circled a puckered nipple with one careless finger. Turning her flushed face towards his, he had drawled out a single word.

'Why?'

And then she'd told him about Richard and her non-consummated marriage. About how he'd insisted on waiting until their wedding night and how flattered she had been by that seemingly old-fashioned restraint. Because she'd thought it was an essential ingredient for a happy marriage—though she had been basing her opinion on guesswork rather than experience, because she had no idea what a happy marriage was like. Because she'd blocked her eyes and ears to the reality of her own parents' marriage for so long, hadn't she? She'd learnt to ignore dark undercurrents and pretend they simply weren't happening. She'd become an expert in normalising dysfunctional relationships. As if by normalising them it would make everything all right…but of course, it never did. She had been the lonely child, caught in the crossfire of two warring parents. And it had been hell. Perhaps that had been another reason why she'd agreed to become Richard's wife. He had felt *safe*—a bit like a small boat discovering a calm harbour after a rocky and unpredictable voyage.

Yet when her own wedding night had come—sex just hadn't happened. It had been embarrassing and disappointing and as time had gone on and still she'd remained a virgin, Jasmine had asked Richard whether it was something to do with her. It was then that he had broken down in tears to tell her he actually preferred men. To be honest, it had come as something of a relief to know the simple cause of their incompatibility and Jasmine had wished him well before they had separated. But it had left her wondering whether she was a bad judge of character not to have picked up on it before.

She had also wondered if Zuhal would think her less of a woman because of her unusual past. Or if her lack of experience would turn him off, but, to her pleasure and surprise, it had seemed to do the exact opposite.

'Perfect,' he'd murmured, while fingering her quivering flesh. 'Just perfect.'

'Wh-what is?' she remembered asking dazedly.

And that was when he'd explained that being a divorcee automatically precluded her from any kind of future with him, just in case she'd been getting any ideas—something she'd denied vehemently.

But afterwards she'd wondered just how true her denial had been. She'd told him she never expected anything from their relationship other than pleasure, so how did that explain the river of tears she'd cried when they'd made love for the very last time?

She needed to remember that. Every bit of it. To remind herself of just how ruthless Zuhal could be—and just how stupidly sensitive *she* could be. He had all the wealth and the power while she had none, but she had something far more precious: her gorgeous little black-haired baby who was the light of her life. She wasn't going to be unreasonable—just as long as Zuhal wasn't. He needed to understand that, despite the huge differences between them, in their roles as parents they would be equals.

She laid Darius down in his crib and went through the lullaby routine she'd begun after bringing him home from the hospital. She remembered how scared she'd been, yet determined to love her little baby with all her heart. But Darius had been easy to love. An easy baby all round. He hadn't cried incessantly at night, nor been difficult to feed. Had he somehow sensed that Jasmine had been having a tough time adapting to life as a single mum and, in some loyal baby way, had made it as simple as possible for her?

Her hair was still damp from bath-time play and she certainly hadn't got around to changing her clothes when Jasmine heard an authoritative rap on the door. But she wasn't planning on trying to make herself look presentable to Zuhal, was she? To slip into something glamorous so he might look at her with admiration rather than contempt. Apart from the fact that it was so long since she had dressed up for a night out, mightn't that send out the wrong message? Zuhal had one role to play in her life and that was as a father. She bit her lip. Which meant she needed to put all thoughts of the other stuff out of her mind. The kisses and the caresses and the scarily fast way he could always make her come. The way she'd almost succumbed in his arms earlier…

Even so, she couldn't quite block out her foreboding as she ran downstairs, because she suspected that remaining immune to Zuhal was going to be easier said than done. Heart racing, she pulled open the door to greet him, wishing his impact weren't always so overwhelming. But it was. Every time she saw him she felt as if someone had squeezed her heart within an iron fist and wouldn't let it go. Unlike her, Zuhal *had* changed his clothes—adopting the casual attire which occasionally permitted him to go as incognito as was possible when you were the possessor of such head-turning good looks. His soft black jacket meant he smelt faintly of leather, underpinned with that subtle scent of sandalwood which was so much a part of him. Dark jeans hugged the powerful length of his thighs and his jaw was shadowed with the new growth which appeared so soon after he'd shaved, reminding her of just how virile he'd always seemed to her innocent eyes.

But these were things she didn't need reminding of. Zuhal's allure and charisma had never been in any doubt. It was his other qualities she needed to remember right now. His ruthlessness and determination. His ability to cast something aside once he was bored with it. She needed to remind herself that she had simply been a diversion. A sexual plaything to amuse himself with before the time came to take a suitable bride.

There was no conventional greeting from him—no pleasant social niceties which other men might have felt duty-bound to make. He walked straight past her and, without warning or ceremony, slapped a Manila envelope down on the table before turning to look at her, his black eyes glittering. 'You might want to read this before we go any further,' he observed.

'What is it?' she questioned.

He hesitated—an uncharacteristic enough gesture for Jasmine to instantly be on her guard.

'In a nutshell?' he responded. 'It's a legal document which requires only your signature.'

Her crushed heart crashed against her ribcage. 'My signature?' she echoed.

'That's right.'

She blinked as she surveyed the envelope with the wariness of someone being presented with an unexploded bomb. 'What kind of legal document?'

Unbuttoning the soft leather jacket, he subjected

her to the full intensity of his ebony gaze. 'One which will make you a very rich woman, Jazz,' he said quietly. 'Giving you the kind of wealth which would make creating your own fashion label a reality rather than a hopeless dream.'

'Really?' she said, trying to stop her voice from sounding as if she were being strangled but wanting—no, *needing*—to hear the full extent of his heartlessness so she could remind herself of it if ever she was stupid enough to entertain a single tender thought about him. 'And what exactly would I have to do to get this money?'

There was a pause.

'I think you know the answer to that. You sign over all rights to my son.'

She'd known he was going to say something on those lines but she hadn't expected his statement to be quite so bald. It was shocking and it was unbelievable. In effect he was asking her to *sell her baby*! To sign over 'all rights' to him and make as if he hadn't grown in her womb for nine whole months before he'd finally flopped, red-faced and bawling, into the world, after a long labour which had had her screaming with pain and gripping onto the hand of the nearest midwife, because she had birthed Darius alone.

She remembered the kick of his little heel against her distended belly during the long, hot summer of her pregnancy. The sight of his little heart fluttering frantically during the ultrasound appointments at the hospital, when she had blinked at the rapidly moving image and thought how it seemed like magic. Could he really be asking her to just give her son up, to hand him over for an inflated sum of money?

She searched his face for some sign that he might feel bad about making his brutal request, but there was no guilt or shame on his hawk-like features. Nothing other than a grim determination to get what he wanted, as befitted an all-powerful sheikh. And even though she wanted to fly across the room and rake her fingernails down that hard face while demanding to know how he dared to be so cruel and ruthless, Jasmine resisted the urge to retaliate in anything other than a calm and reasoned manner. Because drama wouldn't serve her well. In fact, it wouldn't surprise her if he had one of his palace doctors listening at the door recording their conversation, waiting for the first opportunity to pronounce her as hysterical and unfit to care for the baby prince. A new determination began to rise up inside her, made stronger by her fierce and protective love for her little boy. 'You must know I could never agree to that, Zuhal,' she said, equally quietly.

He subjected her to an assessing look. 'I had hoped you might be reasonable, Jazz.' The tightening of his jaw was the only outward sign that he was irritated by her response. 'But if you really think that maintaining contact across two such dramatically different cultures would benefit the child's welfare, rather than unsettling the hell out of him—then we will have to negotiate some sort of visitation rights for you.'

Some sort of visitation rights? Had he taken leave of his senses? Jasmine stared at him in confusion before comprehension dawned on her and she gave a sudden laugh. 'Oh, I see,' she said slowly. 'That's the first rule of successful bargaining, isn't it? You go in high, then negotiate down. You make your initial proposition so outlandish that I'm then supposed to be grateful for every little concession you make afterwards. Isn't that right? But we aren't talking about oil or diamonds or territory here, Zuhal, or any of the things you usually bargain for—we're talking about a baby.' The breath felt thick and tight in her throat. She felt as if she could hardly get the words out. 'I'm not going to just hand him over to you and *visit* him! Apart from missing him more than I can imagine—I wouldn't put it past you to veto my visa and ban me from ever entering Razrastan! How can you possibly ask such a thing and claim to have any humanity in your heart? Every child needs its mother!'

Zuhal met her furious glare. She was wrong about that, he thought bitterly. No child *needed* a mother. He had managed well enough without his, hadn't he? Even though the Queen had been there *physically*—a glamorous and ethereal presence in the royal palace—she had never been there for him. Shamelessly devoted to his older brother, she had taken parental favouritism and elevated it to a whole new level. Many times he had thought it would be preferable growing up without her, for she used to look through him as if he were invisible. She had made him *feel* invisible.

'Having a mother isn't *necessary*,' he bit out. 'Many successful men and women have managed perfectly well without a maternal influence. You have only to examine the pages of history to realise that.'

In frustration she shook her head and a lock of buttery blonde hair fell against her flushed cheek. 'I'm not talking about mothers who die or who for some reason can't look after their children. I'm talking about mothers who have a choice. And I do have a choice, Zuhal. Oh, I may not have your money or power but I have something which is worth a whole lot more than any of those things, and that is love. I love Darius with all my heart and I would do anything for him. Anything. And I can tell you right now that, no matter what you say or try to do, you won't succeed in taking him away from me!'

Zuhal's eyes narrowed as he absorbed the passionate fervour of her words. She was daring to argue with him in a way she would never have done in the past, when her role in his life had been nothing more than his compliant mistress, whose role had been to bring him pleasure. She had become a lioness during their separation, he realised with grudging admiration, before wondering how he was going to talk her out of her convictions.

Once it would have been easy. A soft smile and seeking look would have been enough to get her to capitulate to his wishes. But back then their roles had been very different and no one would ever have described them as equals. And things had changed. She'd just told him she had no power but she was wrong. She had all the power because she had his son and it seemed he was going to have to move strategically to get what he wanted.

Taking a few moments' respite from the unresolved thoughts which were racing around his mind, he looked around her cramped cottage, registering again how cheap it looked. For the first time it occurred to him that, despite her earlier promise to 'rustle up' some food, there was no evidence of this. No table lovingly set with candles or flowers. No napkin elaborately folded to resemble a fan or some other such nonsense. In short, none of the lavish attention to detail he was used to whenever he had allowed a woman to cook for him.

'I mean what I say, Zuhal,' she continued, her terse words falling into the uneasy silence which had fallen. 'You're not rubbing me out of Darius's life and behaving as if I didn't exist.'

Turning away from his scrutiny of the decor, he fixed her with a steady stare. 'The alternative will not be easy,' he warned softly.

She blinked with incomprehension. 'What do you mean?'

'Having a child being brought up as half-royal, half-commoner. Half-English and half-Razrastanian.'

'Then let him be brought up as English.'

'No way,' he growled. 'He needs to be aware of his royal ancestry and the responsibilities which might one day rest upon his shoulders.'

She frowned at him. 'Surely you're not implying that Darius could one day be King—when he is illegitimate.'

Zuhal stilled as a sudden wave of cynical possibility washed over him. Was this what she had secretly hoped for all along? he wondered. She'd accused him of going in with high stakes, but perhaps she was doing the same thing in her determination to drive a hard bargain. Perhaps the reality was that she was ambitious for herself as well as for her son. Perhaps having had a little time to think about it, she was imagining what could be hers, if she went about it in the right way. Because what woman wouldn't want to be a queen of the desert, with jewels and palaces and unrivalled wealth? More than that, who wouldn't want to be married to *him*? Many had jockeyed for that position in the past, but none had succeeded.

'If you're trying to get me to marry you, I can tell you right now it's not going to happen.' His voice took on a harsh and forbidding note. 'Because nothing has changed, Jazz. You are still a foreign divorcee who would be totally unsuitable for the role of Queen. My people would never accept you. Which is why I must put duty first and continue my search to find a suitable bride. But that doesn't mean that Darius can't be my insurance policy—just in case I don't produce another male heir.'

Her look of quiet reflection was replaced by one of incredulity. 'Trying to get you to marry me?' she scoffed. 'Do you really think I'd want to marry a man who treats women like second-class citizens—who regards his little boy as nothing but an *insurance policy*?'

'Fortunately, that question is destined to remain academic, since I have no intention of doing so.' His smile was swift and dismissive. 'Which means we must come to an alternative arrangement which will satisfy all parties.'

'What kind of arrangement?' Defiantly, she tilted her chin. 'What do you want?'

There was a pause. 'Who knows his true identity?'

'Nobody—not even my cousin,' she answered truthfully. 'I couldn't see the point of people finding out his father was a sheikh.'

He nodded. 'Good.'

'I didn't do it in order to get your praise,' she objected. 'I did it because I wanted to be able to trust people's true motives for getting to know us. I didn't want us to stand out, or for Darius to be made into a talking point.'

'If my brother had not died then things would be very different,' he observed reflectively. 'But he did. One day I hope to have a legitimate heir, but if that doesn't happen, then Darius will be entitled to inherit the crown. And since you refuse to let me take him back to Razrastan, then it seems he must grow up here. With you.'

'Well, thank heavens for that,' she said, breathing out a sigh of relief. 'Because I can't think of anything worse for his welfare than being incarcerated in some gilded palace with an autocratic brute like you!'

His nostrils flared. 'Nobody else would dare speak to me in such a way,' he iced out.

'That's about the only piece of information which has given me pleasure during this entire meeting!'

'Enough!' he snapped. 'It is imperative Darius learns about the country he might one day rule, which is why I want him brought up in London, so he can be schooled at the Razrastanian embassy. In a city which is big, and anonymous. Where nobody is going to discover his true identity—not if you don't tell them.'

'But we don't live in London, Zuhal,' she pointed out. 'We live in Oxfordshire.'

'That is not a problem. You will move.'

'I am not a pawn on a chessboard! I will not move!'

His patience seemingly exhausted, he slammed his fist down on a flimsy-looking table which shivered beneath the force and when he looked at her, Jasmine could see a fire-like determination blazing from his black eyes.

'I will take no more of your futile arguments, Jazz— or your defiant show of so-called pride in refusing to accept my support,' he raged. 'Because there are some things you need to understand. And number one is that there is no way a royal prince will be brought up somewhere like this! Why, there is barely room to swing a cat!'

'We don't have a cat.'

'Will you stop interrupting me?' he raged. 'You will need to be rehoused somewhere befitting my son's status. Somewhere secure.' His gaze moved with withering precision to the crack in the peeling window-frame, which was currently sending a whistle of chilly air into the small room. 'A place which isn't offering an open invitation for thieves and has room for the bodyguards our son needs and which I will be providing, whether you like it or not. Money is obviously not a consideration and I imagine you will quickly discover that you'll enjoy living somewhere which is considerably different from this.' His mouth hardened into a cynical line. 'Most women find luxury addictive, in my experience.'

Jasmine felt a mixture of fury and pain—and his reference to the other women in his life wasn't helping matters. He was insulting her home and lifestyle and maybe she should take him to task for that. But couldn't part of her see the wisdom in what he said, much as she hated to admit it? The modest savings she'd accrued while working at the Granchester hadn't lasted nearly as long as she'd expected, and her sewing only brought in enough money for them to keep their heads above water. Life was often a struggle and it was only going to get worse. She knew what it was like to be the poor kid in school. The one who was forced to sign up for free school dinners. Who lived in fear of someone commenting about the too-small hand-me-down clothes or the shoes which badly needed heeling. The last thing she wanted was for Darius to grow up like that—so how could she let pride stand in the way?

She gave a reluctant shrug. 'I suppose what you say makes sense.'

Zuhal's eyes narrowed. It was not the gratitude he had expected—not by any stretch of the imagination. He inclined his head with regal solemnity, but behind the formal mask he seethed at her stubbornness and thanklessness. 'I will have my people arrange somewhere for you to live as soon as possible,' he said coolly. 'Just pack up the essentials and be ready to leave when you hear from my office.'

Again, she was shaking her head, the long plait swinging like a blonde pendulum, and Zuhal was suddenly filled with an urgent desire to see her newly long hair spread out over his pillow.

'Actually, I would prefer to have some choice in our new home,' she said.

He opened his mouth as if to object, before closing it again. 'Very well,' he agreed reluctantly. 'I will have a shortlist drawn up for you to consider. And you'll need a new wardrobe—not just for the baby, but for you.'

She gave a bitter laugh. 'I don't want your charity, Zuhal. I never did. I'll wear what I always wear and make my own clothes.'

'You will do no such thing,' he contradicted icily. 'Because you are no longer a shop-worker living in hotel accommodation, or a single mother struggling to get by. You will be living in an expensive part of the city and it will naturally arouse suspicion if you look out of place—which, given your current appearance, wouldn't be difficult.'

Jasmine might have objected if his words hadn't been painfully true. She'd always tried to keep herself looking nice but it wasn't as easy as it had been in the past. Darius took up a lot of her waking hours and there simply wasn't the time to make new outfits for herself. Or the money. She tucked a long strand of hair behind her ear. It was why she'd stopped going to the hairdresser— why she'd let her trademark bob grow out.

She chewed her lip. It would be awful if she refused Zuhal's charity—because that was essentially what it was—and then got mistaken for a cleaner or a nanny when she was stepping into the elevator in her smart new London home. Because she knew how money worked. She'd worked at the Granchester long enough to recognise that rich people were only really comfortable with people like themselves. Who looked like them and spoke like them. And she didn't. Not by any stretch of the imagination. Not in her cheap jeans and a thrift shop sweater from which no amount of washing could shift the stubborn stain of regurgitated carrot purée which sat on the shoulder like a faded epaulet.

And then something else occurred to her. 'What about you?' she questioned.

He had been gathering up the Manila envelope which he had dumped on the table on his arrival but he looked up when she spoke, his black eyes watchful. 'What about me?'

'Where will you be living?'

He shrugged. 'I shall make sure I have a base in London close enough to see my son, but for the rest of the time I shall be in Razrastan, preparing for my future. For the formal signing of government papers to allow me to rule until...' his voice faltered slightly '...until my brother can be legally declared dead.'

She nodded, forcing herself to remember the human tragedy which lay at the heart of all this. 'Of course,' she said, sympathy softening her voice despite his harshness towards her.

There was a pause. He seemed to hesitate. 'And of course, I have another important matter to consider.'

'Oh? What's that?'

'My marriage,' he stated coolly.

Jasmine started, her heart jolting as if someone had just pulsed an electric shock right through it. 'Your marriage?'

He nodded. 'I still need someone by my side to help me rule my country—and as soon as possible. Which is why I must find a suitable candidate. I just wanted to warn you in advance, in case the press start speculating.' His gaze seared over her like a dark laser. 'I know what you're thinking, Jazz. That the discovery of my son and heir is a complicating factor in my matrimonial plans, but I don't anticipate any problems.' He smiled. 'My future wife will need to be a very understanding woman, for that is one of my requirements. And during access visits, she will love our son and treat him as her own. I will make sure of that.'

Jasmine prayed her face wouldn't betray her feelings. Had he really said he knew what she was thinking? He didn't have a *clue*. The hurt. The anger. The shame. The *fear*. She told herself she didn't care what Zuhal did with his life or who he took as his wife. But she did. Of course she did. She wanted to rail against the thought of another woman becoming stepmother to Darius, but there wasn't a lot she could do about it. It was a fact of modern life. She'd had a stepmother herself, hadn't she?

And look how that had turned out. Her father's much younger wife had resented all evidence that he'd been married before. She hadn't even allowed Jasmine to play with her baby stepsister—though that had actually worked in everyone's favour, because Jasmine's mother had been hysterical at the thought her daughter might prefer her new 'blended' family.

Painful memories of the past dissolved and Jasmine met the ebony ice of Zuhal's stare. She wished she could tell him to go to hell and that she had no intention of letting him move her into an apartment in a strange city, no matter how luxurious it happened to be. But she couldn't do that, because she recognised that Zuhal wanted the best for his son and maybe anonymous London was a better option than a rural little village. But that didn't mean that she had to roll over like a puppy dog and accept whatever he was prepared to throw her way, did it? Which meant she didn't have to entertain him for a second longer than she needed to. This man who was impervious to her pain.

'Would you like to look in on Darius before you leave?' she questioned in a calm voice, slightly mollified by his look of bemusement.

'Leave?' He frowned. 'Weren't you supposed to be cooking me supper?'

Her expression didn't change. 'There's nothing on the go, I'm afraid. But even if there was, I seem to have lost my appetite. And quite frankly, you're the last person I feel like sharing a meal with right now, Zuhal.'

CHAPTER FOUR

'So.' Zuhal's deep voice was clipped and matter-of-fact. 'What do you think of your new home?'

Jasmine wasn't sure what to think. She was still whirling from the speed with which her move to London had happened, and, with Darius now fast asleep in his luxury new baby seat, this was the first chance she'd had to get her bearings since arriving in the city that morning. To get used to her new accommodation. Home, Zuhal had called it—yet it didn't feel a bit like home.

She glanced around the sitting room—trying to get used to a room the size of a football pitch, with its stunning views over the bright green treetops of Hyde Park. It was the place she'd liked best out of the shortlist of properties the Sheikh's office had drawn up, mainly because it was the only one which didn't make her feel as if she was hemmed in by other buildings. This high up the traffic was just a distant hum—like bees—so it almost felt as if you were in the country rather than in the middle of a city. Jasmine had seen the apartment when it had been empty and cavernous—but in the interim, it had been completely and luxuriously furnished by an unknown hand.

She would have liked some say in the furniture herself and although she couldn't fault the decor, it had a distinctly impersonal feel to it—as if some top-end designer had simply thrown a lot of money at it. Giant velvet sofas were coloured in shades echoing the soft hues of the silken rugs which adorned the gleaming wooden floors. Vibrant oil paintings hung on the pale walls and a bronze sculpture of a horse's head was silhouetted against one of the tall windows. There were even glossy unread magazines artistically placed on one of several coffee tables and coloured glass vases full of fragrant roses. It looked like a set from a film—a room designed in a single day—not built up with memories, bit by bit, like a normal home. But whoever had said any of this would be normal? It wasn't normal to have been whisked here by darkened limousine, was it? Nor to have been followed by a fleet of bodyguards who, as far as she knew, were still lurking outside with those suspicious-looking lumps beneath their loose jackets.

Zuhal had arrived soon afterwards, sweeping in without any of his usual coterie of aides, which meant she was now alone with him, something which was making her pulse race and her breasts to become engorged and she hated it. She hated her body's instinctive reaction to a man who had proved how cold and heartless he could be. Who had announced his intention to take a royal bride and who regarded his firstborn son as his 'insurance policy'. But she was trying her best not to pass judgement, because that wouldn't benefit Darius in the long run, would it?

She wondered if she would ever get used to living somewhere which had three bathrooms—three!—all gleaming white and flashing silver and now crammed with the same bath products she'd sold in the Granchester Hotel boutique, so she knew exactly how eye-watering their cost.

She had chosen her own bedroom after the most cursory of glances because she had no desire to be in any room containing a bed, not with Zuhal breathing down her neck and creating the kind of flashbacks she could have happily done without. The most beautiful room of all was the nursery, which had been prepared for Darius. There was a curved crib fashioned from wood which felt satin-soft to the touch and a mobile full of planets and stars dangling from the ceiling above it. On a pristine window sill was a line of toys—fluffy bears and a soft little monkey with bright eyes. And somehow, the simple comfort of this room made Jasmine feel that the decision to move here had been the right one, if only for her son's sake.

She walked over to the window—away from the subtle sandalwood of Zuhal's scent—and peered down into the park, where she could see people braving the light spring breeze and sitting on benches to eat their supermarket sandwiches. A teenage boy was doing gravity-defying things on a skateboard. Around the line of the lake, she could see the yellow blur of daffodils, all dancing and fluttering in the breeze—just like in the poem she'd learnt at school. She'd been hopeful back then—until her mother's final meltdown about her father's supposed sins had made schooling something she'd just had to fit in whenever she could, and attention to homework an impossible dream.

But something about that memory made her think about the future. Her own ambitions might have tumbled along the wayside, but Darius still had a lifetime to look forward to. Shouldn't she try to put a positive spin on everything which was happening, despite her many misgivings? To answer the Sheikh's question with enthusiasm rather than doubt.

'It's lovely,' she said, as she turned back to face him.

If he had been expecting a slightly more ringing endorsement, he made no reference to it. 'And do you think you can be happy here?' he persisted.

Happy? It was a funny question. Since Darius's birth, all Jasmine had wanted was to ensure security for him and now she'd done just that—even though she hadn't planned it. From now on the two of them were going to be living in unbelievable splendour, while Zuhal picked up all the bills. She should have been relieved, and yet...

How could she possibly be relieved—or relaxed—when part of her still wanted the Sheikh so badly, even though she knew it was wrong to feel that way? Her body ached whenever he was in the vicinity and she was poignantly reminded of how it had felt when he used to make love to her, and a big part of her wanted that to happen all over again. Yet he'd blithely told her he was going in search of a bride who would one day become her baby's stepmother. Wouldn't that kind of cold cruelty fill most people with anger instead of desire?

Unwillingly, she began to study him—wondering if she would be able to do that objectively. But for now, at least, objectivity was a fruitless expectation. His dark grey suit flattered his broad-shouldered body to perfection, subtly showcasing all the muscular power which lay beneath. He had been born to make women look at him, with those hawkish good looks and eyes of ebony fire. She remembered the way she used to stroke her fingers through his hair—giving him the Indian head massage which one of the spa therapists at the Granchester had taught her to do. She remembered what an overdeveloped feeling of pleasure it had given her—to have the powerful and alpha Sheikh purring like a pussycat and relaxing under her rhythmical ministrations.

With an effort she dragged her gaze away from him and glanced out of the window, where sunlight was bouncing off the fresh green leaves which were shimmering in the distance. 'I'm going to do everything in my power to be happy,' she said truthfully.

'Good. That is the kind of positive attitude I like.'

She shrugged as she turned to meet his eyes. 'I'm not doing it for your benefit, Zuhal. I owe it to my son.'

'Our son, Jazz. Please don't ever forget that,' he corrected smoothly, shooting a quick glance at his watch as the doorbell rang, its peal sounding unnaturally loud as it echoed through the spacious apartment. 'Excellent. Right on cue. Come with me, please.'

Jasmine blinked. Surely they weren't expecting visitors? During several heated debates about privacy during the choosing of this apartment, she'd got the definite message that she and Zuhal weren't going to be doing any socialising together. In fact, their relationship—such as it was—was very definitely to be kept under the radar. Which suited her just fine. She wanted to spend as little time with him as possible. No. Why not put it another way? She *needed* to spend as little time with him as possible, if she wanted to hang onto her sanity. 'Come where?' she questioned. 'Who's that ringing the doorbell?'

'Wait and see.'

Jasmine clamped her lips shut, annoyed at his high-handedness but, her curiosity alerted, she followed him past the blissfully sleeping Darius, towards the front door.

After a low-voiced command in his native tongue, the door was opened from the outside by a bodyguard, to reveal a woman standing there. Aged around thirty, she was dressed in what Jasmine recognised instantly as traditional Razrastanian robes and her hair was coiled on top of her head in an elaborate fretwork of black waves. She directed a kind smile towards Jasmine before bobbing a curtsey to Zuhal, who immediately indicated that she should stand at ease as he gestured for her to enter the apartment.

'Jazz, I'd like you to meet Rania,' he said. 'She is going to be helping you look after Darius. His new nanny.'

'I am very pleased to meet you, mistress,' said Rania in perfectly modulated English. 'And I am very much looking forward to meeting Darius.'

'Why don't you come and meet him right now?' suggested Zuhal smoothly.

'He's asleep,' said Jasmine quickly, still reeling from this latest development and yet another demonstration of Zuhal's high-handedness.

'I will not wake him, mistress,' said Rania softly.

What else could she do other than lead her to the baby? Jasmine told herself it was pitiful how hard her heart clenched as she watched the Razrastanian woman crouch down and fix her dark gaze on the sleeping Darius, as if committing every atom to memory.

'The son of the Sheikh is a truly magnificent baby,' said Rania at last, as she straightened up.

Jasmine couldn't fault the sentiment but her smile felt forced. She felt like a puppet. As if everyone were pulling her strings. Moving her this way, then that—leaving her with no idea of where she was or what she was doing. And all she could think of were the words Rania had spoken and which were now circling inside her head. *The son of the Sheikh. The son of the Sheikh.* Was the Razrastanian nanny, despite her kind smile and soft voice, planning to push Jasmine to the side-lines and edge her out of the picture, so that his royal father could assume complete dominance? She could feel her mouth growing firm with determination. Well, that was never going to happen.

Never.

'He bears such a strong resemblance to his father,' Rania was cooing.

Jasmine wished she could deny it. To say that, actually, the baby had *her* eyes or *her* hair—but there was no evidence of her features, or her hazel eyes or blonde locks. With his olive skin and black hair, there surely couldn't be another child on the planet who was more a mini-me of his darkly handsome father than Darius. His limbs were sturdy, his eyelashes outrageously long, and the baby clinic had already told her how tall he was going to be.

'Indeed he is, Rania,' Jasmine said, trying to regain her composure as she turned her attention to more practical matters. 'Whereabouts…um, where will you be staying?'

She could see Rania looking uncertainly towards Zuhal as if for guidance and the Sheikh interposed instantly.

'Rania has her own apartment, which is connected to this one,' he said, with the smooth assurance of a man who had thought of everything. 'I don't think you can have paid it very much attention during your first viewing.'

Jasmine's lips tightened. Obviously not.

'I was here yesterday, putting the final touches to it,' said Rania proudly. 'Would you care to see it, mistress?'

'I most certainly would,' said Jasmine, shooting Zuhal a furious glance. 'And really, there's no need to call me mistress. Jasmine will do just fine.'

'But—'

'*Please*,' said Jasmine firmly, wondering if Rania—despite all her linguistic skill—had any idea that the word mistress had a very different meaning in English. One which she definitely did not wish to be associated with *her*. She forced a new brightness into her voice. 'Let's go, shall we? I can't wait to see where you'll be living, Rania.'

In silence, the three of them walked along the long corridor, until they reached a door at the far end, which Jasmine hadn't noticed before. Or rather, it was the one thing the agent hadn't bothered to point out during an otherwise extensive tour—perhaps if she'd been feeling a little less dazed she might have discovered it herself. The Razrastanian woman pushed open the door and gestured for them to step inside, which Jasmine did—although she noticed that Zuhal remained standing broodily on the threshold.

Inside, was a separate and very beautiful little apartment, with a door leading to a bedroom and another to a neat kitchen. A sitting room with its own small terrace overlooked the park and on one of the walls was a framed poster of a place Jasmine instantly recognised. She felt as if someone were twisting a knife inside her as she studied the imposing building in the foreground of the picture. A golden palace with soaring towers and cobalt cupolas which glinted in the bright sunshine. Jasmine swallowed, for she knew that this was Zuhal's home. The home he would soon share with his royal bride.

And, for half the year—with Darius, too.

'What a beautiful view you've got, Rania,' she said weakly.

Did Zuhal guess how churned up she was feeling? Was that why he stepped forward, to take her by the elbow to support her, as if she were an old lady he was helping to cross a busy road. Quickly she brushed his hand away because she didn't want him touching her—and not just because she couldn't trust her body's reaction to him. Did he really think that an outward show of concern could make up for the fact that he was behaving like an overbearing brute? First, he'd announced that he intended marrying another woman—and now this!

'Why don't we let Rania get settled in?' he suggested smoothly. 'You can both talk baby routine later.'

Rania nodded, quietly closing the door as she disappeared into her rooms, and Jasmine waited until she and Zuhal were back in the sitting room before she said anything. Waited until they were completely out of earshot and made sure that Darius was still asleep—and that her breathing had settled down-so her words didn't come out in a senseless babble.

'You let me vet the apartment!' she accused him hotly. 'But you didn't think to give me the opportunity of telling you whether or not I liked the woman you have employed to help take care of our son?'

'Everyone likes Rania,' he said.

'That's not the point!' Dangerously close to yelling, Jasmine sucked in a deep, unsteady breath. 'And what's more—you know it! So don't give me that *I don't know what you're talking about* look and expect me to be taken in by it!'

Zuhal found himself taken aback by her rage and, in another situation, might almost have been amused by it—because didn't such passion always change into something much more agreeable when it was transferred to the bedroom? But that was never going to happen, judging by the way Jazz was glaring at him—with emerald fire spitting from her eyes.

Undeterred, he loosened his tie a fraction. 'He is a desert prince, Jazz,' he said. 'And having a nanny is a given for all royal children. He will be looked after by someone who speaks my language and who knows the myths and legends of my country. He will grow up bilingual, which is essential for a boy who might one day be King.'

'But I've only ever looked after him myself. I told you before—I've never left him with a stranger.'

'Rania is the daughter of my own nanny at the palace—my favourite, as it happens. She speaks perfect English and received her training at one of the finest establishments in England, one which provides childcare for your own royal family, just in case you're interested.'

'Not particularly. And that isn't the point. You should have asked me first.'

His patience was beginning to wear thin but Zuhal bit back the impatient retort which was on the tip of his tongue, telling himself to go easy on her. To treat her with impartiality as they negotiated their way through these tricky new waters. But how was such impartiality possible when his mind and his body had been in constant conflict, since he'd walked up the weed-strewn path of her little cottage less than a fortnight ago? When every night since he had been plagued by memories of her soft breasts and curvy hips. By the disturbing recall of the way she used to wriggle over his body like some kind of sexy eel, mounting him with a yelp of exultant pleasure as she rode them both to fulfilment. And then afterwards run her fingers through his hair, digging their firm tips into his scalp and massaging away the tension, so that he'd been left feeling almost *boneless* with pleasure.

The other day he'd kissed her and the kiss they'd shared had been as potent as any he could remember. Was that because it had been abruptly cut short and not allowed to proceed to its natural conclusion? Was that why his subsequent sense of frustration had been more pronounced than any he could remember? Zuhal acknowledged the hard jerk of his groin, feeling as if his body was somehow taunting him.

There were a million reasons why he shouldn't want her, even if you discounted her basic unsuitability. She had deceived him. Had tried to keep their child a secret from him. Why, even when Darius had cried out, when he had still been ignorant of his identity, Zuhal had seen the distress clouding her pale face—and then her deliberate manipulation as she had sought to distract him.

If she could have got him out of her cottage without disclosing he was a father, then she would have done, he reminded himself grimly.

But even that knowledge did not lessen her allure, or stop him from wishing he could carry her into one of those conveniently empty bedrooms to slake his hunger for her, once and for all. And then maybe rid her memory from his mind for ever.

He sighed. Compromise wasn't something he was often called upon to use, but maybe he should make an exception in this case. Slowly he inclined his head, determined to acknowledge her concerns. 'If, for any reason, Rania proves unsatisfactory...' he saw her visibly brighten '...any *sensible* reason,' he added swiftly, 'then we can use someone else. Do you think I would do anything to threaten or disrupt the life of my son, Jazz?'

'Now you're making me sound unreasonable.'

'That was not my intention. Darius needs someone in his life other than his parents,' he said. 'Someone to trust and feel safe with. Surely you must see that?'

She was nodding her head now, as if determined to match his own mood of compromise with one of her own. Smoothing her dress down with fingers he noticed weren't quite steady, she met his eyes with a rare expression of complicity. 'I suppose you're right.' She shrugged. 'Especially since he doesn't have any grandparents.'

Zuhal's mouth hardened, but he was unable to manufacture any sorrow that this was the case, for he had grown up without knowing his own grandparents, which might have helped dissolve some of the tensions which had existed in the palace. But he had survived, hadn't he? Deliberately, he focussed his gaze on Jazz because that was infinitely more pleasurable than thinking about the toxic environment in which he had been raised.

In just a fortnight the chill weather had turned into something more usual for this time of year and her simple cotton dress was sprigged with blossom—she had clearly made it herself—with her soft pink cardigan a shade lighter than the tiny flowers. She looked young, vibrant and utterly desirable and Zuhal was filled with a powerful desire to touch her. To crush his lips down on hers and to slide his fingers beneath her floaty skirt and touch her where she was warm and sticky. His throat thickened. Yet despite the undeniable allure of her appearance, she looked like a student on her way to lectures, not a young woman who now occupied one of the most expensive pieces of real estate in London.

'I thought I told you to buy yourself some new clothes,' he observed.

'What's wrong with what I'm wearing?'

'There's nothing *wrong* with them. But your clothes are not appropriate for your new position in life, Jazz,' he said softly. 'We both know that.'

She gave a quick nod of her head, as if she was preparing to say something difficult. 'And how exactly would you define that position, Zuhal—that's something we haven't discussed, have we?'

Zuhal tensed. Was this an invitation to be completely frank with her? To reach a new understanding which they could both enjoy to the max? What was it the English sometimes said? *To make hay while the sun shines.* He felt his pulse quicken. Her eyes were no longer flashing green fire, obscuring the golden lights which usually glinted there. But in place of the anger he could detect a distinct smokiness—and Zuhal had known enough women to recognise what that meant. Hadn't she made it obvious when he'd walked in here today and looked at him with desire in her eyes? When he had observed the instinctive hardening of her nipples beneath the cheap cotton of her dress.

'That's up to you, Jazz,' he said silkily. 'The decision is yours.'

Her eyes narrowed with suspicion. 'You're being very…oblique. I'm still not quite sure what you mean.'

'Then let me state my words plainly, so there can be no misunderstanding.' He paused, aware that his throat had dried, so that it resembled the dust of his beloved desert homeland. 'When we kissed the other day, there was no doubt that the passion which burns between us was as strong as before. I looked at you and I wanted you. I still do, despite your determination to keep my son from me and your subsequent defiant behaviour. But I am willing to overlook your stubbornness, because you were the best lover I've ever had.' He glittered her a smile. 'And I am eager to taste such pleasures with you again.'

She nodded her head solemnly, as if she was giving his words careful thought before responding to them. 'You're saying you want us to take up where we left off last time, is that it?'

He slanted her a smile. The kind of smile which women had told him was like being caught beneath the full force of the sun. 'I couldn't have put it better myself,' he said softly.

'Even though you are currently in the market for a royal bride?'

His smile died. 'That isn't going to happen overnight, Jazz. Even though speed is of the essence—I don't anticipate taking a wife before the end of the year.'

'And during that brief window of opportunity, we'll be lovers?'

'I knew you would understand,' he breathed.

'Oh, I understand all right.' The fire in her eyes was back and so too was the mulish tilt of her chin. 'I understand that you're an arrogant man with an overdeveloped sense of entitlement, who treats women like toys he can just pick up and toss away once he's had enough of them.'

She took a step closer, like a boxer squaring up to an opponent in the ring.

'Do you really think I'm going to hang around here, waiting for one of your rare visits—ready to drop everything when you deign to show your face-and then simply fall into bed with you?'

'How dare you speak to me this way?'

'While in the meantime,' she continued remorselessly, 'you're out there courting every eligible princess the desert region has to offer in order to find yourself a suitable bride?'

'That's a very extreme way of looking at it,' he bit out.

'It's the truth, Zuhal,' she said. 'What other way is there to look at it?'

He glowered at her. 'I have been completely straight with you, Jazz. Perhaps you would do me the honour of returning the favour. And if you don't want to be my lover, then how do you intend spending your time?'

Jasmine sucked in a deep breath, knowing she needed to be strong. Or at least she needed to *appear* strong. Zuhal didn't have to know she wanted intimacy just as much as he did—the difference being that for her it spelt emotional danger. 'You are planning to live your life as you see fit, Zuhal,' she said quietly. 'And I'm going to do exactly the same. I'm going to be the best mother I can, and to accommodate your wishes where Darius is concerned. But I'm also going to live my own life. I plan to make friends and forge a future for myself.'

'With a man?' he shot out instantly.

Jasmine couldn't deny the pleasure she got from the dark look of jealousy which crossed his features and made his shadowed jaw clench. And although the thought of being anywhere near any man other than Zuhal made her feel violently sick, he didn't have to know that.

'Who knows what I will do? I'm young and free and single,' she said, with a carelessness she hoped didn't sound faked. 'And this is England, Zuhal. Where men and women are equal.'

He gave an angry snort, a pulse flickering wildly at his temple as he walked away without another word, and Jasmine was surprised that the loud slamming of the front door hadn't woken the baby.

CHAPTER FIVE

'HIS ROYAL HIGHNESS is waiting for you in the drawing room, mistress.'

Pausing in the middle of unbuckling Darius from a buggy the size of a small car, Jasmine hid her frown as she was met by a nervous-looking Rania. She'd learnt it was pointless to ask the nanny not to call her 'mistress', just as she'd learnt she had absolutely no control over the Sheikh's movements in her life. That he turned up when he felt like it and, of course, could walk right in whenever he wanted to because there was always Rania or a bodyguard to let him in. And because he owned it, of course. She might be the one who was living here, but Zuhal was the one who had paid for the apartment and everything it contained. Sometimes it felt as if he *owned* her, too.

It wasn't an ideal situation, because every time he arrived she had to fight an instinctive urge to touch him—and how crazy was *that*? Just as she had to fight the desire to stare at him and drink in all his power and his hard, masculine beauty—because remembering just how good it felt to be in his arms would do her no favours at all. He flew into London once a week on business and Jasmine tried to make herself scarce whenever he arrived to see his son, although Rania was always on hand to meekly obey his orders. Because pretending they were a happy family was nothing but a mockery of the harsh reality.

And because she didn't want to get stuck into a doomed pattern of togetherness, which would be shattered when he found himself a royal bride.

But every time Zuhal left, she had to go through the process of eradicating him from her mind, telling herself that meaningless sex with her ex-lover was a bad idea in every respect, no matter how much her body craved it or how fierce the unspoken attraction which always seemed to sizzle between them. She'd had her chance and she'd done the right thing in turning it down. That ship had sailed.

Rania stepped forward. 'Let me take Darius for you, mistress.'

'Thanks, Rania—but I'll do it. I think he's teething because he was up for most of the night. He was a bit cranky in the clinic this morning, but the nurse said he's coming on leaps and bounds.'

Nervously, Rania cleared her throat. 'This is excellent news, mistress, but His Royal Highness will not enjoy being kept waiting.'

'I'm sure he won't,' said Jasmine, a renewed cheerfulness washing over her, despite her lack of sleep. 'But maybe it will do him good.'

'You think so?' A silken voice came filtering through the air and Jasmine felt all the little hairs on the back of her neck prickling in anticipation as Zuhal entered the hallway with noiseless stealth. She could sense his presence with every soft footstep he took towards her and it took a moment for her to compose herself so that her expression would register indifference, rather than desire. She looked up to meet his gleaming eyes as, pausing only to trace the tip of a finger over his son's soft cheek, he turned to the Razrastanian nanny. 'Rania, will you mind taking care of Darius so that I can speak to Jazz in private?'

'Certainly, Your Royal Highness.'

Eagerly, Rania complied, removing Darius from his buggy with the tender efficiency which Jasmine had grown to like and trust—although she didn't like the way the nanny always deferred to the Sheikh. She looked down at the baby's black curls with a rush of fierce, maternal love, but her heart sank a little as Zuhal gestured for her to accompany him to the sitting room, where, outside, the spring flowers in the park had given way to the bright blooms of early summer.

'You didn't think to warn me that you were coming?' she said, bending down to unnecessarily straighten a velvet cushion which the cleaner had placed at perfect right angles to the one beside it.

'Why would I do that?' he questioned blandly. 'Unless you were planning to do something which you know would anger me, should I walk in on you unexpectedly. Is that the case, Jazz?'

'Please don't talk in riddles, because I haven't got the energy to work them out, Zuhal,' she said. 'Like what?'

'Like being here with another man,' he accused, all

blandness gone now as a cold note of steel entered his voice.

'I don't know what you're talking about.'

'I think you do.' He began to pace the room, more agitated than she'd ever seen him. 'There was a man here yesterday.'

Jasmine narrowed her eyes as memory came flooding back to her. 'How on earth do you know that?'

'How do you think I know?' he demanded. 'Because my bodyguards informed me!'

'So you're having me *spied* on now, are you?' she returned. 'Bad enough you sent someone to investigate the playgroup I decided to join—as if I wasn't capable of making a judgement about it myself—but now I discover that I'm not even allowed to invite friends back to what is supposed to be my *home*, without your heavies reporting back to you!'

'Please don't be so naive, Jazz,' he hissed, his pacing footsteps coming to a halt as he turned round to fix her with a blistering stare. 'My son is currently under your care and naturally my staff keep me informed if anyone unknown to them should visit the apartment. You're lucky he wasn't stopped at the door and sent on his way. So I will ask you…who was he?'

For a moment Jasmine was tempted to call his bluff. To tell him that the man in question was her new lover and they'd both been eagerly waiting until the baby was fast asleep so that they could jump into bed together and enjoy a wild night of passion. But there was being independent and there was being downright stupid—and no way was she going to mess with Zuhal, not when he was in this kind of mood. When a dark and dangerous anger was radiating from his powerful body in waves which were almost tangible.

Reluctantly, she shrugged. 'He's an Italian waiter I used to know when I was working at the Granchester.'

'An Italian waiter?' he repeated, as if she had just told him she'd been entertaining a mass murderer. 'What the hell was he doing here, Jazz? Practising his silver service technique, or was he teaching you how best they like to kiss in Roma?'

'Don't be so ridiculous,' she answered stiffly. 'He's actually been getting experience—'

'What kind of experience?' he shot back immediately.

'*Work* experience—before he goes back to join his father's restaurant in Lecce—not Rome,' she completed witheringly. 'His sister is pregnant and he knew I liked to sew, so he asked if I would design something especially for the new baby which he could take back to Italy with him. Which I have, although it's not quite finished. Here…' She slipped from the sitting room to one of the unused bedrooms, which she had turned into a makeshift sewing room, before returning with a tiny, hand-smocked romper suit which she waved in front of him. 'See for yourself if you don't believe me.'

As she held up the impossibly small garment, Zuhal felt the tight knot of tension which had been building up inside him dissolve—to be replaced by the instant rush of relief. Had he really imagined Jazz in the arms of another man? But that was the trouble. Of course he had. Many times. Because he was frustrated. Because he felt powerless. Because for once in his life here was a woman refusing to do what he wanted her to do, which was to fall into bed with him. He'd tried telling himself he could understand why she no longer wanted to be his lover and, as the mother of his son, her proud morality should please him. He told himself it was better all round if their relationship entered a new, platonic phase, yet still he couldn't stop thinking about her—even though logic told him that her chilly refusal to resume her tenure as his lover was only feeding his desire. That same logic had convinced him that sex was the only way to get her out of his system for good—for what woman didn't lose her allure when a man was repeatedly exposed to her?

And perhaps he was going about it the wrong way.

'I have seen something like this before,' he said slowly, his eyes still on the impossibly small garment.

'Of course you have. Darius has one which is very similar—although his is a different colour. Here I've used boats rather than ducklings.'

He nodded. 'It is an exquisite piece of work,' he said, his gaze taking in the delicate blue and white embroidery.

She was looking at him expectantly, as if waiting for the punchline. 'And?'

'And…nothing.' He shrugged, before producing a smile. 'You obviously have great talent.'

She shook her head in self-deprecating denial. 'I wouldn't go that far.'

'No arguments, Jazz. Why not just accept the compliment in the spirit in which it was intended?'

'Okay,' she said cautiously. 'I will. Thank you.' Her cheeks a little flushed now, she regarded him warily. 'So what can I do for you today, Zuhal? Apart from giving you a platform to demonstrate your unreasonable jealousy?'

Trying not to focus on the fecund swell of her breasts, Zuhal attempted to put his jumbled thoughts into some kind of coherent order.

'There are a couple of things I need to discuss with you.'

'That's fine. Discuss away,' she said. 'But could you please do it quickly because I'm planning to take a walk in the park while the sun's still out.'

'But you've only just got back!'

'Rania will be here while Darius has his nap, so I thought I'd have a bit of a snooze in the fresh air, because your son kept me awake for a lot of the night. Forgive me for having such an outrageous plan for my afternoon—but I wasn't aware I had to clock in and out every time I left the apartment, although maybe that was stupid of me,' she added sarcastically. 'Perhaps the reason you bought the whole penthouse floor of this block was because it resembles a fortress.'

'You don't like living here?' he questioned. 'This was your favourite out of the shortlist, if you remember?'

Jasmine hesitated because usually he didn't ask her opinion—riding roughshod over her wishes was much more his style. She knew she really ought to count her blessings now that she had security for her son and no financial worries. But despite these things, she'd quickly found London very different from Oxford—especially when you had a baby in tow. When she'd been work-ing at the Granchester she'd had no responsibilities and her time off had been her own. But not any more. Now she was achingly aware that her baby needed pals his own age, which was why she had joined an infant play-group—the one Zuhal had insisted on vetting.

Darius loved it when they sang songs and jangled tambourines and she'd met plenty of other young women her age. But they'd all been nannies, not moth-ers, which had made Jasmine feel even more of an out-sider. She'd made friends with a couple of them on a very superficial level, but hadn't dared ask them back to her home. Because if they saw all this wall-to-wall luxury, wouldn't they inevitably start asking questions? In fact, hadn't one of them—Carrie—already tried? Questions Jasmine couldn't possibly answer because then it would all come tumbling out that she was the one-time mistress of a future king, and mother to his illegitimate heir.

'It's very comfortable,' she said, in careful reply to the Sheikh's drawled query. 'But sometimes I get stir-crazy living all the way up here. I mean, I know there's the balcony to sit on but it's not quite the same as walk-ing outside. Sometimes I feel...'

'What?' he prompted softly.

'Oh, I don't know...' She shrugged her shoulders. 'Trapped.'

His eyes narrowed. 'I can understand that. Very well. I will grant you your wish. We will take a walk to-gether.'

Startled, she looked at him. 'And how's that supposed to work? I thought we weren't supposed to be seen together.'

'Nobody will notice us. We will simply be a couple out walking in the sunshine, one of many such couples. My military training taught me that I can always blend into the background if I try,' he explained. 'And my bodyguards have been trained to observe from the shadows.'

Blend in?

Jasmine stared at him. Was he deluded? Dominating the vast sitting room with his powerful presence, his outward appearance wasn't so very different from the other successful businessmen who frequented this part of the capital. In his exquisitely cut charcoal suit and a silk shirt the colour of buttermilk, he was certainly dressed like your average billionaire. But he *was* different, no two ways about it. He was a desert sheikh and that affected the way he did things. The way he thought about things. She didn't particularly want to go for a walk with him yet the alternative was being cooped up inside, with the four walls closing in on them and a sensory overload on both her imagination and her body, so Jasmine nodded her head.

'Okay,' she said.

While Zuhal spoke rapidly into his cell phone in his native tongue, she went off to get ready, checking Darius and assuring Rania she wouldn't be long. Pausing only to pull on a pair of espadrilles and cram a straw hat over her head, she exited her bedroom to find Zuhal waiting for her in the hallway, looking at his golden wristwatch with ill-disguised irritation. He had removed his tie and undone the top two buttons of his shirt, offering a distracting glimpse of dark chest hair just beneath the pale silk.

Did she imagine his jaw tightening when he caught sight of the summery espadrilles whose matching pink ribbons were criss-crossed over her lower legs like a wannabe gladiator? No, she didn't think so. She might have been innocent when she met him and been subsequently accused of naivety—but she wasn't deluded enough to deny the unmistakable sensual charge which entered the atmosphere whenever they were alone together. It was the same sensory overload which made her itch to touch the slashed angles of his darkly handsome face, and to cover his lips with hungry kisses. A response which she tried her best to batten down, usually with remarkably little effect—like today—when the tug of heat low in her belly was inconveniently reminding her how big he used to feel when he was inside her.

But it was strange and curiously satisfying being outside with him as Jasmine realised that fresh air or daylight had never really featured in their relationship. In some ways it had been more of a vampire affair. There had been those badly lit restaurants of their early dates, and afterwards her being smuggled into a borrowed mews house for snatched nights together. But the combination of blue sky and sunshine glittering on the water of the lake was making her feel curiously carefree, in a way she hadn't been for months. And Zuhal had been right about his bodyguards slipping into the shadows, because even when she looked very hard, she couldn't see them.

He hadn't exaggerated about blending in himself, either. Was it the fact that he had removed his tie, or was it just his unusually relaxed stance rather than his regal demeanour, which made him into just a spectacularly handsome man who was taking a summer stroll with his…?

What?

How would she describe her role in the future King's life? Not his girlfriend, that was for sure. Not even his lover—not any more. And mother of his child made it sound as if they'd been married, which of course they never had been. She bit her lip. She'd never had any status at all, really—which begged the question of why she had tolerated it so happily. Was that because her sexual awakening had been so powerful that it had rocked her world in a way which nothing else had come close to? Because she'd been so totally caught up in this new way of living and feeling—of being somebody's *lover*?

Or was it because at the time she'd thought herself in love with him? Crazy, really. How could you be in love with a man who treated you as a convenience—flitting in and out of your life as the mood took him? She hadn't really known him at all—and, as she was starting to get to know him now, she was seeing a ruthless side which he'd never shown before.

His deep voice broke into her reverie.

'I thought the whole point of a walk in the sunshine was that it was supposed to be relaxing, but instead you're looking as if you have all the cares of the world on your shoulders. Relax, Jazz. It's a beautiful day.'

Jasmine blinked to find the Sheikh's black gaze

trained on her. The edges of his lips were curved into a smile and silently she reproached herself. She had to stop analysing stuff and wishing for things which were never going to happen. Why couldn't she just live in the moment and enjoy it?

'You're right. It is. Gorgeous.' Tilting her hat back, she breathed in, half closing her eyes until a vaguely familiar tinkle of music made her open them again. There was an ice-cream van in the distance, with a small queue of children forming at the front, and maybe it was the powerful collision between difficult past and difficult present which made something hard and hurtful coil itself around her heart.

'Jazz? Is something wrong?'

Zuhal's deep voice snapped her back to reality and she blinked at him, momentarily disconcerted. 'Why?'

'You've gone pale.' His voice had become a silken whisper. 'As pale as milk.'

If she'd been in the apartment she would never have told him, but high up in that expensive citadel, he would never have asked. And maybe that was another thing which being outside did. It freed you from inhibition. It allowed memories to rush back and with them came all the feelings, so that in that moment she was no longer a puzzled new mother, but a bewildered little girl again.

'There was an ice-cream van outside my house when I was little,' she said, her voice sounding as if it were coming from a great distance away. 'I heard the music and went outside to listen—more to drown out the sound of my parents arguing than in any great hope of getting an ice cream.'

'And did you get one?'

'Actually, I did.' She gave a quick smile, because the Sheikh's calm question meant he was able to slip almost unnoticed into her memory. 'My father came outside and bought me a cone—the biggest I'd ever seen. A massive thing heaped with pink and white ice-cream with one of those flaky chocolate bars sticking out of the top. I was surprised because he would never normally have done that and it made me wonder why he was there, in the middle of the day, when he should have been at work. He kissed me on top of my head and said goodbye in a funny kind of voice, and I remember watching him walk down the road just as my mother came flying out of the house.'

'And?' he prompted, into the silence between them, which was broken only by the far-off sound of children playing.

She shrugged. 'My mother told me he was leaving. That he had another little girl with someone else—a new daughter he loved much more than me. She said some other stuff, too—stuff I've done my best to forget—and then she had a complete meltdown. Actually, so did my ice cream,' she added flippantly as she stared at the sun-scorched grass, willing her eyes not to fill with tears. 'Amid all the drama I'd completely forgotten about it and it fell off the cornet and lay on the pavement in a big, creamy puddle.' It had been the end of her childhood and the beginning of a new and very different phase, where she had become the mother, and her mother, the child.

'Jazz,' said Zuhal softly. 'Are you crying?'

She looked up, surprised by the sudden touch of his fingertips to her face. When had he moved close enough to touch her?

'No,' she answered proudly. 'Crying is a waste of time.'

Was she imagining the gleam of understanding in his black eyes, or was it a case of just seeing what she wanted to see? A pulse began to jump at her temple as he rubbed the pad of his thumb against her chin and that simple brush of skin against hers reminded her all too vividly of the days when their bodies had lain naked together. Jasmine swallowed, praying that he would continue, knowing that if he pulled her into his arms she would not resist. Because didn't she want that? More than anything? To feel his lips on hers and be locked in his embrace, so she could let his lovemaking melt away all her pain. Wasn't she sick and tired of the celibate stand-off which had sprung up between them?

The air between them seemed to shift and change. She could feel the sudden tension in her body as he took another step towards her. A flash of hope and longing swept through her as his hawk-like features clicked into focus, when the unexpected sound of her own name made Jasmine jump back in alarm.

'Jasmine! Hey, Jasmine!'

She turned around to see Carrie, the nosy nanny from the toddler group who today had neither of her twin charges with her. She was wearing cut-off denim hot pants which made the most of what was obviously a spray tan, and a T-shirt bearing the legend *Luscious* was stretched tightly across her generous chest.

Jasmine shot a swift look at Zuhal but he wasn't ogling the brunette stunner, unlike just about every other man in the vicinity. Instead, he was regarding Carrie with an expression of cool disdain.

'Well, hi. Fancy seeing you here,' said Carrie, looking him up and down, the gleam in her eye suggesting she found his disdainful expression both a turn-on and a challenge. 'You must be Mr Jasmine?'

'This is Zuhal,' said Jasmine quickly, only to see the Sheikh glare at her. 'We were just—'

'Leaving,' said Zuhal firmly, cupping Jasmine's elbow with the guiding clasp of his palm.

'Oh.' Carrie pouted. 'Must you? I see we're all childless. Thank. The. Lord. Why don't we go over to that Pimm's tent by the bandstand? It's a perfect day for getting sloshed in the sunshine.'

'I don't drink,' said Zuhal repressively.

Jasmine thought afterwards that it was a pity Carrie took a confident step towards him because her slightly predatory action was misinterpreted as one of aggression by his phalanx of bodyguards, who immediately swarmed from behind various trees, to surround them. Carrie was blinking at them in astonishment and Jasmine noticed that one of the bodyguards was having difficulty averting his gaze from her heaving breasts.

'Oh, wow,' breathed Carrie softly. 'Now I think I'm spoilt for choice!'

The next few minutes passed in a blur. Jasmine was aware of being virtually frogmarched out of the park and back to the apartment, with Zuhal's angry words ringing in her ears. And all that softness and understanding she'd thought she'd seen in his face had vanished, replaced by a cold censure which made his eyes glint like steel.

'I cannot believe that you associate with such people!' he stormed, as the elevator zoomed them up towards the penthouse.

'I don't think she meant any harm,' she defended. 'She's just…just a young woman who likes to work hard and play hard.'

'She is a predator!' debated Zuhal fiercely. 'Who dresses like a tramp! And I do not want my son associating with someone like her—that is simply not going to happen. Do you understand, Jazz?'

'What, are you planning to vet everyone I come in contact with?'

Grimly, he nodded. 'If I need to, then yes.'

She hated the way he just breezed in and out of her life, making changes as the mood took him, before waltzing back to Razrastan again. He needed to understand that although she was living in one of his properties, she was still a free agent and she would see whoever she wanted to see. But Jasmine clamped her lips shut, telling herself there was no point in discussing it now, not when he was in this kind of mood.

Yet she felt distinctly flat when he delivered her back to the apartment. His rugged features were still dark with rage as he bid her a terse farewell before striding out of the apartment without another word.

She stood in the empty sitting room after he'd gone, looking out as the golden sunlight bounced off the bright green of the treetops, realising how unsatisfac-

tory the situation had become. She wanted him, yes—
she had never stopped wanting him, if the truth were
known—but for reasons of pride and self-preservation,
she was no longer prepared to settle for what little he
was prepared to offer her.

CHAPTER SIX

JASMINE FIRST REALISED something was wrong when she got a call to her mobile phone from an unlisted number. Deciding it was probably a sales call, she nonetheless picked it up, mainly because it had been ages since anyone had rung her.

'Hello?' she said cautiously.

'Is that Miss Jones? Miss Jasmine Jones?' The caller's voice was female, smoky and very confident.

'Speaking.'

'Just a couple of questions for you, Miss Jones. Is it true that you're the mother of the Sheikh of Razrastan's baby?'

Jasmine nearly dropped the phone. 'Who is this, please?'

'My name is Rebecca Starr from the *Daily View*,' said the voice. 'And I notice you're not issuing a denial to my question.'

Jasmine cut the connection with shaking fingers, wondering how the smoky-voiced Rebecca Starr had got hold of her number and wondering how best to respond. She swallowed. If in doubt, do nothing—wasn't that what people always said? She certainly wasn't going to bother Zuhal with it—not when he had stormed out in such a bad mood yesterday after that incident in the park with Carrie and her hot pants.

The phone rang again and Jasmine snatched it up, afraid that the shrill ringtone would wake her sleeping baby.

'Miss Jones? It's Rebecca Starr again. Do you have any immediate plans to marry Sheikh Zuhal Al Haidar of Razrastan?'

'Where did you get this number from?' Jasmine demanded uselessly.

'Because we understand there is a vacant role for a new royal Sheikha,' continued the journalist smoothly. 'Now that Zuhal is to be crowned King.'

With an angry squeak, Jasmine cut the connection, resisting the temptation to hurl the phone against one of the velvet cushions which were lined up neatly on the nearby sofa, knowing that if she did someone would just put them right back again. That was the trouble with having a fleet of cleaners at your disposal, she thought—there was never any mindless domestic work with which to displace your angry thoughts. No floors to clean or cobwebs to flick away from the ceiling.

She tried to convince herself that the press would soon lose interest if she didn't fan the flames of their story but she still felt faintly uneasy as she went about her normal routine. When he woke from his nap, she took Darius out for a stroll in his buggy and the warm sun beat down on the bare skin of her upper arms. Trying to ignore the discreet presence of the accompanying bodyguards, she found herself hoping she wouldn't bump into Carrie again, dreading having to bat away a stream of curious questions about Zuhal. But sooner or later she was going to have to see her, wasn't she? And what then? She couldn't pretend he didn't exist and she couldn't spend the rest of her life avoiding questions because she wasn't sure how to answer them.

She was just rounding the path to skirt the edge of the glittering lake when she sensed movement nearby and, glancing up, saw a blinding flash. Blinking, she watched as the black blur of one of the bodyguards hurtled towards a copse of trees while three others hurried forward to surround her.

'What's going on?' she questioned.

'Paparazzi,' one of them answered succinctly.

'What do they want?'

'Photos of you. And of the royal Prince. We need to leave, Miss Jones.'

'But—'

'Right now, Miss Jones,' he interrupted.

Jasmine forced herself to stay positive as she was practically marched back to the apartment—because having a baby meant you couldn't afford to indulge in introspective gloom—but she was glad when Rania stepped in to take Darius for her. And once she was on her own, reaction set in and Jasmine could do nothing to stop the jittery feelings which flooded over her. Her skin felt cold. Her hands were shaking and her heart was racing like a train. She wondered if this was how the future was going to look, with her locked away in her luxury apartment, hiding from anonymous people who took photos of her baby son without anyone's permission.

She wanted to pace the room. To talk to someone, but mostly she wanted to talk to Zuhal—and that surprised her. Maybe it was because he was the only person who would understand. The only person who *could* understand, because Darius was his son too. She went into her bedroom—with its pristine bed and neatly folded nightdress on the pillow. The framed photos of Darius and the portrait study of her mother taken before disillusionment had set in were the sole signs that this room actually belonged to anyone. A single woman's bedroom, she thought, as she scrabbled around in one of the drawers for the phone number Zuhal had given her.

With fingers which were still shaking, she keyed in the numbers and Zuhal's almost instant pick-up brought her up with a start, because for some reason it hadn't occurred to her that he might give her his direct line. She pulled a face at her pale reflection in the mirror.

Did she really think so little of herself?

And why wouldn't she, when she had been cut so comprehensively from his life once before?

'Zuhal?'

'What's happening?' he demanded, his voice underpinned by something she'd never heard there before. 'Are you okay?'

'Yes. But I've been…been…' The words trembled on her lips and she found herself unable to say them.

'Ambushed by paparazzi?' he provided harshly.

She sucked in an audible breath. 'So your spies have already got back to you, have they?'

Amid the opulent surroundings of an aircraft which was more like a flying palace, Zuhal scowled. 'Of course they have,' he bit out. 'What do you think I pay my staff to do, Jazz? They are guarding my son. It's their duty to tell me exactly what's happening in his life at any given time and I gather someone was photographing you in the park.' Silently, he cursed the distance between them and her stubbornness in not having let him bring up Darius in a country where people would not have access to focus their long-range lens on an innocent little prince. And then he realised that she was ringing him and that was something new. Fear coursed through him in a way it had never done before. 'Has something else happened?' he demanded as dread rippled down his spine. 'Is Darius okay?'

'Darius is fine, but I…' He could hear her swallow. Could hear her try to piece her words together, even though her voice was shaking. 'I had a phone call from a journalist.'

He froze. 'Saying what?'

'Asking if I was the mother. Asking if…'

'If what, Jazz?'

He could hear the embarrassment in her voice. Or was it distaste? he wondered bitterly.

'If I was planning to marry you.'

Zuhal closed his eyes and allowed the prolonged silence to send its noiseless scream down the international phone line before hearing her cough.

'Zuhal? Are you still there?'

'Yes, I'm right here—but don't worry, I'll be with you very soon.'

'With me?' He could hear the confusion in her voice. 'But you told me you were going back to Razrastan.'

'I was,' he agreed grimly. 'But the moment I heard about the incident in the park, I had my jet made ready. I'm on my way back to London.'

'You're on your way back to London,' she repeated dully. 'And just what is that supposed to achieve?'

'I don't intend discussing it with you now, Jazz,' he snapped. 'I've always found the phone a particularly unsatisfactory form of communication.'

'Which is presumably why you avoided it in the past,' she said waspishly.

He scowled, but he wasn't going to get into an argument with her now. Especially not about things which had happened between them in the past. It was the future which needed addressing now, he thought grimly. 'Expect me in around three hours' time,' he said briefly, and cut the call.

Jasmine couldn't settle to anything as she waited for Zuhal to arrive. He didn't bother to ring the doorbell, he just let himself into the apartment—in a cruel parody of a husband returning home from work.

For a split second she almost didn't recognise him because for once he was wearing traditional robes and she'd only ever seen him dressed that way in photos. Her heart clenched in her chest and she felt a moment of aching awareness as she acknowledged his powerful and almost primitively alpha presence in the pristine apartment. His black hair was completely covered by a white silk headdress, knotted with a circlet of scarlet.

The stark lines made his hawkish profile appear more autocratic than usual, just as the flowing robes emphasised the hardness of his body, rather than disguising it with its swishing folds. Maybe it was because she was all too aware of what lay beneath—all that muscular physique honed by years of riding.

He flicked her an unfathomable look as he strode towards the sitting room and what choice did she have but to follow him? But Jasmine was aware of a new tension about him and something indefinable glittering from his black eyes.

'Is this what you wanted all along?' he queried silkily.

She blinked at him in confusion. 'What are you talking about?'

'I'm talking about the sudden press interest, which seems to have come out of nowhere.'

'And I'm supposed to have provoked it, is that it?'

He shrugged. '*You* were the one who wanted to walk in the park yesterday, remember?'

'Only because I was feeling positively claustrophobic stuck in here with you!'

His eyes grew hard. 'Did you set it all up so that we'd bump into that woman Carrie—who has clearly run straight to the newspapers about us?'

'How could I do that when I had no idea that you were going to take a walk with me?'

Zuhal sliced the condemnatory palm of his hand through the air. 'You could have phoned her when you were putting on your hat!'

'Well, I didn't!' she flared. 'I can't believe you'd

think me even capable of such a thing—of putting my son at risk like that. How dare you?'

Zuhal was so taken aback by the fury in her voice that he let his hand fall to his side. And the crazy thing was that all he wanted to do was to kiss her—long and hard and deep. He wanted to take her in his arms and strip them both bare and lose all this anger and these recriminations. He scowled, because now was not the time to be distracted by the lure of sex, no matter how much he ached to be inside her again. The whole situation had got completely out of hand and it was now time for him to rein it all in, using the most effective means at his disposal.

He was going to have to do what he should have done the moment he found out about his son.

'You will have to come back to Razrastan with me,' he said.

'I beg your pardon?'

His mouth twisted. 'I don't think my statement requires any clarification.'

'You don't think your statement requires any clarification?' she repeated. 'Well, I do! What happened to keeping me here, with Darius as your insurance-policy heir, while you went out seeking a suitable bride?'

'I'll tell you exactly what happened,' he gritted out. 'My son has been discovered by the press. It hasn't hit the newspapers yet because my lawyers currently have an injunction out—but it will, because the courts will probably throw it out on the grounds that it's in the public interest to announce that Razrastan has a new heir. Even if they don't you can't keep something like this quiet for ever. Which is why the best kind of damage limitation is for you to agree to return to the guaranteed safety of my homeland.'

She shook her head. 'I can't do that, Zuhal,' she whispered.

Beneath his silken robes, Zuhal's body stiffened. Was she really refusing the gift he could offer her—a place of sanctuary while he worked out some kind of future for them all, even though he didn't yet know what that future could possibly be? She was a mass of contradictions, he conceded unwillingly—a woman who continually perplexed him. Who kept him at arm's length with a determination which was in itself a turn-on.

Yet he found himself remembering that moment in the park when he'd touched her and had seen her whole demeanour soften. Her green eyes had blazed with something passionate and unspoken. If that woman— Carrie—had not burst in on them, might he not have taken Jazz into his arms and kissed her? Brought her back here and spent the rest of the day having sex with her, so that once again she would become his compliant lover of old, eager to agree with whatever he suggested? When, instead, she was returning his gaze with a cool confidence which was making him seethe. So how best to proceed? He couldn't exactly drag her kicking and screaming back to Razrastan, could he? No matter how vivid *that* particular fantasy was turning out to be!

'You must realise that now I have discovered the existence of my son, nothing can ever be the same, Jazz.'

'You didn't discover him,' she answered. 'You came across him by chance.'

'However you care to define it,' he iced out, 'the facts remain the same. You are the mother of the Sheikh's son and you both remaining here in England is no longer a satisfactory option. You have no experience of press harassment but I do. You will be given no space until you provide them what they want, which is a story.'

She tipped her head back, her green eyes on a collision course with his. 'You really think I'd sell a story to the papers?'

'Actually, no. I don't.' He shook his head. 'But the story won't go away and in the meantime rumours will abound.'

'Rumours?' she questioned wryly. 'Or the truth?'

'The fact of our son is undeniable.' He gave a heavy sigh. 'I just need to figure out the best way to present it to my people and I can't do that if I'm constantly worried about you being besieged by all and sundry.'

'I don't know,' she hedged.

Sensing weakness, he swooped. 'Come back to Razrastan with me, Jazz,' he urged. 'Which will at least give us the space to think about the future.'

Jasmine turned away, touching her tongue to her dust-dry lips, her heart pounding as she acknowledged his words. He was promising nothing—certainly not on the emotional front. He'd spoken as if she were a plant he was eager to pluck from her native soil, to transplant her in his own, but with no assurances that she could thrive there. He wanted her to go to *his* palace and *his* country—where he literally ruled the roost. She would have absolutely no power there, and very little say in matters. And all this was complicated by her feelings for him, which wouldn't seem to go away. Because she still wanted him. Not just her body, but her heart, too. She wanted him in a way which was never going to happen and she knew that to go to his desert home would be to make herself vulnerable.

But what alternative did she have? Staying here and playing a constant cat-and-mouse game with the press? Continuing to obsess about him finding himself a suitable wife—a scenario which made her want to batter her fists against the walls of this elegant apartment which still didn't feel like home.

Would the royal palace feel any different?

She bit her lip.

The chances were that it wouldn't but, for her son's sake, shouldn't she give it a *try*? To see if Zuhal's suggestion was in any way workable, even if she had no real faith in the idea?

'Very well,' she said slowly. 'I will bring Darius to Razrastan and we will consider our options.'

Zuhal nodded, but there was no sense of triumph or satisfaction in his heart at having won round one of what he suspected was going to be a difficult battle. Was he going to have to make Jazz his bride in order to get her to comply with his wishes?

His mouth hardened. She was not the kind of woman he had ever imagined marrying and he did not know if his people would accept her—but Razrastan required an heir, just as it required a king.

His country had never needed him before but it seemed that, suddenly, it did now.

CHAPTER SEVEN

ZUHAL WALKED INTO the lavishly appointed drawing room and suppressed a rising feeling of apprehension as he thought of what lay ahead. Forty-eight hours had passed since he'd arrived here in the palace, with the blonde Englishwoman and her son in tow. A child who was very obviously the fruit of his loins, although nobody had dared comment on that fact to his face. He'd been aware that his courtiers and staff were buzzing with questions they wouldn't dream of asking their ruler, but he also knew that sooner or later the subject would need to be addressed.

And this morning, he had done just that. He paced the room, the silk of his robes rippling over his bare flesh. His meeting with his closest advisors had concluded there was only one satisfactory way to provide the best possible future for his son.

Zuhal's throat constricted. His son. The small but sturdy scrap of humanity who bore his genes. He'd thought the disappearance of his elder brother had been the most seismic thing which could happen to him but he had been wrong. Becoming the unexpected ruler of this vast desert kingdom was certainly momentous but the thought of fatherhood was far more significant and he was still processing it.

His jaw tightened. During the flight here he had surreptitiously observed Darius during those moments when Jazz had been sleeping. Registering the coal-black curls and golden dark skin of the baby, he'd felt an unexpected thrill of accomplishment and pride shivering through his veins. He had managed to produce an heir to continue the powerful Al Haidar line, without even trying. And in that moment he had vowed that whatever happened between him and Jazz he would never allow her to remove Darius from the country he would one day rule.

Did she realise that?

He heard the sound of footsteps and looked up. Her footfall was soft on the marble floor and as he saw the pale gleam of her hair in the distance, he felt the instinctive jerk of his groin. He ran his gaze over her as she approached and found himself approving her unfamiliar appearance, thinking how perfect she looked in the part of would-be desert Queen. Surprisingly, she had made no resistance to the assortment of 'appropriate' clothes he had insisted on providing for her—as if recognising the need for the kind of high-specification wardrobe required of his fiancée. Her measurements had been dispatched to one of the palace couturiers and an array of soft silken robes in a muted spectrum of colours had been waiting on her arrival in the capital city of Dhamar. With a compliancy he hadn't been expecting, she had also approved the exquisite garments which had been procured for the infant Prince, despite her own ambitions in that particular area. In fact, the only things she'd brought with her from England were something called a baby monitor, which she had insisted on being installed as soon as they arrived, and a soft toy monkey, with bright eyes.

'Ah, Jazz,' he said, as she grew close and he could not help his gaze from drinking her in, as a thirsty man might drink after a long day in the desert. She was wearing a silky gown the colour of a ripe mango, which brought out the golden lights in her unusual eyes. He could see the luscious thrust of her breasts as their curved weight pushed against the fine material and he thought longingly of the way he used to trace patterns on them with his fingertips, before taking her nipple into his mouth and teasing it until she gasped aloud. He felt the rush of lust and it was with an effort that he dragged his eyes away to meet her gaze. 'I trust you've settled in well?' he questioned benignly. 'And that your quarters meet with your satisfaction.'

She gave a flicker of a smile. 'That's a bit of an understatement. They're absolutely amazing. I've never seen anything quite like them. Not even when I worked at the Granchester.'

Zuhal didn't like the implication that a hotel—no matter how grand—could possibly be compared to his royal palace, but he made no comment. She would soon learn what were and were not acceptable topics of conversation, but now was not the time for a short lesson in diplomacy! He inclined his head. 'I'm glad you think so,' he said. 'And now, we will feast. I trust you have some appetite tonight, Jazz—for the servants inform me that you have eaten remarkably little since our arrival.'

She raised her eyebrows. 'Does that mean I'm still being spied on—despite living in your palace with practically no contact with the outside world?'

'I prefer to think of it as looking out for your welfare,' he corrected spikily. 'So why don't you sit down over there?'

The sweeping movement of his hand indicated an ornate table which had been laid up in one of the recessed windows overlooking the floodlit rose garden. On golden platters were elaborate displays of glistening fruits and savoury dishes, as well as tall decanters of iced fruit juice. Since he'd dispensed with all his servants, it meant Zuhal now found himself in the highly unusual position of having to serve her with food and drinks himself. And he thought she seemed completely oblivious to the honour he was affording her.

'Thank you,' she replied, perching on one of the gilt-edged chairs, before accepting the glass he was offering. 'Mmm… Delicious,' she added, as she sipped at the iced pomegranate juice.

He sat down opposite her and spooned some stewed aubergine onto her plate. 'How is Darius settling in?' he questioned.

'Better than I thought he would,' she said, as she lifted up her fork. 'Even the change in climate and the fact that we've leapt ahead by a few hours doesn't seem to have perturbed him. He's just had his bath and I've read him a story and now he's fast asleep. He won't wake until morning.'

'How can you be so certain?'

'Because that's his routine.' She hesitated for a moment, as if gauging his interest was genuine, before forging on. 'It's a routine I deliberately established, because I knew I'd never get time to get any sewing done otherwise. He's broken it a few times of course and once, when he was running a temperature, he was awake all night long.'

'And what was that like?' he questioned, his curiosity aroused.

'It was a nightmare,' she admitted. 'He screamed from dusk to daybreak. It was…' she gave a rather helpless shrug '…a long night.'

'I'm sure it was.' He realised with a start how much she'd had to deal with. That, despite Darius being an easy child, there had been nobody else for her to turn to—and surely that must have been hard, to have done it all on her own. Unexpectedly, he felt the stir of his conscience and suddenly he found himself wanting her to relax. To lose that pinched look which was making her face seem so pale. To become more like the Jazz of old, rather than this new, wary version. With this aim in mind, he coaxed her with food and watched as she tried a thimble-sized glass of Razrastan's famous lychee dessert wine, and it was with pleasure that he saw some of the tension leave her. 'Is there anything else you require?' he questioned solicitously. 'Anything my staff can help you with?'

Jasmine tried to concentrate on his question, but it wasn't easy. All she could think about was how frustrating it was to be within touching distance, when they hadn't actually touched at all. And while she knew this was probably the most *sensible* outcome—it certainly wasn't what her body wanted.

She couldn't seem to stop staring at his olive-dark face, wishing she could tug off that cream headdress and tangle her fingers in the rich blackness of his hair. She could feel her breasts tightening beneath her robe and the insistent tug of desire low in her belly as she surreptitiously ran her gaze over him. Suddenly it seemed like an awfully long time since she'd had sex. Well, it was. Over eighteen months, to be precise—and increasing exposure to the father of her child was reminding her all too vividly that she was a healthy young woman with physical needs of her own.

She found herself wanting to touch him—just as she had done when he had unexpectedly reappeared in her life again and had kissed her so passionately in her run-down little Oxford cottage. Maybe even more, because being with him again reminded her just how much she had always fancied him. And it wasn't his royal status which set her heart racing, or the fact that he was one of the wealthiest men on the planet. To her he was the man who had awoken her sexuality—the only man she had given her heart and her body to—and a woman never forgot something like that.

This was the man who used to flutter soft kisses over her belly before licking his tongue between the eager parting of her thighs. Who had brought her to orgasm that way, his hungry lips drinking in every shuddered spasm she made. The first time he'd done that she'd been incredibly nervous—self-conscious, even.

But Zuhal had taught her that sex was a gift to be enjoyed and there should be no barriers between consenting lovers. He had known her body inside and out, and sometimes, when he'd been deep inside her, it had been difficult to know where he began and she ended.

But she hadn't been thinking about that when she'd reluctantly agreed to come to Razrastan. She'd been thinking about her son. And now all her guilt about Darius not having had a father figure had been replaced by the fear that she'd walked into some sort of gilded trap. From the moment she'd entered the palace, the glittering walls seemed to enclose her with all their heavily guarded splendour. She'd looked around the vast and ornate citadel, slightly dazed to realise that Zuhal owned everything as far as the eye could see.

But he didn't own her, and that was what she needed to remember.

He had brought her and Darius here to get them away from a curious press and work out some kind of plan for the future—even though he had given her no indication of what that plan might be. He'd made it clear about the kind of woman he expected to marry and it certainly wasn't her—not that she'd want to marry such a cold-hearted brute in any case. Surely he wasn't expecting her to stay here indefinitely, while they lived separate lives?

She sighed, knowing she was going to have to make an effort. She needed to get on with the father of her child, no matter what happened between the two of them. So she nodded in response to Zuhal's unusually solicitous questions. 'There's nothing more we need,' she told him. 'Our rooms couldn't be any more comfortable and the view over the palace gardens is breathtaking. I had no idea that you could grow so many flowers in such a hot climate.'

'Fortunately, we do have access to water,' he commented sardonically, a dismissive wave of his hand indicating he was done with horticultural small-talk. 'And what of the nursemaids who will assist Rania? I trust they also meet with your approval, Jazz.'

It was a statement rather than a question and Jasmine hesitated, recognising once again that negotiation was better than confrontation. 'I have no complaints,' she said. 'They seem very…capable.'

'They are,' he agreed. 'Like Rania, many of them are the daughters of the women who used to care for Kamal and I when we were young.'

Jasmine nodded, his words reminding her that his upbringing was a million miles away from hers—a young prince surrounded by an army of servants. She realised she'd hardly ever heard him mention his own mother, not even when they'd been at their most intimate—actually, he'd barely mentioned his early years and neither had she. But back then their focus had been solely on pleasure, rather than the exchange of confidences which might have brought them closer as a couple. She met the black burn of his eyes. 'I wanted to talk to you about that,' she said hesitantly. 'You know, there's no need for a nurse to sit in the same room, watching Darius while he sleeps. I'm sure Rania and I can manage perfectly well on our own.'

'But I want something more for my son than just

managing,' he bit out. 'Darius will one day be King, and will need to get used to the presence of servants.'

Jasmine narrowed her eyes. 'You can't just come out and say things like that,' she objected, all thoughts of compromise forgotten. 'He might want to be a bank manager, living in the English countryside.'

He shook his head. 'No, not that. Not ever that. He will be King of Razrastan.'

'And how is that ever going to happen?' she demanded baldly.

His lips twisted into an odd kind of smile. 'I think you know the answer to that, Jazz,' he said softly. 'Darius will be my legitimate heir—and in order for that to happen, you must become my wife.'

A brittle silence entered the atmosphere as Jasmine stared at Zuhal with disbelieving eyes. 'Become your wife?' she repeated faintly.

'Surely the idea doesn't come as a complete shock to you?' he suggested sardonically. 'I have spoken with my closest advisors and government this very morning. They think my people will accept you, since you are the mother of my son. And, if the subject is handled with delicacy and tact, see no reason why we shouldn't marry. In fact, they concluded that marriage is the only appropriate solution to this particular dilemma.'

'*Dilemma?*' she echoed, outrage beginning to bubble up inside her. 'Is that how you see me?'

'Please don't fixate on the words I'm using but think instead about the meaning of what I'm saying, Jazz,' he continued remorselessly. 'I am proposing marriage. I, the Sheikh, am asking you, the commoner, to be my bride. Don't you realise what a great compliment that is?'

Jasmine shook her head. It didn't feel like a compliment. It felt like…

As if Zuhal was being forced into doing something he didn't want to do. As if he had been backed into a corner with no other way out. And wasn't that the truth of it? He didn't love her. He'd never loved her—so what were the chances of having a successful marriage? She thought about her own parents. About her mother's reaction when the relationship had started to crumble and the desperate way she'd tried to cling on. *I don't want to become like my mother,* Jasmine thought suddenly. And I don't want an uncaring sheikh's power to diminish me as a person, just because he wants to claim Darius as his rightful heir.

'It's too early to talk about marriage,' she said, quickly getting up from the table, unwilling to be subjected to Zuhal's look of disbelief as she gave him her answer. Resolutely, she walked over to one of the huge windows, glancing up at an indigo sky and thinking how far away the spatter of silver stars looked. 'Way too early.'

'Your attitude is more than a little *insulting,* Jazz,' he said, and she could hear the scrape of his chair and the sound of his footsteps as he walked over to join her. 'Don't you realise that most women would be eager to become my Queen?'

He was standing beside her—so close that they were almost touching. The warmth of his body was almost palpable and his presence was so powerful that Jasmine could scarcely breathe as raw longing clogged in her throat. 'Maybe they don't know you as well as I do!' She turned her head to look at him, detecting a brief flicker of outrage in the inky blaze of his eyes. 'I think we should take things slowly. I think, right now, that caution is probably the wisest choice.'

He gave a low laugh, which trickled over her skin like warm honey. 'Forgive me if I disagree,' he murmured, 'but I think a little recklessness might work better in our favour.'

She saw something in his eyes which was achingly familiar, as was the sudden tension which entered his hard body. And then suddenly Jasmine was in his arms and she never knew which of them instigated it, only that it seemed as inevitable as the rising of the giant moon outside the window, which was bathing them with a strange, silvery light. The Sheikh's mouth hovered briefly over hers and Jasmine gave a yelp as he brought it down hard to kiss her—before kissing him back with an urgent hunger which seemed to make her world spin. It felt as if she were falling. Or drowning. Drowning in a sweet, molten tide of desire.

Last time he'd kissed her, she'd felt a certain amount of restraint for all kinds of reasons, but mainly because she'd been concealing the knowledge of her son. Now she was concealing nothing. Not a single thing. She felt naked—despite the flowing material of the robes which covered her. She could feel the shameless spring of his erection pushing hard against her belly and felt the corresponding opening of her thighs as if she were silently girding herself to accommodate him. She heard his soft laugh as he acknowledged her submission, and his arms tightened around her back.

And Jasmine hugged him back because, oh, how she wanted this.

Now.

Here.

Just like this.

The real world retreated and all that mattered was the incredible sensation Zuhal was provoking by the tantalising whisper of a fingertip which traced its way down her spine. It was a gesture which felt almost innocent, yet how could it possibly be innocent when her nipples were hardening into tight buds which felt as if they were about to explode? He gave a low laugh of pleasure as he tilted her chin so that she was dazzled by the close-up fire of his eyes.

'Oh, Jazz,' he said softly. 'You want me, don't you? You want me so much, baby. You always did.'

His mocking smile dared her to deny it, but how could she deny it when it was the truth? When she'd dreamed and fantasised about this in weak moments when her defences had been down. Gazing up into the hectic gleam of his eyes, Jasmine was aware of her almost imperceptible nod of consent and the Sheikh's low growl of pleasure before he bent his dark head to kiss her again.

CHAPTER EIGHT

HIS HUNGRY HANDS were on her breasts, her bottom and her belly as sexual heat ripped through Jasmine like a desert storm. Zuhal's fingers were moving urgently over her as if he couldn't wait to reacquaint himself with every inch of quivering flesh. She clung to his shoulders for support as he pulled her closer with a possessive mastery which made her feel weak with desire.

'Zuhal,' she breathed, the warmth of her breath mingling eagerly with his, the heat in her lower body starting its restless throb.

He didn't reply. Not at first. His only response was to deepen the kiss—his tongue exploring her with breathtaking intimacy. Her heart was racing like a piston as her fingers touched the unfamiliar headdress and she gave an impatient little tug to remove it. It slithered redundantly to the marble floor and suddenly his head was bare, just like in the old days. Exultantly, her fingertips explored the thick silk of his hair, before kneading at the base of his neck in a way which made him give an instinctive murmur of appreciation. Her hands moved to his biceps—powerful and supremely strong beneath his desert robes. She began to massage the rippling flesh and felt a familiar tension enter his body as he circled his hips in a way which made her intensely aware of his erection.

Jasmine closed her eyes as she felt that steely column pressing into her belly, suddenly aware of everything which had happened since they'd last made love. She recognised that her body had done some amazing things during that time. It had grown and given birth to a baby—an accomplishment which seemed both unreal and marvellous. But this was different. This was hunger. Sexual hunger. A raw and primitive need which was fierce and all-consuming. It was eating her up from the inside and igniting a yearning so powerful that she felt almost unable to stand.

Did Zuhal realise that? Was that why he drew back and stared down at her for a long moment—his eyes glittering like polished jet—before scooping her up into his arms with a moan which called out to her aching heart? When for a moment he seemed like the embodiment of all things alpha as he towered over her, dark and strong and vital as he carried her across the shiny marble floor towards an arched entrance at the far end of the vast chamber, his robes flowing like liquid silk as he walked.

'Where are we going?' she gasped, as he dipped his head to enter a narrow corridor, whose ceiling gleamed with exquisite inlaid tiles depicting erotic scenes of cavorting lovers.

'Somewhere where we'll be more comfortable.'

She looked up into the hectic gleam of his black eyes. 'Somewhere?'

'My bedroom,' he clarified unsteadily. 'It is connected to your apartments through this passageway, which is unseen by anyone else and which only the King is permitted to use. But I grant you my permission to use it any time you wish, Jazz.'

They emerged into a room which was way more magnificent than the suite which had been assigned to her and Darius, but for once Jasmine wasn't daunted by the size or splendour of the accommodation. Exquisite furniture and several statues swam in and out of focus, but all she could see was the vast bed, which Zuhal was striding towards.

Dimly she became aware of him impatiently brushing aside a litter of cushions before laying her down on it, his black gaze raking over her with a look of hungry speculation. Her hands were lying above her head and her legs were splayed out beneath the soft silken robes. And in that moment she felt like a sacrifice about to be offered up to the gods—a feeling which should surely have repelled the modern woman she was—yet the expression on his face spoke to some deep need inside her and she knew there was no power on earth which could have made her resist him.

'Oh, Jazz,' he groaned as he lay down beside her, his lips at her neck, his practised hand already rucking up the slippery fabric of her gown as his mouth drifted to her ear. 'You look so beautiful lying there.'

'D-do I?'

'Utterly.' he husked. 'Do you know how much I want you?'

'I think…' She closed her eyes as he began to drift kisses over her neck. 'I think I can just about work it out.'

'Then double it,' he growled. 'Better still, triple it.'

His hungry words thrilled her—they made her heart race even harder. She remembered the first time he'd taken her to bed, when her heart had swelled up with so much joy. When she'd cried—she wasn't quite sure why—when he had taken her virginity, and he had dried away her tears with a touch which had seemed almost tender.

And although some tiny voice in her head was telling her this was different—was urging her to employ caution—Jasmine refused to listen. Because how could she possibly be cautious when Zuhal's fingers were at her breasts? When they were cupping each swollen mound so that the mango silk appeared bright against his burnished flesh. And now his hand was inching its way up her leg, his featherlight fingertips brushing against the silky flesh of her inner thigh so that goosebumps were flowering beneath his touch. She could feel a syrupy rush soaking her panties and Jasmine closed her eyes before opening them again. 'Zuhal,' she said weakly, and just saying his name out loud was making her even more excited.

'Do you like that?'

'You…you know I do,' she managed to say, but only just—because now he had reached her panties and his finger was tracing a teasing path over the delicate fabric, which stretched tightly over her aching mound. Jasmine swallowed. How could she have forgotten that her body could ever feel like *this*?

'And this?' he questioned, almost carelessly.

She almost shot off the bed as skilfully he targeted her quivering clitoris. 'Oh, yes,' she groaned. '*Yes.*'

'How much do you like it?' he murmured.

'A…a lot,' she breathed.

'Then let's see if we can do something you like even more, shall we? Any ideas, Jazz?'

'I'll… I'll leave those to you,' she gasped. 'You were always the one with the ideas.'

Pushing aside the damp fabric, he began to thrum his finger against her moist flesh and Jazz began to quiver as his hand took on that slick rhythm she hadn't felt for so long. Already she felt crazily close to coming, knowing that if she let him continue she would succumb to the intense orgasm which was building up inside her. And wasn't that what she wanted? Wasn't that *all* she wanted? A quick, physical release to satisfy her aching body—with no danger of compromising her heart. Fractionally she lifted her hips and squirmed, her silent invitation to continue with his ministrations all too obvious. But Zuhal obviously had other ideas. Pulling his hand away and allowing it to rest indolently against the springy curls of her pubic hair, he pressed his lips into her ear.

'No,' he breathed hotly. 'Not like that. Not the first time. I want to feel myself inside you again, Jazz. Deep inside you, where I belong.'

His erotic words rocked her. They set up an answer-

ing clamour in her body which made her long to accommodate him. But even as her trembling thighs were
spreading open to welcome him, that cautious voice of
earlier was louder now, and less easy to ignore. It was
reminding her that his words weren't true. That this
wasn't the *first time*. Far from it. She was countless epi-
sodes and almost two years away from that initial de-
flowering, which had taken him by surprise. She was
no longer the virgin divorcee he had rapturously introduced to sex. Nor was she the idealistic innocent who
believed that just because a man groaned out heartfelt
words of desire when he was orgasming inside you, it
meant any more than just physical satisfaction. With
Zuhal it had only *ever* been about physical satisfaction.
But now there was something else he wanted even more
badly. His baby son. Was that what this was all about?
Softening her with seduction while he plotted to take
what he saw as rightfully his?

Did he think that if she had sex with him now she
would instantly agree to marriage?

Because that had been part of the trouble before—
she'd allowed passion to sweep her away, so that she
wasn't really thinking straight. Was that why she had
tolerated her very part-time role as his mistress and
been content to live in the shadows of his life? Maybe
that was what amazing sex did to you…it robbed you
of your strength and logic—and she needed both those
things like never before. For her son's sake, but also
for her own.

Her thoughts blurred as he slipped a finger inside
her panties and she knew that if she didn't stop him

soon, she would be past the point of making a rational decision…

Wriggling free of his intimate caress, she somehow managed to scramble off the day-bed, steeling herself against the sight of Zuhal still lying there in his rumpled robes, two high lines of colour flushed across his autocratic cheekbones, his black eyes burning with an expression she couldn't quite work out.

'Was it something I said?' he questioned mockingly.

Flattening her fingers against her heaving breasts, Jasmine struggled to get her breath back. 'That…that wasn't supposed to happen!'

'No?' He raised his black brows. 'So just what did you *think* was going to happen when I carried you in here, Jazz? Did you think we were going to have a discussion about world politics, or that I was about to start regaling you with stories of Razrastanian history?'

She realised that although outwardly he appeared cool and in control, his sarcastic words were underpinned with unmistakable irritation as he folded his arms behind his head to cushion it. She couldn't blame him.

'I'm sorry.' Distractedly, she shook her head. 'I wasn't thinking.'

There was a pause as his black eyes bored into her. 'Why don't you want to have sex with me, Jazz?'

She could feel the burn of her cheeks. She shouldn't have allowed him to bring her in here, putting herself in a situation she couldn't handle. Because wasn't the truth that she wanted to go right back over there and have him touch her with all that sweet unerring accu-

racy again? Didn't she long to feel him inside her—
deep inside her—as he himself had groaned out a few
minutes ago?

But a few moments of pleasure weren't powerful
enough to make her forget why she was here. He'd offered her marriage but she was still unsure of what
her answer was going to be. Because surely she could
only accept if she felt equipped enough to cope with
a loveless union. The last thing she needed was to be
blinded by desire. 'Because sex will just complicate
things. Surely you can see that.'

'You're saying you don't want us to be intimate?' he
queried softly.

Her voice was stiff as she tried to give an honest answer. 'I'd be a liar if I said I didn't want it. I just…just
don't feel ready for it at the moment.'

'Maybe that's something you ought to think about
next time you start batting those big green eyes at me,'
he observed, a little pulse hammering frantically at his
temple.

She gave an awkward nod of acknowledgement. 'We
were both responsible for what just happened, not just
me. We got…carried away.'

'And then some,' he agreed drily.

Attempting to put some space between them, Jasmine walked across the room to stand beside a marble
statue of a winged creature which was half-falcon, half-
goat—before turning back to face him. But he was still
tempting her. She suspected that he always would. 'I'll
try to be more circumspect in future,' she said.

There was a pause. 'Even if that means resisting your own desires?'

She met the curious question gleaming in the depths of his ebony eyes. Could she explain what was making her so cautious, without coming over as vulnerable or needy in the process? 'Here in your lavish palace, the only thing I have is my integrity and I don't intend to compromise it,' she said. 'I won't be able to think straight if we become intimate again. I'm afraid that desire will cloud my judgement and I can't afford to let that happen.'

'These are fighting words, Jazz,' he observed softly.

'They aren't meant to be. I don't want to fight with you, Zuhal.' She drew in a deep breath, praying her new-found conviction wouldn't leave her. Praying she wouldn't morph back into that docile Jasmine of old who had been content with the crumbs of affection the powerful Sheikh had thrown her way. 'We're no longer two occasional lovers who can't keep their hands off each other. We're parents. We have a lifetime bond through our son. We rushed into a relationship once before without really getting to know one another. This time, I think we should take things more slowly—to decide whether or not we could make a marriage work.'

'And am I supposed to admire your reluctance?' he questioned. 'Is your elusiveness part of some complex female game of playing hard to get in order to make yourself seem more of a prize?'

'I can assure you I'm not playing games, Zuhal. This is much too important for that. I have to believe that there's a basic compatibility between us before I agree to become your wife—otherwise it's just a recipe for disaster.'

Zuhal shook his head, unable to believe that Jazz of all people was turning him down. A woman who had been eager to learn all he could teach her—who had been the most delightful of all his lovers. Was she holding out for what women always demanded—words of love he would not provide? *Could* not provide, he reminded himself bitterly. If Jasmine wanted violins and moonlight she was doomed to be disappointed.

He looked at her. During that tantalising tumble which had just taken place on his bed, her hair had come free from its ribbon and was now tumbling down in waves of golden silk. She looked like an angel, he thought reluctantly, her long lashes shuttering the verdant beauty of her green eyes. He watched her smoothing down her robes as she struggled to catch her breath and in that moment she looked like the Jasmine he remembered—young and wild and passionate. But this Jasmine had just pushed him away in a way she would never have done before.

For a moment he was tempted to walk over there and attempt to change her mind. Would she have the strength to resist him a second time? He suspected not as for a moment he imagined being inside her again, his length encased inside her molten tightness as he rocked them both towards that blissful goal.

But he wasn't going to do that. She would regret soon enough having turned him down and discover that he had no intention of chasing after her all the way to the altar. Did she really think a man in his position would ever have to grovel to a woman? His lips hardened into a smile.

Let her come to him.

'So what exactly is it you want of me, Jazz?' he enquired casually.

It was a question Jasmine had never thought he'd ask. She knew what she'd wanted when they'd been together before but had accepted she was never going to get it. Because you couldn't demand love when instinct told you that love was an alien concept to a man like Zuhal. But she could discover more about the man who had always been a closed book to her when they had been casual lovers, couldn't she?

'Obviously, I'd like to learn about your country and your culture, Zuhal. But I'd also like to learn more about you.'

'Even though you've just turned down a method guaranteed to do exactly that?'

'I didn't find out much about you in all the time we were together, did I? And we were having plenty of sex back then.'

He raised his eyebrows. 'There are official biographies you can look at,' he said coolly. 'Which have always been in the public domain. We even have the authorised versions here in the palace library, which you are perfectly at liberty to read.'

She shook her head. 'That's not what I meant.'

'Oh?'

It was the most forbidding of looks and maybe if so much hadn't been at stake, Jasmine might have heeded its silent warning. But there was a potential marriage

133

to consider, and it had to have the makings of a good one for her to risk putting Darius at its centre. And how could she consider marrying a man who remained little more than a stranger?

'I want to hear it from you, Zuhal,' she said. 'From your lips, not somebody else's.'

She saw his face darken with frustration, irritation and then a grim kind of acceptance. 'Very well,' he said at last, bending to pick up the discarded headdress which she had pulled from his head. 'You'd better speak to my diary secretary.'

'Your diary secretary?' she echoed in confusion.

'Of course.' He gave the flicker of a smile edged with undeniable *triumph*. 'How else did you think I was going to find time to see you? I am King now, with many demands on my time. Speaking of which…' he glanced at his watch '… I must leave you now, since I have work to do.'

She blinked. 'What, now?'

His black eyes glittered. 'There is always work to do, Jazz, no matter what the clock says. And since the evening has fallen far short of my expectations, I might as well put what remains of it to good use. I will show you back to your rooms and anything you require, just ring and one of the servants will attend to you.'

A peremptory wave of his hand indicated she should precede him. But it did more than that—it made it very clear who was in charge.

Jasmine opened her mouth to object before shutting it again, because what could she say? She had turned down his proposal and now he was suggesting she make an appointment to see him, in the same way he might schedule in an appointment with his dentist! And meanwhile that vast and rumpled bed was mocking her with all its unused promise.

The bubble of the evening seemed to have burst. She walked ahead of him, hearing the soft shimmer of his robes brushing over the marble floor as he followed her. And all she could think about was the powerful perfection of his brooding body and the way it had felt when he'd held her in his arms again, as she tried to quash a deep and overwhelming sense of regret.

CHAPTER NINE

IT SHOULD HAVE been a fairy tale. At least, that was how it might have looked to an outsider. A one-time single mother plucked from her humble abode and transplanted into a glittering, golden palace by a sheikh who was eager for her to be his bride.

A lump rose in Jasmine's throat. Because this was no fairy tale. This was living in a gilded prison.

It was true she'd been meeting all kinds of new people—from royal monarchs who ruled neighbouring countries to the noblemen and women of Razrastan itself. She'd sat beneath sparkling chandeliers, wearing a fortune in diamonds around her neck—while discussing with the American ambassador the proposed trip by the President of the United States of America!

Those were the facts.

The irrefutable facts.

But facts only told you so much. They only showed you the supposedly smooth surface—not the dark undercurrents which were swirling beneath. She might be the mother of the Sheikh's baby, and they might be polite and perfectly civil with each other in public. But in reality they'd barely spent any time alone since she had rejected Zuhal's sexual advances, and the subject of marriage was still unresolved.

She'd wanted to get to know him before making any firm commitment, but how was that possible when palace life seemed the enemy of intimacy? When meals were distinctly formal and featured guests Zuhal thought it prudent she meet. During course after endless course, streams of servants weaved their way in and out, bearing extravagant dishes heaped with Razrastanian specialities, whose very names dazzled her. None of the servants ever met her eyes. They seemed to look right through her. She suspected they disapproved of this Englishwoman who had entered their royal palace with an illegitimate baby in tow. Maybe they were glad there had been no official acknowledgement of her role in the Sheikh's life.

And none of these functions offered any opportunity for private conversation with Zuhal because he was always sitting at the far end of the table, looking impossibly aloof and regal. Why, the physical distance between them was so great, that just getting him to hear her meant she almost had to shout. Just as there had been no shared moments of parenting with him. It seemed he made time to see his son only when he was certain Jasmine wasn't around and she wondered if he was punishing her for refusing his proposal, by deliberately keeping his distance. On more than one occasion, she had emerged from her dressing room, her hair still damp from the shower, to see the silky shimmer of the Sheikh's pale robes disappearing through the tall, arched doorway.

Sometimes she would wake early when the baby was still asleep and the palace all but silent. Once, unable to get back to sleep, she had gone to the stable complex, just as Zuhal was dismounting from his horse after his morning ride. Hidden away in the shadows, he hadn't seen her, but Jasmine had watched as he'd peeled a silk shirt from his torso. Like a woman hypnotised, she had observed his slow striptease with a racing heart which had threatened to burst out of her chest. With hungry eyes she'd drunk in the gleam of his burnished skin and bronzed definition of his powerful physique. There wasn't an inch of surplus flesh on his hard body and his washboard abs were glistening like the cover shot of a fitness magazine. She'd found herself wanting to run over and to slowly slide her way down over his body. To lick her tongue over his chest, revelling in the taste of each salty bead of sweat, knowing they were all a part of him. And then to unzip his jodhpurs and feel his proud length springing free, first against her fingers and then into the moist and waiting cavern of her lips.

She began to question if she'd been too hasty. If she had driven him away with her proud stance, which had masked her fears about getting intimate with him again. Yet how was she ever going to find out whether they were compatible if they were never alone? When the days were ticking away, bringing closer the formal signing of the papers which would make Zuhal the official ruler of Razrastan. She hadn't actually ruled out marriage, had she? She'd just told him she wanted to get to know him better before she committed. So maybe it was time for action instead of all these fractured thoughts. Maybe she should take Zuhal at his word and book herself an appointment to see him, since he obviously had no intention of backing down himself.

Which was how one sun-dappled morning she found herself in Zuhal's offices in the south-west corner of the palace, which overlooked a sylvan courtyard of trees. At its centre was a cool pond, in which red-gold fish swam—giving the place a curiously peaceful feel. Inside, it was completely different—a modern hive of activity hiding behind the ancient doors. Assistants tapped feverishly at the keyboards of sleek computers and rows of clocks indicated different time zones from around the world. She was asked to wait in an anteroom, before being shown into an inner sanctum for a meeting with Zuhal's chief aide—a shuttered-faced man in traditional Razrastanian robes, who looked up from his desk as she was ushered in.

'Miss Jones,' he said smoothly, rising to his feet to greet her. 'My name is Adham. This is an unexpected pleasure.'

Jasmine recognised his voice instantly. She would never forget it, not in a million years. A chill rippled down her spine. This was the same aide who had blocked her attempt to tell Zuhal she was pregnant all those months ago. Was that why his face was so unfriendly when he looked at her? Why she detected a glimmer of darkness in his expression as she entered his plush office? Or was he just more open about expressing what she suspected most of the palace staff really felt about her? Quashing down her instinctive apprehension, Jasmine composed her face into a look of polite enquiry. 'I hope I'm not disturbing you?'

'Not at all, Miss Jones,' he said, his forced smile seeming to contradict his benign words. 'What can I do for you this morning?'

Jasmine felt the sudden pounding of her heart, recognising that this was the moment. She was here to try to deepen her relationship with the father of her child and to address seriously the possibility of being a future queen. So maybe it was time to start acting like one. To show Adham that she was no longer some inconvenient lover he could dismiss as if she didn't matter, but part of Zuhal's life, whether he liked it or not.

Adopting the wide smile which had always been super-effective when dealing with tricky customers at the Granchester boutique, she gestured towards the sunlit garden outside. 'It is an exceptionally beautiful morning, isn't it?' she observed, with diplomatic politeness.

'Indeed. The weather in Razrastan is especially temperate at this time of year,' Adham answered, the faint elevation of his eyebrows silently urging her to get to the point.

Jasmine did exactly that. 'I'd like to see the Sheikh, please.'

'I'm afraid that won't be possible, Miss Jones. His Royal Highness is busy at the moment. I'm sure you are well aware of the demands on his time at this key stage in the country's future,' he said, his tone smooth and pleasant, although the icy gleam of his eyes suggested a certain insincerity. 'In fact, he is on the phone to the Sheikh of Maraban, as we speak.'

'Oh, I didn't mean *right now*,' said Jasmine quickly. 'Obviously, he's tied up most of the time. I appreciate that. I just wondered if you could make an appointment for me to see him.'

A flicker of incredulity passed over the shuttered features. 'An appointment, Miss Jones?'

'If you would. Zuhal did say we should coordinate our diaries in order to make time for one other.'

'His Royal Highness mentioned nothing to me.'

'Does Zuhal run everything past you, then, Adham?' questioned Jasmine innocently.

It was the first time in her life that she'd ever pulled rank—not that she'd ever had any rank to pull before now—and to her astonishment it worked. As if realising that this time she wouldn't be thwarted, the aide reluctantly bent his head to study the leather-bound diary in front of him before returning his shuttered gaze to hers. 'Very well. I believe I can fit you in, if you are prepared to be flexible. Shall we say tomorrow morning at ten o'clock? His Royal Highness has a window of thirty minutes he can allot to you, after his morning ride.'

Thirty minutes! Not even an hour alone with the man who had asked her to marry him! And just around the time when Darius would be having his post-breakfast playtime, which wasn't what you'd call convenient. But if this was the best she could hope for, then she was going to grab it with both hands. 'Perfect,' she said brightly.

The aide consulted some sort of grid chart in front of him. 'If you would like to make your way to the Damask Room at the allotted time, His Royal Highness will join you there.

Jasmine nodded. 'Thank you, Adham.'

Despite the somewhat lukewarm response she'd received, Jasmine felt a fizz of excitement as she returned to her suite, where Darius was waiting with Rania. The baby gurgled with pleasure as she held out her arms to him and her mind was buzzing as she wondered how to make the most of her time alone with Zuhal tomorrow.

Was that being super-needy?

No, she told herself, as she waved a noisy rattle in front of the baby's nose. Not needy at all. It was being grown-up and sensible. Accepting that she wasn't dealing with just *any* man. She closed her eyes with pleasure as Darius wrapped his chubby little arms around her neck and snuggled up close. Zuhal was a man who would soon be King and she needed to make allowances for that.

But that night, during a pre-dinner drinks reception for a cluster of visiting Argentinean diplomats, she looked up to find the Sheikh's eyes fixed on hers more often than usual. The expression in their ebony depths was one she couldn't decipher, but it was enough to set her heart racing as she walked forward to meet the line of guests.

She had decided to treat these functions in the same way she used to regard shopping evenings at the Granchester boutique, trying to put people at their ease—and for the most part this made them bearable. Yet tonight it felt different. Or maybe it was just she who felt different. She'd broken the deadlock and from tomorrow, she would start learning more about the Sheikh whose narrowed gaze was currently sweeping over her like a dark spotlight. She wished he wouldn't look at her like that in public. Making her dress feel as if it had suddenly become two sizes too small. Making her brow break out into tiny little beads of sweat beneath her carefully coiffed hair.

As usual, she and Zuhal left the reception at exactly the same time but tonight, instead of going to his own suite, he insisted on accompanying her to Darius's room where he remained while she checked on him, before dismissing Rania for the night. The main reception room of her private suite seemed very large and echoing as she shut the door to the nursery and turned to Zuhal, realising that, for the first time in a long time, they were completely alone. She swallowed. She could detect the subtle yet very masculine scent of sandalwood radiating from his powerful body, making her uncomfortably aware of his raw virility as she regarded him with cautious question in her eyes.

'I understand you paid a visit to Adham this morning,' he said, without prompting.

'I did.'

'And insisted on a meeting with me tomorrow morning.'

Wasn't his expression more than a little *smug*? Jasmine wondered, with a touch of indignation. 'Insist?' she echoed lightly. 'I thought that's what we agreed. Appointments in the diary. A rather unconventional way of a couple getting to know each other, it's true, but that was the only way you could guarantee allotting me any time.'

'It's true, that's what we agreed,' Zuhal conceded, feasting his gaze on her luscious body and letting it linger there. He'd said it to make her realise that he had neither the time nor the inclination to play games with her. He'd imagined his cool indifference might make her reconsider her foolishness in rejecting him and bring her running into his arms. That without further prompting she would slip along the secret corridor to his bed and seek the pleasure she was guaranteed to find there.

But it hadn't worked out that way.

His remoteness hadn't had the desired effect of taming her or bringing her into his bed. There had been no delicious blonde lying waiting for him between the slippery silk of his sheets, eagerly taking him into her arms before spreading those delicious thighs for him. Instead, she had remained as prim as a maiden aunt and ironically this had only increased his hunger for her. His mouth dried. As if he needed any more hunger than was already coursing around his frustrated veins!

'So you've got what you wanted,' she observed thoughtfully.

A pulse flickered at his temple as she tilted her chin with faint challenge. 'On the contrary, Jazz,' he demurred softly. 'I'm still waiting for the thing I want most.'

Her eyes narrowed as she looked at him and suddenly all that old sexual shorthand was back. The flush to her cheeks and the darkening of her eyes. The spring of her nipples against the silk of her robes and quick writhe of the hips, which was almost imperceptible to anyone else but him.

'Jazz,' he said, on a throaty note of hunger he couldn't disguise and he heard her answering intake of breath. Did she move first or did he, and wasn't that something he needed to know—in order to establish whose victory this was? But suddenly Zuhal didn't care—not about the method, only the result. He didn't care which of them had backed down as, with a hungry moan, he closed his arms around her and desire reverberated through him as never before.

Her mouth opened beneath his kiss and her moan echoed his as he explored her with his tongue. Sweet heaven, but she tasted good. So good. His shaking hands were on her robes, tugging at them impatiently with none of his usual restraint, and she was doing the same thing to him—touching his body through the delicate material as if she were discovering it for the very first time. But this was nothing like the first time. Back then she had been a virgin and now she was a sexually experienced woman who knew exactly what she wanted. And so did he.

Her hand pressed boldly against his erection as he deepened the kiss and, urgently, he backed her up against the wall, peeling off her tunic and flinging it aside before dispensing with his own the same way. He ripped off her panties so that they fluttered onto the Persian rug, his fingers quickly finding the moist heat now exposed to him and beginning a deliciously familiar rhythm. The scent of sex filled the air as he strummed against the warm syrupy feel of her and she bucked immediately.

'Yes,' she gasped, brokenly, and suddenly she forgot everything. Forgot that she probably shouldn't be doing this and that Zuhal wasn't using any protection. All she could think about was it. And him. The word burst out of her lips again. 'Yes.'

His hands clamped around the cool flesh of her buttocks, he lifted her up so she could lock her thighs around his hips, positioning herself perfectly for that first, deep thrust which made her gasp in the way he remembered so well For a moment he had to still in order to compose himself, terrified he would come straight away—like some over-keen schoolboy whose wildest fantasy had just been realised.

'*Oh*,' he breathed, as control returned to him and he resumed his thrust. Each. Hard. Hungry. Thrust. 'Isn't that good, Jazz?' he demanded unsteadily. 'Isn't it the best thing you ever felt?'

Her breath was hot against his neck, her words slurred with pleasure. 'Is it praise you're seeking, Zuhal?'

No, it wasn't praise. He told himself it was orgasm he wanted—all he had ever wanted—but orgasms were easily attained, weren't they? And then he stopped thinking altogether, focussing instead on how tight she felt as his balls slapped softly against her molten heat. On how his heart was pounding like a regimental drum as he increased his speed. He drove into her while doing all the things he knew she liked best. Grazing her nipples with his teeth—so that she was balancing on the fine edge between pain and pleasure. Stroking his thumb down the enticing valley which cleaved between her buttocks, so that she moaned softly with pleasure.

When she came, he followed almost immediately, kissing away her shuddering moans as his seed spurted long and deep into her body and he felt the inexplicable clench of his heart. Long minutes passed as her head flopped against his shoulder and he could hear her breathing fanning his neck. At last she unfolded her legs and slid them down so that she was standing again, her weight now pressed against the wall instead of into his body. But when he tilted her chin to stare into her eyes, she was having none of it and shook her head.

'No. Don't say anything,' she said.

'Not even to ask you whether you'd like to do it all over again?'

Her emerald gaze was very clear. 'And if I did, would you use some protection this time?'

He nodded. 'Of course I would. I wasn't thinking. At least, not about that.'

There was a fraction of a pause. 'Neither was I. But I need to do some thinking now, so will you please go?' She shook her head as if to pre-empt further argument. 'I mean it, Zuhal. Just go.'

It took a moment or two for him to realise she meant it and slowly he expelled a long breath. It was the first time he'd ever been ejected from a woman's bedroom but to Zuhal it suddenly felt more like a reprieve than a punishment. Because wasn't it a relief to be spared the inevitable analysis of what had just happened, in that tedious way women had of always overthinking things?

They both knew exactly what had just happened.

Sex. Amazing sex—nothing more and nothing less.

His lips curved into a satisfied smile as he allowed himself the brief luxury of a stretch. 'Sure,' he said, as he bent to retrieve his discarded robes.

CHAPTER TEN

THE SUN WAS rising in the dawn sky as Zuhal headed towards the stables next morning. He felt the tension leaching from his body—something he attributed to the amazing sex he'd had with Jazz last night, an erotic encounter which was making him grow hard just thinking about it. Because tension was an integral part of his life now, he recognised. It went hand in hand with the many new challenges facing him as monarch. Yet he found himself relishing those challenges in a way he hadn't been anticipating, because he had never imagined he would be King. To rule had never been his destiny, but already his people were beginning to accept him, even to warm to him, and he was confident that he would be able to do his best by them.

Wasn't that the silver lining to the dark cloud which had descended on him when Kamal had disappeared? The realisation that he no longer felt the outsider in the country of his birth?

The distant sky was a flamboyant display of flamingo-pink and orange as he swung himself into the saddle and urged his horse forward. Last night had been pivotal in all kinds of ways. He had spent the evening watching Jazz perform admirably as Queen-in-Waiting and her subsequent sexual capitulation boded well for the future. Surely now there was no further barrier stopping him from making her his bride? No reason for her to keep him dangling while she tantalisingly refused to give him her answer.

His mouth curved into a speculative smile. He remembered the way he had ripped the robes from her body and the way she had moaned as his fingers found her wet heat. Pride was all very well, but sexual satisfaction was a far more powerful motivator. Wouldn't that fast and furious encounter encourage her to go ahead with the marriage as quickly as possible, so that they could become husband and wife?

He rode for nearly an hour and was galloping back towards the stables when, suddenly, he caught sight of the gleam of blonde hair in the distance. Jazz. He felt his groin tighten as his gaze drank her in. In the light desert breeze, the folds of her robes had moulded themselves to her delectable body and he was reminded of clasping those luscious curves before bringing them both to orgasm. Was she eager for an early replay? he thought with hungry amusement Was that why she was here? Perhaps she wanted him to tumble her onto the stable floor and take her amid all the bales of hay, rutting into her like a stallion?

'So this time you don't mind being seen?' he questioned as he slowed his horse and drew up beside her.

She blinked up at him in alarm. 'Seen?'

He jumped down onto the dusty ground. 'Didn't I

once observe you watching me from afar? Standing in a corner of the stables and watching while I took off my clothes?' Her answering colour told him that her shadowed presence hadn't been a figment of his over-heated imagination and, although she was now glaring at him, he smiled. 'Don't worry, I rather liked you in the role of voyeur.'

'I'm not worried!' she flared back at him, her cheeks still flushed and pink.

'So why are you here?' he mused softly. 'As far as I'm aware, we aren't supposed to be meeting for another hour and I need to shower first. Unless what happened last night means you're thinking you might like to join me? I'm quite happy for you to soap me off, my beauty. It's far too long since we had a shower together.'

Jasmine wished he would stop making sexual allusions every time he opened his mouth because they were drawing her attention to his body, which she'd been trying very hard to forget. But how could she forget when the memory had kept her awake most of the night, as she'd recalled the way he had driven into her. Her cheeks grew hotter as she remembered her eagerness to have sex with him—backed up against one of the palace walls, of all places, with her legs wrapped tightly around his bare back as he had taken her on a quick trip to paradise. What had happened to her determination to keep things on an impartial footing until she had discovered whether she wanted to marry him? It had vanished the moment he had taken her in his arms and kissed her.

'I don't want to talk about that,' she said. 'Last night shouldn't have happened.'

His eyes glittered. 'Are you quite sure?'

'Quite sure. I'm supposed to be getting to know you,' she continued. 'In a rather more formal way than that.'

'As you wish. I've never had to beg a woman for sex before, Jazz—and I'm certainly not going to start now.'

'It was usually the other way round, was it?' she queried mischievously.

He gave a brief smile as they began to walk towards the stables, and Jasmine suddenly became aware of a sense of wistfulness as she breathed in a long-forgotten fragrance. 'I love that smell,' she said suddenly.

He turned to look at her. 'What smell?'

'You know. Horses. Leather. Dust. Sweat. The whole thing. Stables, I guess.' She gave a sigh, which seemed to bubble up out of nowhere. 'You're very lucky to be able to ride out in the desert with no fences or houses or roads to get in the way. You must get a real sense of freedom out here—the kind you don't really get back in England.'

He narrowed his eyes, as one of the grooms led his horse away. 'You sound as if you know what you're talking about.'

'You seem surprised.'

'Maybe I am. I thought you were the quintessential city girl. Are you telling me you can ride, Jazz?'

'Yes, I can ride,' she said quietly. 'I used to love all things equestrian until the age of ten. Or did you think I'd always been poor and that riding is a rich person's sport?'

He lifted his hand by a fraction, but the quirk of his lips indicated a signal of acknowledgement rather than command.

'So what happened when you were ten?' he continued curiously as they began to walk back towards the palace.

Jasmine tried to avert her gaze from the thrust of his thighs against his jodhpurs, but it wasn't easy—particularly when she thought of her fingers roving over their hair-roughened power last night and the memory of what lay at their apex. She cleared her throat. 'It was a continuation of the fallen-ice-cream episode,' she said.

'The fallen ice cream?' he repeated blankly.

'You remember. I told you about it in London. When my father left home.' She gave an impatient shake of her shoulders. 'Weren't you listening?'

'Yes, of course I was listening. Forgive me. I am feeling a little *distracted*. You can't blame me for that, in view of what happened between us last night.' With what looked like an effort, he dragged his gaze from her torso to her face. 'So what happened—after your father left home?'

He had stopped walking and was looking at her, waiting for her answer.

'We had to sell the house and the car,' she explained. 'And my pony was the first thing to go, obviously.'

'Why?'

Jasmine felt a flicker of irritation at his incomprehension. Did he really lack the imagination to work it out for himself, or was he just incapable of putting himself into the shoes of a normal person? She stared down at her feet, aware of a fine layer of dust from the yard which was now covering her toes and wishing she'd worn something more substantial than beaded flip-flops.

She lifted her gaze to his. 'Because as well as making his much younger secretary pregnant and causing a scandal at work, my father had also been living beyond his means—and once it was discovered, everything started to tumble down. The banks needed to be paid and there was no money to pay them. It meant my mum was left with very little. In fact, with almost nothing. We had to start renting a tiny apartment.' She sucked in a deep breath. 'And Mum had to go back out to work—but the only work she could get was cleaning. Overnight she went from being a middle-class wife to what she called a "skivvy" and she never got over it, really. She got ill soon after that. Perhaps the two things were related.'

Zuhal met the sombre expression clouding her green-gold eyes. It must have been tough, he acknowledged, as they resumed their step and the soaring blue cupolas of the palace swam into view. Maybe everyone's childhood was tough, he concluded grimly as several servants spotted him and lowered their gazes in natural deference. Or maybe it was family life itself which created all the problems. He thought about his own parents. About the so-called 'love' which had corrupted the atmosphere with so much poison. His mouth twisted. Who needed it? Surely mutual tolerance and good sex were a better long-term bet than all the chaos wreaked by love?

He observed the glint of sunlight on Jazz's pale hair and imagined her as a horse-mad young girl. He could picture her in a smart jacket, her hair in a net and a crop in her hand. A bright rosette pinned to her pony as she leaned forward to pat the forelock. It must have hurt to have lost all that, he realised with a sudden flash of insight, which wasn't usually his thing. Because although he didn't have quite the same affinity with horses as his brother did—*had done*—he corrected painfully, he still valued his daily ride above most things.

'Would you like to ride out with me tomorrow morning?' he said as she began to move away from him.

She turned back and he could see the uncertainty on her face. 'I haven't been on a horse for years,' she said. 'I don't know if I can still do it.'

'There's only one way to find out.'

'I don't know, Zuhal.'

'Is that a yes?' he prompted softly, and suddenly it mattered. It mattered a lot.

There was a pause and then she nodded, her blonde ponytail shimmering like the tail of a horse in the early-morning haze as her green eyes met his. 'It's a yes. And thank you. But there's no way I'll be able to keep up with you. Give me the most gentle horse in your stable and I'll be happy just trotting around the yard.'

'You will do no such thing,' he vowed. 'You can have my undivided teaching skills, if you like.' He felt the flicker of a pulse at his temple and the more insistent one which was throbbing deep in his groin. 'And don't they say it all comes rushing back, the moment you're back in the saddle?'

'I guess they do,' she said and the smile she gave him lingered long after he had watched her retreating into the palace.

He spent longer in the shower than usual—mainly because his newly ignited sexual hunger refused to be doused, even by the prolonged jets of icy water over his heated skin. He found himself bemused and intrigued by her determination to ignore what had happened last night. Unless her prudishness was all for show and she was planning to seduce him during their ten o'clock appointment in the Damask Room. Yes, that could work. That could work very well. He felt the flicker of a pulse at his temple and ordered Adham to ensure that he was not disturbed for the duration of the meeting, telling him it was possible it might run over.

But his anticipation was dampened the moment Jazz was shown into the room and he saw a new light of purpose glinting from her green-gold eyes. She was wearing a demure cream gown which covered her from head to ankle and his heart sank. Sinking down gracefully into one of the soft chairs, she pressed her knees together and he couldn't help contrasting her demure image with the wildcat lover who had greedily met his urgent thrusts last night.

'I'd like to discuss bringing the high chair into the dining room,' she began, without any kind of fanfare.

He narrowed his eyes. 'Excuse me?'

'I think it's best if we make some attempt to live as a normal family, even if these surroundings are far from normal, and neither is our situation. But I think it would benefit Darius if he joined us at lunchtime. That's all.'

Zuhal frowned. 'Have you forgotten that we often have international delegations with officials present during lunch?' he demanded.

'No, I haven't forgotten. But it will do them good to see the powerful King living as other men do. It would make you seem more…approachable.'

'You think I'm unapproachable?' he demanded.

She hesitated. 'I think as King you're still an unknown factor and interacting with your son will show people a softer side of you. Can you see any reason why we shouldn't give it a trial run, Zuhal?'

He met the determination in her eyes and felt a smile begin to build. 'I guess not,' he said, as grudging admiration for her sheer tenacity washed over him.

Then followed a debate about the installation of a small sandpit—'It's not as if we're short of the raw material, Zuhal!'—and before he knew it the half-hour was up. The meeting had not gone as he had hoped and yet, for some reason, he found himself whistling softly underneath his breath as he went off to his next appointment.

Next morning she joined him at the stables and he discovered that she was a good rider who possessed a natural affinity with the horse he had chosen especially for her. At first their routes were slow and unambitious—rarely venturing too far from the palace, until Zuhal was confident that Jazz herself was at ease. He watched her walk and canter and gallop with a growing feeling of satisfaction. He observed her increasing confidence as she and the horse became better acquainted before increasing the scope of their rides by taking her a little further into the desert.

And the stream of questions she'd implied she'd wanted the answers to had somehow failed to materialise. Maybe the sheer physicality of riding demanded all her attention, or maybe she was cleverer than he'd given her credit for by not pushing him into a corner. Her occasional queries were light—like butterflies dropping onto a blossom rather than rocks falling into a well. They seemed to encourage confidences rather than making him clam up, as had happened so often in the past whenever women had tried to delve beneath the surface. Once or twice, he found himself offering an opinion which hadn't been asked for. Like the time he'd admitted missing the banter and friendly rivalry he'd shared with his brother. Or confessing that being a ruler was harder than he'd envisaged and perhaps he had judged Kamal too harshly—something which troubled him now. He didn't tell her that for the first time ever he felt as if his life had true meaning. That he was no longer just the royal 'spare', and as ruler he found he had the power to make a difference.

But after an entire fortnight of uneventful rides, Zuhal had decided that enough was enough. He wanted her in his arms again and her body language was sending out a silent message that she wanted him just as much. This celibate existence had gone on long enough. He would put her in a position where she couldn't distract herself with horses or babies and this time *demand* she marry him!

The ride they embarked on the following day was

their most ambitious yet and for most of it he rode beside
her, his headdress streaming in the wind as they tracked
the golden sands in silence, the pounding of hooves
and the snort of the horses the only sounds to be heard.

'Look over there,' he said after a while, slowing
down to point into the distance. 'See anything?'

Screwing up her eyes, Jasmine noticed a tiny dot on
the horizon which was growing bigger as they rode towards it, until she saw the outline of a large tent with a
conical roof. Nearby was an unexpected copse of trees
and a group of smaller tents. In the shade of the trees
they dismounted and Zuhal tethered the horses before
two male servants appeared from one of the smaller
tents, bringing bowls of water for the animals to drink.

'Is this what you call an oasis?'

'Ten out of ten, Jazz,' he murmured.

He motioned for her to follow him into the cool interior of the largest tent, which stood some distance away.
Dipping her head to enter, she gave an audible gasp as
she gazed around the deceptively vast interior where
intricate bronze lamps hung from the ceiling and silken
rugs were scattered over the floor. A large day-bed of
silver brocade stood beside an exquisitely carved table,
on which reposed tiny glasses studded with the rainbow
colours of what looked like real jewels.

'Oh, Zuhal—it's beautiful,' she breathed, unable to
conceal her wonder or her delight. 'I don't think I've
ever seen anything quite so beautiful.'

'Not even at the Granchester Hotel,' he questioned
sarcastically.

A smile played at the edges of her lips. 'Not even there!'

He inclined his head in acknowledgement. 'Please, sit,' he said formally.

A little saddle-sore after the long ride, Jasmine obeyed, sinking into the heap of cushions he was indicating, while Zuhal called out something in his own language before lowering himself down beside her.

'What is this place?' she asked, as one of the servants appeared at the door of the tent, bearing a large stone jug and dispensing cool liquid into two tiny jewelled glasses.

'It is my refuge,' he said slowly, once the servant had left. 'It was my brother's refuge too, and our father's before him. It is traditionally the place where kings have come to escape from the pressures of court and palace life.'

Jasmine nodded as she took a sip of the refreshing drink. She had been treading on eggshells for days, afraid of driving him away with her curiosity and trying to establish some kind of trust between them, but something told her that now was the time to dig a little deeper. 'What was it like?' she asked, putting her glass down and leaning back against the soft nest of cushions.

'What?' he queried obliquely.

'Growing up in a palace.'

'You've experienced something of that yourself,' he answered carelessly. 'You will have noted the presence of servants. Of days which are governed by form and by structure. Of the innate need for formality—despite your single-handed mission to disrupt that formality by having our son eat his lunch with us.'

Jazz felt an inner glow because it was the first time he'd ever said *our* son. 'You can't deny that he's been very well behaved!' she defended.

'No, I cannot deny that,' he agreed gravely.

There was a pause before, encouraged by his relaxed demeanour, she asked a little more. 'So how did being a royal impact on your family, when you were a child?'

He shrugged. 'I never knew anything different. My blood is blue on both sides. My father came from a long line of desert kings and my mother was a princess from the neighbouring country of Israqan.'

Her voice was cautious. 'So was it an arranged marriage?'

'Unfortunately, no. It was not,' he answered repressively. 'If it had been there might have been a chance it might have worked. As it was, they met at the Razrastanian embassy in New York and *fell in love.*'

Jasmine registered the unmistakable contempt which had coloured those last three words. 'And was that so bad?'

'It was disastrous,' he said, his lips twisting with derision. 'Experience has taught me that love is nothing but an illusion which justifies desire and such...*passion* cannot possibly be sustained. At first it is an explosion—but explosions inevitably destroy whatever is around them. And then there is drama. Endless drama—with scenes and fights and tears. How I hate drama,' he added bitterly.

'And is that what happened—to your parents?'

'That is exactly what happened.' His black eyes glittered. 'It quickly burnt itself out and all that was left were two people who were essentially incompatible and who hated one another.'

'I'm sorry to hear that,' she offered, pausing for a moment before asking, 'So how did they deal with it?'

Again, he shrugged. 'My father sought comfort elsewhere and my mother threw all her energies into preparing my brother for his accession to the throne, in order to make him the finest ruler this land has ever known.'

'Did she indulge him?' she asked sharply.

'You could say that.' He took a last mouthful of juice before putting the jewelled beaker down. 'He grew up feeling he was capable of anything. That he was indestructible.'

'And where did you come in all this?' she questioned suddenly. 'Where did you fit in, Zuhal?'

Zuhal's eyes narrowed. Perceptive of her. But also perhaps a little too close to the bone. He prepared to bat away her question with flippancy before something stopped him and he frowned as he became aware that he had never admitted this to anyone. He'd never really been in a position to before, because he hadn't seen the point in confiding in any of his lovers, knowing that to do so would have been a potential security breach.

Yet suddenly the desire to connect was stronger than his innate desire to conceal. Was that because, as his potential wife, Jazz needed to know what kind of man he really was—so she didn't foster any unrealistic fantasies which could never be met? 'I didn't fit in anywhere,' he grated. 'Not then. I was the forgotten son. The invisible son. There's no need to look so shocked, Jazz. Don't they say every mother has her favourite? Well, it wasn't me. But I was well fed and well cared for and that was enough.' He saw the pain in her eyes and reached out to tilt her chin with his finger. 'Have I told you enough for one day? Don't you find the discussion of dysfunction a little…tedious? Surely you can think of a more pleasurable way of passing the time other than talking about a past which is lost to us for ever?'

The air between them thrummed. The breath left her lungs. Glancing up into the inky gleam of his eyes, Jasmine felt an erratic quickening of her pulse. She wanted to know more but she sensed that now was not the time, just as she sensed that Zuhal needed her now in a way he hadn't needed her before.

'I can think of several things,' she said huskily. 'It depends which one you're referring to.'

'You know exactly what I'm talking about.' He sprung to his feet to close the tent flaps, so that the interior instantly grew dim and mysterious. Now the cavernous space was lit only by the silvery brocade of the day-bed, the silky colours of the rugs and the bright sheen of metal lamps as he returned to join her on the floor and pulled her into his arms again. 'This,' he breathed. 'I'm talking about this.'

Jasmine knew he was going to kiss her but underpinning her desire was an overwhelming rush of emotion as he put his arms around her, as she thought about the little boy who nobody had wanted. But then he sank her into the soft cushions and her thoughts were forgotten as their mouths met in a hard and hungry kiss which left them gasping for oxygen.

His fingers were unsteady as he unbuttoned her shirt and tugged it from her shoulders, so that she was lying there in just her jodhpurs, riding boots and a black lacy bra. 'That's better,' he murmured.

'Do you—?'

'No. No more words, Jazz,' he said, with a shake of his head as he bent to pull off her riding boots. The jodhpurs were next to go, each movement a sensual torture as he slowly stroked them down her thighs, his fingers whispering tantalisingly over the black lace wisp of her panties. She gasped as he unclipped her straining bra, so that her breasts spilled out—one nipple finding itself positioned perfectly for his waiting lips to suck on.

'Oh!' she gasped.

'I thought I said no words.'

'I couldn't help myself.'

His eyes swept over her, as he swiftly removed his own clothes before taking her hand in his. 'Is this what you want?' he questioned, directing her fingertips to his groin. 'I think it is. It's certainly what *I* want.'

And Jasmine needed no further guidance as she wrapped her trembling fingers around his mighty shaft, enjoying the sound of his murmured pleasure as she began to slide them up and down the silken skin. Lying down beside her, he kissed her until she was quivering—touching every inch of her with a taunting skill, until she was making strangled little pleas. At last he positioned himself over her and she could feel the heaviness of his body and the hard brush of his erection between her thighs. And then he gave one hard, long thrust, to tunnel up deep inside her—and as he did so, another rush of emotion threatened to overwhelm her. Closing her eyes, Jasmine sank her lips against his sweat-sheened shoulder. Because this wasn't some *wham-bam* bout up against the wall. This was heart-stoppingly intimate and terrifying in its implications. And only Zuhal could make her feel like this. Respond like this.

'Zuhal,' she said brokenly, but maybe he didn't hear. Maybe he was so intent on giving her pleasure that he was oblivious to her turbulent feelings—or maybe he just preferred to ignore them. And then everything was forgotten as her body began to spasm helplessly around him.

She was dimly aware of the choked cry he gave as her back arched and the spurting rush as he filled her with his seed. When the world came back into focus at last, it was for her to find his dark head resting on her breast, one bent arm around her neck, his breath warm against her damp skin. And wasn't it infuriating how stupidly *mushy* she felt? Wasn't she in danger of falling for him all over again, despite his emotional distance and his obvious mistrust of anything to do with love? But then something occurred to her—something which drove all these thoughts clean from her mind.

'That's the second time we've omitted to use any protection,' she said.

He stirred and yawned. 'Doing it with you as nature intended just seems to come naturally to me,' he admitted. 'Do you mind?'

Jasmine hesitated, aware that something had shifted and changed between them. Say it, she urged herself. Don't expect him to guess what you're thinking and then be angry when he gets it wrong. 'I think it's better if we decide if and when to have another baby,' she said carefully. 'Rather than just leaving it to chance.'

'Do you want another baby, Jazz?'

There was a long segment of silence. 'If we're to be married, then yes, I think I do,' she answered eventually.

'You mean the marriage you've been dragging your feet about?'

She didn't deny his accusation, just shifted her weight a little as she looked up into his eyes. 'Because up until now, we've seemed more like strangers than anything else.'

His black gaze burned into her. 'But now we're no longer "strangers"—you're happy for it to go ahead?'

Happy? It seemed a strange word to use in the circumstances. It felt a long time since she'd experienced that particular emotion. When she'd found herself alone and pregnant, it had been independence which Jasmine had strived for and, against all the odds, she had achieved it. Even though it had been a bit of a struggle, she had forged a decent life for herself and Darius. She had been her own woman—in charge of her own destiny—and she recognised that her growing feelings for Zuhal threatened to destabilise everything she had achieved.

She met the dark gleam of his eyes. Yet today he had shown a chink in his armour and a vulnerability she hadn't expected. He'd described the awful atmosphere in the palace when he'd been growing up. He'd described how his parents had made a mockery of love and how he despised and mistrusted the word and all it stood for as a consequence. She got that. But she could show him by example that it didn't need to be like that, couldn't she? She loved Darius and maybe Zuhal would come to realise that love wasn't always a dirty word. And if that happened, then couldn't they learn to love each other—or was that a wish too far?

'Yes,' she said gravely. 'I am. And I'm prepared to give our marriage my very best shot.'

'Good.' He inclined his dark head. 'Then it is agreed. We will wed as soon as possible. We will become husband and wife and have shared goals for a stable future, not just for the monarchy, but for Darius—and for any brothers and sisters he may have.'

She thought how business-like they both sounded— as if they were dealing with a business merger rather than a relationship. But his mouth was soft as he reached out for her and most of her misgivings melted away beneath the sensual onslaught of another heady kiss.

She kissed him back with a fervour which matched his own and his face was tight as he lifted her up and brought her down onto his aching shaft, groaning as she began to ride him. And suddenly it was all happening so fast. Indecently fast. She felt that first sweet clench which began to dominate her world as she began to come, aware that he was watching her closely. His fingers were tight on her breasts as her back arched and she threw her head back with a fierce shout which was quickly echoed by his own.

Afterwards they lay there very quietly, and it was with a beat of something which felt like hope for the future that Jasmine agreed to Zuhal's suggestion that they head back to the palace. With a sense of torpor, they dressed and drank some juice before going back outside, where the rested horses seemed infected by their laziness, making the return ride slow and leisurely.

Zuhal wasn't quite sure at which point he noticed that something was different. Was it the barely perceptible flash from one of the palace windows, as if someone was looking out for them, which made his body grow tense? Or was it just the sight of three of his aides waiting for them in the stable yard—Adham among them, which was highly unusual?

There was an expression on his chief aide's face which he'd never seen before—one he couldn't quite decipher—and Zuhal's heart gave a lurch of foreboding as he tried to work out exactly what was going on. But then he saw a rare smile break out on Adham's face as he rushed forward to greet the Sheikh.

'Your Royal Highness!' exclaimed the aide, not even waiting until Zuhal had leapt from his horse. 'I have wondrous news! Your brother is returned. The King is alive!'

CHAPTER ELEVEN

'WHERE THE HELL have you been?'

Zuhal stared into the face of his brother—a brother he hardly recognised. Kamal's face was gaunt, his eyes sunken, and his ragged clothes unlike any he would usually wear as royal regalia. He must have lost at least twenty pounds, and his black hair flowed down past his shoulders. Only his proud deportment betrayed the fact that this was no ordinary man who had been lost in the desert for months and months, but in fact a desert king.

'Well?' Zuhal's demand rang out through the echoing Throne Room. The blonde gleam of Jasmine's hair reminded him she was sitting in the window seat, but he barely noticed her—his only focus on the brother he had thought was dead. Utter relief at seeing his only sibling alive suddenly transformed itself into righteous anger. 'Are you going to give me some kind of explanation about how you've just miraculously returned, after we've spent months sending search parties out for you?'

Kamal nodded, his gaunt expression becoming tight and tense, as if he had no desire to relive what had happened to him. 'The sandstorm came down on us suddenly and my horse and I were lost—'

'That much I know,' Zuhal interrupted impatiently. 'And if you'd bothered letting someone know where you were going then we could have found you.'

'No. You could never have found me,' said Kamal, his voice suddenly bleak. 'For I was swallowed up in the most inaccessible part of the desert, heavily concussed, with my leg broken.'

'Oh, my brother,' said Zuhal, his voice suddenly trembling with an emotion he did not recognise.

'Were it not for the nomadic tribe from the Harijia region who found me and took me in and helped me back to health, I would surely have died.' Kamal looked down at his hands. 'I lived in their tents as one of them for many months and they taught me much about the land I thought I knew. I liked living there.' He lifted his gaze to his brother. 'For a while I thought I wanted to stay. Maybe a part of me didn't want to come back and continue to be King.'

There was a silence.

'So what changed your mind?' asked Zuhal slowly.

There was silence. 'I heard you were getting married to the Englishwoman.' Another pause. 'And that she had a child.'

Noiselessly Jasmine rose to her feet and left the Throne Room, but nobody noticed her go. Of course they didn't. Ever since they'd returned to the palace she'd felt invisible to the man she'd spent the afternoon having sex with and the reason for that was as plain as the nose on her face. The King had returned and her place here was now redundant.

* * *

An exhausted Kamal retired early and Jasmine spent that night in Zuhal's bed, but his lovemaking—although satisfying—felt almost *perfunctory* and he resolutely refused to discuss the impact of the King's return on their future. The following morning he had already left for his early ride when she woke and Jasmine was aware of a sharp sense of disappointment that he hadn't taken her with him, as was usual. Had he only tolerated her accompanying him on his daily ride because he'd wanted her to marry him?

But now there was no longer any need for him to marry her, was there?

Jasmine found herself in a strange position. She felt alone and scared—more scared even than when she'd found herself pregnant. She didn't want to put any more pressure on Zuhal but this sense of being in limbo wasn't doing her any good. She needed to face up to the facts and calmly ask the Sheikh what he really wanted now that his brother had returned—perhaps when they were in bed, soft and satiated by sex. Perhaps when her arms were around his waist and he was nuzzling her neck in a way which made her shiver with something deeper than desire. Or would it be easier if they were face to face across a table, so that she wasn't naked and vulnerable? So that she could calmly get up and leave and go and cry with dignity and in private…

Trying to work out the best way to approach such a delicate matter, she took Darius out for an afternoon stroll, planning to sit in the palace rose garden and sing him the soft lullabies he loved. Rainbow light arced through the spray of the ornate fountains, and the blousy blooms of perfumed flowers made her feel as if she'd tumbled into a kaleidoscopic fantasy-land as she walked through the spacious gardens. She was going to miss this beautiful place, she thought, with a sudden clench of her heart.

The air was soft and drowsy with the buzz of bees and Jasmine thought she heard the drift of voices coming from the interior of the rose garden. She wondered who it might be as her sandaled feet moved silently towards the sound, until the familiar velvety caress of her lover's voice indicated he was deep in conversation with his brother.

She didn't mean to eavesdrop. In fact, she was just about to turn away and go somewhere else in order to give them peace, when she heard her name mentioned. She told herself afterwards that it was only human nature to stand there for a moment or two. To want to know what was being said about her. She told herself it was a good thing she *did* listen—because otherwise, how would she have known the truth? Wouldn't she just have carried on weaving impossible dreams about the future and hoping that one day Zuhal might learn to love her, if only a little?

'Jazz?' Zuhal's voice was drawling. 'What about her?'

'Won't she mind not being Queen—now that I'm back?'

'It is not in her remit to *mind*.'

'But she is a woman, Zuhal—and women are notoriously ambitious for their men.'

'Not Jazz.' There was a pause. 'We don't have that kind of relationship.'

'What kind of relationship *do* you have, then?'

'It defies definition,' said Zuhal flippantly.

'Oh?' Kamal's voice probed further. 'Are you still going to marry her, now that I'm back?'

'I haven't decided.'

Jasmine bristled at his arrogance—his innate certainty that *he* was the one who called the shots—when Kamal's next question made her heart pound violently against her breastbone.

'Do you love her?'

There was another pause, during which Jasmine could hear some unknown bird singing high from one of the treetops, and its sweet, drenching song sounded unbearably poignant.

'No,' said Zuhal, in a hard, empty voice. 'You must realise by now that I don't do love, Kamal.'

She'd known that all along, but even so Jasmine was surprised by the fierce intensity of the pain which ripped through her as she registered that cold and unequivocal statement. She wanted to gasp with shock and pain—but somehow she held it back, because now was not the time. And really, she'd learned nothing new, had she? Because nothing had changed.

Zuhal had told her he didn't do love. He mistrusted it and didn't want it—for reasons which were perfectly understandable. He'd told her that emphatically and now he was stating it loud and clear to his brother. Perhaps he was doing her a favour. Would she really have been content to spend her life here with him, not daring to show her feelings for fear it would make him angry, or suspicious that she had started to love him again? What kind of an example would that set to Darius?

She was trembling as she silently turned the pram and pushed it away as fast as she dared go, knowing that there was only one solution which lay open to her—and she took the baby to Rania, before going to Zuhal's offices to find him. Ignoring Adham's protest, she walked straight into the Sheikh's office without knocking to find him talking on the phone. Something in her face must have sent out an unspoken warning because he uttered a few terse words in his native tongue before terminating the call and rising slowly to his feet.

'This is unexpected,' he said, a faint note of reproof in his deep voice.

'I overheard you,' she said.

His brow darkened. 'What are you talking about?'

'In the garden, talking to your brother. I heard you say you didn't love me.'

He didn't look in the slightest bit abashed. 'But you knew that already, Jazz. I've never lied to you about that.'

'No, I know you haven't.' She drew in a deep breath. 'And while part of me respects you for your honesty, I've realised I can't live like that. It's not good for our son to live like that either.'

'So what do you expect me to say in response to this?' he demanded. 'To tell you that I didn't mean it?'

'No. I don't expect that, Zuhal. If you must know I admire your honesty and the fact that you've never spun out lies or empty promises.' She took a deep breath. 'But

I just want you to arrange for me and Darius to return to England, and as soon as possible.'

He raised his dark brows. 'To do what?'

She shrugged. 'To live somewhere—not London, but close enough for you to be able to access us easily. And a house, I think—not an apartment—because I want Darius to have a garden of his own. I'd like to go back to Oxfordshire until I can find something which meets with your approval. You can even appoint your body-guards if you wish—since I recognise that as Darius is your son we need protection. But I want to go back, Zuhal.' Her voice suddenly became low. Urgent. 'And as soon as possible.'

Zuhal's mouth hardened with anger and contempt as he acknowledged Jazz's manipulative demands. Well, if she was hoping he would start grovelling in an attempt to persuade her to stay, then she was in for a disappointment. He didn't argue with her, because this kind of conversation felt like one he'd had too often with women in the past—though never with Jazz, he conceded. It was emotional blackmail. She was making a statement. She was leaving.

And she was taking their son with her.

He kept his cold resolve through all the arrangements for their departure and maintained it as he saw her and Darius off from the airfield. But he couldn't deny the inexplicable lurch of his heart as he saw her disappearing inside the private jet, his son's dark curly head bobbing over her shoulder. It felt as if a dark cloud were descending on him as he recalled saying goodbye to his child, who'd naturally been too young to realise what was happening. But *he* had known, hadn't he? Had known and felt guilty and resentful, all at the same time—half tempted to tell Jazz that he wouldn't allow her to take his progeny from the country, but knowing deep down that the child needed his mother.

The powerful engines roared but he turned away so that his back was to the plane during take-off, mainly because he'd got a damned speck of dust in his eye and infuriatingly, it was watering. On returning to the palace, he worked solidly for the rest of the day, checking his phone with unusual regularity.

But the only thing he heard from Jazz was after she'd touched down in England and sent a miserable little text saying, I'm back. Which, of course, he had already known, because his security people had alerted him.

He sent back an equally bald text:

I will be in touch to discuss arrangements about Darius.

But she didn't reply, which infuriated him even more.

His handover to Kamal almost complete, he decided to reward himself with some extra riding, deciding that some hard physical exercise was exactly what he needed to rid himself of this strange frustration which was burning away inside him. But for once the exertion and beauty of the desert failed to work their magic and he realised he was missing Darius more than he would ever have imagined. His mouth thinned. He would travel to Europe and see him, but he would do it in his own time and on *his* terms.

Stopping in Paris en route for a long-overdue meeting, he checked himself into a sybaritically indulgent hotel with glittering views over the river Seine, for an overnight stay. He wasn't really in the mood for socialising but unexpectedly ran into the dashing ex-polo player, Alejandro Sabato, and agreed to have dinner with him. He'd forgotten how the charismatic Argentinean attracted women like wasps buzzing towards uncovered food and several times their meal was interrupted while one of them gushingly requested a selfie with the ex-world champion. And then, much to Zuhal's annoyance, they were papped leaving the upmarket restaurant.

Zuhal's eyes were gritty when he woke next morning and, although he tried ringing Jazz from his plane before he touched down in England, the call went straight to voicemail. But she didn't bother ringing back and neither did she pick up the second call he made as his limousine—with diplomatic flag flying—sped from the airfield towards Oxfordshire.

A house had been purchased for her, not far from where she'd lived before—but her new home was a world away from her old, rented cottage. Set like a jewel in an acre of walled garden, the detached villa had mullioned windows which glinted like diamonds in the sunshine and a soft grey front door. Two bright pots of scarlet geraniums stood on either side of the front door and the sporty little saloon he'd insisted on buying for her was parked in front of the garage. But when Zuhal lifted the shiny bronze knocker to sound out a summons through the house, nobody came to the door. He tried again with the same result and he scowled.

Where the hell *was* she?

His anger grew as he waited in his limousine, drumming his fingers against his knees and glancing out at the lonely lane, wondering if she was safe and wondering why he had allowed her to live this kind of existence in the English countryside. By the time she returned, a bag bulging with groceries on the bottom of the pram, he was seething, as his eyes raked over her.

She was back to wearing jeans and a shirt, and her hair was twisted into a plait as she returned his gaze with shuttered eyes. She couldn't have looked less like the perfumed Queen she'd been poised to become, yet something twisted deep inside him as he stared at her. Something he didn't want to acknowledge for fear of where it would take him.

'Wouldn't it be more sensible to have one of the bodyguards do your shopping for you?' he demanded, as he carefully helped her manoeuvre the pram into the spacious hallway of the house to avoid waking the baby. 'Rather than struggling like this on your own?'

'Not if I want to have any semblance of living a normal life,' she responded. 'I thought you were coming yesterday.'

'I tried to ring but you didn't pick up.'

'And? You could have left a message.'

'I don't like leaving messages.'

'We all have to do things we don't like, Zuhal—but it would have been common courtesy to have informed me that you weren't going to be here when you said you were. I have to be able to rely on you. Darius is too young to know the difference right now, but in the future he needs to know that you're going to turn up when you say you are.'

He frowned, knowing that she had a point and realising that nobody—nobody—had ever spoken to him quite so caustically before. 'I had business to attend to in Paris.'

'So I saw in the papers.'

His eyes narrowed as he detected a faint crack in her voice. 'I thought you didn't read the papers.'

'I...' She seemed a little lost for words at this and swallowed, before tilting her chin with the stubborn gesture he had grown to recognise. 'Why are you here, Zuhal? If it's to see Darius then perhaps you'd like to wait in the sitting room until he's awake? If it's to organise access arrangements, then wouldn't it be better if it was done officially, through your office and your lawyers?'

He studied her. 'And that's what you want, is it?'

She swallowed again, but even so when her words came out they still sounded as if she had a foreign body lodged in her throat. 'Yes, that's what I want.'

Zuhal stilled as something inside him twisted. Something which felt like pain. Not the brutal kind, which came from a cut or a blow, but something much more insidious—and yet it was sharp. Crushingly sharp. He held his palm over his chest, as if that might steady the erratic beat of his heart as he looked into green-gold eyes which contained the hint of unshed tears.

'Jazz?' he said huskily, even though he wasn't really sure what it was he was asking.

'I'm not sure I can deal with this,' she said, with a brisk shake of her head. 'Not right now. I'm not in the mood. You told me you didn't like drama—that you saw enough of it during your childhood to put you off it for ever—well, neither do I. I wasn't expecting you and I'm not…prepared.'

'Why do you need to be prepared for my visit?'

She shook her head. 'It doesn't matter.'

'It does. It matters to me.'

Jasmine stared at him. Was he completely *stupid*? Didn't he realise that since returning she'd realised just how much he'd burrowed his way underneath her skin? That the memory of his proud hawkish features swam into her mind at pretty much every opportunity? That she missed him. She missed him more than she had any right to miss him.

But why tell him any of that? Why *should* she admit her weakness—and her love—for a man who didn't want it? That would completely disrupt the delicate balance of power which existed between them, which they needed to maintain in the future. It wasn't as if they weren't ever going to see each other again. Because of Darius there were bound to be lots of times over the years when they would bump into one another and she needed to ensure things stayed dignified and civilised between them. And that was never going to happen if Zuhal thought she was pining for him. Suddenly Jasmine could picture him laughing about her behind her back, perhaps when he was lying in bed with a new lover. Could imagine his drawled, cruel words as he dissected their relationship with forensic accuracy.

Jazz? Oh, she's nobody special. Just the mother of my child. There's nothing between us. The pregnancy was a mistake. Does she love me? She could even imagine his arrogant smile. *Yeah. I guess she does.*

Well, she wasn't going to give him that pleasure. Pointedly, she looked at her watch. 'So which is it to be, Zuhal? Either way, I need to get on, so you must excuse me. I've got someone coming over to look at some of my baby designs.'

Zuhal frowned and still he felt a burst of dark restlessness as something occurred to him. He remembered one morning when he'd found Jazz in the nursery, just before Kamal had returned. She'd been sitting on the floor flicking a balloon in front of their gurgling son, while dappled sunlight from the rose garden had streamed in on them both. She'd looked up at him and smiled, with a look of simple joy in her eyes, and he had smiled back. His heart pounded as he remembered going off to his office, whistling softly beneath his breath. He thought about the hard morning rides he'd taken since she'd gone, which had failed to work their magic, mainly because she hadn't been there to talk to. The space at the lunch table, which seemed so bare without her. The high chair which had been put away, as if Darius had never even been there.

His jaw clenched and the pain which had been twisting inside him grew unbearable. He knew he could walk away after he'd seen his little boy. He could agree that all such future meetings would probably be best conducted on neutral territory, through their respective lawyers. Or he could tell her the truth, which was only just beginning to dawn on him. A shocking truth which seemed to have come at him out of nowhere.

He thought back to when he'd discovered he had a son and told Jazz he would continue to seek a suitable bride, before blithely announcing that Darius would be his 'insurance policy' in case his new wife proved infertile. Suddenly he recognised just how wickedly cruel his words had been, though he'd never really stopped to consider the consequences of saying them before now. He thought how tolerant she had been, even in the face of all that heartlessness. How strong and brave in withstanding the undoubted suspicion and coolness of the palace servants when he'd first taken her to Razrastan. And determined, too. She had rejected his advances when they'd arrived at the royal palace—with a single-mindedness he suspected most other women wouldn't have displayed in her place. Didn't that make him respect her even more?

'Jazz, listen to me.'

'We've said everything we need to say.'

'But that's where you're wrong. I haven't even started but I need to start now by telling you just how much I miss you—'

'No!' she butted in, urgent desperation in her voice, as if she couldn't bear to hear what he was about to say. 'One thing I've always admired about you is your honesty—so please don't ruin that by telling me lies!'

'Not lies but the truth,' he argued doggedly, as the certainty inside him grew. Like when your plane dropped down, out of the cotton-wool blur of the clouds—and suddenly there was a whole clear landscape below you. 'I've realised why I ended my relationship with you the first time round—long before I planned to.'

'Don't,' she whispered, with a shake of her blonde head. 'Just *don't*.'

'It was because you used to make me *feel* stuff,' he continued, undeterred. 'Stuff I didn't want to feel. I listed all the reasons why you were unsuitable for any kind of future and I forced myself to believe them. But I never forgot you, Jazz. Not ever. Why else do you think I chose to come to you when I needed comfort and succour after my brother disappeared?'

'Because you thought I would be a walkover?'

He shook his head. 'No,' he said simply. 'Not that. And not just because you were the best lover I've ever had but because something told me that with you I would be able to break the rule of a lifetime, and talk. Why else did I never...' his voice deepened, and cracked '... take another woman to my bed, since parting from you?'

She was staring up at him, disbelief widening her green-gold eyes. 'Are you trying to tell me you haven't had sex with anyone else since we split up?'

'I am telling you, because it's the truth,' he clarified unsteadily. 'And I'll you another. That my morning rides haven't been the same without you by my side to talk to. That the palace has seemed empty without you there. But I'll tell you something else, something which eclipses all those other realisations and that is that I love you. I love you, Jazz. I love you so very much.'

She shook her face from side to side, her expression disbelieving and mulish. 'But you don't want love. You don't do love.'

'That's what I thought and that's what I said—only now I discover I was wrong. Because I don't want to live without it. Without you. Without Darius. My family—the most precious thing in the world, which I almost let slip through my fingers.' He reached out and took her hands in his, and even though they lay there—inert and cold—she didn't pull them away. 'Will you forgive me for all the cruel and unthinking words I've said to you, my beautiful Jazz? Will you give me another chance to show you that I am capable of change, and of love? Will you allow me to become the husband you deserve? To cherish you and protect you for as long as I live?'

There was a pause during which she shook her head again as she stared down at the exquisite silken rug he'd had shipped here from Razrastan. But when at last she lifted her gaze to his, he could see bright tears brimming over in her extraordinary eyes, making them look like new leaves which were drenched with the morning dew.

'Yes,' she whispered, at last. A tear was trickling down her cheek but her fingers were curling into his. 'How could I refuse when I love you, too? When I've never stopped loving you, no matter how hard I tried.'

He smiled but it took an effort as he realised just how close he'd come to losing her. And as he pulled her close, he discovered that the wetness on her cheek was mingling with tears of his own. 'But now you don't have to try any more, my love. The only thing you have to do right now is to seal our love in the most traditional way of all.' His words grew unsteady as he positioned her face so that her mouth was within claiming distance. 'So kiss me, Jazz. Kiss me and convince me all this is real.'

EPILOGUE

IT WAS A perfectly warm English evening. The sinking sun was gilding the edges of the sky as dusk glimmered on the horizon. On the veranda of their large, white house overlooking green hills and rolling countryside, Jasmine kicked off her shoes, which were sinfully high to walk in, but which were her husband's undoubted favourite, which was why she wore them. Briefly, she closed her eyes because she still got a sharp hit of pleasure whenever she thought about those two words.

My husband.

The man she had married and the man she loved. The man who loved her back and who had no qualms about showing her just how much.

As if on cue, Zuhal emerged from the house where he had been kissing their three children goodnight after reading them one of the many Razrastanian fables which Jasmine was eager to see translated into English because they were just so *good*. Darius particularly liked the one about the desert falcon who discovered the lost rubies before turning into a prince and marrying the Princess. Unbelievably, their son was nearly five now and a bright tearaway who loved teasing his twin sisters, Yasmin and Anisa—eighteen months old and the apples of their father's eye.

She looked up at him and smiled. 'Everything quiet?'

Zuhal's answering smile was slow, the glint in his eyes provocative and his murmured reply contented. 'Fast asleep. Which means we have the whole evening ahead of us. What would you like to do, my love?'

What Jasmine sometimes wanted was to pinch herself, to ask herself whether this could really be happening, if life could possibly be this good. But it could, and it was. From difficult and rocky beginnings there had emerged the kind of relationship she had never imagined would exist between her and the Sheikh of Razrastan.

She and Zuhal had married in a lavish ceremony in his country, attended by the great and the good from around the globe and, in the absence of a father, his brother Kamal had consented to give her away. She had become close to the King in the time leading up to their wedding and during their subsequent visits, though, as she sometimes said to Zuhal, he had hinted at something which had happened to him during his period away from the palace—something to do with a woman, which had not yet been resolved.

And then something else wonderful had happened. Her ex-husband had seen the reports of her marriage in the newspapers and had wished her every happiness, telling her that he had remarried himself. In fact, Richard and David had managed to track down a rare, first edition of Razrastanian poems and had sent it to her and Zuhal as a wedding present and, with that simple gesture, yet another scar of the past had been healed.

As newly-weds, she and the Sheikh had decided to settle in England, moving to an enormous estate in the beautiful county of Sussex, where Zuhal had achieved a lifetime ambition and, in addition to his thriving property and shares portfolio, had opened up his own polo club, which was currently breaking all records. It had taken him a while to adjust from the idea of being a prosperous king to being a prosperous businessman again, but he had seen the many benefits his new life offered him. And these days he articulated all his hopes and fears to his beloved wife.

In the early days of the polo club, he had received practical advice from the dashing ex-player Alejandro Sabato, who had assured Jasmine that Zuhal had played no part in the photograph which had been plastered all over the press, of the two men emerging from a restaurant with several blonde women in pursuit that night in Paris.

'He was unusually quiet that night,' Alej had mused. 'And several times he mentioned your name. I knew then that he was in love with you.'

Jasmine smiled, as Zuhal walked over to her and began to massage her shoulders. In love. Yes. Her previously closed-up lover had become the most demonstrative and affectionate of men.

'You haven't answered my question,' Zuhal murmured, as he bent to kiss her neck. 'About what you'd like to do tonight?'

She turned her head a little, so that she could catch the ebony gleam of his dark eyes. 'Any suggestions?'

'Plenty,' he murmured. 'But you are a remarkably difficult woman to please. I try to shower you with jewels, but you aren't interested.'

She held up her left hand as she surveyed the rare blue stone which had been purloined from the palace vaults in Razrastan. 'That's because one diamond is enough.'

'And I offer to fly you to Paris for the weekend, but you refuse.'

'That's because there's no place like home.'

He smiled. 'You didn't even want to go out for dinner tonight, despite the fact that the chef of the restaurant I was planning to take you to has just won his third Michelin star. Which makes me wonder what exactly you would like to do tonight, my beautiful Sheikha Al Haidar?'

With a soft laugh Jasmine rose to her feet, wiggling her now bare toes against the cool tiles as she looped her arms around her husband's neck and planted her lips just a few centimetres away from his. 'I think I'd like to take you to bed,' she murmured. 'To show you and tell you just how much I love you, and how much I value having you in my life.'

Zuhal nodded, his throat suddenly constricting. 'And I shall tell you yet again that I became the luckiest man in the world all those days ago, when I walked into a hotel boutique and saw you standing there, blushing and not quite meeting my eyes.'

Her beautiful face was so close to his. And, as he always did in times of great emotion—which he no longer attempted to bury or deny—Zuhal used the poetic words of his native tongue, a language which Jazz was gradually coming to understand.

'If I stood you next to all the planets which glow in the mighty desert sky,' he said huskily, 'then you would be the very brightest, my darling Jazz.'

He lowered his head to hers and began to kiss her—tenderly at first, but with a fast-growing passion which soon had her moaning with pleasure. And the stars were shimmering like diamond dust in the darkening sky by the time Zuhal lifted his wife into his arms and carried her into the bedroom.

* * * * *

CONTRACTED FOR THE SPANIARD'S HEIR

CATHY WILLIAMS

CHAPTER ONE

'SHALL I BRING the girl in now, sir?'

Sprawled back in his swivel chair, Luca Ross looked at his housekeeper, Miss Muller, who was standing to attention by the door.

In short order, he had sacked the nanny, sat his god-son down for a talk to find out what the hell was going on and now, item number three on the agenda, was the girl waiting in the kitchen. It was fair to say that his day had been shot to pieces.

He nodded curtly at his housekeeper, who was as forceful as a sergeant major and one of the few people not intimidated by her aggressive and powerful boss.

'And make sure those hounds don't come with her,' he said flatly. 'Lock them outside if you need to. If it's raining, then they'll get wet. They're dogs. They're built for that. Just make sure they don't destroy any more of my house.'

In the cold confines of his home office—which was better equipped than most commercial offices, with all the accoutrements necessary for him to keep in touch with his myriad companies that spanned numerous time zones—Luca Ross sat back and contemplated this latest, unwelcome development.

He had failed. It was as simple as that. Six months ago, out of the blue, he had inherited a six-year-old cousin once removed, a boy he had briefly met when he had accepted—with cavalier nonchalance, he now realised—the role of godfather.

Luca had few relatives, and certainly none with whom he kept in active contact, and the request, coming from his cousin, had seemed perfectly acceptable. A compliment, even.

His cousin had then set off for foreign shores to seek his fortune, breathtakingly naïve in his assumption that the streets of California were really and truly paved with gold, and Luca had promptly lost touch.

Life was hectic. Emails had been few and far between and his conscience when it came to the role of godfather had been easily soothed by the occasional injection of cash into the bank account he had set up for his godson shortly after his cousin and his young wife had set off to sail the seas and make their fortune.

Job done.

He had not banked on actually being called upon to take charge of anyone, least of all a six-year-old child, but fate, unfortunately, had had other plans.

Jake's parents had been tragically killed in an accident and Luca had been left with a godson who had no place whatsoever in his highly controlled and extremely frenetic life.

Naturally, Luca had done his best and had flung money at the unexpected problem. But now, sitting back in his office while he waited for the tiny, dark-haired thing who had returned his godson two hours earlier, he had to concede that he had failed.

That failure was an insult to his dignity, to his pride

and, more than that, signalled a dereliction of the duty he had blithely taken upon his shoulders when he had accepted the position of godfather.

Once this chaotic mess was brought to a conclusion, he would have to rethink the whole situation or else risk something far worse happening in the not-too-distant future.

What, precisely, the solution to that problem might be, Luca had no idea, but he was confident he would be able to come up with something. He always did.

Standing outside the door, where she had been delivered like an unwanted parcel by the fearsome middle-aged woman with the steel-grey hair and the unsmiling face of a hit man, Ellie wasn't sure whether to knock, push open the door which was ajar or—her favoured option—run away.

She instantly and regrettably ruled out the running away option because right now, in the pouring rain, the dogs she was looking after were mournfully doing heaven only knew what in the back garden of this stupidly fabulous Chelsea mansion. She couldn't abandon them. If she did, she quailed to think what their fate might be. Neither the hard-faced housekeeper nor her cold-as-ice employer struck her as the types who had much time for dogs. They would have no problem tossing all three dogs into the local dogs' home faster than you could say 'local dogs' home'.

She licked her lips. Hovered. Twisted her hands together. Tried hard not to think about the towering, intimidating guy to whom she had spoken briefly an hour and a half previously when she had rung the doorbell to deliver one runaway six-year-old back to his home. She'd had no idea to whom the blond child belonged, but she certainly hadn't envisaged the sort of drop-dead gorgeous man who had greeted them with an expression that could have frozen water. He had looked at her and the dogs and then taken charge of the situation in a manner that had brooked no debate, dispatching her to the kitchen where she had been commanded to *sit and wait; he would be with her shortly.*

She tentatively knocked on the door, took a deep breath and then walked into the room with a lot more bravado than she was currently feeling.

Like the rest of the house she had glimpsed, this room positively screamed *luxury*.

In her peripheral vision, she took in the cool greys, the marble, the built-in bookcase with its rows of forbidding business tomes. On one wall, there was an exquisite little painting that she vaguely recognised. On the opposite wall, there was an ornate series of hand-mounted clocks, all telling different times, and of course the vast granite-and-wood desk on which were three computers, behind which...

'My apologies if you have been kept waiting.' Luca nodded at the leather chair facing his desk, his cool, dark eyes never leaving Ellie's face. When she had shown up at his front door, with Jake in one hand and a series of leads attached to dogs in the other, Luca had thought that he had never seen such a scrappy little thing in his life. Small, slender, with short hair and clothes he associated with the sort of people with whom he had minimal contact. Walkers, ramblers, lovers of great open spaces...

He'd barely been able to see what sort of figure she had because it had been hidden under a capacious jumper that was streaked with muddy paw-prints. Her jeans had been tucked into similarly muddy wellies and she had forgone the nicety of an umbrella as protection against the driving summer downpour in favour of a denim hat from beneath which she had glared at him with unhidden, judgemental criticism.

All in all, not his type.

'Sit. Please.'

'I don't know what I'm doing here, Mr Ross. Why have I been made to hang around, waiting to see you? My whole day has been thrown out of kilter!'

'Tell me about it. And I'm betting that your out-of-kilter day is somewhat less catastrophic than mine, Miss… Edwards, is it? When I left for work this morning, the last thing I anticipated was being called back here because my godson had done a runner.'

'And it was a good job I was there to bring him back!' Ellie stuck her chin out defiantly, recalling in the nick of time that she was really furious with this man, who clearly ran such a rubbish ship on the home front that his godson had absconded, crossing several main roads and endangering his life to get to the park where anything could have happened, because this was London.

Anger felt very good, because the alternative was that unsettling *awareness* in the pit of her stomach because the guy staring at her, as grim-faced as an executioner, was also one of the most ridiculously good-looking men she had ever set eyes on.

An exotic gene pool was evident in the rich bronze of his skin and the midnight darkness of his stunning eyes while his features were perfectly and lovingly chiselled to exquisite perfection. One look at him had been enough to knock the breath out of her body and, sitting here, the effect of those remote, thick-fringed dark eyes on her was threatening to do so again.

'You have no idea how dangerous London can be,' she emphasised, tearing her gaze away from his with visible difficulty. 'A young boy wandering through a park…? That's a disaster waiting to happen.'

'Yes. There is no doubt about that.' Luca sat back and stared at her coldly and thoughtfully. 'Incredibly fortuitous that you were on the scene, ready to return him.'

'Yes. Yes, it was.'

'Should I tell you at this point how fortunate you are that you're not currently being quizzed by the police?'

Ellie stared at him blankly while her brain tried to crank into gear and make sense of what he was saying.

'Police?'

'My initial reaction when my housekeeper phoned to tell me that Jake couldn't be found was to suspect kidnap.'

'Sorry?'

'Look around you, Miss Edwards.' Luca waved his hand carelessly to encompass the luxurious surroundings of his office, where an original Picasso rubbed shoulders with an impressive sculpture of an elongated woman that rested on a glass stand.

Ellie duly looked.

'I have never,' Luca continued, 'considered the necessity for bodyguards—or kidnap insurance, for that matter—but then I have never been in charge of a young and unpredictable child. Had you not shown up when you had, my next phone call would have been to the police, and you would now be sitting here being interrogated by them. However, here you are, and, in answer to your original question, the reason I kept you waiting was because I thought it necessary to establish what role, if any, you played in my nephew's disappearance.'

'I'm sorry, but I'm not following you.'

'In which case, I'll give you a few moments to digest what I've just said. I think, once you've done that, you'll know precisely where I'm going with this.'

'You think that I…that I…'

'I'm not a man who takes chances. I've always found that it pays to take what people tell me with a generous pinch of salt.' Luca shrugged. 'For all I know, you could have lured the boy out with the bait of those three hounds frolicking in my back garden.'

'*Lured him out?* Why on earth would I do that?'

'Now, Miss Edwards, you must surely realise that anyone living in a place like this would be able to pay whatever money you might ask for in return for the safe return of his charge? I won't go so far as to say that you kidnapped the boy. Perhaps it was an opportunity that presented itself, one you decided to take advantage of. Maybe you saw Jake out with the nanny at some point? Noticed where he lived? Temptation and opportunity often have a way of finding one another.'

'That is the *most outrageous* thing I have *ever heard* in my entire life!' Cheeks flaming, Ellie sprang to her feet and then stopped dead when he commanded her to sit back down.

'When you're sitting on a fortune, you find that people will do anything to try and get their hands on some of it. Had the police been called, trust me when I tell you that the line of questioning would have been far more intrusive.'

'Perhaps in your world, Mr Ross, people will do anything to try and steal your money—maybe you're surrounded by people who have no scruples—but I can assure you that I'm not interested in getting my hands on any fortune of yours! I had no idea that Jake lived in a place like this. Thank goodness,' she added sarcastically, 'that he was wearing a convenient dog tag so that I knew his address.'

Luca had the grace to flush. 'He's six years old and he's only been in the country for a few months. It was important that he carried some form of identification on him, just in case he ended up lost for some reason. His nanny was instructed never to let him out of her sight, but as you can see for yourself my instructions were lamentably ignored. Jake is a bright boy, but he can't be expected to remember an address he is not familiar with.'

'Do you believe me when I tell you that I just happened to find him in the park, Mr Ross?' Ellie said tightly. 'Because I don't have to stay here and be accused of…being a criminal!'

'Yes.' Luca sighed and twirled the pen on his desk between his fingers before fixing his riveting dark eyes on her. 'I had a word with my godson and it would seem that he got bored. Alicia, the nanny, was on her phone—doubtless on a personal call, which is clearly against the rules—and he thought he'd go and do a little exploring.'

Luca preferred not to dwell on that conversation which, as with most of the conversations with his godson, had been monosyllabic and unsatisfactory.

He had sat on the bed, while Jake had conspicuously refused eye contact, and had done his best to elicit information from him.

'What did you think you were doing, leaving the house without the nanny?' Luca had asked, tempering an inclination to be impatient and critical.

Jake had shrugged.

'Not a good enough answer,' Luca had gritted, which had met with another shrug.

In the end, he had managed to drag a 'I hate it here and I was bored so I went outside to play' from Jake and that had been the sum total of words exchanged.

'It's what six-year-old boys do, unfortunately. They explore, especially when outside looks like more fun than inside.' Her voice was cold. She was still bristling at his insulting insinuation that she might have had something to do with his godson's absconding from the less-than-happy home sweet home. Whatever world Luca Ross inhabited, did he honestly think that everyone around him had some sort of underhand motive and had nothing better to do than to try and access his bank account?

That there wasn't a person out there who wouldn't do what it took to get their hands on what he had?

Except...

She, of all people, was uneasily aware that she should have known what power money and wealth could exert.

She had grown up with the disastrous consequences of a beautiful mother who had been one of those people Luca had talked about; one of those people who would have done anything for money.

Her mother had yearned for that very thing Luca Ross accepted so casually, and that yearning had created a war zone within the Edwards household. Andrea had, as she had made patently clear over the years, married beneath her. She had married a lowly clerk who had failed to rise to the heights she had initially hoped when they had both been young and hopeful. Riven with bitterness and disappointment, she had focused all her energies on ensuring that her youngest daughter, Lily, a beauty like her, could make good on the dreams and aspirations *she* had had to watch wither away.

And the casualty had been Ellie, studious, hardworking and a sparrow to her little sister's shimmering peacock.

Oh, Ellie knew just how damaging the quest for money could be. She had grown up loathing the way people were prepared to behave to get it. Her father had been the one with the strong moral compass and she had adhered to him from a very young age.

The arrogant billionaire sitting in front of her was just the sort of guy she loathed.

The fact that he could sit there and casually accuse her of deliberately trying to con him out of money by snatching his nephew and then returning him in the guise of a Good Samaritan said it all.

'If that's all, Mr Ross…? I have to return the dogs to their owners. I've texted to tell them that there's been a bit of a situation but I can't afford to antagonise any of them.'

'Let me have the addresses of these people. I will ensure that their pets are returned to them.'

'I've already been here for nearly an hour and a half. I have things to do. You said you wanted to talk to me and I'm thinking that you wanted to establish whether you had to bring the police in to arrest me. Now that you've seen I'm not a criminal, I shall leave and take the dogs back to their owners myself. They're tired and they need to be fed.'

'There are a couple of things I still want to straighten out. I can assure you that the dogs will be delivered safely back.'

'By your housekeeper?' Ellie smiled at him without warmth. 'I think she blew the bonding bit when she chucked them out into the pouring rain and locked the door behind them.'

'My orders. I had no intention of letting those dogs drag any more mud into my house than they already had. They're dogs. Enjoying the great outdoors is what they do. My driver has two dogs. He will deliver them, unless you want to hang onto them for another hour or so. Your choice.'

'What else is there to say, Mr Ross? I've told you everything that happened. I saw Jake playing with the dogs and, when I went over, he let slip that there was no adult with him. At first I didn't believe him, because kids are clever when it comes to twisting the truth to get what they want, and I thought that perhaps he wanted to have a bit more time with the dogs, but I very quickly realised that he was telling the truth. He was in that park on his own. Naturally, I was horrified.'

'Naturally.'

'And I got him back here as fast as I could. And, no, I don't want any money for returning your nephew. I'm just relieved that—'

'Yes, got the drift. As for the money element to your statement, why don't we return to that later?'

'There's nothing to return to, Mr Ross.'

'You rescued my godson. I feel we can step away from formalities. Why don't you call me Luca? And you… Ellie, I believe you said?'

Ellie flushed. Luca. Strong, aggressive name for a strong, aggressive male, was the thought that ran through her head. She squashed it flatter than a pancake and gave him a little half-shrug.

'You seem to imply that you're familiar with children.' The dark eyes watching her were careful and speculative as he continued to command the conversation, thinking on his feet as he talked, observing—something he was extremely good at. 'Have you any of your own?'

'I'm twenty-five. I would have to have started very early.'

'And you're not married…'

'How on earth do you know that?'

'No ring on your finger. Jake took to you as well as the dogs. If he hadn't, he would never have allowed you to walk him back to the house. He would have scarpered. It's obvious he trusted you. He was also holding your hand when he returned.' He tilted his head to one side and inspected her in silence for a few long seconds. 'None of this may seem like much of a big deal to you, Ellie, but I can assure you that it is. Since he came over here, he has found it difficult to…settle.'

'Can I ask what happened?'

Luca's initial response to that was to shut down, because answering questions posed by other people was seldom within his remit, unless those questions were work-orientated. Personal questions were off-limits. This was a personal question, but for once he wasn't going to drop the shutters, because he was in a jam and he was beginning to think that part of the solution could be sitting right there in front of him.

'His parents were killed in a car accident,' he intoned flatly. 'Freak situation. They left Jake an orphan. By virtue of the fact that I was Johnny's closest blood relative—his cousin, to be precise, not to mention Jake's godfather—and the fact that Ruby, his wife, had no close family members, I inherited Jake.'

'So you're Jake's second cousin as well as his godfather…'

Luca frowned. 'As I have just said.'

'And yet, despite that connection, things must be a bit strained between you for him to have run away.'

Was he being called to account? For a few seconds, Luca's mind went blank because *being called to account* was not something with which he was familiar.

'A bit strained?' he questioned in a voice that would have had grown men quaking, a voice he had perfected over the years, one which was very handy when it came to controlling anyone who had the temerity to breach his barriers.

The slender, dark-haired gamine sitting opposite him wasn't quaking.

'It happens,' she said, her voice rich with sympathy. 'Just because you're family doesn't always mean that the relationship is close.' She thought of her own relationship with her sister, which was anything but close even though, once upon a time, they had been far closer than they were now.

'Jake and his parents,' Luca said heavily, 'went to America to live. Keeping in touch was difficult.'

'I'll bet.'

'I'm an extremely busy man.' Luca heard the irritation in his voice and was exasperated with himself for launching into explanations that were, frankly, unnecessary.

'It wasn't meant as a criticism,' Ellie murmured, lowering her eyes and thinking that that was exactly how it had been meant—because what she was deducing was that Luca would have been way too busy making money to remember some cousin on the other side of the world.

'The fact is that we have both found ourselves in a situation where adjustments have had to be made and Jake has found those adjustments somewhat difficult.'

'Poor, poor kid. No wonder he's had trouble settling down. I've come across that sort of thing a couple of times, usually involving kids who have come to London from another country, and in one instance to stay with a distant relative they really didn't know very well. Adjusting was an issue.'

She sat up straighter, on more solid ground now that she was in possession of a few facts. 'I don't suppose...' she had nothing to lose by speaking her mind '...it's helped that he's been farmed out to a nanny and a housekeeper, and heaven only knows who else, when all he probably needs is one-on-one time with you as the adult responsible for his welfare.'

'Is that a criticism?' Luca asked coldly. 'Because I've been sensing a few of those under the demure replies and the polite questions.'

Ellie dug her heels in and shrugged. 'I can tell you don't appreciate it,' she said eventually, when the silence threatened to become too tense, 'but I'm just speaking my mind. I'm a teacher, and I have quite a bit of experience when it comes to young kids.'

'So you're a teacher? That's very interesting.' Luca dropped his eyes and doodled something on the pad in front of him.

'Is it? Why?'

'I feel I would have worked that out eventually,' he murmured, and she reddened.

'Why is that, Mr Ross?'

'Luca.'

Ellie stared at him, lips tightly pressed together, and just like that Luca smiled.

Her expression—thorough disapproval even though she was let down by having such a delicate, feminine face, all huge green eyes, short, straight nose and a mouth that was a perfect Cupid's bow. The more defiantly she tilted her chin, narrowed her eyes and aimed for severe, the more amused he was.

'I'm not seeing the joke.' Ellie's heart was slamming against her rib cage, and not just because she knew that he was laughing *at* her. That smile was so *sexy* and, just like that, she glimpsed someone other than the ice-cold billionaire who had rubbed her up the wrong way the second she had met him and who represented everything she had no time for.

And this *someone other* was dangerous. She felt it. This *someone other* wasn't just drop-dead gorgeous. He was sinfully sexy, the sort of *sexy* that should come with a health warning.

'You should see your face,' Luca drawled. 'Tight lips, pursed mouth, disapproving eyes. Could you be anything *but* a school teacher?'

He made that sound like a source of amusement instead of consternation, which somehow made his criticism all the more offensive.

'Maybe most of them are too scared,' she snapped with reckless abandon.

'I don't care for that tone of voice.' Cool eyes fastened on her flushed face. He realised that she had signally made no effort to try and impress him from the second she had walked into his house, just as he realised that most people did, which was something he took for granted.

'And I don't care for the fact that you think it's okay to sit there and laugh at me. I'm a teacher, an excellent teacher, and if you think that it's hilarious that I speak my mind then too bad.'

'Not hilarious,' Luca said slowly, speculatively. 'Refreshing.'

His mobile buzzed and he took the call, which lasted a matter of seconds. Not for a second did his eyes leave her face.

Ellie had the strangest sensation of intense discomfort under that scrutiny. It was as if her body was on hyperalert, sensitive in ways she couldn't quite understand. She felt restless in her own skin and yet frozen to the spot, barely able to breathe.

'The dogs have gone. I'm sure their owners will be overjoyed to have them home.' He sat back and inclined his head to one side. 'Can I ask you something, Ellie?'

Ellie felt that he would anyway, whatever answer she gave, so she tilted her head to one side and didn't say anything.

'Why are you walking dogs when you have a job?'

That wasn't what she had been expecting and she went bright red.

'I don't see what that has to do with anything,' she muttered.

'The nanny has gone.' He changed tack so abruptly that she was left floundering and wrong-footed.

'The nanny...?'

'Second in six months.'

'That can't be a good thing. The poor boy probably needs continuity,' Ellie said when he made no attempt to elaborate on this. 'Children really need defined boundaries and, especially in Jake's situation, stability would be very important.' *Tight lips...pursed mouth...disapproving eyes...* Ellie was impatient with herself for letting him get under her skin, because who cared what the man thought one way or another?

'I fully agree with you. It's been disappointing but what can one do? The first nanny was a middle-aged lady who was clearly out of her depth dealing with Jake. He's extremely clever and very strong-willed underneath that quiet exterior. It would seem that he simply refused to go along with any plan he didn't agree to.' Luca paused. 'He also created such a fuss about going to school that, as it came out in the wash, the woman was browbeaten into keeping him at home on a couple of occasions which, naturally, didn't work.'

'Has he not settled into school life either?'

'It's been a difficult period,' Luca murmured with exquisite understatement.

Confused, because she had no idea where this roundabout conversation was leading, but very much aware that there was a definite destination in sight even though it eluded her at the moment, Ellie stared at Luca with fascination.

Everything about him was compelling, from the graceful, economical movements of his hands when he spoke to the proud angle of his head and the harsh beauty of his features.

For the first time, she was awkwardly conscious of the gaping chasm between them—and not just in the money stakes.

He was so breathtakingly beautiful that he made her aware of her shortcomings, and that was a place she hadn't visited for a long time.

Growing up, she had learned to accept that when it came to looks she was second-best.

Lily was the one with the looks. Like her mother, she was tall, willowy and blonde, her vanilla hair dropping like a waterfall down her narrow back. From the day she'd been born, she had been attracting attention, and that had only become more pronounced as she had grown and eventually matured into a stunningly beautiful adolescent.

With a sister blessed with such spectacular looks, Ellie had quickly learned to fade into the background, developing skills that did not rely on physical appearance. She had studied hard, got A grades in everything, helped out during summers at the local kennels and played as much sport as she could, because being outside the house often beat being inside it.

So it was irritating now to find herself thinking about her looks and wondering what Luca saw when he stared at her with such a veiled expression.

'I had hoped,' Luca said truthfully, 'that Alicia might have worked out. I'd come to the conclusion that it might have been a mistake relying on experience to deal with Jake, without taking into account that experience might come with the downside of being a little too stuffy to handle a kid of six.'

'Mr Ross… Luca… I'm sorry that your nephew hasn't settled over here as well as he might have. I would advise you to try and bond with him a bit more, but I'm sure you'll ignore me. Perhaps, after this little incident, his nanny will be a little more vigilant. Maybe she just needs to get him out and about a bit more. It's the summer holidays and there's an awful lot going on in London at the moment for kids. Or she could even take him out of London. To the seaside, perhaps.'

'That would be difficult,' Luca said gently, when she had finally tapered off into silence, 'considering the nanny has been sacked.'

'Sacked? But why?'

'Why do you think?'

'Yes, well… I'm sure she will have learned from this episode…' Ellie vaguely wondered whether the sacked nanny could take him to some kind of industrial tribunal for unfair dismissal but somehow she couldn't envisage anyone, least of all a young nanny, having the courage to do anything of the sort.

And sadly, whilst the poor girl probably did deserve a second chance, it was fair to say that letting her charge escape did come under the heading of *dereliction of duty*.

'I would hope so but it doesn't matter because it's not my problem.' Luca pushed himself away from the desk and linked his fingers on his washboard stomach. 'My problem isn't what the sacked nanny does now. My problem is what *I* do now…'

CHAPTER TWO

LUCA HAD REACHED a decision. He'd done what he did best. Faced with a problem, he had brought his natural creativity to the situation, thought on his feet and come up with a solution.

He'd sacked the nanny. He needed cover. And it wasn't going to fall on his shoulders because he didn't have enough hours in the day.

Miss Muller, efficient though she was, could hardly be expected to turn her hand to child minding a six-year-old. She'd never had children and, from the little he had glimpsed of her interaction with Jake, an eagerness to make up for that lack was not there.

And the agency wasn't going to be much help in the immediate future. They were painstaking when it came to the business of sourcing nannies. Leave it with them and he could be collecting his pension before they came up with a replacement, especially given the short, chequered history of the previous two, both sacked.

Cover was staring him in the face. The girl was perfect. He was good when it came to reading people and he could read that this one would be up to the job.

He would lay his cards on the table soon enough but first he would find out as much as he could about her personal circumstances because her personal circumstances could be used to his advantage.

He would at least have to determine her availability.

It didn't occur to him to ask her directly whether she would be able to step into the breach because getting what you wanted always panned out better once you'd got a feel for the lie of the land. A lifetime of dealing with people had given Luca a healthy scepticism when it came to making sure he got the best possible deal from them.

This girl was no gold-digger, but that didn't mean she wouldn't be tempted to try her luck if she thought she could pull a fast one.

'You never told me why you were walking dogs.' He lazily returned to the question he had earlier directed at her. He tilted his big body at an angle that allowed him to watch her closely from under lowered lashes. 'You have a job. I don't know what teachers get paid, but I'm assuming it's not so little that they have to take a begging bowl onto the streets.'

'Walking dogs isn't the same as *taking a begging bowl onto the streets.*'

'Figure of speech. Shouldn't you be enjoying your respite from tetchy kids and classrooms?'

'I…' Ellie reddened. 'I like dogs,' she said lamely. 'And I like walking.'

'And that's very commendable, but you surely must do it because of the money?'

'I… As it happens, I find the additional income very useful.' Ellie heard herself stutter out the truth and immediately told herself that it was nothing to be ashamed about and that she shouldn't let herself be cowed into editing her personality which was, by its nature, open and honest.

'Why?'

'*Why?* Mr Ross, *Luca*, I'm not one of your employees. I don't actually have to tell you anything.'

'Instead of getting worked up because I'm asking you a few questions, you need to sit back and listen to me without interruption for a few minutes.'

Ellie's mouth dropped open.

'You probably want to get back to your house as much as I need to return to work, but there *was* something I wanted to propose to you, and I think you would be open to my suggestion—especially if you tell me that you need money.'

'I never said that I *needed* money.'

'You don't have to but I'm good at joining dots. I heard the anxiety in your voice when you talked to me about reuniting those dogs with their owners. You were apprehensive about upsetting them. You don't want to upset them because, however much you love dogs and love walking, it's not a labour of love for you. Ergo, you need the money.

'Now, don't get me wrong. I don't give a damn what you want the money for—addiction to fine wine, an obsession with designer clothes…or maybe you're saving for a round-the-world cruise. I don't care. It's all the same to me. You have no criminal record, because checks would have been done on you before you became a teacher. Here's the deal.'

He leant forward, palms flattened on the desk. 'I no longer have a nanny and I can't afford to spare the time out for babysitting duties. Miss Muller isn't going to be able to step up to the plate here and I would not ask her to. However, as I said to you, my nephew took to you and that in itself speaks volumes. Combined with the fact that you clearly need the money, we could work together towards a satisfactory solution to my problem.'

Ellie stared at him in a daze. She was accustomed to controlling situations. It was part and parcel of her job, but right now she felt as though she had handed the reins over to someone who was cheerfully steering her in the direction he wanted her to go.

'I'll admit my immediate reaction to you showing up at my front door with my godson was one of instant suspicion.'

Ellie was fascinated by Luca's lack of apology for behaviour that frankly had been pretty outrageous. When she had walked Jake back, she had anticipated gratitude. She had mentally prepared an informative speech about the importance of family and of understanding the psyche of children. It was going to be a severe speech, as befitted the situation. She had even mulled over the possibility that she might step into a quagmire that would necessitate outside intervention. She worked in a school where that sort of thing had occurred on a couple of occasions, although something about Jake had made her think that his family life wasn't going to be a disaster zone. His clothes had been dishevelled and muddy from the dogs but expensive all the same.

She hadn't anticipated a series of events that had seen her told coolly that she could have been hauled down to a police station, accused of staging the whole thing for money and then eventually been given the all-clear without a hint of remorse.

'I got that,' Ellie said tightly as her mind continued to whirr. She couldn't take her eyes off him. He was larger than life in every sense of the word and in his presence every nerve-ending in her body was on red alert, every sense and pulse stretched to breaking point. From the proud angle of his head to the luxuriant dark hair and exotically sculpted features, the man oozed more than just sexuality and it knocked her for six.

And now he was offering her a job?

'Naturally I would do my own background check on you anyway,' he murmured, half to himself.

'You're offering me a job?' Just in case she'd got hold of the wrong end of the stick.

'The circumstances are a little unusual,' Luca admitted. 'It's not in my nature to jump into anything without first testing the water, but I need someone to look after Jake, and sooner rather than later...'

'But you could always just take a couple of weeks off work. Maybe go on holiday with him whilst the agency finds a replacement. If he's had trouble settling down then a holiday might be just the thing he needs.'

'I don't have time for holidays,' Luca said flatly.

'Never?' Ellie asked incredulously, wondering what the point of being rich was if you never took time out to enjoy your hard-earned cash. If *she* had money, then she would travel the world. It was a luxury she had never had.

'There's no time off when you're running a business the size of mine.' Luca shrugged. 'It may sound harsh but I'm simply being realistic.' He leaned back and sighed heavily, with a hint of impatience. 'This escapade has made me realise that Jake needs someone who is not only capable of taking him from A to B and making sure he is fed and watered, but someone with whom he has some kind of bond. He clearly didn't bond with either of the previous nannies, but in the space of a very short time he managed to do that with you, and I'm guessing your

experience as a teacher has something to do with that.'
He looked at her shrewdly. 'So here we are.'

'I already have a job,' Ellie said. As job offers went,
this one certainly hadn't been wrapped up in any pretty
packaging. He was in a jam and she was a possible solution. No beating about the bush with any niceties.

'Teaching, and walking dogs for the additional income.'

She decided not to go down the 'needing money' road
again. Luca made her nervous and uncomfortable and
she couldn't think of anything worse than working for
him. 'There's no way,' she said politely, 'that I would ever
consider jacking in my full-time job to become a nanny
to your godson. I love my job. I enjoy working with lots
of different kids.'

He would make a terrible employer. It was obvious that
he was as warm and cuddly as a rattlesnake. He thought
nothing of getting rid of people who didn't live up to his
high expectations and, while he was quick to blame, he
didn't seem prepared to accept that he might be the root
cause of Jake's behaviour.

Work for him?

She would rather walk on a bed of burning coals. Part
of the reason she enjoyed what she did, aside from the
satisfaction of working with the kids, was that she really
loved the people she worked alongside.

They were on her wavelength. They were all part of
the greater caring community who didn't rush to put
themselves first.

Luca Ross was part of the cut-throat community who
thought nothing of taking what they wanted whatever the
cost. He was arrogant, ruthless and manipulative. She'd

been in his company for a handful of hours and already she felt wrung out.

'I'm not talking about a long-term position,' he clarified, still fully confident that he was going to get what he wanted because, frankly, he always did. 'Of course, a suitable nanny will be found in due course, but that's going to take time, and this time around I will have more input to the procedure than previously.'

Ellie was making a mental list in her head of all the things she disliked about him and she tacked this new one on. *He probably left choosing the nannies to his secretary because he was too busy and couldn't be bothered...*

'I'm sorry,' she said, standing up so that he could take the hint that their conversation was at an end. Her body broke out in light perspiration as he slowly rose to his feet. He strolled towards her, in no hurry.

His long, lean body oozed latent strength and suffocating masculinity. She could almost see the flex of sinew and muscle under the charcoal-grey trousers and the white shirt, which he had cuffed to the elbow. His forearms were liberally sprinkled with dark hair. She wondered whether his chest would likewise be sprinkled with dark hair and she furiously stopped herself in crazy mid-thought.

He cast an ominous shadow as he finally paused to stand in front of her, and Ellie had to will herself not to cower.

The mental checklist of things she disliked about the man was growing by the second. Not only did he think he could get whatever he wanted but he was not averse to using sheer brawn and intimidation tactics to get there.

'Sorry?'

'I'm not interested in working for you.' She cleared

her throat and their eyes collided, causing the air to rush out of her body in a whoosh. 'I appreciate the offer, but you're better off going back to the agency, and maybe taking more of a hands-on approach this time, because you seemed to imply that you hadn't on the previous occasions.'

'How can you appreciate my offer when you haven't heard the details?'

'I don't need to.'

'Care to tell me why?'

'I know you think that you can get whatever you want because you're rich, but you can't.' She tore her eyes away with difficulty. He was standing so close to her that she could breathe in whatever woody, intensely masculine aftershave he was wearing.

Breathing was proving to be a problem. It was unnerving. She forced herself to remain calm and composed because he was just standing there; he wasn't trying to prevent her from leaving the room. She remembered how to breathe and then looked at him.

'Jake ran away for a reason.' Her voice, thankfully, did not betray the utter turmoil his proximity was bringing on. 'Okay, so maybe he didn't like the nanny very much, or perhaps he got bored and decided to venture out, but the bottom line is that there's obviously something missing on the home front and that something can only be provided by you.'

'We're going round in circles.'

'Because we're on completely different wavelengths.' She cleared her throat and wished that he would back off by even a couple of inches so that she could get her act together. 'And that's just one reason why I could never work for you. We're from different worlds.'

'Since when do people have to think alike in order to have a satisfactory working arrangement?'

'It matters to me,' Ellie persisted. Since she had nothing to lose, she said, bluntly, 'I don't like what you stand for. I'm not into money and I don't approve of people who focus all their energy on making it. I'm happy doing what I'm doing, and I wish you all the best in your search for a replacement for the nanny you sacked.'

Luca stared at her in silence then he nodded slowly.

He backed away, leaving a cool void behind him. Desperate to leave only seconds earlier, Ellie now hovered uneasily. He had moved back to the desk but was now perched on the edge and was watching her with a thoughtful expression.

'So...' She licked her lips nervously.

'You were on your way out?'

'Yes, I was!' She pulled open the door and an odd thought suddenly sprang into her addled brain—*this will be the last time you set eyes on this man.* She blinked, surprised and bemused at the discomfiture that thought provoked out of nowhere.

Ellie thought he might have tried to stop her, one last stab at persuading her to hear him out, and she was disconcerted to find that she was almost disappointed when he remained in the office while she let herself out of the house, pausing and looking up the stairs on her way out.

Should she try and find Jake? Say goodbye? She wanted to. In a short space of time, he had touched her with his shy overtures of friendship.

No. She'd already become way too involved in his backstory. She'd done her good deed for the week and delivered him back to his home and it was doubtful she would lay eyes on him again.

Whatever nanny Luca got, Ellie's money was on the poor girl being monitored more closely than a convict on parole. She would be manacled to the poor child while Luca carried on making money and kidding himself that he was being a good guardian by flinging cash at the problem that had landed on his doorstep.

Hateful and obnoxious, she thought, barely aware of the walk back to the park and then on to the nearest bus because she was so busy thinking of him.

Ellie shared a house with three other girls. Every time she approached the front door, she recalled the far nicer little place she had rented previously where she had been able to relax in peace; where she hadn't had to jostle for space in the fridge; any time she wanted to herself now had to be spent in a bedroom that was only just about big enough for a bed, a chest of drawers and a wardrobe that was a whisker away from being held together by masking tape. But needs must.

She wondered, but only briefly, whether she should have listened to whatever offer Luca had been prepared to put on the table…

Twenty-four hours later, Ellie was on her way back home when she noticed a long, sleek, black car pull away from the kerb, picking up speed and then slowing down until it was right alongside her.

The persistent rain of the past couple of weeks had stopped and, at a little after six-thirty in the evening, a watery sun was trying to remind everyone that it was still summer.

The road was quiet, practically deserted, and with a flare of panic she quickened her steps, only almost to col-

lide into the passenger door of the car which had been
flung open, barring her path.

'Hop in, Ellie.'

She recognised the voice instantly and, when she
peered inside, her heart did a quick flip and her breathing hitched. Luca was the last person she had been expecting to see again.

The tinted windows had prevented her from seeing
the driver and now she wondered how on earth he had
managed to do that? Show up just when she was on her
way back to her house. Did he have some sort of tele-
pathic X-ray vision?

She blinked, her mouth opening and shutting while
Luca looked at her in total silence.

'How did you find me?'

'Hop in.'

'No!'

'Don't slam the door. Just get in the car and listen to
what I have to say.'

'How did you find me?' she repeated, reluctant to get
in the car yet not wanting to draw attention to herself.
She slid into the passenger seat and slammed the door
behind her.

In the enclosed space, she was uneasily conscious of
the raw sexuality that had accosted her last time she
had been in his company. He was so staggeringly *male*,
so devoid of any soft side, so unapologetically masculine.

She looked at him and didn't know whether it was
because he had been on her mind, or whether it was just
the shock of seeing him when she hadn't expected to,
but her body was suddenly filled with a disturbing electric charge.

Her nipples pinched, scraping against her tee shirt because she seldom wore a bra except to work. What was the point when there was precious little to hold in place? And there was a stickiness between her legs that horrified her, made her want to slam her thighs together tightly.

'Don't forget, I know where your dog-walking clients live,' Luca intoned smoothly. 'I asked them whether you were out with their dogs. Actually, I struck jackpot with owner number one. You're a creature of habit, Ellie. Same routine. It was a pretty simple process of deduction that you would be heading back to your house around now. Mrs Wilson was kind enough to let me have your address. She also gave me your mobile number but I thought it best if I surprised you.'

'She had *no right* to hand over my private details!'

'Maybe she could tell at a glance that I wasn't a homicidal maniac.'

'That's not the point.'

'Which is your house?'

'I don't want you in my house!'

'Then we can sit here and have this conversation,' he said calmly. He killed the engine and reclined in the chair, angling his big body so that he was facing her.

'We've covered everything there is to say. I'm not going to work for you.'

'You've moved.'

'I beg your pardon?'

'You never used to live in this part of London. You used to rent a tidy little flat in West London, but you gave that up two months ago so that you could move to this area which is, at the very best, dodgy.'

'How did you find all of that out?'

'I can find out anything I want to,' Luca told her without batting an eyelid. 'And I wanted to find out about you because I want you. You're saving money, and a brief background check leads me to believe that it's because you're helping your father out of a hole.'

Ellie stiffened, shocked and dismayed. How far was his reach?

'Tell me about it,' he said, but his voice was curiously gentle. 'And don't let your feelings for me and your pride get in the way of your common sense, Ellie. Like I told you, we can help one another. As business arrangements go, this could be an extremely rewarding one for both of us. I need someone there for Jake. Did you know that he's asked after you?'

Suspicion poured out of every pore in Ellie's body but that question, tacked on at the end, made her hesitate, even though she suspected that he was a man who would work the cards in his hand any way he chose if it could get him what he wanted.

You didn't get to the top by being kind and caring and making allowances for the weak and feeble. You got to the top by being ruthless, and he was at the very top.

'It's the first conversation I think I've had with Jake since he came over here. Or, at least, the first conversation that wasn't like squeezing blood from a stone.'

Ellie opened her mouth to inform him that she wasn't interested, and besides she resented the fact that he had been investigating her behind her back, but instead she heard herself say, 'What do you mean?'

'We've barely spoken. I've had reports from the nannies but the times we've sat down together over a meal, he's only managed to mutter a few monosyllabic answers to the questions I've asked. This morning, he asked after you, and after those mutts you introduced him to. He wanted to know whether he would be able to return to the park so that he could walk with you.'

His expression was shuttered but Ellie was good at reading body language and what she was seeing was genuine emotion from a man who probably found it difficult to express himself in terms of feelings and who was at a loss with a situation he couldn't control.

'This would not be a permanent position,' he told her softly, shifting, because a car was not the most comfortable of places in which to have a protracted conversation. 'It would be a matter of a few weeks, no more than the duration of the summer holidays, during which time you could perhaps help source a replacement nanny for Jake. I think your input would be helpful on that front. It's clear you have an instinctive empathy with children, which is something I clearly lack.'

Ellie opened her mouth and he raised his hand.

'No, allow me to finish before you start digging your heels in.' He shot her a crooked smile and Ellie blinked because, shorn temporarily of that authoritarian streak in him that she had previously glimpsed, he was curiously *human*. It was unnerving.

'I could have found out the details of whatever commitment you may have towards your father, but I stopped short of that because it doesn't matter, and I also felt that if you wanted to fill me in then you would. I will pay you enough to more than cover the entire debt your father has incurred.'

'That's a crazy assurance,' Ellie said shakily. Her eyes dropped to where he was resting his hand lightly on the gear shaft and she inconsequentially thought what shapely hands he had.

'My pockets are shockingly deep,' Luca returned without a trace of false modesty. He paused and inclined his head to one side. 'What happened? Do you want to talk about it?'

The vision of being released from the stranglehold of a debt that would take her years to clear dangled in front of Ellie's eyes like an oasis in the desert.

'If you'd rather not go into the details, then that's fine. All I want to know is this: are you prepared to consider my offer? In return for a handful of weeks working for me, your father will never have to worry about his debts again. You don't have to like me to agree to this. That doesn't enter the equation. All you have to do is ask yourself whether you're willing to prolong your father's unhappy situation because of misplaced pride.'

As trump cards went, Ellie knew that he had pulled out the ace of spades. Her father was stressed beyond belief and frankly so was she.

Did she want him to know the situation? Ellie already knew that she would agree to what he wanted. He'd somehow managed to find the precise spot where his appeal would hit pay dirt.

'It would be a relief to clear my father's debts,' Ellie said stiffly.

'Before you continue, do you want to carry on this conversation in your house? I'm too big to sit in this car indefinitely. I need to stretch my legs.'

'I share the place with other girls.' She involuntarily grimaced. 'But I guess we could go to a pub. There's one not far from here. I could direct you.'

Having secured the deal, Luca had no intention of letting the grass grow under his feet. They were in the pub with a bottle of chilled wine in front of them within fifteen minutes.

'So...?' he pressed urgently.

'My dad has found himself in a bit of a pickle.' She opened up, because she did want him to know more than just the bones of why she was taking this job. He'd found out so much about her that he could easily have found out the entire story and the fact that he hadn't softened her impression of him. Just a little. If she chose not to explain anything, she knew that he wouldn't try to find out off his own bat but, for some reason, she didn't want him to be left with the suspicion that her father had blown away his savings on rubbish.

'He got taken in by a scam on the Internet. He didn't admit to what had happened for a while. In fact, I only found out because I happened to come across a letter from the bank he had left on the console table in the sitting room. When I asked him what was happening, he admitted to everything. The bills have been piling up and he hasn't been able to meet his mortgage payments for the past few months. He's been having panic attacks.'

She looked down quickly. 'Apologies,' she said huskily. 'My dad and I are very close and I can't bear to think what he must have been going through. Anyway, of course I earn enough to keep body and soul together, but I've had to move into somewhere smaller temporarily. It's been very stressful and you should know that if it weren't for...this situation there is no way I would be sitting here having this conversation.' She looked at Luca, her green eyes challenging.

The clarity of her gaze was so disconcerting that for a few seconds words failed him.

He was staring at someone from another planet. He had offered her an easy, hassle-free job and instead of biting his hand off and naming her price she had turned him down. She was only accepting the offer now because she would have been insane to refuse it.

Luca was accustomed to women who accepted his generosity without batting an eyelid. He was made of money and he had never yet come up against any woman who didn't enjoy spending some of it when it was on offer.

He hadn't cared why she'd needed money when he had first suggested the job. He'd been confident that she would snap at the chance to get her hands on some to fund whatever lifestyle had left her in debt. He'd assumed a credit card crisis and had banked on her trying to manoeuvre to get the maximum out of him.

He was quietly pleased that he hadn't been able to buy her.

'Tell me how much your father owes,' he said, not beating around the bush, and Ellie reddened and hesitated.

'Do you think I'm going to laugh because he's been the victim of a scam?'

She didn't answer that, instead naming a figure that seemed so huge to her that she looked away in embarrassment.

'Naturally I don't expect you to cover that stupid amount...'

Luca told her what he was willing to pay her, and for once in his life he wasn't interested in driving a hard bargain.

The woman had such fundamental integrity that he was surprised to discover a side to him that wasn't utterly cynical. Born into wealth, Luca had seen from the sidelines how ugly the pursuit of money could be after his mother had died. As an eligible middle-aged widower, his father had become a magnet for women from the ages of twenty to seventy. Many of the women, having admitted defeat with his father, had turned their attentions to him, even though Luca had been a mere boy of seventeen at the time.

His own experiences as an adult had hardly served to change his opinion that there wasn't a woman alive who wouldn't do whatever it took when the stakes were high.

Luca didn't mind. He was happy to be lavish with the women he dated but he had no intention of settling down with any of them. He had no intention of settling down, full-stop.

He was fascinated by Ellie's clear-eyed gaze as their eyes met.

Predictably, she was staggered by the sum he was willing to pay. Even more predictably, she hotly refused to allow him to part with such a vast amount of cash.

'You're overreacting,' he dismissed, reaching to top her glass up. 'I'm not offering you the crown jewels...'

'As good as. It goes against my nature to accept a sum as large as that.'

'And it goes against my nature to be stingy when it comes to a situation like this. You'll be doing me a service, and I'm a man who rewards good service.'

A quiver of excitement rippled through her as their eyes met and tangled. This was a business arrangement, but right now it felt like an adventure...

CHAPTER THREE

THE FOLLOWING DAY, Ellie finally made contact with her sister.

Lily had called their father the night before and it hadn't taken him long before he phoned Ellie to tell her all about their conversation. But by then Ellie was on her way out to meet Luca for dinner. He would have her contract of employment and had told her that it was essential she knew what was expected of her. Ellie thought that top of the agenda would be not making personal calls while her charge slipped out of the house.

'Did she leave a number, by any chance?' Ellie asked when there was a break in the conversation.

She was going to be late for dinner but if she didn't talk to Lily now then there was no guarantee that she would talk to her at all. Over the years as Lily had pursued fame and fortune, using her incredible looks to open doors, she and Ellie had grown increasingly distant. It took a lot of will power to resist the temptation to let things slide until their contact was reduced to birthday cards and polite conversation over the turkey with their father on Christmas day.

Ellie had no time to beat about the bush.

'Did Dad mention anything…er…about his situation

over here?' she asked bluntly, because the long-distance call was costing her money, and if she didn't stop her sister in mid flow then she would have to spend the entire phone call listening to Lily wax lyrical about all the exciting things happening in her life and the agents who were hunting her down with scripts for movies.

'What situation?' her sister questioned cautiously, so Ellie explained.

She decided that throwing out hints wasn't going to work. 'I thought that since you've found your feet over there you might think about helping me out, Lily. I earn a teacher's salary and I don't have to tell you that it's not much…'

'*You* chose to be a teacher,' Lily snapped defensively. 'So please don't tell me to start feeling sorry for you because you haven't got any money!'

'This isn't about me, Lily. It's about Dad. I've had to take…er…another job to help raise money to clear his debts, but if you could contribute then it would give me some flexibility…when it comes to accepting the offer. Luca will clear the debt but obviously it goes against my pride to accept that level of generosity.'

'What job?' Lily asked curiously. 'Luca? Who's Luca?'

In a mad rush to leave, Ellie briefly explained the situation, that Luca was a Spanish businessman who had hired her to look after his godson for the summer. Lily knew where she stood when it came to money. She would know that accepting such a vast sum of cash would have been tough.

'Oh, for God's sake,' Lily said, although her voice was more thoughtful now. 'Stop with the pride thing and just accept what's on the table. Jeez, the guy is obviously loaded and he needs you to look after the kid. Instead of beating yourself up about it, you should be trying to suss whether you can't get more out of him! Anyway, I can't commit to anything, Ellie, and even if I could I'd be nuts to hand over hard-earned cash when there's some rich guy willing to clear all Dad's debts for a few weeks of playing happy families with his kid.'

So that was that.

Despite the fact that her sister was in the enviable position of having producers banging on her door, she was being true to who she was and refusing to help.

In a rush, Ellie barely glanced at herself in the mirror before flying out of the house.

She was meeting Luca at an Italian bistro in Covent Garden. He had only ever seen her in clothes used to walk dogs, but this was going to be a more formal meeting, and she had dressed accordingly, in the same outfit she pulled out of the wardrobe for parents' meetings. A neat grey skirt, a white blouse and a pair of ballet pumps.

It was an outfit that reminded her of the businesslike nature of their relationship, and for that Ellie was grateful, because when she thought of him her mind started playing games, and what she saw in her head wasn't someone in a suit discussing terms and conditions and holding a fountain pen, it was a man with smouldering sexiness and a smile that could give her goose bumps.

She was half an hour late by the time she stepped into the bistro and looked round her, spotting Luca instantly.

She smoothed down her skirt and took a few seconds to gather herself. The restaurant was busy, with every table filled, and despite the casual sense of waiters hurrying with trays, the open-plan kitchen and the unfussy furnishings, Ellie could tell that the food would cost a fortune.

The clientele was all well-heeled. The food passing her on plates was delicate, artistic creations.

She weaved her way towards Luca and, the closer she got, the more nervous and self-conscious she felt. Her outfit, which had seemed sensible and appropriate when she had put it on an hour earlier, felt cheap and drab and she slid into her chair with a palpable feeling of relief.

'You're late,' Luca opened.

Ellie's initial reaction was to snipe back at him. Her glass-green eyes were narrowed as he glanced at his watch and then relaxed back in the chair to look at her.

Unlike the other people in the restaurant, who were all clearly kitted out in designer gear, Luca looked as though he had dressed in a hurry and without any thought for the end result. His dark hair was combed back and there was a scraping of stubble on his chin. Yet it suited him—he looked even more dangerous with a five o'clock shadow and her nervous system went into free fall.

He was in black. Black tee shirt. Black jeans. Loafers without socks.

Her mouth was suddenly parched and she gulped down some of the water that had been poured into a glass in front of her. A glimpse of her prissy grey skirt was a timely reminder of why she was sitting in this up-market bistro.

And she also realised that his observation was pertinent. If she was going to be working for him, then punctuality was going to be important.

'I'm sorry,' she said, composing herself. 'I was delayed by a phone call. My sister phoned and I haven't spoken to her in quite a while. I couldn't brush her off.'

'Your sister? For some reason I thought that you were an only child.'

'Lily lives in America.'

Luca picked up something in her voice and he inclined his head and waited. This woman was going to be a key part of his life for the next few weeks. Two or three at the very least but almost certainly longer. The contract sitting in the envelope in his pocket offered a clever inducement should she need to stay longer than she might have anticipated. A sliding scale of pay, rising with each week over a two-week tide mark. Irresistible to someone who needed the cash.

Under normal circumstances, he wouldn't be sitting here right now. When it came to employees, it was pretty simple. He paid them well and they either did their job well, and were further rewarded, or else they didn't and they were booted out.

But the last nanny had been a learning curve for Luca. Normal rules didn't apply when it came to something as personal as his godson.

He had hired Alicia, paid her handsomely but he had taken his eye off the ball. In other words, he had treated her the same as he would have treated any of the people who worked for him.

And where had it got him? A runaway child who had had the good luck to be found and delivered back safely by a woman who was obviously charity and goodwill on two legs.

This time round, he was going to have to liaise with the woman looking after Jake and not simply rely on reports, emails and a debrief once a fortnight.

If he was going to have a more hands-on approach, then it would pay actually to find out about her. He needed her to feel comfortable with him because, if she did, she would be a lot more relaxed and forthcoming.

As things stood, she felt about as comfortable with him as a minnow felt in the company of a shark. He knew that. She didn't like him, she disapproved of him, and she'd only taken the job because he had done what he knew how to do so well. He'd put her in a position of being unable to refuse what was on the table.

Luca knew the power of money and he knew how to use it to his advantage.

But you couldn't buy trust and you couldn't buy openness and he would need both if he was to make headway with Jake—and that was what he needed to do.

'Whereabouts?'

'Los Angeles, as a matter of fact. Or at least,' Ellie couldn't help tacking on in the name of perfect honesty, 'I'm assuming that's where she is.'

'Do I hear the sound of the pot calling the kettle black?' Luca asked coolly. 'If I recall, you were pretty vocal on the subject of my losing touch with my cousin when he moved with his family to the very same place your sister now lives. Coincidentally they both ended up in America…'

'Not really. Lots of people go there because they see it as a land of opportunity.'

'But you weren't tempted?'

'I… I don't chase dreams. I'm too grounded.' Ellie flushed. 'Lily and I are very different. Anyway, to get back to what you said, my sister was the one who lost touch with me,' she said uncomfortably. 'Not the other way around.' For some reason, she didn't want to carry on talking about Lily. She remembered the curiosity in her sister's voice when she had mentioned Luca and the huge amount of money he was paying her, enough to clear their father's debt. 'This is a brilliant place.' She looked around her but she could feel his dark, penetrating gaze boring into her. 'You can imagine that, on a teacher's salary, this kind of restaurant is way out of my league.'

A waiter came and Luca gave his order without bothering with the menu, which he hadn't opened, while Ellie made a deal of scrutinising hers and picking what she wanted carefully.

'I have a stake in this place,' he said, casting his eye around him briefly. 'A decade ago, I decided to dabble in the restaurant business, so I bought a few failing ones to add to my portfolio. This was one of them.'

'Right,' Ellie mumbled. 'Of course. It's really important to have a varied portfolio, I've found.'

Luca burst out laughing, then he sipped his wine and was still smiling as he looked at her. 'Is that why you chose to teach? Because your sister was the one who had the monopoly on dream-chasing?'

Startled because he was closer to the truth than he probably imagined, Ellie stared at him for a few seconds. 'Like I said, I'm grounded. I don't have that risk gene in me that's willing to take a chance that everything's going to work out the way I want it to.' Ellie wondered why that made her sound so dull. She was no different from the majority of the human race.

She looked at him with a trace of defiance but his expression was bland and, when he next spoke, it was to change the subject. He had the contract, he told her, fishing it out of his pocket and sliding the envelope towards her.

'We said two to four weeks. I think it's possible that it might be longer. The longer it is, the more you'll be paid.'

Ellie opened the envelope and read the contract. It couldn't have been more straightforward but the sums of money involved made her feel even more uncomfortable now because it was all officially written down, waiting for her signature.

'The job isn't worth what you're willing to pay me,' she said simply and Luca clicked his tongue impatiently.

'We've been over this.'

'I know, but seeing the amount now, in black and white...'

'You need to dump the social conscience, Ellie, or else we'll be having this conversation on a loop, and it's not going to get either of us anywhere. Take the money and run. That's what any sensible person would advise.'

'You'd probably have a lot in common with my sister. You both think along the same lines because that was exactly what she said.' Plus, she thought absently, looking at the lean, beautiful lines of his face, he would probably do what every other guy did when they were confronted with Lily—he would want her.

Ellie thought that she had grown out of feelings she had had when she'd been an impressionable adolescent but now, suddenly, as though Pandora's box had been opened, they all flew out at her and she blinked in dismay.

Lily had always stolen the limelight, but that had been fine. It had only been less fine when she had stolen the one and only guy Ellie had been serious about.

Serious, hard-working, head-firmly-screwed-on Paul had been such a sensible choice and Ellie had liked him a lot. He had been the PE instructor in one of the local schools and she had met him on a night out with some friends. They'd got along and then, of course—oh, why hadn't she seen it coming?—he had been introduced to Lily and Lily had done what she had always done. She had charmed him. She had paraded in front of him in next to nothing, long, slim legs everywhere, blonde hair tousled, blue eyes wide and innocent.

'He actually asked me out,' Lily had said later. 'So really, I did you a favour, because if you'd ended up with him then it wouldn't have lasted. Besides, he was boring.'

The fact that Ellie had not suffered serious heartache following the break-up didn't detract from her annoyance that her sister had had no qualms about proving the point that she was prettier, sexier and more appealing to the opposite sex. After that, Ellie had quietly determined that she would keep any involvement with guys under wraps until she was sure that they were interested in *her* for who she was.

That hadn't been difficult because none had appeared on the horizon since. She had backed away from involvement with the opposite sex because it was easier than risking disappointment.

She was annoyed at the direction of her thoughts and even more annoyed when Luca asked casually, 'If your sister is on the other side of the world making her fortune, why have you been walking dogs to help pay off your father's debts?'

'Because…'

'Got it. So, moving on, you'll have to sign the contract. That will include an agreement to extend cover as necessary.'

'I haven't signed up to an indefinite situation…' *What had he meant by 'got it'?*

'I'm not asking for anything beyond the official school summer holidays—and have a look at the fine print. Stay on and you'll retire with enough money to do more than pay off your father's debts.'

He handed her a pen and nodded. 'You're doing me a favour, Ellie,' he said quietly. 'I'm not just paying you to look after Jake because I've sacked the last nanny and I'm in a tight corner. I'm paying you to be much more than a competent babysitter. I'm paying you because I think you'll be able to bond with Jake and I know that he's going to benefit from that.'

Ellie saw the raw sincerity in Luca's face and any hesitation was wiped out of her mind faster than dew melting on a summer morning. She signed the paper and shoved it back to him.

'Did you mean all that?' she asked, 'Or were you just making sure that you got what you wanted?'

'You think I'm ruthless enough to lie in order to get what I want?'

'Probably,' she said truthfully, and he delivered another of those rare, utterly charming half-smiles that made her thoughts go into a tailspin.

'Lying's not my style,' Luca told her. 'I don't need to use underhand tactics to get what I want in life. I've always found that the art of persuasion is far more successful.'

'And an ability to throw money at a problem.'

Luca shrugged. 'Money talks and usually has the loudest voice. Now, when will you be able to start?'

Since she had nothing planned for the long summer holidays—having assumed that they would be filled with the joys of dog walking to earn some money and perhaps, if push came to shove, some bar work, which she thought she would have rather enjoyed—the answer was *immediately*, but she took her time giving it a lot of undue thought.

'I should go and visit my father before I start,' she answered. 'I'm going to have to explain how it is that I'm suddenly in a position to pay off all his debts, and that's a conversation best had face to face.'

'Understood. Want me to accompany you to do the explaining?'

'No!' Horror laced her voice and she looked at him in alarm.

'Why not?' Luca asked bluntly, irritated by her reaction, because since when had women rejected the offer of his company?

'My father would be astounded if you showed up and he was told that you and I had worked out a deal whereby you were going to be paying me a fortune for looking after your godson for a few weeks.'

'Why?'

'Because…you're not the sort he would ever associate me coming into contact with, far less doing business with.'

'Ah. I'm not the sort you would get along with…unlike the elusive sister. We're back to the sliding scale of your disapproval, are we?'

'It's just easier if I handle this on my own. But thanks for the offer.'

'How long do you intend to stay there?'

'A couple of days at most and then I can start.'

'I should tell you that my preference would be for you to live in, Ellie. I can't always account for my working schedule and it's going to be a nuisance having to find someone who can fill in when necessary. Naturally, you will be compensated.'

'I'm not sure about that,' Ellie muttered, flushing. She thought of the discomfort of her shared house and, when their eyes met, she had a sneaking suspicion that he could read her mind.

He said, 'You'll have your own suite on the top floor. I assure you it will be very comfortable. Very quiet.'

Ellie had missed quiet. She'd never realised how important that was until she'd been thrown into the situation of sharing her space.

'Okay,' she agreed. 'On one condition.'

Luca raised his eyebrows in a question and she told him firmly, 'No extra money. Please. You're already paying me enough to do something that I will enjoy doing anyway.'

The spendthrift and the saver, Luca thought with curiosity. *One seeking fame and fortune in America, the other teaching and working her butt off to clear debts her father had incurred.* In his head, a picture was being put together, and for the first time he was genuinely interested in knowing the dynamics behind the relationship between the woman sitting opposite him and her family.

He felt the stirrings of something inside him. Something novel. His love life had become all too predictable and, yes, whilst he enjoyed the predictability, and certainly wouldn't have traded it for anything out of his control, with predictability came a certain amount of boredom.

He'd been celibate for the past two months and the last woman he had dated had only been on the scene for a few weeks. He couldn't really remember what she looked like although he knew that she had run to type—beautiful, blonde, leggy and very amenable. He hadn't been interested in her backstory, although she had insisted on filling him in anyway.

And since then? His libido had gone on holiday.

Luca sat back and looked at Ellie, his lush lashes veiling his expression.

God only knew where she had bought her outfit. Had she specifically looked for something designed to do absolutely nothing for the female form?

And yet the delicacy of her features was strangely arresting, and the fact that he wanted to find out more about her wasn't just about him knowing that he needed to get her onside if the situation with Jake were to work out. She sparked his interest. Her unwillingness to confide spurred on his curiosity. Her lack of interest in his money tickled him pink. She wasn't impressed and she didn't bother to pretend, and that seemed to fire up his jaded soul.

'Now that you're working for me,' he drawled, 'you'll find certain things will be at your disposal. I'll arrange a driver to take you to see your father.'

'My father doesn't live in London.'

'I don't care if he lives in Glasgow. You will also have the services of my driver on tap for when you need to go out with Jake. In addition, I will deposit a sizeable amount of money into your account which you can use when it comes to paying for anything Jake might want or need.'

'Anything?'

'Anything.' Luca shrugged nonchalantly. 'Money is no object.'

Ellie drew in a deep breath and tried hard not to be intimidated by the powerhouse sitting across from her. Everything inside her reacted to him in ways that were embarrassing and unwanted. He wasn't the type of man she could ever be remotely interested in, yet her body went up in flames when she was around him, and that unnerved her. How could she be so uncontrolled in her responses? She'd never been that way and, especially after the debacle with her last boyfriend, she had firmly put the lid on her emotions—not that Paul had roused anything like the idiotic sensations Luca seemed to. That had been a measured relationship, which she had liked. If she had been cautious then, well, she was even more cautious now, so why did sitting within touching distance of Luca make her feel all hot and bothered?

The bottom line was that she was going to have to get her act together because this was a business arrangement and there was no room within any business arrangement for a disobedient body. Luca was a staggeringly good-looking man and the fact that she was so keenly aware of him on a physical level just said something about her hormones. They were in full working order. She should be thankful for that, considering they had done a disappearing act after Paul had left the scene. It was good to know that she was *normal*, and maybe when she was back at work she would think about jumping back into the dating scene. This time round she would make sure that whoever she dated wasn't into leggy blondes.

'Now that you've told me all the terms and conditions about my employment,' she said carefully, 'there are just a few things *I* would like to say.'

Luca's eyebrows flew up and she took a deep breath because she knew that, given half a chance, he would tread all over her and the whole point of this exercise would be lost. It didn't matter how much *she* bonded with Jake, it was far more important that *he* did, and throwing money around like confetti wasn't the way to do it.

'Have you sat down with Jake and actually talked to him about what happened?'

'The runaway episode?'

'The loss of his parents. That episode.'

Luca flushed darkly. 'I thought it best not to bring that up because it's sure to revive bad memories. It's better to move on from that place.'

Ellie held his stare. Food had come somewhere along the line but she had been so preoccupied with the conversation that she had hardly been aware of eating what was on her plate. Now, plates cleared, Luca dismissed a hovering waiter who wanted to find out about dessert.

'I disagree,' Ellie told him firmly, ignoring the way his mouth tightened in automatic rejection of the criticism. 'Just because you don't talk about it doesn't mean that it's all going to disappear. It was something momentous. He's only young, but you can mention his parents naturally so that the subject doesn't become taboo. Have you any pictures of them?'

'I…' Did he have any pictures? All their worldly goods had been shipped back to him and he had had the lot put into the attic. He hadn't checked to see what was there and had thought that at some point in the future, when he had time, he would go through it all. That thought had come and gone and he had done nothing about it.

Ellie was looking at him curiously.

'You don't know?'

'It's not that shocking.' For once on the back foot, Luca shifted irritably, his fabulous eyes pinned to her face. 'I haven't had time to go through the crates that were shipped over,' he muttered.

'You're busy.'

'Is that a criticism?'

'It's an observation.' Ellie paused. 'And if we're going to have a successful working relationship then I have to feel that I can be honest and truthful with you when it comes to Jake.'

Luca lifted both hands in a typically Spanish gesture that could have indicated impatience, annoyance, resignation or a combination of all three. Accompanied as this gesture was by a scowl, Ellie thought that it probably wasn't resignation, but that was tough.

'Feel free,' he delivered smoothly. 'I'm all ears.'

'The first thing you should have done should have been to go through those possessions one by one. There are probably all sorts of things there that would have been cherished by Jake, that would have made him feel more secure in an alien environment. He's still very young. He would have had toys that have been with him probably since he was born.'

Luca looked at her in stony silence but she ignored it. So what if he thought she was a prissy schoolmarm who disapproved of pretty much everything about him?

'Also, what about photos?'

'Do photos exist any more?'

'Then his parents' computers or mobile phones, or any place where digital photos might have been stored.'

'I...' Luca was about to repeat what he had said, that time was a valued commodity and he just hadn't got round to finding any to sift through his cousin's bits and pieces. Not much had been shipped over. Johnny and Ruby had not exactly accumulated a treasure trove of memories but then, from what he had gathered, they had rented and had moved on a fairly regular basis. Souvenirs and baby photos on the mantelpiece probably hadn't been their thing.

But he should have done more than just dump the lot in the attic with the vague thought that he would go through it all on a rainy day. In his world, rainy days when you did stuff like that never happened.

'I will ensure that the oversight is rectified,' he conceded and she gave him a nod of approval.

She ordered a coffee, because he was beginning to wear the hunted expression of someone who was keen to leave, but since she had a few more things to say she would have to ensure that he stayed put, at least for a short while longer.

'When?'

'Soon.'

Ellie didn't say anything and eventually, on a note of frustration, and raking his long fingers through his hair, Luca gritted, 'Tomorrow.'

She beamed. 'Brilliant.' She looked at him and her tummy did a flip. When she was talking business, she could almost forget the impact he had on her, but as their eyes tangled she thought how gorgeous he was, how astoundingly, sinfully sexy. On the looks front, no one could deny that Luca was without comparison.

She would have to get past that if she was going to be working for him and she knew that if she could accept the magnetic pull he had over her and shrug it off then there would be no problem dealing with him.

Establishing the nature of their relationship from the outset would be a good start.

'And there's something else. I think you'll need to get more involved with Jake. Money is no substitute for time. I realise you're busy with work, but you're going to have to find the time to leave it now and again so that you can begin to build a relationship with him. He didn't run away,' she said bluntly, 'because he was so happy to be living here in London with you.'

'Anything else?' Luca asked silkily. 'Should I go on a parenting skills course to make sure I'm covering all bases?'

'Not funny.' She tilted her chin at a combative angle and outstared him. 'When I leave, it would be nice to think that you and Jake had built something a bit stronger than what's there now. He needs to really know that he's loved and wanted in order to settle properly.'

His discomfort was palpable. Luca Ross didn't do these sorts of conversations. Ellie waited, half-expecting him to shut down the dialogue and move back into his comfort zone. Instead, he said at last, 'You win. I will take some time off work.' He shook his head and shifted his piercing gaze away from her. 'I've never failed at anything in my life before and I don't intend to fail at this. I'll do what it takes.'

CHAPTER FOUR

WITHOUT ANY FANFARE, Ellie vacated the house in which she had been renting a room. Most of the business of balancing the books was amicable and largely done over text. Rooms to rent in London which were cheap and in a relatively good location were as rare as hen's teeth and there was a list of alternative tenants—mainly friends of friends—waiting in the wings. The girls were all a pleasant bunch and they took her defection without grumbling.

Ellie didn't know whether she was relieved at the lack of fuss or saddened because she'd made so little impact, then she robustly reminded herself of the lucrative nature of her new temporary job and told herself that she would be able to afford something far better by the end of summer. A definite date hadn't been set but it would be determined by the speed with which a suitable replacement nanny was found which in turn, Ellie thought, depended on how fussy Luca intended to be. He might have given the go ahead on the last two with a casual wave of his hand but that was pre-runaway godson. Now, he had been shocked into taking stock.

She'd been bought lock, stock and barrel for the foreseeable future, and as she looked around her vacated room and reminded herself of the small fortune she would be earning over the next few weeks she couldn't prevent an uneasy shiver from running through her.

When she thought back to that conversation three days ago, she realised just how much he had controlled the outcome. He had sought her out, having done his homework, and he had baited his hook in just the right way to catch the fish he needed.

He'd known her weak spot and he had subtly but effectively played on that without appearing to be manipulative in any way—but here she was, room emptied of her possessions and stepping into waters she couldn't predict. Luca would be a fair employer but he would have impossibly high standards and she couldn't afford to let his overpowering personality suffocate her professionalism.

She knew that she would have to do more than just engage with Jake. She would have to try and build a bridge between little Jake and his older cousin. He would be cool and practical and he would expect her to be the same. She would have to squash the temptation to get hot and bothered in his presence, because if she did then all attempts to be cool and practical like him would take an instant nose dive.

Her visit to her father had been brief because, she had said, she had to return to London to start her job.

'It's quite specialist.' She had spun the truth in a way that had somehow justified the exorbitant salary she was being paid. 'This isn't just a normal situation... Jake is a very confused and mixed-up young lad...'

She was guiltily aware that in one sentence she had somehow managed to go from a primary school teacher walking dogs to a top psychologist capable of dealing with a troubled young child but, if she'd stuck rigidly to the truth, her father would have been worried sick. He wasn't an idiot. Why would someone pay over the odds for the simple job of looking after a misbehaving child? Why wouldn't he get a professional in? It would have been impossible to explain either Luca's personality, that was geared to see and take what he wanted whatever the cost, or that he had wanted her because of the peculiar nature of the situation.

Lily, she was told, was making noises about returning to England for a spell, if she could spare the time. Ellie had grimaced and concealed the bald truth that her sister had refused to contribute a penny towards paying off her father's debt.

She had had just one conversation with Luca since their dinner. She had phoned to thank him for the initial sizeable deposit of cash into her bank account and, getting to the point as he always did, he had said bluntly, 'I hope you're not getting cold feet.'

'What makes you ask that?'

'I'm good at detecting anxiety in people's voices,' he had informed her drily. 'If you're worried that you'll be working with someone you don't like, then don't be. It's immaterial whether you like me or not. You just need to respect me. The world is full of people whose values don't happen to dovetail with yours. Being an adult means training yourself not to be affected by that.'

Which had told her!

For the duration of the summer holiday, she would have to be prepared to commit fully to the job, to be there twenty-four-seven for his godson. No last-minute appointments that couldn't be broken, no dog-walking duties that had to be fulfilled and no men claiming priorities over her time.

He had asked her, at the tail end of that conversation,

and almost as an afterthought, whether there was a man in her life.

'You don't have a husband,' he had delivered in a voice that was cool and a little bored and she could picture him doing something else while he was talking to her on the phone—perhaps checking emails on his computer or reading some high-level report. 'And you don't have a live-in partner, but is there someone lurking in the background that you may have failed to mention?'

He had wanted her positioned in just the right place to suit his needs, and having anyone making demands on her time was not going to work, especially as she would be living under his roof. Considering she had only just been gaping at the sum of money in her account, she had realised in that instant just how detailed the trade between them was going to be. In short, he would call all the shots.

'As a matter of fact, I haven't at the moment.' She had stumbled over her words and her cheeks had reddened in embarrassment. Luca didn't have any interest in her personal life, except insofar as it might affect their arrangement, but she had winced with self-consciousness at the picture that admission had painted—the teacher who walked dogs, dressed in shabby clothes, with no one in her life.

Where most girls her age, with eight weeks of summer to fill, would have been booking holidays with boyfriends, she was trying to find a way to save money so that she could bail her father out of the desperate hole he had contrived to dig for himself, and there was nothing going on in her life to prevent her from doing that. She hadn't had to cancel any hot dates or rearrange any holidays with a significant other so that she could fulfil her obligations to Luca.

It had been a moment to think seriously about the direction her life had taken. She hadn't really thought about it before, but now she could see that she had thrown in the towel after her last crash-and-burn relationship. She had buried herself in her job—had breathed a sigh of relief that she hadn't actually *loved* Paul but had more been in love with the idea of being in love—and had taken the safe option of not getting involved with anyone again. She would wait for the right guy to come along.

But having to admit to Luca—sex-on-legs Luca, who had probably never spent more than a handful of nights in an empty bed—that she was resolutely single had been mortifying.

Was this where she wanted to be in a year's time? Two years' time? Okay, maybe walking dogs to earn some extra cash, but still on her own with no particular reason to look forward to the long summer holidays? Maybe getting together with a clutch of similarly single female friends so that they could go somewhere together? Was that how she had been affected by living in the shadow of her fabulously beautiful younger sister? Had she had her self-confidence sapped over the years? Even though she would always have asserted proudly that you didn't have to rely on something as superficial as looks in order to lead a brilliant and fulfilling life, had she known, somewhere deep down, that she had in all truth given up on making any effort?

When she had been dating Paul, she had made an effort. Back then, she had fussed over her appearance and done all those girly things her sister had spent a lifetime doing. She had experimented with make-up, done her nails and grown her hair, and it had all been for nothing, because he had dumped her for her sister. That had been a wake-up call for her, and after that she had promptly lost all interest in stuff that she wrote off as being superficial.

When she met someone, appearance would not make a jot of difference to how he felt about her. He wouldn't be the sort of shallow type whose head could be turned by a sexy blonde with big boobs and legs up to her armpits.

Except, she was never going to meet anyone if she didn't get out there, was she?

She was going to be living in a gilded cage for the next few weeks, and once she was back in her own world things were going to change.

Right now, the gilded cage was a joy to behold, and Ellie did a full circle of the room.

On her bed, Jake was lying in starfish mode, staring up at the ceiling, trying to think of as many things as he could that began with the letter A.

Ellie flung herself down next to him and tickled him until he started squealing for her to stop.

'Shall I tell you a secret?' she whispered, laughing, and Jake giggled.

'What?'

'This is the nicest room I've ever slept in in my entire life.'

'My room's nicer,' Jake whispered back, hugging her. 'I have a Spiderman duvet.'

'You're right,' Ellie said, in a serious hush-hush voice. 'That's the only thing that's missing and I'm going to make sure to put that right as soon as I can. No Spiderman for me, though. Maybe something princessy...'

Jake made a face and she laughed and ruffled his hair. 'Are you saying I'm not like a princess?' she teased, slip-

ping off the bed. 'Because you'd be right! I'm more like…
the big, bad wolf and I'm going to *gobble you up* if you
don't fly down to the kitchen this very minute and start
eating your dinner! Miss Muller called you ages ago,
you little horror!'

She might not have seen Luca since the deal had been
done, but she had seen a lot of Jake, and she could already
feel the bond between them growing.

Luca was prepared to pay the earth for her services
and she realised that this was what he wanted—this bond
between herself and his godson—because that very bond
would be the foundation for his own way in to Jake. To
put it loosely, he would use her, and for that he was willing to pay over the odds. This was the nature of their relationship and it helped to put everything in perspective.

Her settling-in period had been made even smoother
because Luca had had to go to New York on business for
the first few days after her arrival. He had kept in touch
by email and text, and spoken with her every evening
without fail to ask penetrating questions about Jake, but
she had been relieved that he wasn't around while she
found her feet.

She'd had time to relax with Jake and, bit by bit, was
finding out about his background.

The picture he was slowly painting, much to her dismay, was of a broken household with his young and irre-
sponsible parents largely absent. As he gradually opened
up, she realised that he talked more about the elderly couple in the flat next door to where he had lived, who had
obviously borne the brunt of babysitting duties when his
parents had been busy chasing the dream.

As promised, his possessions had been sorted through
while she had been visiting her father, and she had flicked

through a scant amount of photos of his parents on the laptop which had been charged up. A young, beautiful couple, largely posing against dramatic backgrounds that made the photos resemble photo shoots, with only a handful of pictures of Jake as a baby and so forth.

Little wonder that he had shrunk into himself, bewildered and confused, when he had been torn from the familiarity of his surroundings and thrust into the care of an aggressively powerful workaholic who had no patience with having his life disrupted. From the sounds of it, his life had contained precious few rules. He had attended school *sometimes* and had been allowed to do what he wanted whenever he wanted. Luca, with his authoritarian approach to life and his rigid sense of control, would have been a terrifying contrast to Jake's largely absent, easy-going, very young parents.

She would talk to Luca the following evening when he returned to London. It was going to be a two-way street and, if he thought that he could call all the shots, then he was going to be in for a surprise.

She was busy mulling over a scenario in which she could pin her demanding and arrogant employer to the spot, and force him to listen to things he would probably not want to hear, when there was a knock on her bedroom door.

Ellie answered it without thinking. Probably Jake bouncing back up for something or other.

It was Luca. For a few seconds Ellie stood and stared because she hadn't been expecting him.

She'd spent days dismissing her nonsensical response to him and now all of that flew out of the window faster than a speeding bullet as their eyes collided.

She marvelled that she had somehow forgotten how

breathtakingly *vital* Luca was, even when he needed a shave and he looked dishevelled and weary. Nothing could detract from the man's enormous sex appeal. His impact was as powerful as if she'd run headlong into a brick wall and been left dazed and disorientated.

He was in a suit but the tie had gone, as had the jacket, and he had cuffed the sleeves of his white shirt to the elbows.

She lowered her eyes, heart beating harder than a sledgehammer in her chest, and her mouth went dry, because all she could see somehow was his muscular forearms and the sprinkling of dark hair that seemed weirdly, aggressively, over-the-top *masculine*.

'What are you doing here? I thought... I wasn't expecting you until tomorrow evening.'

'Things got wrapped up earlier than expected. It's not yet seven-thirty. I expected to find you downstairs.'

'I was on my way down.' She tried hard not to focus on her stunningly casual outfit—old jogging bottoms, tee shirt and bedroom slippers. These were not clothes with which she could project her professional face.

'I thought that this would be a good a time to have a face-to-face conversation before I start work. I have a hundred emails to get through but I can spare an hour or so.'

'What, now? I realise I'm being paid a lot, but that doesn't mean that you can barge into my bedroom and summon me downstairs for a chat.'

'I'm afraid it does,' Luca returned coolly.

This was what you signed up for, a little voice whispered in her head.

'I can't predict my hours,' he continued in the growing silence. 'With the best will in the world, I can try and have a more reliable work schedule, but there's no guarantee that that will work out.'

'I do understand that, but I don't get why you can't arrange your schedule to accommodate Jake. You keep reminding me that you're the boss of your own company, so why can't you decide when you can leave and when you can't?'

Luca looked at her narrowly. 'I don't care for the tone of your voice.'

Back down now and cower, Ellie thought, and she would set a precedent for their relationship that would last the duration of the time she was under this roof, and it would make for a very uncomfortable situation. There would be things she would need to say to him that he would not particularly want to hear and he would need to be less of a control freak to deal with it.

'I apologise for that,' she said in a composed tone. 'And of course, I do appreciate that you can't tailor your working hours as much as you may like, but I think Jake would benefit from a predictable schedule from you, at least to start with. And that aside…' she drew in a deep breath '… I won't be disturbed any and every time you think you might want to catch up. It's not on.'

Thick, humming silence greeted this and, eventually, Luca raked his fingers through his hair and stared at her, as though debating what he should say next.

Ellie stepped into the breach and continued in a more placatory voice, 'If you give me fifteen minutes, I'll come downstairs. I just need to change.'

She used the fifteen minutes of allotted time to dress quickly into a pair of trousers and a pale blue polo shirt.

On her way down, she passed Jake, who was heading up.

'Read me a story tonight?' He looked at her and then sighed with disappointment when she told him that she couldn't.

'So you get two tomorrow night,' she promised, kneeling down and giving him an affectionate squeeze. 'Plus, Luca is back tonight. Isn't that great?' Her keen eyes noted the way his whole body tensed and he shook his head vehemently.

'Why does he have to come back?'

'Because he wants to spend some time with you.'

'I don't want to spend any time with him.'

Ellie didn't say anything. As far as mountains to climb went, this was going to be a steep one.

Ten minutes later, she was sitting at the long metal and wood table when Luca walked in; she could see he'd had a quick shower because his dark hair was still damp. He positively glistened with robust good health, an alpha male in the prime of his fitness radiating energy from every pore, and no longer looking tired.

'So.' He strolled towards the fridge and peered inside. 'Talk to me.'

Ellie gritted her teeth and wondered whether the word *polite* had ever been used to describe Luca's take on conversation.

Was he *that* short with everyone to whom he spoke? Or maybe just with the people who worked for him? Surely not? There were moments when she glimpsed such overpowering charm and charisma that she could only imagine the guy just didn't believe in wasting any of that charm or common courtesy on her because she worked for him.

And he doubly wouldn't be bothered because not only

did she work for him but she was also a *woman* and therefore would not even register on his radar.

He asked her about Jake, and she repeated a lot of what she had communicated to him via email. He was a very good listener. She could tell that he was taking in every word she was saying, and was probably working out how her activities with Jake compared to the previous two nannies.

He'd abandoned the fridge in favour of a glass of wine, and offered her a glass as a token gesture of politeness, not pressing her when she shook her head.

'I know this is going to work out,' he said when there was a pause, 'because Jake asked for you when you went to see your father.'

'He probably needed a comforting shoulder after everything he's been through. We looked at some of the photos together.' She hesitated. 'Did you go through them with him?'

'I began.' He shrugged. 'But it wasn't a success.' He didn't add that Jake had stared stonily at the ground in absolute silence, his small body stiff with tension, until Luca had flung his hands up in surrender and packed in the exercise.

'It takes time.'

'That's a commodity that's in short supply with me.' He hesitated, then added with hard-won honesty, 'I'm afraid I don't know a huge amount about children. I have no idea how to communicate with them. I don't suppose that helps.'

'You just have to be interested and genuine,' Ellie told him. 'Talk to Jake the way you would talk to…well…anyone, really. Bearing in mind he's six, so discussing world politics isn't going to get you anywhere.' She smiled and he returned it with a crooked smile of his own.

'I prefer giving orders,' Luca said. 'Or else it's down to world politics, I'm afraid.'

'You'll pick it up.' She hesitated, then explained what she had found out about Jake's background and the way he seemed to have been left to his own devices while his youthful parents had got on with their lives.

'I wouldn't say that Johnny and I were the best of friends,' Luca expanded thoughtfully. 'He was much younger and very different from me. I only met Ruby, his wife, once. At the christening. She seemed very much like him.'

'How so?'

'In love with a dream that was never going to materialise,' Luca said flatly. 'And with a baby in tow, to make matters worse. Naturally, I advised against the whole thing.'

'Naturally.'

Luca frowned. 'I'm picking something up here. What is that remark supposed to mean?'

'Being in love with a dream is just another way of saying being hopeful.'

'Which, if you don't mind me saying, is another pointless waste of time.'

Ellie wondered, in astonishment, where that depth of cynicism had stemmed from but the conversation was already over and he was standing up, restlessly prowling back to the fridge and frowning into it until she asked him, reluctantly, whether he had eaten.

'Not since yesterday,' Luca confirmed, without looking at her.

'If I had known, I would have told Miss Muller... She

stayed on later this evening because she left early yesterday. Her neighbour was poorly. She had to do some shopping for her. She prepared something for Jake and I would have—'

'Forget it. I didn't know myself that I would be returning a day early.'

'I could do something for you. Make something...'

Luca swung round to face her. 'Cooking for me isn't one of your duties,' he said flatly.

'It's no trouble,' Ellie said, standing up and making her way over to one of the cupboards, but he halted her in mid-stride, one hand on her wrist.

At that fleeting contact, a charge of electricity raced through her, sending hot sparks through her body and igniting all her nerve endings. Her nipples pinched into urgent, responsive buds and she could feel a horrifying melting between her thighs that made her want to rub her legs together. Her mouth ran dry and she stared up at him, pupils dilated, only galvanising her treacherous body into action when he removed his hand and stood back to stare at her narrowly.

Dismayed that she might have revealed far more than she wanted to, Ellie stepped back, but her heart was thundering and her skin was hot and prickly.

It didn't matter how much she told herself that she needed to be businesslike and efficient, she couldn't seem to help the way her body reacted when it was around him.

She had never suffered that sort of weakness before and she was baffled as to how she could suffer it now with a man who, however drop-dead gorgeous he was, did not appeal to her on any other level at all.

'No.' Luca pinned his fabulous dark eyes on her flushed face as he helped himself to bread and unearthed some cheese from the fridge. He didn't bother with butter or anything else. 'Like I told you, cooking for me isn't part of the deal, and I won't have it.'

'Right.'

'You're offended,' he said shortly, sitting down and then relaxing back to look at her with brooding intensity while she hovered in the middle of the sprawling kitchen like a fish out of water, wanting desperately to leave, but knowing that she would have to be formally dismissed before she could do so.

'Why should I be? Of course I'm not. I was merely being polite. Of course I know that cooking for you isn't part of the deal.'

'I don't do *women cooking for me*,' Luca told her, releasing her from the suffocating stranglehold of his stare and eating the bread and cheese without enthusiasm. 'I don't like it, and I never encourage it, so there's no need to feel piqued because I turned down your offer.'

'I told you, I don't,' Ellie said stiffly. It was now fair to assume that she wasn't going to be dismissed just yet so she sidled across to the chair facing him and sank into it with relief. 'And, while we're on the subject of deals, you've spent the past couple of days abroad and after this you're off to work. Maybe you should look in on Jake? Say goodnight? I'm sure he'd really appreciate that.' She crossed her fingers at the little white lie. Horror would be a more predictable reaction from Jake if Luca were to show up on a godfather-godson bonding mission.

'I...' Luca looked at her and, for a moment, she saw someone who might be top of the food chain when it came to making money, but who when it came to the relationship with his godson was touchingly vulnerable.

'He's probably asleep,' she said quickly. 'You wouldn't want to wake him.'

Luca nodded briskly. The whole thing was a bloody nightmare and he was only now really appreciating the extent of it because he was being called upon to interact instead of throwing money at the problem and leaving it to the professionals. He'd sworn to himself that this was a challenge he would overcome, but how equipped was he to handle the demands of a screwed-up kid?

Highly equipped, a little voice inside him whispered.

Introspection had never played a part in his life. Luca was someone who powered through, eyes firmly set on the present and the future, because nothing about the past could be changed so why dwell on it? He particularly didn't dwell on his emotional past, which had always been better secured under lock and key, but he unlocked that place now.

His background was, on the surface, so different from Jake's. He had known happiness right up to the point when his mother had died. After that, his father had retreated behind impenetrable walls and, when he had, he had taken Luca's childhood with him, leaving behind a young boy forced to grow up fast and to find his independence at an age when he should still have been playing with toy cars and Action Man heroes. All the money in the world had not been able to compensate for the absence of his father.

Had that been a childhood? Yes, he had certainly learnt to thank his years spent at that boarding school for providing him with the sort of backbone that could win any fight. But could you have called it a *childhood*?

You didn't have to be a genius to work out that Jake

would tread a predictable path if Luca didn't get his hands dirty and engage with the situation.

'I'm glad you're here,' he said gruffly. He stood up and she followed suit.

She smiled and he moved towards her, his expression unusually hesitant.

When she looked up, he was so close to her that her heart seemed to skip a beat.

He reached out. She wasn't even sure whether he was aware he was doing anything but what he did was devastating. He brushed her cheek with his finger. A soft, brief gesture that was there and gone in a heartbeat.

'And if I don't tell you that,' he finished awkwardly, 'it's not because I don't think it.'

The moment was gone but her heart was still thumping long after he'd disappeared off to work.

CHAPTER FIVE

'THINKING OF COMING HOME? When?' Ellie was having this rushed conversation on the phone to her father whilst keeping one eye on the front door.

The past week had been a busy one. At the start of this job, she had been determined to keep some distance and to remember that she was doing this purely for the money. She wasn't in it to build a lasting relationship with Jake, far less his complicated godfather.

Unfortunately, she had felt herself being sucked into the family dynamic as the week progressed. Luca had made big efforts to keep to his side of the bargain, to put in more of an appearance than he had previously.

Jake had tolerated his presence. One step forward, two steps back. She had watched and noted Luca's frustration, for once playing a game the rules of which he hadn't made and didn't get.

She had tried to limit her interventions, but they had both turned to her variously to mediate their awkward interaction, where neither side seemed to know quite what to do.

Luca, on the back foot, was not the arrogant guy she had so disliked on first sight.

Jake, tiptoeing around like a shy deer hoping to sneak

past a predator to get to a stream, was increasingly working his way into her heart.

'Not giving a date yet,' she heard her father say with pleasure in his voice. 'She'll be busy over there. Said she can snatch a week or so to return. Can't spare longer than that. Something about agents hounding her.'

'Well, that's nice anyway.' Ellie wondered whether the little chat she had had with her sister a couple of weeks ago had galvanised her into doing something to check up on their father. She hoped so. It was no longer important whether Lily contributed to the financial situation because that was, miraculously, in hand but she knew that her father would be thrilled to have his youngest daughter come and visit.

'Told her you weren't going to be around much to come up here and visit,' her father continued. 'Told her you were hard at it in London, sorting out that little lad.'

'Yes, indeed,' Ellie mumbled guiltily.

'She'll want to see you, Els. She specifically mentioned how keen she was to meet up. Think she might be impressed by what you're doing.'

Ellie couldn't see that herself because Lily had never been particularly impressed by anything that hadn't involved being in the public eye and preferably surrounded by adoring admirers. So why was she suddenly interested in a job that involved looking after a child? But Ellie swallowed back a tart reply while manoeuvring to conclude the conversation.

This evening she would be going out with Luca, leaving Jake with a babysitter who lived three doors down.

This was about business. It was a perfect opportunity to broaden Jake's horizons when it came to interaction with other adults on the home front. They would be discussing progress. There was a script to be obeyed and Ellie was going to make sure she stuck to it.

But she hadn't stopped thinking about the way he had oh-so-casually touched her. She'd been set alight and, deep inside, there remained something smouldering, waiting to re-ignite.

For a few seconds, their eyes had met, and she had felt *something* stir between them, something hot and dangerous, but it had been over in the blink of an eye. It preyed on her mind, though, that brief connection.

It was a relief, in a way, that he had made sure to keep everything between them businesslike since then. They had semi-formal discussions in his office, employer and employee discussing work-related matters. She sat opposite him, perched forward, hands on her lap, and reported on the day's events, and stopped short of actually submitting a written report only by a whisker.

Tonight, though, it would be an experiment in getting Jake accustomed to a change of face. It had been Ellie's idea, because there was no point in allowing Jake to settle into such a comfort zone that any new person on the scene would be viewed, once again, with suspicion and mistrust.

She had suggested the young girl a few houses away because the girl owned a dog and they had chatted briefly on a couple of occasions. She had visited the girl's parents and satisfied herself that she was an excellent babysitting option.

Ellie had imagined the girl popping over to babysit during the day, even if Ellie remained upstairs in her suite catching up on work prep for the forthcoming term. She hadn't foreseen an evening out with Luca, but here she was.

She was alarmed at the level of excitement racing through her, touching all her nerve endings like little electric charges pulsing through every pore of her body. The minute the lines between employer and employee were even a tiny bit blurred, Ellie found that she was frighteningly far from immune to his raw, animal sex appeal which he exuded in punishing waves without even having to try. She had caught herself looking at him—sidelong, surreptitious glances that felt like the stolen glances of a lover. When she was within a metre of him, she could feel the heat of his body as though she was standing too close to an open flame—and the only saving grace was the fact that talking about Jake was a constant reminder that she was in paid employ.

Tonight, though…a meal out.

She had debated whether to wear her parents' meeting outfit of neat skirt, responsible, worker-bee blouse tucked into the waistband and her no-nonsense pumps, but on the spur of the moment she'd opted for something less formal because it was a lovely summer evening.

She had treated herself to a couple of summer dresses and she looked at her reflection in the mirror now. She didn't have the curves of a lingerie model but she looked okay.

The colour suited her dark colouring. It was a pale bronze and made her look ever so faintly exotic. The dress was short and skimmed her slender body lovingly and the shoes, with a little heel, did great things for her bare, brown legs. She'd also made the most of her eyes which she had always considered her best feature.

This wasn't a date and *she knew that*, but why shouldn't she wear what any other twenty-something would wear if she happened to be going out for a meal?

She would have worn this very outfit, she thought, running lightly down the stairs towards the kitchen where Luca had told her he'd be waiting, if she'd been going out with a bunch of girlfriends. No big deal.

She entered the kitchen unhurriedly and took a few deep breaths as Luca, who had been absently gazing through the kitchen window, slowly turned to face her.

He was tugging at his tie, loosening it, and for a few seconds he stilled.

'You're on time. Good.' Luca had perfected the art of glancing at Ellie without really taking her in fully. His reaction to her—one that continually caught him off-guard, the tug she induced in his groin—was unwelcome, inappropriate and incomprehensible because she wasn't his type at all. Too slight, too fierce, too outspoken and too flat-chested.

He had gone out of his way to underline their working relationship. No casual chatting in the kitchen, which would smell of something more intimate than he wanted. In the formal sitting room, they interacted in the way an employer interacted with someone he happened to be interviewing for a job.

He didn't get why she affected his libido the way she did, but he was working overtime to control his wayward response. That one and only moment, when he had given in to the urge to touch her, had galvanised his body into a reaction that had shocked him in its intensity. Her skin had been as smooth as satin under his fingers. He had had to fight down the urge to slip a finger into her mouth, feel her suck it then tug her close to lose himself in her sweetness.

Now, though…

There was no need for this so-called meeting to be conducted at night, nor was it necessary for the venue to be an expensive country pub. Lunch at the noisy local wine bar would have sufficed, but his rational brain had decided to take a break when that choice had been made.

He lowered his eyes, lashes concealing his expression, but he didn't have to stare at her because the image was imprinted in his head. She was in a dress that hugged her slender body and accentuated her ballerina grace. Her breasts were pert and rounded. Her legs were tanned, slim and shapely, and the shortness of her dark hair emphasised the contours of her delicate face and the swan-like grace of her neck.

'I usually am,' she responded quickly, heart picking up speed as she tried and failed not to look at him. 'Last time, there was a reason I was a little late.'

'I believe you. You're not one of these women who shows up late to prove a point or stage a grand entrance.'

Ellie sensed that this was one of those vaguely offensive remarks loosely gift-wrapped as a compliment of sorts.

Old feelings of insecurity rose to the surface like scum. She'd thought she'd put those feelings to rest. Living in her sister's shadow, knowing that she was the plain Jane with the brains, had been tough, especially because their mother had made no attempt to disguise her preference for Lily. But it was only now, in the company of Luca, that she realised just how deeply old wounds could cut.

Luca was so imperfect when it came to every single thing Ellie used as a benchmark for men. Yes, she had had glimpses of someone so much more complex than he appeared on first sight, but the truth was that he was still a billionaire with all the traits of a billionaire. Arrogant, ruthless, intolerant of imperfections, uncompromising. Faced with the arrival of his little charge, he had made no concessions until Jake had absconded, at which point he had got his act together. To some extent. If Jake had never run away, God only knew how much interaction he would have had with his forbidding and powerful god-father, the man from whom he was destined to inherit a multi-billion-euro business. None, Ellie suspected.

All those downsides and yet... Luca was so physically perfect a specimen. So sinfully sexy. Once she started looking at him, she couldn't seem to tear her eyes away, and her brain went into hibernation, leaving her at the mercy of all sorts of confusing, unwelcome reactions.

Ellie knew that she could keep at the forefront of her mind the fact that Luca was the sort of guy who would always be attracted to leggy blondes like Lily. It was galling that she was attracted to him. She could blame her hormones, and tell herself that he *was* ridiculously attractive, so it was no wonder she found him so, but none of that counted for anything. He wasn't her type, so why did she find him so compelling?

The way he was looking at her, his dark, intelligent eyes shielding all expression, made her wonder what was going through his head. Was he amused because she had dressed up? Did he think that she might be getting ideas into her head and maybe thinking that this was some kind of date instead of just an alternative venue for their usual daily debrief about his godson? Maybe he thought she hadn't taken the hint when he'd begun conducting their brief meetings in the more formal sitting room.

'I don't do grand entrances and I'm almost always on time,' Ellie said, grinding her teeth together, because that was just the sort of prissy statement that a truly boring person would come out with. 'It...it goes with the job.'

'Goes with the job?'

'When you teach, there isn't an option to swan in and out of class at whatever time happens to take your fancy. You have to get in at a certain time and it's a habit that's become ingrained. It's not the sexiest trait in the world, but there you go.'

Ellie went bright red and averted her eyes as he smiled slowly and walked towards her.

'I like it,' Luca told her honestly. 'It's a fallacy that men enjoy being kept waiting because a woman needs five hours to apply some war paint. Speaking of which...' He paused, and in that pause Ellie could feel herself tingling all over and waiting for him to *do something*. He had that look in his eyes. The dark depths were lazy and slumberous. He was so close to her, so close that she could feel the warmth of his body heat radiating and enveloping her. 'We should be heading off...'

Ellie blinked. He was still looking down at her. Her throat was parched but she managed to croak, 'Where are we going?'

'I thought we'd get out of London.' For once, he left the driver behind and she followed him to the garage where his Maserati was housed. He opened the passenger door for her and she slid inside a car that smelled of leather and walnut and breathed shameless luxury.

He turned to her just as he switched on the engine which roared into life. 'Forty minutes and we can sample the joys of a country pub. I don't do rural, but I also don't get many opportunities to take this car out, so why not?'

He drove with the skill and confidence of someone comfortable behind the wheel of a fast, powerful car. In between talking about Jake and the advances she was seeing in him, Ellie let herself linger on the flex of his muscled forearm as he changed gears, and the lean beauty of his profile as he stared ahead, concentrating on the road and listening to every word she was saying.

'It's taking longer than I thought,' he mused.

'What is?'

'Relationship building.' Luca shot her a sideways glance.

'It's not an overnight process.' Ellie stared ahead as they left the busy hustle of London and began cruising out towards Oxford. 'Think of your own childhood,' she urged, 'and how complex the relationship you had with your parents was. It's all about having the trust there so that you're free to make mistakes, on either side, knowing it's not going to affect the balance of the relationship. In this case it's made all the more complicated because of the situation.'

'I can't really fall back on personal experience, as I may have mentioned,' Luca said drily. 'Please don't paint rosy images of me as a kid. I was sent to boarding school when I was quite young after my mother died. My relationship with my father was, in actual fact, a very simple one. He paid the school fees.'

'You're so...*matter of fact* about it,' she observed, drawn to the tight line of his lips, the expression of someone who had few touching memories when it came to his past.

'Where's the point in getting worked up over a past that can't be changed? You work in a tough school. You must have encountered kids with more pressing problems than an eight-year-old from a rich background who ends up in a boarding school.'

'I guess that's one way of looking at it,' she said slowly. But the way he had bluntly stated those facts...*mother dying, boarding school, absentee father...and eight years old!* Somehow the situation in Luca's case felt quite different from Jake's insofar as there were alternative parental choices that could have been made. Luca's father had still been around but instead of reaching out he had chosen to walk away.

'You *would* find it difficult to bond if you...er—'

'Let's drop the Good Samaritan take on this. Bottom line is that we need to speed the process up,' he interrupted her. 'Jake is with the neighbour this evening, but sooner or later the hunt for a nanny has to commence, and by the time it concludes he should feel more confident in my relationship with him to make for a happier home environment.'

'Speed it up? How do you intend to do that?' That glimpse of humanity underneath the icy exterior was as fleeting as those other glimpses of him that showed her a man who was not the intimidating powerhouse he projected to the outside world, but it touched her in ways she couldn't explain. She pictured a bewildered child, holding back his grief as he was dispatched into the care of efficient strangers. No wonder he found it impossible to bond with his nephew. He had no experience of family life to fall back on. For all the ups and downs within her own family, who had been far from perfect, she at least had known the ebb and flow of how families operated.

'You're the touchy-feely one with the people skills,' Luca told her flatly. 'You should have one or two ideas. Here's the thing—with the best will in the world, time isn't on my side. You need to busy yourself thinking about how we solve this problem. Anyway, we're here.'

Ellie realised that they had either been driving longer than she'd thought or faster than she'd imagined because they were now in a very civilised part of the world. The houses were all set back from the road and dotted in between fields. Only the distant sound of the motorway served as a reminder that they weren't in the deepest countryside.

The pub was a chocolate box concoction of old beams, cream walls and a sprawling courtyard in which were lined up high-end cars interspersed with a couple of motorbikes.

It was still warm, even though the sun was no longer high in the sky, and the garden at the back was packed, with only a couple of free tables, one of which Luca took, settling her before returning with a bar menu and a bottle of wine.

'My driver can get here and return to London in the Maserati.' He poured them both a glass of wine. 'And we can take a taxi back to London. Now, let's talk ways forward with Jake.'

'I don't know how you think I can work miracles and suddenly speed up his recovery process and cement the relationship you two have.' She frowned and stared off into the distance, seeing but not really noticing the crowd of expensive-looking people filling out the place. She rested her eyes on his cool, beautiful face. 'You may think that you don't need to have any input into trying to find a solution to this, that so long as you unbend enough to get back from work a little earlier than you're accustomed to doing, it's enough, but you're wrong. You won't thank me for saying this, but throwing money at the situation isn't going to work the way it may have done for you when you were a child.'

Ellie didn't mean a word of that. Personally, Luca's cold, unemotional take on the world was probably directly related to the way his father had dealt with the situation and no one could say that the end result had been a blazing success, even if the guy was as rich as Croesus.

She looked at the uncompromising, unwelcoming lines of his lean, striking face and had an insane desire to reach out and stroke his cheek, the same way he had casually reached out and stroked hers. His boundaries were steel-clad and she wondered whether anyone had ever come close to breaching them. Any of those women he had dated? She thought not. He would never allow any of them near enough.

'Don't get me wrong…'

'No need to butter me up before you drop the axe.' Luca grinned because, against all odds, he was amused by the uncomfortable tinge of colour in her cheeks. 'You have amazing eyes,' he murmured, in a voice that implied that he was as surprised by what he had just said as she was.

'I beg your pardon?'

'It's an unusual shade of green, as clear as glass washed up on a beach.'

Ellie could feel herself burning up under his lazy, dark eyes. 'I… I don't think that's…appropriate, do you?'

'Possibly not,' Luca murmured. His eyes drifted to her mouth, full lips the colour of crushed raspberries and made for kissing.

'Stop looking at me,' Ellie whispered, breaking the silence with difficulty.

'You don't like it?'

'No, I most certainly do not!'

Luca raised his eyebrows and smiled and she wondered whether he thought that she might actually *like* him staring at her. She'd never played with fire and this felt as though she had a box of matches in one hand and a tank of petrol in the other. It wasn't a game she cared to begin.

'You need to spend a bit more undiluted time with Jake.' Back to the reason they were sitting here! 'I think that might be the way to go if you want to speed things up. Half an hour in the evening is better than what you were putting in before but it's not nearly enough.'

He surfaced to something she was saying and realised that he'd dropped the ball for a minute there because he'd been too busy looking at her. *Spend more time.* Time was money for him, but he was being pinned into a corner, and somehow his brain wasn't functioning at optimum level.

He heard the voice and recognised it almost before he registered that he was being addressed.

Heidi Troon had been his last girlfriend and she had not accepted the parting of ways with philosophical equanimity. She had screeched and squawked and accused him of leading her on, then she had wept and wailed and finally, in the absence of a suitable response, she had flounced out of his apartment, having called him every unladylike name under the sun and swearing darkly that he would get what was coming to him. That had been some months previously and since then her vitriolic departure, along with a certain boredom with the prospect of wooing a replacement, had propelled Luca into increasing his workload. Jake, in retrospect, had not been a happy beneficiary of the situation.

He turned around with visible reluctance as she arrived at his side, her big blue eyes staring at Ellie with open curiosity before zeroing in on him.

This was a woman designed to make men swoon and bump into lamp posts. With legs up to her armpits and hair that fell in a golden sheet to her waist, she knew how to play up every single asset she possessed to perfection, and her assets were many.

She was wearing a small red skirt and a small, cropped black-and-white sleeveless top that clung to every curve, and the striking length of her legs was accentuated by six-inch strappy sandals.

'I've been trying to get in touch with you,' she crooned and Luca gritted his teeth. 'We left on bad terms and afterwards, well, I thought I could make it up to you. I've phoned and texted…'

'I know.'

'Why haven't you replied?'

'I've been busy. Heidi…this is Ellie.'

Ellie had never seen anyone as stupendous as the blonde towering over their table. She wasn't sure whether to stand, sit, smile, stretch out her hand or explain why she was sitting in a country pub with Luca. Or maybe just curtsy. She opted for the path of least resistance and looked away in silence, leaving Luca to deal with the situation.

'I wanted to talk to you, Luca. Without your…*who are you anyway?*…earwigging.'

Luca sighed and stood up, his lean, handsome face tight with disapproval. 'I'll be back shortly,' he grated, while Ellie grinned like a wind-up toy until her jaw ached.

Hot embarrassment was coursing through her. Had she been lulled into thinking that this was *a date*? Well, she'd been brought right back down to earth with a bump, and let that be a lesson to her.

By the time Luca returned, the blonde was no longer with him, and Ellie was halfway through her food.

'Apologies,' she said stiffly.

'For what?'

'For getting in the way if you would rather have dined with your friend.'

'If I'd wanted the woman around, I would have asked her to stay. I didn't ask her to stay because the last thing I wanted was her company.'

'She must have been curious about me. What did you tell her?'

'Nothing.' His expression was cool and unrevealing. 'Why would I tell her anything? It's none of her business.' He shrugged and said, by way of brief explanation, 'We went out some time ago. It didn't last long but she took the break-up badly, even though I'd been nothing but honest with her from day one. She has been trying to contact me and I've been ignoring her texts. I had said what had to be said and that, as far as I was concerned, was the end of the story. My apologies if you felt uncomfortable with the situation.'

'Not at all,' Ellie lied. 'But don't you care if she gets the wrong impression?'

'Wrong impression?' Amusement lightened his features. 'Ah, I get where you're going with this. I repeat: what she thinks is her concern. I can't legislate over her thoughts and I have never seen the need to explain myself to anyone.' That *had* occurred to him, and he'd thought, so what if she thought that Ellie was her replacement? Wouldn't it stop her thinking that there was still a chance for them and bring an end to the nuisance calls? Why would he shut down that line of thought when it was beneficial to him that she run with the misconception?

'Has it occurred to you that *I* might care what some-one else thinks of me?'

'No,' Luca answered truthfully. 'You don't know the woman so why would you care what she thinks of you? You'll never see her again and, if she chooses to gossip a bit with her crowd, then it won't make a scrap of dif-ference to you because you'll never know.'

Everything he said made sense, but Ellie was still dis-mayed at the thought of having her reputation used as gossip fodder for people like the stalking blonde. Being seen with Luca, being thought of as the latest in his line of mistresses, did not sit well with her. She had noticed the way the other woman had looked at her with those icy blue eyes—with pitying speculation.

'Don't think about it,' he said dismissively. 'If you worried about what everyone thinks, you'd go mad.'

'Thanks for the tip,' Ellie muttered, lowering her eyes and half-wanting to slap him, because maybe that was how it worked in his world, but it wasn't how it worked in hers. Plus, somehow the atmosphere had been ruined, and while she knew that there should have been no at-mosphere to ruin in the first place she still felt flat all of a sudden.

'You're welcome,' Luca drawled. 'You'll thank me for it one day, even though right now you look as though you'd ram your foot on the accelerator and run me over if you happened to be behind the wheel of a truck.'

'Not everyone sees the world the way you do.' Ellie looked at him defensively but he had obviously put that moment of unpleasantness behind him and was already half-smiling at her.

'What a shame.' The smile turned into a grin. Her breathing hitched, and some of that determination to remind herself that this was *business and not pleasure* was chipped away. 'Now, moving on, there was something I wanted to discuss with you before that untimely interruption. You say that I need more time with my godson and I happen to agree with you. The only way I can think of doing that is to remove myself from the office altogether.'

'What does that mean?'

'Take time off. Two weeks. I won't be able to fully escape the workload, but there will be considerably fewer demands on my attention. I own a villa in Majorca. I can't remember the last time I went there and I'm thinking that this would be a good opportunity to pay it a visit. Naturally you would have to come along.'

'Two weeks? Out of the country?' Ellie was thinking *sun, sea, sand...and Luca. What kind of a mix was that?*

'You'll find that it will be a luxurious two-week holiday. Yes, it'll be a busman's holiday insofar as your interaction with Jake is concerned, but I can guarantee relaxation. The villa is a short walk down to a private cove. When we return to London, the hunt for your replacement can begin in earnest, and I'm hoping that some undiluted time with Jake will build more of a bridge between us than currently exists.'

'When would we leave? I had hoped to go up north next weekend. My sister is planning on coming over and seems keen to meet up...'

'I should be able to tie up all loose ends and get my calendar cleared within three days. Aim for that. The sister can be put on hold. Three days should give you time to buy whatever you want to take with you in terms of summer clothes, as well as whatever Jake needs. It'll be hot out there. Questions?'

None, Ellie thought, as her life hurtled into fifth gear

and the predictability which had been the mainstay of her existence threatened to vanish altogether. She'd taken his deal and signed her soul away in the process. So how could she have any questions?

And then, at five the following evening, questions became redundant anyway because fate decided to speed things along. In the kitchen with Jake, Ellie was startled by the sound of the front door slamming and then, seconds later, Luca strode into the kitchen, face as black as thunder.

He tossed two tabloids on the table and said, before Ellie could recover from her astonishment at seeing him, 'Turn to the gossip column. Jake.' He spun to look at his godson. 'Exciting news. We're going on a trip. Find Miss Muller and start packing whatever you want to take with you. Ellie will be up in a minute.'

'We bought some Lego. Can I take it?' Jake hovered, nervous eyes locking on Ellie.

'Whatever you want.' Then Luca seemed to think about it because he knelt to Jake's level and said, tone slightly softened, 'But there will be a lot to do out there. A pool, the sea... There's even a boat.'

'A boat?' Jake's eyes lit up and, for the first time, Ellie could see real interest there in what Luca was saying just as she could see the effort Luca was making to remember that he was dealing with a six-year-old child and so had to exercise patience.

'Nothing fancy, but you don't need fancy to do a bit of sailing.'

'Will you teach me how to sail?'

'I could do that.'

Luca smiled and Ellie felt a lump form in her throat.

Something inside her bubbled up, something quite different from the fierce sexual awareness that gripped her whenever she was in his presence.

The way he was now with Jake—a certain softness in his manner, as though he was deliberately slowing himself down—touched her.

Then, Jake gone, things were back to normal and Luca was focusing on Ellie, striding forward to help himself to some water while he tugged off his tie with one hand and flung it on the table. 'It seems that my ex has had a little mischief at our expense. You're the newest acquisition in my long and chequered line of women.'

The colour drained from Ellie's face. She snatched up the paper and there, in bold print, were riveting revelations about a non-existent relationship which, Heidi had made sure to reveal, could really be serious because, for once, the most eligible man on the planet was not dating to type.

'I'm even more furious than you are,' Luca said with audible loathing in his voice.

'You have to tell these reporters that none of this is true!' Ellie was horrified at what her dad would think. He would be bitterly disappointed. She had never been the type of girl to sleep around and get herself emblazoned in tabloid papers. He might never find out, but Lily was going to be around, and she read tabloids as thoroughly as a student cramming for an end-of-year exam.

'I don't discuss my private life with reporters,' Luca informed her, his movements restless and lacking their usual grace. 'And for the record, never get into a dialogue with the paparazzi unless you want every word misconstrued.'

'So what do you suggest? You might not care about any of this but *I do*!'

'It'll be a five-minute wonder. You can tell your father the truth but that isn't going to make the article disappear. There will be reporters trying to take pictures of you out and about and embellishing a non-story as much as they can until some other nonsense comes along to distract them.'

'Pictures of me?' Ellie squeaked, paling at the thought of that intrusion into her privacy.

'Not if we leave the country. I have my private jet on standby. You just need to pack your bags and I'll ensure we leave this house without being followed. My villa is more secure than the Bank of England and, by the time we return, all of this will have blown over.' He glanced at his watch, dumped his empty glass in the sink and looked at her. 'I will see you in the hallway in an hour, Ellie.' Then unexpectedly his voice was gentle when he added, 'I realise I have a different take on this to you, Ellie, but everything will be fine in the end. You just have to trust me on this…'

CHAPTER SIX

WITHIN AN HOUR and a half, they were being driven in his Jag out to the airstrip where his private jet would be ready and waiting for them. There were no reporters in sight, but there were two black Range Rovers driving behind them at a discreet distance, and they had been ushered out of the house via a side door straight into a waiting chauffeur-driven car.

She hadn't managed to cobble anything together by way of summer clothes, so her case was full of the stuff she wore every day. Jeans and tee shirts. A couple of pairs of shorts and some flip-flops. Jake, fortunately, had an ample supply of designer summer gear, which had been provided along with all the expensive trinkets and gadgets that Luca had ordered in for him as a replacement for *quality time.*

The sun was fading by the time they made it to the airstrip which was forty minutes outside London. In the car, Luca worked and Jake stared excitedly out of the window before asking repeatedly when they were going to be there, and Ellie...

Ellie marvelled that her well-ordered, neat little life had detonated without her even realising that there had been a hand grenade waiting to go off.

This was an adventure, and it felt like one. Except she didn't do adventures. Her sister did. Which, for most of the silent drive, brought her right back to the business of her father and hoping he didn't read all the rubbish that had been circulating in the tabloids...

The private jet—which clearly Luca took for granted, as he barely glanced at it—was amazing.

Sleek, black and powerful, bearing the logo of his company in dull, matt silver along the side, it oozed crazy wealth and Jake was so impressed that he sidled closer to Luca, who had paused to look down at his godson.

The promise of a sailing lesson had opened a crack in the door between them, even if neither of them was quite aware of that, and Ellie took a back seat, allowing them both awkwardly to try their hand at communicating without her intervention.

Jake asked questions about the jet and Luca broke down his answers into bite-sized replies, easily digested by a curious six-year-old.

'Perhaps you could teach me how to fly?' Jake asked as they boarded, and Luca burst out laughing.

'That might have to wait,' he said, looking down as Jake strapped himself in. 'A pilot's licence is the one thing I haven't yet had time to get. But don't worry. You want to fly my jet? You'll get the chance in time.'

'Wow,' Ellie murmured with heartfelt sincerity when Luca was sitting next to her, while behind them Jake occupied himself with something on his tablet. 'I think you're working out how this whole father-son thing works...' Then she blushed and clumsily amended, 'I meant godfather-godson.'

'Stick to the former.' Luca pulled out his laptop, eyes

not on her. 'It's more appropriate considering he will inherit the throne.'

'Inherit the throne?'

'What I have will one day be his.' He looked at her thoughtfully. 'I would like to have a meaningful relationship with the child who will, one day, take over my empire.'

'More than the relationship you have with your own father,' Ellie heard herself say, but instead of slamming down the shutters hard Luca nodded abruptly.

'Something like that.' He stared at her for a few seconds, then adjusted his position and murmured softly, 'And, Ellie, don't think about what other people are going to say or how they're going to react to a couple of trashy articles printed in some tabloids. I can see it's on your mind. Don't focus on it.'

She nodded but didn't answer as the jet began taxiing for take-off. It thundered into the heavens with the power of a rocket and she couldn't contain a gasp of excitement, which took her mind off the whole sorry business for a couple of minutes.

'Did you get through to your father?' Luca asked as soon as they were airborne.

'No,' Ellie told him glumly.

'It's more than likely he won't read those articles. Is he the sort who has a penchant for trashy tabloids?'

'One of them isn't a trashy tabloid.' Her green eyes were filled with anxiety. He lived in such a different world from her, she thought again. He occupied a world where he was such a top dog that other people's opinions didn't matter and he had complete freedom to do exactly what he wanted. Looking at him was like looking at an alien from another planet.

'You're getting lost in the details.' Luca smiled. Her worry was palpable. He should have been irritated because he disliked hand-holding, especially when it came to situations where the hand-holding concerned something he personally considered trivial, but he wasn't irritated. In fact, he wanted to smooth away her anxiety. He felt a tightening in his groin as his gaze dropped to her full mouth and he breathed slowly and deeply, regaining control. It would help if she wasn't staring at him with eyes that could have melted ice.

'It's a storm in a tea cup. Trust me on this one. The paparazzi are fickle. I might be marginally newsworthy but I'm a businessman, not a celebrity. The only reason they've picked up on this at all is because I'm rich and because Heidi is a model who enjoys getting her name and face out there. Reporters love her and she knows just how to throw mud around.'

'Your storm in a tea cup is my personal nightmare,' Ellie said, worrying her lower lip and then leaning back against the leather seat to close her eyes briefly. 'And even if my father doesn't read tabloids, which he doesn't, my sister devours them, and she'll be reporting the incident in great detail.'

'Ah, your sister, the one who has so much in common with me. I recall you saying something of the sort.'

Ellie shrugged one narrow shoulder and kept her profile averted. She didn't want to talk about Lily. She didn't want him to be curious about her sister. Why was that? she wondered. It wasn't as though they were ever going to cross paths. She hated the thought of that happening but refused to analyse why.

'I'll try and take it all in my stride,' she said, eyes still closed, which made this awkward conversation a lot easier. 'But I don't live in your world where this kind of thing happens. You're used to dealing with it, and besides, you don't really care what people think anyway. We're chalk and cheese.'

'I won't argue with that.'

'That's why this whole situation is so stupid,' she thought aloud.

'Why?'

'Because...' Ellie turned to him then drew back a little because it felt as if he was way closer to her than she'd thought. She could smell the clean, woody scent of whatever aftershave he used and could see the tawny glitter in the dark depths of his eyes. 'Because anyone would take one look at us and know that there was no way we could be anything other than employer and employee.'

'You don't do justice to yourself,' Luca said softly. 'What makes you think I don't find you sexy?'

Ellie's eyes widened and then she said, angrily, 'Please don't think you have to compliment me to make me feel good about myself. I feel very good about myself. I'm just realistic.'

'Look in the mirror, Ellie.' Luca's voice was mild and unrevealing.

Ellie's head was swimming. She couldn't maintain eye contact. What was he saying? That he found her *attractive*? She refused to believe it. She had seen his last girlfriend and she was nothing like her.

If she had looked like Lily, well, that would have been a different matter.

Ellie hated all the old insecurities that had somehow been revived ever since she had met Luca. She didn't understand why that was so and it was frustrating that those insecurities were pursuing her so doggedly when she thought she'd left all that behind a long time ago. Was it because he was the sort of beautiful person she had trained herself to ignore over the years? She'd hunkered down after the boyfriend that never was. She knew the limits of her sexual appeal and was very content to work with what she had. But Luca's compliments? Why should he be allowed to feel sorry for her?

'I look in the mirror every day,' she said crisply, 'and I'm not exactly a six-foot blonde whose best friends are reporters and who enjoys having her face splashed across gossip columns in tabloid newspapers, am I?'

'No, you're definitely not that.'

'And thank goodness for that!' Ellie was stung by his easy acceptance of what she had said.

'But as my ex made clear in that article, what about the theory that opposites attract?'

Ellie laughed shortly. 'I don't think so.' She was beginning to squirm because the conversation seemed to be meandering down all sorts of unpredictable roads and, the more it meandered, the more out of control she was beginning to feel. 'Men always go for the same types.'

'Is that your personal observation?'

'As a matter of fact, it is,' Ellie said coolly. Their eyes tangled and she powered on, determined not to be the first to look away. 'Not,' she added gamely, 'that my private life is any of your business.'

'No, of course it isn't,' Luca murmured, his interest piqued in ways that took him by surprise. 'And I won't muddy the waters by pretending that it is. Although...'

'Although what?' The lengthening silence threatened to wreak havoc with her fragile composure.

Ellie hadn't had much choice when it had come to this arrangement. In fact, she'd had *zero* choice. For the amount of money he was paying her, she would have been obliged to follow him to Timbuktu for the job, had she been asked. In the absence of any choice, she had tried not to give house room to the tricky technicality of what it would feel like being cooped up with him all day for hours on end with very little reprieve.

Trepidation soared inside her as he continued to look at her with lazy, brooding intensity, his dark eyes so unsettling and so compelling.

'We're going to be in one another's company for longer periods of time than we have been so far.'

'Yes, I realise that, but I'm here for Jake, and I suppose it's no different than if you were to go somewhere on business with your secretary.'

'Very, very different,' Luca corrected without batting an eyelid. 'I've never shared a villa with my secretary before. Not to mention the fact that the business of Jake takes this to a very personal level.'

'Perhaps *personal* is the wrong word.'

Luca shrugged. 'My point is that there's a limit to how formal things are going to be once we get to the villa. I feel it's only fair to warn you of that in case you're beginning to feel nervous about the situation.'

'Thank you for that,' Ellie said politely, eyes sliding away from this dark, beautiful face.

The jet began dipping and she jumped up to check on Jake.

'Come sit up by us,' she urged, and by the time they were both buckled up the jet was descending to land.

The villa was breath-taking Ellie thought when, two short hours later, the four-wheel drive Luca had hired finally came to a stop. They had driven through lush mountains, where both she and Jake had exclaimed at the glimpses they'd caught of turquoise strips of ocean in the distance.

Far behind them lay the buzz of the nearest town, replaced by hillsides dotted with whitewashed houses, and ribbons of tarmac winding away from the main road climbing the sides of the hills to disappear into the greenery.

All of it was barely visible because night had descended, although the villa itself was brightly lit.

It was peaceful, it was tranquil and it was telescopic-lens-proof.

'CCTV,' Luca pointed out as they headed to the front door. 'And the perimeter walls are crawling with cameras.'

'Extreme for somewhere you don't visit very often,' Ellie returned as she was offered a glimpse of how the really rich conducted their lives.

'I like my privacy.'

Which made Ellie think how furious he must be that it had been so efficiently invaded by his ex.

To Ellie, it had seemed like overkill. It was only after the first couple of days that she thought just how *safe* the place felt.

No prying eyes, and that lack of any intrusion from the outside world was like a pick-me-up tonic.

She had got through to her dad on the first evening they'd arrived and had stammered through an explanation for whatever tacky article he had read which, thanks to Lily, who was now back in the UK, had been all of them.

Then she had spoken to Lily who had been barely able to contain her curiosity and had asked so many questions about Luca that Ellie's head had been aching by the time she'd hung up.

But she hadn't been able to hold on to her worries for long because the villa was magical. Pale colours, shutters everywhere and a veranda that circled the entire house like a bracelet and was strewn with sitting areas. The breezes wafted through the open windows like a lullaby. The infinity pool was stupidly stunning, like something lifted straight out of a classy house magazine.

All the tension drained out of her body and, whatever charm the place wielded, Jake wasn't immune to it either.

His thin, pale face relaxed and the tentative advances he had shown towards Luca continued, slowly but surely. He began to play without reserve and to show some of the spirit a normal six-year-old boy should have.

On day one, they took it easy. Luca showed them around the villa. They strolled down to the private cove where Ellie sat in the shade reading while Luca spent an hour with Jake in the shallow water before calling it a day and retiring to take a series of business calls.

From where she was sitting, Ellie was able to hear their conversation, with Jake asking what fish lived in the sea, squealing apprehensively when the water got too frisky around his ankles and then finally drifting back towards her so that he could sit and focus on building a sand castle.

It was relaxed in the villa because Juanita, the house-keeper, was there, popping up with furniture polish and dust cloths in a very reassuring fashion.

She came in once a week, Luca told Ellie, regardless of whether the property was in use or not, to air it and make sure the roof hadn't fallen in. While they were there, she would come daily and also be responsible for all the cooking.

'So if you don't use this villa,' she asked, bemused by this display of wealth, 'then who does?'

'Friends.' He'd shrugged. 'Employees. Clients occasionally.'

'It's so beautiful. What a waste for you.'

'It's an investment. What's wrong with that?'

Ellie thought it was sad that he really couldn't see where the flaw in that argument was but she wasn't going to go down any more personal roads with him.

She was relieved when, on the first night, Juanita was bustling in the kitchen while they ate the dinner she had prepared after Jake had been settled. Luca had spoke to Juanita in fluent Spanish and then, meal over, Ellie excused herself and retired to bed.

Bit by bit, Ellie noted that the periods of time Luca spent with Jake increased. It was very small steps but all heading in the right direction.

She took a back seat, explaining to Luca that it was a good idea for him to have one-to-one time with Jake without her being there twenty-four-seven because when she was there Jake's attention was conflicted.

'Right now,' she confided when, on their third day, Luca and Jake had spent close to an hour together without Luca climbing the walls with boredom and looking at his watch, 'you're really making strides. Keep this up and by the time we get back to London, you can really begin the search for another nanny. Jake will be comfortable enough around you to see you as the primary adult in his life with the nanny as a secondary figure. He'll feel he belongs and that'll be more than half the battle won.'

They were on the sprawling veranda, Ellie sitting in a wicker chair with her book on her lap while Luca leaned against the wooden railing, looking down at her from his towering height.

Inside, Juanita, who had taken an instant liking to Jake, was continuing with her project to teach him Spanish. After all, as his godfather's heir, he would need to speak the language like a native.

Ellie stared up at Luca, shielding her eyes with her hand. Being alone had been rare so far. Juanita was around all the time, arriving at eight in the morning and leaving at seven, and when she wasn't around Jake filled the gap. Being alone with Luca was unexpected, and she had been lulled into complacency, so out here alone with him she was jumpy.

Just a handful of days in the sun had turned his skin to burnished gold, and there was a lot of that burnished gold on display, because he hung around in loose khaki shorts and tee shirts that did a brilliant job of showing off his lean, muscular physique.

Right now, his hands were jammed into the pockets of his cream shorts, dragging them down, which emphasised his lean hips and hard, washboard stomach.

She looked away quickly but her skin was prickling all over and she was suddenly self-conscious in her tidy pair of denim shorts and loose cotton tee shirt. And her bare feet. Somehow a pair of sandals went a long way to making her feel suitably attired.

'I hope,' she said into the lengthening silence, 'you don't feel that by giving the two of you time together I'm somehow shirking my duties…'

'If I felt that, trust me, I would tell you.' Luca raked his fingers through his hair. 'I can see that there has been an improvement in my relationship with Jake,' he admitted. 'So the last thing I would feel is that you're shirking your duties. You're doing exactly what I'm paying you to do. That said, you can relax in your spare time, Ellie. Have you been to the pool once since we got here?'

'I… Not yet…but I plan to…' She'd cringed at the thought of getting into her very proper, sporty black one-piece in front of him, choosing instead to watch from the sidelines while he and Jake took to the water.

'You can swim, can't you?'

'Yes! Of course I can swim! I was very sporty when I was a teenager!'

'Then enjoy the pool, Ellie. You can take the working hat off now and again.' He pushed himself away from the wooden railing and strolled towards her, then he leaned down, hands on either side of the chair, caging her in and bringing her out in a fine film of nervous perspiration.

'Luca…'

'You're beginning to make me feel like a taskmaster.' Luca watched the delicate sweep of colour in her cheeks and his keen eyes noted the way she had pressed herself so far back into the chair that she was in danger of breaking it. 'I'm not keeping tabs on you, Ellie.' His voice had sunk to a low murmur.

She smelled of flowers, fresh, clean and *young*. He found that he couldn't move because he was entranced by the delicacy of her face. She glowed over here. Her short hair had lightened in the sun and a sprinkling of freckles had appeared from nowhere on the bridge of her nose. She looked like a fairy. A ridiculously sexy fairy. He had to will himself to stand back, and when he did he made sure to put some distance between them, but his breathing remained thick and uneven.

'I know you're not,' she said evasively.

'Good. I'm going to work now and I'll be busy until early evening. Something has come up with a deal in Hong Kong and I have a series of conference calls to chair. Jake's busy with Juanita. You can sit out here reading your book or retire to your room, but you can also explore the grounds and enjoy yourself. If you like, I can arrange for you to be driven into the village. No one knows where we are so there's not much chance of any flash bulbs going off in your face. Besides, the village is small, and even if I don't get here very often I contribute quite substantially to various projects and organisations. They are reassuringly protective of my privacy.'

'I... I'm fine here, Luca. Thank you.' Her heart was thumping as though she'd run a marathon. 'I like reading, and I'm very relaxed, so please don't worry about me.'

For a few seconds he stared down at her, his expression veiled, then he straightened, eyes drifting downwards to the small, delicate points of her breasts. A surge of hot blood made his groin ache. He felt giddy, out of control, and he abruptly stepped back, scowling.

'Good.' His voice was cool and sharp. 'Just so long as you know that you can actually have fun—that you're not my servant, or on call twenty-four-seven.' At which, he swung away and headed at a pace towards his office.

Hurt by the abruptness of his voice, Ellie realised that whatever occasional shiver of camaraderie she sometimes felt with him, whatever weird feeling that he sometimes *saw her as a woman*, was an illusion because it was obvious the guy thought she was a bore. The sort who faded into the background and had to be forced to enjoy the massive grounds, the gardens and all the things that were on offer. She had brought her computer over and had mentioned that there was a backlog of school stuff to do, which had so far been put on the back burner. Hardly riveting stuff for a twenty-something singleton to be doing in a place the likes of which she would never, ever see again.

On the spur of the moment, Ellie headed straight up to her bedroom, slipped into her swimsuit, armed herself with sun lotion, a towel, a sarong and her oversized sunglasses and headed straight down to the cove.

Jake was with Juanita and, really, she'd had no time to herself since they had arrived.

It would be good to relax and enjoy the scenery without feeling self-conscious that Luca was around, or in teacher mode because Jake was there. What with all the business with her dad and his debts, relaxation had been a distant dream for so long now. She would be an idiot to pass up the opportunity to grab some while she was here in this little slice of paradise.

It was a little after five but the sun was still warm and the sound of the water whispering against the sand was soporific.

On the very verge of falling asleep, Ellie decided to take to the water. She'd represented her school in swimming and it felt great to be scything through the sea. It had been a long time. Public swimming pools were fine, but usually far too crowded to do anything but weave in and out of other swimmers, and there was nothing like the freedom of the open water.

Oblivious to everything but the feel of the water as she sliced through it, she was barely aware of the distance she was swimming.

After twenty minutes she stopped, lay on her back,

floated and let her thoughts drift in and out of her head. She closed her eyes.

Luca's sexy image swam into her head and she didn't bother trying to chase it out.

She shivered when she recalled how her skin had burned when he had touched her. She thought about the dark beauty of his face and the way his eyes lingered, watching her and thinking thoughts she couldn't begin to imagine but about which she could speculate for England.

She wondered...

Floating like driftwood, she wondered what it would feel like to have him touch her intimately. To have those long, clever fingers explore her body, rouse her passion. She could feel the warmth of her wetness mingle with the sea and she shifted, restless and suddenly aching between her legs.

She wanted to touch herself to ease the tingle there.

She wasn't expecting her lazy reverie and the pleasant ebb and flow of her fantasies to be brought to a sharp halt by the feel of someone grabbing her, gripping her waist and sending her into a panicked meltdown.

She thrashed like a wild thing as the sea water poured into her eyes and her mouth until she was spluttering and quite unaware, for a few terrified seconds, about what was happening.

Then she snapped out of it when Luca growled into her ear, 'What the hell do you think you're playing at!'

Her stinging eyes flew open and there he was, like a dark, avenging angel, glaring at her, out of his depth in the deep water but still holding her as though she was as light as a feather.

Ellie pushed, hands flattened against his rock-solid chest, and he circled her wrists with his fingers.

'What are *you* playing at? Let me go!'

'So you can bloody carry on drifting out to sea while you're in La-La Land? No way! You're coming right back to shore!'

'I'm fine!' Ellie yelled, dropping all pretence of professionalism, because she'd been taken by surprise, and because the feel of him so close to her, wearing next to nothing, was making her feel giddy and faint, especially when she'd been having such pleasurable and such, such taboo fantasies about him.

'You can't see the shore line, Ellie!' He was treading water but now he began to swim, making sure that she kept pace with him.

He was a strong swimmer, but so was she, and pride made her swim as strongly as she could so that he didn't think she was a wilting female in need of being saved from her own idiocy by a knight in shining armour.

By the time they finally made it to land, she was exhausted as she staggered upright.

He didn't wait for permission. Water pouring off him, he picked her up and ignored her half-hearted struggles against him.

'Put me down!'

'Shut up.'

'How *dare* you tell me to shut up?'

'Have you any idea how long you've been out here?'

'I must have forgotten my waterproof diving watch back in my room!'

'The sun's practically disappeared!' Luca roared, striding up the beach towards a rug that he had brought with him and dumped alongside her towel. 'You've been missing in action for over an hour and a half, Ellie!'

'No, I haven't!' The sun *had* begun to fade and… *An hour and a half?* Where on earth had the time gone?

In her raunchy thoughts! That was where!

She stopped struggling, choosing to hold herself as rigid as a plank of wood against him, which he ignored, and then she found herself on the rug, staring up at him and hastily shuffling herself into a half-sitting position, resting on her elbows.

She could barely catch her breath because the swim back had been so tiring.

Legs apart, Luca stared down at her, thin lipped, eyes narrowed, oozing anger through every pore.

'You suggested I take some time out,' Ellie said weakly. Okay, her eyes had been closed, and she might have dozed off out there, because darkness was rolling in at speed. Her heart was beating hard and fast.

'I didn't suggest you head out on a suicide mission into the open ocean! Do you know *anything* about the currents that can sweep along these shores without warning? Have you any idea how many people get into difficulties because they think that the sea is a safe place just because it's calm? No lifeguard here, Ellie!'

'Well, then.' She sprang to her feet, because lying on the rug just made her feel helpless with Luca towering over her like a skyscraper. 'Good job *you* came along to rescue me, isn't it?'

She was breathing brimstone and fire. This was a side to her that Luca had never seen. Her eyes were flashing, her hands were placed squarely on her hips and she was leaning into him with open aggression.

'Damn well is,' he growled. 'And there's no way you're going to attack me for being worried about your bloody welfare!'

'Well, I'm very grateful! Even though I *wasn't in any difficulty whatsoever*! How would you like me to thank you, Luca?'

'How? Well you can start with this…'

CHAPTER SEVEN

HE KISSED HER. Even when he reached to cup his hand behind the nape of her neck and lowered his head Ellie still wasn't expecting him to *actually kiss her*.

The touch of his mouth against hers was as potent as an electric shock ripping through her body, heating her blood and firing her nervous system into frantic overdrive.

A soft kiss…but only for a second, just long enough to break down all her defences, and she stepped towards him, hands positioned to push him away but instead curving over his warm, naked skin and seeking out his flat, brown nipples.

She was straining up, on tiptoe, and she sighed into his mouth. She'd just been fantasising about this and it felt unreal for the fantasy suddenly to become bone-melting reality.

The teasing delicacy of Luca's kiss changed tempo and he pulled her towards him, tasting her with urgent hunger, tongues meshing, and their damp bodies sticking together, salty and hot.

Ellie's head fell back as he carried on kissing her and she wound her hands around his neck.

He was so impossibly strong and muscled and she

dropped her hands to trace the contours of his corded shoulders.

She was on fire, flames licking through her slender body, tightening her nipples and causing her legs to tremble unsteadily. As if sensing that, he swept her off her feet, without his mouth ever leaving hers, and this time when he rested her on the rug he lay down next to her.

Ellie moaned softly.

The sun was disappearing rapidly and they were bathed in soft twilight.

She squirmed against him, half of her aghast at what she was doing while the other half was sinking into the physical contact like a man deprived of water suddenly led to a flowing stream.

She'd never wanted anyone as badly as she wanted this man. She never wanted to come up for air, and she was so overwhelmed that 'right and wrong' and 'crazy and sensible' were just a jumble of words that made no sense.

Luca flattened her, hand on her hip, and he began stroking her thigh.

Her legs dropped open and he placed his hand over her crotch and gently massaged.

For a few seconds, she couldn't breathe. His touch was firm but he was caressing her in such a leisurely manner she could barely think straight.

She sifted her fingers through his dark, spiky hair and then felt the rough stubble on his chin and arched up to push her small breasts against his chest.

The damp swimsuit was an intolerable barrier, and when his hand drifted away from her crotch to cover her breast she hooked her finger under the strap, wordlessly leading him to do what she was desperate to do.

It was funny but *lust* was a word that had never exerted any curiosity for Ellie. She'd read a million articles about women who flung themselves into bed with some guy because he was irresistible.

Privately, that was a concept she had always held in contempt.

Really! Irresistible? No wonder the world was full of miserable divorced couples! If they were guided by lust, then where was the longevity in that? She'd always reckoned that her mum had married her dad because she'd been carried away by lust, only for reality to insert itself and begin its destructive work once the lust had tapered off.

She could never have imagined being swept off her feet and doing anything that went contrary to good, old-fashioned common sense.

She had watched and seen the way boys hung around Lily with their tongues out and their hormones all over the place. 'Recipe for disaster' was what she could have told them, and sure enoug, they always ended up retreating, wounded.

Even when she had had her one big affair with Paul, yes, Ellie had found him attractive enough, but she hadn't found herself wanting to fling herself at him.

In fact, the whole sexual side of things had been controlled and pleasant and that had suited Ellie fine.

She'd been devastated when he had succumbed to Lily's charms but not particularly surprised when, like all the others, he had fallen by the wayside as soon as her sister had decided it was time to move on.

Lust, Ellie had worked out a long time ago, was for the birds.

Except, caught in the grip of it now, she was finally discovering what all the fuss was about.

Luca's hands on her had the same effect as fire melting wax and her body was molten hot with need. She clung to him shamelessly and, when he eased the straps of her swimsuit down, she shuddered with heated anticipation.

It was dark now on the beach. The calm, glassy water was inky-black and the trees and rocks dark silhouettes against a starless horizon. The breeze was as ineffective when it came to refreshing their bodies as the whirring of a sluggish overhead fan.

But Ellie cooled as the swimsuit exposed the pert, rounded orbs of her breasts, pale in contrast to the rest of her, which had turned pale gold over the past few days in the sun. Against her pale breasts, her nipples were dark-pink circles, enticingly large compared to the size of her breasts.

Luca bent down, took one nipple into his mouth and began to suckle on it. He lathed the tight bud with his tongue and Ellie groaned and wriggled, feverish in her want.

Hand cradling the back of his dark head, eyes squeezed tight and mouth open as she breathed thickly, Ellie pressed him harder against her aching, sensitive breast, desperate for some attention to be paid to the other one.

She shuddered when he did just that, turning his attention to her swollen, pulsing nipple and, at the same time, easing his hand underneath the stretchy swimming costume to feel the slick wetness between her thighs.

'This is what heaven feels like,' Luca broke free to mutter. He meant it. She was so hot, so responsive and so damned sexy. It was as if he had discovered a different person behind the armour of prissy clothes—or had that person always been there? Had he seen the passion lying dormant behind the calm exterior? Surely he had, because she had piqued his sexual interest long before now.

His erection was rock-hard and he had to control his breathing so that he didn't do the unthinkable. One touch from her and he knew that he would come as fast as a randy teenager, and he didn't want to do that. He wanted to take his time even though, at the back of his mind, he knew that they would have to stop. Right now, time was definitely not on their side.

But when?

Luca had no desire to lose the moment.

But the moment was lost when they both heard the distant reedy voice of Jake calling out for Ellie.

There was no way that either Jake or Juanita would take the steps that led down to the cove. They were lit but at this time of the evening it would be a hazardous trip down for a six-year-old and Juanita, despite living close to the sea, was terrified of water.

No matter.

That voice penetrated their cocoon and Ellie pushed Luca away with shaking hands and stumbled to her feet.

'What are you doing?' she cried, and it was such a stupid question that Luca didn't bother responding.

Ellie spun round and began running along the cove, grabbing her stuff en route, heading for the stone steps up to the villa.

Horror was spreading through her with toxic ferocity. How on earth had they ended up doing what they had? What had possessed her? How could she have lost all control like that?

Lust...was the word that sprang into her head, mocking and jeering at her prim, horrified reaction.

She recalled the feel of him in the water when he had

surprised her, the hardness of his body lying next to her and the sensation of his mouth on hers, on her lips...her breasts...her nipples.

She wanted to groan with frustration and despair because this sort of thing just *wasn't her*.

She headed up the steps at speed, half-stumbling as she neared the top to see Jake and Juanita on the lawn outside the front door.

Behind her, Luca was taking his time and not saying anything, and Ellie was more than happy to ignore him.

What sort of conversation could they have? The thought brought her out in a cold sweat.

She threw herself into scooping Jake up and hurrying inside. She knew she was chatting far too much, with high-pitched, feverish intensity, and she knew that it was to distract herself from the horror of remembering what had happened down there on the beach.

To her relief, Luca vanished, probably to bury himself in whatever he had been doing before he'd been rudely interrupted and taken it upon himself to play knight in shining armour.

It gave Ellie time to shower quickly, change and then return to the kitchen where she took up where she had left off with Jake.

'I was scared,' he confided in a small voice.

'And I was silly,' Ellie admitted, giving him a huge cuddle. 'I swam a little too far out, and that was incredibly naughty.'

'But Luca saved you,' Jake piped up in a voice that was full of admiration. 'When I told him I was scared, he told me there was no need to be because he'd make sure you were okay, and you were. He saved you.'

'I'm sure he'd like to think that.' Ellie couldn't help

injecting a touch of sarcasm into her response. 'Although I used to swim a lot when I was your age, right up until I was a big girl.' Which led to a long discussion about sports, hobbies and swimming and allowed her mind way too much freedom to roam and agonise over what she had done.

Ellie knew there was no way she could lay the blame on Luca's shoulders.

He had been dragged away from his work and had been furious at having to rescue her. Yes, he might have instigated that kiss, but she had flung herself wholeheartedly into it and had practically accosted the poor guy.

As if there was any chance that he could actually fancy her! Ellie cringed when she thought about that. He was a man and he had responded the way any man would have when a woman flung herself at him with abandon.

He had probably gone into hiding just in case she wanted a repeat performance.

Juanita had gone, Jake had been settled and Ellie was finishing the salad she had prepared for herself when she looked round to see that Luca had quietly entered the kitchen behind her.

She froze. She desperately wanted to blank him out but instead hungrily took in the lean, muscular lines of his body and remembered the way it had felt pressed up against her, wet, slick and hard.

'What are you doing here?' she questioned tightly.

He'd changed, as she had. Where she had got into some faded jeans and a tee shirt, he was in all black—a black V-necked tee shirt that clung in just the right way and black jeans. And he wasn't wearing any shoes. That seemed disproportionately intimate.

'It's my villa.'

'I... I've just eaten,' she gabbled, backing away as he strolled towards her then swerved to fetch a bottle of water from the fridge. 'I was just on my way up. I...: I... I hope you remembered to say goodnight to Jake! It's a brilliant routine. Have I told you that? He really enjoys that.'

'We need to talk, Ellie.'

'Talk? Talk about what?'

'What do you think?' He raised his eyebrows and shot her a dry look.

He raised the bottle to his lips and began drinking and Ellie frantically asked herself how it was that someone drinking water from a bottle could look so sexy.

It was an effort to tear her eyes away and she had to work hard at channelling her thoughts into some kind of order.

So beautiful, she thought weakly. It wasn't fair! How was she supposed to stand a chance against someone so beautiful? She'd thought she was as tough as nails when it came to making judgement calls on men. She'd always found it easy to scoff at people who were swept away by something as superficial as *looks* because, after all, there was so much more to a person than appearances.

Yet here she was! Scratch the surface and what you found was a guy who had nothing at all in common with her, whose principles contravened everything she believed in, whose arrogance got up her nose...

It angered her so much that none of that seemed to count for anything because she took one look at him and something inside her melted. And then there had been those moments, like when she had seen him stooping down to Jake, slowing down, trying so hard to connect, willing to step out of his comfort zone. Those had been moments when something inside her had opened up, letting him in.

'I don't want to talk about that,' Ellie whispered.

'You want to pretend that none of it ever happened?'

'And none of it would have if you hadn't overreacted! I'm an extremely strong swimmer! I represented the county at one point when I was a teenager!'

'Academic.'

'What does *that* mean?'

'It means that whether you swam in the Olympics makes no difference to the fact that if we hadn't been interrupted we would have ended up making love on that beach.'

The colour drained from Ellie's face and then, just as quickly, rushed back to turn her cheeks beetroot-red.

'We wouldn't.' She turned away to busy herself by the sink. When she felt his hands on her shoulders, her whole body stiffened. For a few panicked seconds she forgot how to breathe. She didn't dare turn around to look at him.

'Why can't you just drop it?' she half-cried under her breath.

'And why do you find it so impossible to talk about it?'

'We would have come to our senses. *I* would have come to my senses. There's no way...'

'I wanted it, Ellie.'

'No! That's crazy!'

'And so did you.'

'Stop putting words into my mouth, Luca! Yes, I admit you're an attractive man, but that doesn't mean that I'm a complete fool!'

'Why don't you look at me when you say that? Or are you afraid to?'

'Afraid?' Ellie burst out laughing but even to her own ears her laughter sounded hollow. He'd thrown down a gauntlet and she turned slowly to look at him.

Luca dropped his hands and stood back.

'I apologise,' she said stiffly.

'For what?'

'For throwing myself at you.'

'I'm a big boy, Ellie. If I hadn't enjoyed it, I wouldn't have ended up lying on that rug with you, with the straps of that swimsuit down, feasting on your breasts.'

Ellie closed her eyes. Her breathing was laboured. She didn't understand why he had to be so provocative, so graphic.

'It was a moment of madness,' she whispered, helpless against the onslaught of wild emotion Luca's words had roused in her. Her body was responding in just the way she didn't want it to; she folded her arms protectively across her breasts and looked at him with deep reluctance.

'I want you,' Luca said flatly. 'I'm not saying it makes sense.' He raked his fingers through his hair, suddenly ill at ease but utterly unable to back away from what he wanted to say. 'I'm not saying that it's something I need. That either of us needs. But since when does everything have to make sense?' In his world, everything *always* made sense, and he was annoyed and frustrated that in this instance he couldn't bring his formidable intellect into play to control a situation that was, as she had said, no more than a moment of madness.

'I work for you, Luca.'

'And I have always kept very distinct lines between business and pleasure.'

He reached out to touch her cheek and felt her shiver under his touch. 'Until now.' He heard the unsteadiness in his voice with some surprise.

She was gazing at him, lips parted, pupils dilated, and she didn't pull away when he lowered his head and oh, so gently covered her mouth with his.

He tasted her.

This wasn't frantic and urgent, as it had been on the beach. This was slow and tender, and she lost herself in the moment, curving her body into his, her softness moulding against his hardness.

Their tongues were entwined and her eyes were closed as he took his time exploring her.

He wasn't rushing. He wasn't touching her anywhere at all and, the less he touched, the more she wanted him to. When he finally pulled back, they stared at one another in silence and he was the first to break it.

'I want to make love to you.'

'I don't understand why.'

'You do something to me. Have done for a while. There's something about you. I want to take you to my bedroom and I want to taste every inch of your body.'

'Luca…'

'Yes or no, Ellie? It's a simple question that needs a one-syllable reply.'

'I've never been the kind of girl who does this sort of thing. We're chalk and cheese…' She thought of the towering blonde mischief-maker who had been his last conquest. Men ran to type. Men who were attracted to towering blondes didn't suddenly find themselves unable to resist small brunettes.

But then again, small brunettes who went for serious, relationship-focused guys with a social conscience didn't suddenly find themselves unable to resist arrogant billionaires who expected the world to obey their commands.

So what was this about, for either of them? Was it because being here, in a place that was so peaceful and so magical, had turned their heads? Had it taken those first stirrings of attraction she had felt for him and magnified them into something irresistible? And was it all about novelty for him? A change being as good as a rest?

He was waiting for her answer. He said it was a simple yes or no but she knew it was far from that.

'Maybe opposites attract,' Luca murmured, because he couldn't think of any other explanation for why he found her so incredibly enticing. 'Yes, Ellie, or no? Say no and this is something that will never rear its head again.'

'Yes.' Apprehension and excitement flared inside her like a blowtorch. She looked at him and cleared her throat. 'Opposites attract. I guess that must be it.'

Luca wasn't sure whether to be flattered that she had agreed with him or disgruntled because it was hardly the level of adoring enthusiasm he was accustomed to from the opposite sex.

He wasn't going to waste time debating the issue.

'My bedroom?'

'This is so crazy…' But her head was so full of him that crazy made sense in a weird kind of way.

Wordlessly they headed for his bedroom. The effect of the silent villa felt like tacit encouragement, egging her on to do something that felt wildly, madly daring. She'd played it safe all her life and especially when it came to men. Living with a beauty queen for a sister, and a mother who wasn't backward when it came to drawing comparisons, Ellie had made a virtue out of never punching above her weight. Sensible choices meant she'd never be let down. Although that hadn't exactly worked with the boyfriend who had leapt for her sister faster than a Jack-in-the-Box, had it?

But still…

Heart racing, she paused as Luca pushed open the door to his bedroom and stepped inside.

Two banks of windows overlooked the sprawling back gardens and the windows were both open so that a cool breeze blew through, rustling the nude-coloured voile drapes. The bed was enormous. Ellie stood still and gazed at it. Was this really what she wanted—a meaningless one-night stand with a guy because she happened to find him irresistible?

Because she knew that, if it wasn't, then this was the time to back away.

'Cold feet?' He switched on the overhead light but then immediately dimmed it so that the room was infused with a mellow, warm glow. He turned to look at her, his beautiful face all shadows and angles.

'No,' she whispered, although she hadn't actually stepped into the room, but was hovering just outside, as though an invisible but impenetrable force field were keeping her out. 'You?'

'I don't get cold feet when it comes to sex.' Luca reached out and linked his fingers through hers, gently guided her into his bedroom and then shut the door behind them.

'Will you promise me one thing?'

'What's that?'

'We don't talk about this in the morning. I mean, we pretend it never happened.'

'We pretend it never happened…?' Luca murmured with low incredulity. Had any woman ever said that to him before? Nope.

'A one-off…' She placed her hands on his chest and stared at her pale fingers then raised her eyes to his. 'I've never done a one-off.'

'Nor have I.'

'Don't tell lies, Luca.' But she smiled and some of the tension left her. Of their own accord her hands were stroking his chest and loving the hardness of his torso under the tee shirt.

She was fascinated by the perfection of his physique. She itched to feel the flatness of his nipples again and to explore lower, to feel the throbbing pulse of him.

'I don't do one-night stands,' he murmured, cupping her rear and inching them both towards the bed. 'I may not do permanence but I don't do one-night stands.'

'So this is a first for both of us…'

'Both virgins when it comes to this, yes.'

Everything she said made sense and was what he should have wanted to hear. It was a complication that could end up a massive headache. She wasn't built like him. She still had ideals and illusions. She still believed in the power of love and all those fairy-tale stories that got people walking up an aisle before everything turned sour and the starry-eyed sweet nothings became high-pitched arguments in a divorce court.

She could get hurt.

'Just don't go falling for me.' He kissed the side of her face, trailed his mouth along her jawline, tasted the sweetness of her lips.

'That would never happen.' Ellie sighed and curved against him.

'That's good. We both know the score. This is an itch that needs to be scratched.' He nuzzled her neck and then broke apart to hook his fingers under his tee shirt, stripping it off in one easy movement.

He guided her hand to his erection, which was a prominent bulge under his jeans, and she gasped.

'My turn now,' he murmured into her ear, and he undid the button of her jeans and pulled down the zip, then worked his way into her panties until he found her sweet spot, the throbbing nub of her clitoris. 'Now touch me.' He groaned unsteadily as he slid his finger along and into her.

Ellie unzipped his trousers. She felt clumsy and gauche, and then nearly passed out when she actually touched him. He was huge, his shaft rigid and thick.

Touching one another without taking it any further was making her head swim. She was so wet between her thighs that she just couldn't keep still.

He broke from her but his eyes never left hers as he stripped off the rest of his clothes and then stood in unashamed glory in front of her. So lean, so beautiful, his physique perfect in every way. He let his hand rest loosely on his erection and smiled crookedly when she found she couldn't tear her eyes away from the sight.

'Your turn,' he commanded, watching.

Lack of experience showed in her first nervous fumblings, but when she looked at him the flare of desire was so apparent in his dark, intense gaze that her inhibitions were discarded along with her clothes.

She'd never thought of herself as desirable before and

that look in his eyes made her heady with feminine satisfaction.

It seemed hard to believe that this drop-dead gorgeous guy wanted her but he did. It was there in the flare of his nostrils and the burning darkness of his eyes.

In the grip of lust, Ellie was realising that there was so much more than love when it came to relationships.

There was...*this*. Wonderful, incredible, short-lived, like a firecracker burning bright until it was extinguished in a poof.

Somehow they made it to the bed. Her breathing was staccato-ragged.

He straddled her, and Ellie wriggled up to lick his thick, pulsing manhood, then he shifted and lowered himself to kiss her.

With a groan, she pulled him closer. He couldn't get close enough. She wanted to feel his body against hers, his heartbeat in tune with hers, his breathing warm against her skin.

Their lips met and she arched up to him, one hand behind his head, the other in a closed fist under the small of her back so that she was pressed against him.

Tongues meshed. Her groans merged with his. When he finally reared up, she wanted to do nothing more than yank him back again so that they could carry on kissing.

She had never dreamt that the physical demands of her body could be as powerful as this.

He pushed her gently on her shoulders and she tilted back, her small, pointy breasts a succulent feast waiting to be enjoyed.

She gasped as his mouth circled a breast, sucking deeply as his tongue teased the rigid peak. She couldn't contain her mounting excitement and she shifted her hips from side to side, and up and down, desperate and greedy for him in a way she would never have dreamt possible.

She was barely aware of panting his name or begging him to *hurry up because she couldn't take it any longer*.

She was breathing fast, and even faster when that devastating mouth finally left her breasts to trail a path down her flat stomach, pausing only to circle her belly button.

Luca parted her legs and with expert fingers stroked through her wet folds to tease her clitoris until her pants became hitched cries of pleasure.

Then he dipped down to taste her with the tip of his tongue, a gentle, delicate exploration that made her whole body stiffen in urgent response.

She curled her fingers into his dark hair, pressing him lower even as she opened her legs wider. She felt the waves of her climax begin to build, stiffening her body, and then, with explosive force, she spasmed against his questing mouth, bucking just as he'd said he wanted her to do.

She'd become a slave to her body. She'd reached heights that made her cry out in a voice she didn't recognise. She had no time to apologise for her premature climax, because surely it would have left him frustrated? She came down from her high and slowly he began to build her back up with expert finesse.

He knew just where to touch and how so that her sensitised body was once again roused.

When he sank into her, thrusting hard and deep, she was taken to whole new heights of pleasure, soaring and cresting, higher and higher as he plunged harder inside her, filling every ounce of her body.

Her climax this time was so powerful that it swept her away, and she cried out, jerking and arching as he angled his hips and his shaft in just the right way to take her soaring.

She felt him come, felt him stiffen on one final thrust, and then she was sated and so satisfied that what she wanted to do most was fall into a deep sleep.

Luca rolled off her, disposing of the condom she'd hardly noticed him donning, but then he immediately turned and pulled her close against him so that their naked bodies were pressed against one another.

'I should go,' Ellie said drowsily, although she didn't want to.

'I've decided to renege on my promise,' Luca responded without a hint of shame.

'What do you mean?'

'I still want you and I have no intention of waking up in the morning and pretending that nothing happened between us. A lot has happened between us, and one night isn't going to be enough for me. So, if you want to play the pretend game, then you're on your own.'

'But you promised!' Ellie said with consternation.

Luca shrugged. He circled his finger over a rosy nipple that was peeking out above the cover.

'Promises get broken. This one has.' He fastened his dark eyes on her. 'Are you going to tell me that one night will be enough for you? Because, if you do, then I'll say now that I won't believe a word of it. We're here and I don't intend to watch you from a distance and kid myself that I don't want to touch you.'

'We're not children, Luca! We're grown up enough to know that you don't always get what you want!'

'That's right. We're not children, we're adults, and we still want one another and we can have one another. Ten more days and then we return to London and this thing between us...this virus...gone. It's as easy as that...'

Luca was in no doubt that he would be more than ready to conclude things by then anyway. He bored easily and, though she might be stimulating now, in a fortnight that allure would have worn off, and it would certainly disappear under the weight of reality that would be waiting there for him. Besides, whatever ground rules had been agreed, he was still uneasy at the thought that she might start looking for more than was on the table.

'It's not as easy as that, Luca.' Her brain was refusing to function. It really wasn't as easy as that. Was it?

'Oh,' he murmured silkily, 'but it is. Trust me...'

CHAPTER EIGHT

LUCA LOOKED ACROSS the width of the infinity pool to where Ellie was teaching Jake some swimming tricks of the trade. She swam like a fish. She could have rescued *him* if he'd been in trouble in deep water as efficiently as he had thought he'd been rescuing *her* a week ago when he'd spotted her on the distant horizon.

Now that he was looking at her, he decided that it beat reading the *Financial Times* on his tablet. She was so graceful, so slight, so supple when she moved, and she had a laugh that could light up a room. From behind his dark designer sunglasses, reclining on the lounger in the shade, Luca indulged in thinking about all the things he found strangely attractive about her, from the way she looked to the way she smelled and definitely the way she responded to him when he touched her. She was a firecracker between the sheets.

He was guessing that this was what a lot of people might call paradise. Overhead, the sky was a milky blue with just a few wispy clouds here and there to interrupt the perfect turquoise expanse.

The sun was beating down. At a little after five, it no longer bore the fiery intensity of the midday sun, but it was still warm enough for them all to be out here fooling around in the swimming pool.

Luca hadn't been to this particular property for some time and the last time he *had* been, with a handful of high-achieving employees being rewarded for their hard work on a particularly fruitful deal, he had spent the majority of the long weekend working, signing off on yet another deal, barely venturing outside except to a couple of highly rated local restaurants. He hadn't been tempted by the swimming pool and, indeed, he had barely spared any time actually to appreciate his surroundings.

He was appreciating them now. Maybe it was because, for the past week, he had seen them through Ellie's eyes, and viewing his possessions through other people's eyes was not something he spent a lot of time doing.

He had always been indifferent to the fact that women found his wealth impressive. It came with the territory.

With Ellie it was…different. She was impressed, but fundamentally she didn't attach a huge amount of importance to money, and she certainly didn't have pound signs in her eyes at his displays of wealth. She teased him about how much he owned and told him that he was too rich for his own good. She was insistent that she do her bit around the villa, always tidying up behind Jake, even though the hired help descended every morning, paid to do that. He didn't get it but he had to give her credit. She took absolutely nothing for granted and was at pains to explain to him that, when you grew up with not very much, you learned to appreciate everything you had.

When pressed, she admitted that, yes, some people reacted by realising the importance of all those things that money couldn't buy while others reacted by doing their utmost to get rich, whatever the cost.

Luca, in this roundabout manner, had found out about her sister and had formed a picture in his head of a woman who was very different from Ellie.

And of course, on rote, she reminded him how grateful she was for the way he had rescued her father.

'Which makes me think,' he had drawled as they had lain entwined in the sheets after a particularly energetic bout of love-making, 'that filthy lucre does, actually, have its uses.'

'Yes,' Ellie had said, 'it has purchase power. I can't deny that, but there's a lot more out there that can't be bought and, when you sell your soul for it, you lose sight of all those other things.'

'Very philosophical.' But Luca wasn't buying any of that because he'd seen too much avarice in his lifetime, and way too many women who would have sold their souls to the devils a thousand times over for money, but he was tickled pink at her sincerity.

'I have no idea how we got where we have.' She'd shaken her head in wonderment. 'Our perspectives on life are polar opposite.'

Luca didn't know, himself, how things had got to where they were between them.

The one-night-stand plan had been kicked to the kerb on night one, and their original intention to keep their liaison within the four walls of the bedroom had quite quickly got lost when he had absently held her hand in front of Jake.

Was that when, subtly, the relationship with his godson had changed? Had that been the turning point when Jake had begun to trust him? Yes, he had been making headway before, but things had definitely taken an up-turn at that point.

Luca guessed that this was as good as it got when it came to playing happy families.

It wasn't about love and it wasn't about selling your soul to someone else safe in the knowledge that sooner or later you were going to get hurt. Those were options he had shut the door on, and that was a door he would never thinking of opening, but yes…there was something to be said about this arrangement.

He gazed idly at his phone then re-read the text he had received from his PA, who knew how to handle the press with the dexterity of a magician, and whose contacts within those dubious circles had always been invaluable.

The salacious rumours started by his ex were about to go up a notch. It was becoming a headache. Being linked with a woman in a six-inch column in a tabloid was one thing. Taking the rumour that step further was something else.

Across the pool, Ellie was laughing at something Jake had said. She had a wonderful, engaging laugh, and for a few seconds, eyes concealed behind sunglasses, Luca watched her thoughtfully.

He thought that sometimes life had a funny way of dealing hands that looked unfortunate until you sat back and worked out how to play with them.

Under normal circumstances, he shouldn't have been here, but here he was.

If life had carried on as it had been, he would have been working and Jake would, in due course, probably have ended up in therapy because of him. Who knew? He might have suffered an even worse fate. Drugs…drink…

There was a world of temptation out there for kids who had been screwed over by life.

But this turnaround... Well, he couldn't have asked for better.

Luca stood up, glanced at his watch and strolled down to where the pair of them were recovering on the semi-circular marble steps in the warm, shallow end of the pool, exhausted after frolicking in the water.

Ellie shielded her eyes and watched as he approached.

Her heart flipped in her chest and her mouth went dry, her nipples pinched into tight buds, and every pore in her body responded in ways that were all too familiar now.

She didn't think she would ever tire of watching him, of listening to him, of the way he touched her, the way he made her body come alive.

For as long as was humanly possible, Ellie had kidded herself that the way he made her feel was down to lust. He was irresistible. She was too inexperienced to ward off the potent effect he had on her. She had capitulated and fallen into bed with him because her body had refused to listen to common sense, but the nature of lust was that it didn't last. She wouldn't be the first and she wouldn't be the last. Blah, blah, blah.

She didn't know when she wised up to the truth that what she felt for him—and it was a feeling that seemed to grow ever stronger by the second—left lust standing in the shade.

Unguarded, protected by all those common-sense check lists she had always had when it came to the opposite sex, or so she'd thought, she hadn't been prepared for her heart to be ambushed by the very sort of guy she should have been equipped to walk away from. She'd been side-swiped by his arrogance, his self-assurance, that way he had of always assuming that he was the leader and the duty of everyone else was to follow and obey.

She had barely really noticed when the little things had started piling up. The way he laughed. The occasional look of searing vulnerability she had seen when he looked at Jake, when he thought no one was observing him. His quick wit and the way he balanced his outrageous arrogance with magnificent generosity. He was a contradiction and he had sucked her in until it was hard to think of a time before him.

Where she had always imagined that love would be something that grew, after months of watering and nurturing, she had discovered, to her dismay, that it was something that just appeared from nowhere like a weed, with the power to smash her foundations to smithereens, and there was nothing she could do about it.

Except enjoy him while she could.

The end of their allotted time out was a heartbeat away and she intended to lose herself in loving him and then face the consequences when it was all over and she returned to normality.

She took great care in making sure he didn't suspect a thing, because she had her pride, and she couldn't bear the thought of him laughing at her, or looking at her with pity from the depths of those dark, fabulous eyes.

'Are you coming in?' she asked lightly now. She was already moist between her legs at the unconscious hunger in his gaze as he stared down at her.

She had brought her one and only black one-piece swimsuit, something she wore to the public swimming baths near her in London, because her other two were at the family house. It was so modest that she could have gone and done her weekly supermarket shop in it and no one would have batted an eye but, when Luca looked at her in it, it was as though she was the most stunning lingerie model on the planet.

Nothing could have made her feel more wonderful and more at home with herself and her body than that fierce gaze of unhidden approval and appreciation.

She'd discovered that it was like a drug and she knew that she was guilty of feeding off it, hungrily taking it in, because pretty soon it would no longer be available.

'Tempting,' Luca drawled. His dark eyes followed Jake who was splashing around with a toy Juanita had bought for him the day before. He turned his gaze to Ellie. 'Will you make it worth my while later if I do?'

Ellie blushed. 'Is sex all you ever think about?' she asked in a low voice as he settled on the stair next to her, leaning back and closing his eyes.

'No, work takes priority, but there's not a lot in it.'

'We should go in.' She stood up and called to Jake, then went to towel herself dry. Sex, sex, sex. It really was all Luca thought about. On every other level he was so complex and three-dimensional but, when it came to relationships, he was as shallow as a puddle.

'Just a minute, Ellie.' Luca held her arm, staying her, and when their eyes met his were so serious that she felt a shiver of panic ripple through her. 'Juanita's there. She can play with Jake for a couple of minutes, and I've arranged for her to babysit this evening.'

'Oh, okay.' His words were unthreatening but her panic levels were up all the same. 'I guess you want to discuss progress with Jake. I'm sorry. It's been far too easy to lose track of the fact that this isn't a joy-ride for me.'

'Stop.'

'Stop what?'

'Apologising for things you should never feel obliged to apologise for. We don't need to have formal discussions about Jake any more. We're lovers. Interviewing you across a desk is no longer relevant. I think we've gone past that point, don't you? But…there *are* other matters I need to talk to you about.'

'What other matters?'

'This isn't the right place. We need to talk and what I have to say will require a certain amount of privacy, hence the reason why I've arranged for Juanita to stay on. I'm going to book us into one of the local restaurants I recall as having excellent food, as well as a certain amount of privacy.'

Ellie felt the surge of tears prick the backs of her eyes because she knew what this talk was going to be about. She was about to get the 'Dear John' speech and icy fear settled in her heart. She looked away quickly but, when she next spoke, her voice was light, in keeping with the no-strings-attached, sex-only non-relationship they were supposed to be having.

'I know…' She shrugged and stared off into the distance. '"The time draweth near". We're going to have to wrap this up and actually start putting our heads together about finding a replacement for me. I've got a good idea of the sort of girl Jake would take to, and I don't think there's going to be any problems with adjustment.'

'Save the bracing words of encouragement, Ellie. Like I said, we need to talk, and a rushed conversation here isn't appropriate.' When he glanced down, he was treated to the sight of her cleavage, and the small bumps where her breasts were outlined by the fine fabric of her swimsuit.

He veered his eyes away from the delectable sight and breathed in deeply.

'I've got work to do. I wish I hadn't, but you're right. The time is drawing near and the rabble in London are getting tetchy.' He stood up. 'I'll swing by when Jake's in bed to tell him goodnight and then I'll meet you in the hallway.'

'Sure.' She followed suit, moving to fetch her towel from the lounger, along with all the other stuff that followed her out whenever she came to the pool. Sun cream, sunglasses, her sarong, her e-reader, her phone and an assortment of puzzle books she never got round to doing but always felt she might.

Luca veered off ahead of her to his office and she called out to Jake, but this time not even his six-year-old chatter could distract her.

It was the first restaurant they'd been to together since they had arrived at the villa and it felt odd to dress up when most of her time had been spent in shorts and tee shirts with flip-flops. She wondered whether his taste for shorts and tee shirts with flip-flops had reached the end of its natural cycle.

For the first time Ellie was nervous, and she wished that he could just text her the bad news, give her some advance warning so that she could get her facial muscles to behave and not let her down. Her stupid facial muscles were always letting her down when she was around him and she didn't want to give him any sign that there was anything amiss about calling it a day.

She'd brought a couple of summer dresses and, like

Cinderella stripped of the fancy ball gown, she looked at her reflection critically. Yes, she'd got a good colour out here in the sun, and, sure, her short hair was now streaked with auburn and gold, but aside from that… Now that she knew what this dinner was all about, now that her walking papers were about to be handed over, the ridiculous self-confidence he had inspired in her was seeping away like water down a plug hole. She was back to being who she really was. Just an ordinary woman whose moment in the spotlight was over.

Luca was waiting for her and she plastered a bright smile on her lips.

'I'm not late, am I?' She chatted as she slipped on the shoes she had carried from her room, dangling them on one finger. She didn't look at him but she was ultra-aware of him standing within touching distance of her.

He was coolly, elegantly sophisticated in a white linen shirt and a pair of dark jeans and loafers. The ultimate dream man, the stuff that women's fantasies were made of. She would have to work hard at making sure not to use him as a benchmark when it came to future relationships because, if she did, then she was going to be in for a rough ride.

'How was Jake when you went in to see him?' She settled on something impersonal as they headed out to the rugged four-wheel drive he had rented for the duration of their stay.

'Jake was…' Luca turned to her once they were in the car, before switching on the engine. 'Unrecognisable as the sullen little boy who first walked through the front door of my house seven months ago, but then you know how far I've come with him.' He smiled and slid his gaze across to her. 'Two days ago you gave me a gold star for progress.'

Ellie blushed when she remembered how he had demanded she reward him for that particular gold star. She also remembered telling him that he should aim for several a day because she quite liked the reward schedule he had in mind.

Bad time for that kind of memory. She decided to bring it down to business. It was what Luca understood best. Business and sex, and there was no way she was going to talk about sex. Or even remind him of what they had shared. She'd seen the way he had dealt with the ex who had ended up with her walking papers. She'd seen the annoyed impatience on his face because, once he'd dispatched a woman, the last thing he wanted was to have to go through the bother of working to disentangle her from clinging to his neck.

'Let's put the business chat on the back burner for the moment,' Luca drawled after she'd made a few fruitless attempts to discuss the qualities a replacement nanny might need. 'Talk to me about something else.'

'Like what?'

'Surprise me. I want some soothing conversation. I don't want to exercise my brain just yet with an in-depth discussion about what a successful nanny needs to be.'

'Well…what's the restaurant like? I… I hope I'm dressed okay. I haven't been abroad very much. Well, I can't tell you the last time, to be honest, but I always think that in hot countries the dress code is casual, even if the restaurant is fancy.' At this rate, Ellie thought desperately, she was going to exhaust her repertoire of nervous, pointless small talk before they made it to the restaurant.

For a few awkward minutes, Luca didn't respond, and

when he did it was to say, pensively, 'I had an interesting message from my PA.'

'Yes...?' Ellie shot him a confused look from under her lashes.

'My expectations that gossip about our so-called relationship would die a convenient death over the two weeks we were here seem to have been misplaced.'

'I don't understand what you're saying.' Ellie frowned because, in truth, she'd barely given a second thought to the silly rumours that had hastened their departure from London. She'd spoken to her dad when she'd first arrived. Her sister had been frantic with curiosity and Ellie had taken to dodging the calls and ignoring the text messages.

She was living in a bubble and there was no way she was going to let Lily burst it.

'My feeling is that Heidi had hoped for a more dramatic response from me when she spoke to the press. Anger, retaliation, a dialogue. Anything but silence. So she decided that leaving well alone wasn't going to do.' He looked at her and grimaced. 'There's nothing more dangerous than a woman scorned.' His voice had cooled. 'Especially one who clearly had a great deal more ambition when it came to our relationship than I ever had. Or, for that matter, ever hinted at. But we can talk about that over dinner.'

They'd arrived at the charming restaurant, white-fronted and cluttered with clambering, colourful flowers. The courtyard at the front was half-filled with high-end cars and she could see diners inside, outlined in mellow lighting. Inside, there were sofas, rustic wooden tables, little honeycomb-shaped private areas and so many plants that the oxygen levels must have been through the roof.

However, Ellie was too tense by this point to take it all in.

'What's going on?' she asked urgently, as soon as drinks orders were taken, menus inspected and decisions made about food.

'Hear me out without interruption.' Luca leaned towards her, elbows on the table, his lean, beautiful face unsmiling. 'The rumour about us has gathered pace and, on hearsay alone, the paparazzi will be printing a piece about our secret engagement. My PA has only managed to unearth this gem because she has some contacts with the tabloid press—a consequence, I'm afraid, of working for me. Naturally, she has neither denied nor confirmed the rumour. She thought it best to get in touch with me immediately.'

'Engagement? Secret?' Ellie blanched.

'The last thing I intended to do was to give credence to my ex's ridiculous rumours, because there would be nothing that would please her more than to think that she'd managed to throw my life out of joint.'

'You should have denied all that rubbish from the start!'

'I don't do conversations with hacks.'

'This isn't just about you, Luca!'

'There's no point crying over spilt milk.'

'Well, you're going to have to say something now. You're going to have to tell them that they've got it all wrong.' She thought about her friends who had been texting, and Lily who hadn't *stopped* texting.

'And naturally I will.' Luca sat back, sipped some wine and gazed thoughtfully at her over the rim of his glass. 'Although…'

'There's no *although* about it, Luca!' Ellie exclaimed

in dismay. Running through her head were the horrible and embarrassing ramifications of an article printed about an engagement that didn't exist. Luca might be able to ignore the gossip, because he didn't care what anyone thought about him, but *she* wouldn't. She would have to be the one to face inquisitive reporters and tell them that it was all a load of nonsense. She'd managed to laugh off the original article as malicious nonsense, and no one had questioned it because they all knew her, knew the sort of person she was. But *an engagement*?

'This is awful.'

'It's true that it's an unexpected development and yet… it's made me think.'

'Think about *what*?'

'Strangely enough, marriage. Not something I've wasted much time on.' He swirled his glass of wine, swallowed some and looked at her thoughtfully. 'My father never loved anyone but my mother and, when she died, so did he—or so did the better part of him, but you know that. However, he was a rich widower, and there was no shortage of gold-diggers trying their luck. They would have sold their mothers for a slice of his fortune. From every angle, love and marriage have never come out tops when put under the microscope. But…'

'But?'

'But although I don't do love…' he absently reached for her hand and played with her slender fingers '…and hence never considered marriage because the two seem to go together, I'm beginning to think that there can be another aspect to a very successful union. The situation in which we now find ourselves has opened up that possibility to me.'

'I have no idea what you're talking about. I *know* you don't do love so *what* situation and *what* possibility?'

'The second you entered Jake's life, things began to change. It was almost as though fate had decided that the wheels had to start going in a different direction. He met you and he immediately responded to you and you've brought out a side to him that I don't think anyone else would have been able to.'

'Thank you very much.' *She* did love, and it was just her bad luck and rubbish judgement call that had landed her where she was. Loving a guy who *didn't do love*.

'And things have only got better since we've been over here. I've talked more to him than I have done in the six months before and, if you don't think that we have extensive conversations now, then you're getting the picture when it comes to how little communication there was between us before.'

She opened her mouth to say something and he raised one hand to stop her.

'Hear me out, Ellie. Someone coming in to replace you isn't going to work in the way I originally thought it might. What Jake has with us, what this little holiday has made me see, is that we're family for him. The two of us. Not exactly the traditional family but one that seems to be working for him.' He raised his eyebrows. 'When it comes to traditional families, who's to say that they're any better than the non-traditional ones? So now it seems that, in the absence of denial, we're engaged. And why not?'

'I beg your pardon?'

'If the world thinks we're engaged, then who are we to tell them they're mistaken?'

'But we're not engaged.'

'Every word I say will probably jar with you, but I'm proposing that we continue our relationship, because it works, and not just for us, but for Jake.'

'Continue our relationship?'

'I'm asking you to marry me. For me, it's something that makes sense, and what I bring to the table would be considerable.'

Ellie's mouth dropped open. She wondered whether she had misheard him or maybe misinterpreted what he had just said. Or maybe that snazzy little fish starter she'd just eaten had contained some hallucinogens.

'You would never want for anything in your life again. You would have security and stability, and let's not forget the sex.'

'You're asking me to *marry you*? Because Jake's happy and because you and I rub along okay and have a good time between the sheets?'

'Doubtless, it's not exactly the romantic dream you've been harbouring…'

'No, it's definitely not that.'

She had a load more to say on the subject but she was side-swiped by the thought of her parents' marriage. That had started out as the romantic dream. It had descended into bitterness and resentment when the romantic dream had turned sour and her mother had realised that the middle manager she had married was never going to become anything more than a middle manager. A good man who would have done anything for her but who wasn't enough. She thought of her own upbringing. The way she had been casually side-lined by her vain and shallow mother, the way the relationship with her sister had suffered for that. She had had the traditional upbringing but it certainly hadn't been an entirely positive one.

'It's a crazy idea!' She robustly pushed that interrupting thought aside.

'Why? Because I'm not your ideal man?'

'And I'm not *your* ideal woman! You're in a different place to me, Luca. You see marriage as a business proposition with plus and minus columns that should all tally up to determine whether it's successful or not.'

She thought of Jake. Okay, so maybe he'd been lulled into a false sense of security, and okay, yes, maybe she and Luca had been remiss in being openly demonstrative in front of him, but she wasn't going to be steamrollered by Luca into thinking that the natural outcome of that was a walk up the aisle because Jake was in need of a family unit.

She could feel a tension headache coming on.

'There's no such thing as an ideal soul-mate, Ellie. We could make this work.'

'You don't love me.' *But could he learn to?* That possibility crept into her head like a thief in the night, and she shivered. 'And what happens when someone comes along to capture your interest? One of those women you've always been attracted to? Where would that leave this so-called business arrangement?'

'We could let this rumour stand and see how it plays out.' He sat back and watched her with a keen gaze. 'But when it comes to someone else coming along? You turn me on and I like you. Why would I want to look anywhere else?'

Ellie could think of a hundred reasons, starting and finishing with six-foot blondes with long, tanned limbs and big hair. He could talk the talk here, where there was no temptation, but what about when temptation *did* appear? What then?

'Don't dig deep to find faults with my idea,' he counselled levelly. 'Let's finish dinner, talk about anything
but relationships and you can sleep on it.' He lowered
his midnight-dark eyes then raised them slowly to look
at her with frank appraisal. 'You can tell me what you
really think when you're warm and drowsy after we've
made love.'

CHAPTER NINE

WITH THE DEXTERITY of a magician, Luca had spared no effort in pulling out all the stops to persuade her to his way of thinking.

He knew that she had her theories about soul-mates and the flowery promises of romance. He knew that his sensible suggestion for a union based on practicality was not high up there on her wish list... But there was this amazing chemistry between them and, however much she might waffle on about the importance of love, he knew that she had been sucker-punched by the power of their mutual physical attraction. She hadn't seen it coming.

She had never thought to work *that* into her long-term happy-ever-after plans.

And then there was Jake. He had watched them together and had seen the affection in her eyes when she looked at the boy. Would she be able to walk away from her little charge with the suspicion that she might take with her all the good work she had achieved?

From the heights of his cynicism, Luca knew that what he wanted was selfish. She was the glue between him and Jake. How successful would the happy family scenario be if a critical component of it went missing in action? He'd come far, but had he come far enough?

That aside, she was also a woman who appealed to him on many levels. The sex was stupendous but he could also appreciate her easy wit and the way she never deferred to him. Without the hindrance of wanting more than was possible, it would be a match that stood a better chance of working than any rush down the aisle between two starry-eyed people.

With the sharply honed instincts of a born predator, a man who always got what he wanted, Luca knew that making love was the way to get to her. He saw no down sides to using that ploy because to him it made perfect sense and bolstered his argument.

What he was proposing transcended the coldness of logic because it was infused with the passion of lust.

His fingers were linked through hers and he urged her up the stairs, stopping on every other stair to touch her. Action always spoke louder than words and he planned to put a lot of his persuasive powers into action.

Once in the bedroom, he kicked the door shut with the heel of his foot and propelled her towards his bed, stripping her off as they made progress across the floor until she was practically naked, with the dress pulled down and dropping to the floor as she shuffled backwards.

'Luca…' Did he think she couldn't see through his ploy?

'Shh…' He placed a finger over her mouth and then replaced the finger with his lips, kissing her without letting her surface for air.

He was doing what he did best. Pesky conversations could always be put to rest between the sheets, but this was bigger than a pesky conversation.

Ellie knew that there was still a lot more to say, but

when he was touching her like this, kissing her sense-less, rubbing his hands over her breasts, skimming them across her stomach, touching her between her legs…she lost the ability to think and turned into a mindless rag doll.

She fell back onto the mattress, arms spread wide, and watched with the usual level of shameless fascination as he stripped off in a hurry.

She could spend a lifetime doing this, she thought ab-stractedly, if she married him. They could give Jake the sort of stable home he would thrive in. *If* she married him. She'd be able to touch him whenever she wanted. *If* she married him.

But…but…but…

The agonising battery of questions tried to press onto her consciousness, but she didn't want to think of any of that, so she pushed them away and concentrated on the luxury of watching him stand for a few taut moments in front of her at the side of the bed, naked and unasham-edly aroused.

She propped herself up, then knelt and took him into her mouth. He had been a masterful tutor and she an en-thusiastic pupil, and she put all his lessons to use now as she licked and sucked him, feeling the rough ridges of his shaft, knowing just how to tease him until he was on the verge of losing control.

He juddered and urgently tugged her away from him, but then held her still for a few seconds while he re-grouped his self-control.

The sex was fast and furious, a tangling of bodies as they met their needs, pleasuring one another in ways that were so finely tuned that neither could put a finger on why, really, they seemed physically to meet with such ease and freedom.

Afterwards, spent, they lay back and eventually Luca turned to her, propping himself up on his side. He pulled down the sheet which she had hoiked up to cover herself because, to his amusement, she was always strangely prudish in the wake of their love-making; he traced a line over her collarbone with his finger.

'I won't lie to you, *querida*, my proposal is something that works for me. I don't do love and empty promises, but you add something to my life, and you add something to Jake's. Like I said, I never gave house room to thoughts of marriage, but this is an arrangement that has an excellent chance of success. It would certainly put paid to the nuisance of having to return to London and start pouring water on all the engagement rumour fires stoked up by my vindictive ex.'

Ellie knew that this level of honesty was commendable. He wasn't wrapping things up with pretty paper and ribbons and trying to pretend that what was in the box was more than it actually was. He was being truthful when he said that rumours of a phoney engagement had made him consider the advantages of a union that was actually for real. Jake would have a family. Luca would not have the bother of explaining himself to nosy reporters. As a bonus, he would have the satisfaction of knowing that whatever his ex had hoped to gain by stirring false rumours would be scuppered. And if he changed his mind? Well, it wasn't as though there was a wedding ring on her finger, was it?

'It all sounds very selfish, Luca.'

'Jake wouldn't agree.'

'So Jake wins and you win...and what about me?'

'You really think that love is a guarantee of happiness?'

'That's not the point, is it?'

'Well, Ellie, I think it is. We go into this with our eyes wide open. We respect one another. We get along. You'll have financial security for the rest of your life but, if you want to continue working, then that would be fine by me. I'm not a dinosaur who expects his woman to stay at home. Added bonus…the sex is great.'

'And what about when the sex isn't great any longer? Your track record doesn't exactly promise longevity on that front, does it?'

'You've broken the track record already. I'm not even beginning to be bored by you.'

'Because we've known one another for five minutes!'

Luca looked at her seriously. 'I've spent more undiluted time with you than I've ever spent with any woman in my entire life.'

Ellie hated the way hope had taken root and was making inroads. Hope that that meant something. Hope that he could come to love her. Hope that she could become indispensable. Things like that happened, didn't they?

'No girl dreams of a marriage proposal in the form of a business deal.'

'I don't get into bed with anyone I've ever done business with.'

'You know what I mean.'

'I can't force your hand, Ellie.'

'So if I say no, you wouldn't care one way or another?'

'I've found that life goes on, whatever disappointments crop up along the way. There's not much I've ever found I can't handle.'

'Because you've had to handle quite a lot from a young age…'

'Playing the therapist on me?' He wasn't nettled because he was enjoying looking at her. She was here, in his bed, flushed from love-making. This wasn't a woman who was going to turn him down flat.

'You're asking me to get engaged to you, and yet we don't even know one another.'

Luca burst out laughing, then manoeuvred himself so that she was resting in the crook of his arm. He played with her breast and brushed her hair with his lips.

'I think you'd be surprised at how much we know one another.'

'I'm not talking about sex.'

'Good,' Luca purred, stirring back into heavy arousal at the sight of her pink, pouting nipple. 'Because right now, there's too much talking going on. I'm happy to talk, Ellie, but only if the conversation is of the dirty variety. And don't tell me you don't want it. You know it turns you on when I tell you just what I want to do to your body…'

She opened her mouth and he shifted so that he was straddling her. He lightly ruffled the soft down between her legs and, while her body was busying itself trying not to succumb to what he was doing, he lowered himself, edging down to lick gently between her legs.

He teased the swollen bud of her clitoris until she was shifting with urgent little mewls of pleasure. He pressed his finger into her until she squirmed. He parted her thighs and hoisted her so that her legs were wrapped around him, allowing him to explore her wetness without hindrance.

He touched her everywhere until there were no more words and no more questions.

If she had doubts about his proposal, then this was as effective a way of showing her what, exactly, would be on the table.

Ellie wondered whether the proposal and her ambivalent response would affect their relationship but the following morning nothing was mentioned and there was no coolness from him.

Had he forgotten about it or just shrugged off her negative response as *'one of those things, you win some you lose some'*?

She didn't bring it up and nor did he. Luca wasn't accustomed to obstacles and either he had decided to jettison the idea because he'd hit a bump in the road, or else he was playing a waiting game.

Either way, Ellie wasn't going to be put on the back foot by bringing it up.

Nerves all over the place, she could barely focus on the day trip to a secluded bay that Luca took them on on a small motor boat he kept. It was a billionaire's plaything that was small, compact and kitted out to an eye wateringly high standard. The fabulous picnic which had been prepared for them tasted like cardboard to Ellie. She swam and did a little nature tour with Jake, and she knew that she said all the right things and held his interest for the full forty-five minutes as they walked and looked at stones, plants and rock pools, but she was so keenly aware of Luca, there right alongside her. So sexy, so tempting…so *suddenly attainable*…

It was a relief when seven o'clock rolled round and Jake was settled in bed. For the first time, when Ellie asked whether he wanted Luca to read him a story, he shrugged and said, 'Okay, I guess so.'

Major headway. Prompted by the security of the family unit he thought he now had…?

Luca was waiting in the kitchen when she entered at a little after seven-thirty, his back to her as he stared out of the window. But, before she could say a word, she felt the buzz of her mobile phone in her jeans pocket and she absentmindedly pulled it out as she headed into the kitchen, moving towards Luca.

'Lily!' For a few seconds, Ellie was so disorientated that she couldn't quite match the sound of the voice on the end of her phone to the sister whose nosy text messages she had been studiously ignoring. 'Is Dad okay?' A feeling of nausea crept into the pit of her stomach. She'd been living in a bubble. The sound of Lily's voice was the pin that had been stuck into that bubble, bursting it immediately. It was the harsh sound of reality and it made Ellie feel suddenly sick.

'You haven't been answering any of my texts!'

'Sorry, Lily. I'm back in a few days and I thought I'd… er…wait and, you know, talk to you face to face.'

'I've looked this guy up online and he's loaded, Ellie! Plus he looks like a rock star. So what the hell is he doing getting engaged to you?'

'Thanks very much!' Ellie bit down the temptation to press the disconnect button on her phone. She knew her sister so well. Lily wasn't about to congratulate her on landing a great catch. Lily was thinking ahead, working out how much more suitable a guy like Luca would be for *her*…

'You know what I mean. Remember boring Paul Jenna?'

'I try not to, Lily,' Ellie said through gritted teeth.

'Dad says you told him that it's just a load of nonsense. Is it?'

'Let's not talk about me.' She glanced at Luca who was shamelessly earwigging into the conversation and staring at her with undisguised interest. 'Let's talk about you.' Usually this was guaranteed to get Lily off the thorny subject of Luca. 'Tell me what you've been up to in America. Lots of important…er…exciting jobs and offers?'

'Have you slept with him?'

'Lily!'

'Okay. Out of order. Sorry.'

'How are you enjoying being back in the UK?'

'Finally! She's asked the question! I'm not in the UK! I'm calling from your part of the world! Dad told me where you were and I thought I'd fly over and pay you a visit! He's worried.' Lily's voice was suddenly pious. 'So I offered to check and make sure you're okay.'

'You're…*here*?' Ellie looked around her wildly as though anticipating a dramatic entrance from her sister via a cupboard.

'Just making sure you're not in a pickle! You have to admit it's not every day you get engaged! I know what Dad said, that it's all a load of rubbish, but still…what are sisters for if not to look out for one another? Anyway, Els, I'm running out of juice on my cell phone, so text me the address, would you? I'll take a taxi.'

Put in a position from which there seemed to be no easy way out, Ellie gave Lily the address. Her head was swimming, though. How long would it take her sister to hit the villa? How long did she intend to stay? As expected, there was no shame on Lily's part when it came to showing up uninvited at a stranger's house.

Because there would be an agenda.

If, once upon a time, her sister had nabbed the guy Ellie had been seeing just for the hell of it, then what might her intentions be when it came to a man like Luca, the most eligible man on the planet?

Only now did Ellie realise that she had actually begun to give house room to Luca's crazy proposal. She might have laughed at his preposterous marriage proposal but it had set up a series of tantalising scenarios. Lily showing up on the doorstep? It didn't bear thinking about.

Five minutes later, Ellie was staring at the phone and feeling as though she'd been run over by an HGV.

'Family?' Luca encouraged.

'My sister.' She heard a note of dismay creep into her voice and she summoned up a smile from somewhere. 'Guess what? She's here, right here, a taxi ride away, and she's coming to visit. I can't wait to see her. It's been months and months...'

'Ah, the famous sister you think is right up my alley.'

Ellie stiffened and remained silent. He extended a glass of wine to her and she swallowed it in one gulp.

'Dutch courage?' he murmured with keen interest, and Ellie blushed.

'Thirsty.'

'For wine. Interesting. Normally a glass of water does the trick when it comes to quenching thirst. You should sit down. You're looking a little green round the gills.'

'I should tell you that she knows about the...er...fact that...well... I happened to tell Dad ages ago that if he read some silly nonsense about us being together then it was a complete lie and he wasn't to believe a word.'

'And now that there's an engagement story doing the rounds and your sister thinks that there's no substance to it...'

'Something like that.'

'And would she be right?'

Something wicked and daring nudged past the sudden onset of anxiety Lily's call had generated.

Wow. How dared her sister be so openly shocked that Ellie could actually be engaged to someone gorgeous, rich, exciting and *eligible*? How dared Lily take it as read that the engagement thing was obviously a sham?

And why should Ellie automatically begin surrendering at the thought of her sister coming along? Why should she just lie down and wave a white flag simply because she knew that Lily would get the guy, as she always did?

Ellie was suddenly sick of all the insecurities she always seemed to have to put to bed whenever Lily was around.

Luca had given her confidence she hadn't known she possessed—why should she dump it all because Lily was coming out here on a fact-finding operation? A so-called fact-finding mission because sisters had to look out for one another. Since when had Lily ever played by those rules?

For the first time in her life, Ellie had done the unthinkable and stopped playing it safe. And it felt good.

'We could take a chance.' She threw caution to the wind along with her long list of pros and cons.

Engagements didn't always lead to weddings… They *could* take a chance. So Luca didn't love her, but she could have some stolen time to try and make herself indispensable to him and, if that was through Jake, then so be it.

She couldn't bear the thought of never seeing him again and why kid herself that that was something she would be able to handle?

Luca smiled a slow, lazy, satisfied smile and drew her towards him. Then he kissed her and all the doubts she had had about this wild decision flew out of her head with a whoosh. She reached up to link her hands around his neck and kissed him back with hunger and abandon.

Was she doing the right thing? This felt like a little rebellion but it also felt good. She couldn't suffocate that little sliver of hope that what she and Luca had cultivated over the weeks would be strong enough to counter the Lily effect.

She was trembling as her slight body pressed against his rock-hard erection.

For some reason, that phone call had galvanised her into accepting his proposal and Luca wasn't going to question it.

'You're making the right decision,' he murmured, drawing back to look at her, while gently sifting his fingers through her short hair.

'You *would* say that.' Ellie's voice was breathless and teasing. 'If someone agrees with you, then you're always going to think that they're making the right decision.'

Luca grinned. 'But I'm always right,' he said piously, making her smile, relax and momentarily forget the fact that her sister was heading towards her at speed, a force to contend with.

'Stop looking so anxious,' he counselled, kissing her again and pulling her against him.

'My sister has always had that effect on me,' Ellie confessed, resting her head in the crook of his neck.

'Makes you anxious? Charming.'

'Charming,' Ellie muttered inaudibly, 'is exactly how you'll probably end up describing her.'

'Come again?'

'Nothing.' She smiled up at him and squashed the thread of apprehension running through her. 'Anyway.' She stepped back and tidied herself and decided that some more wine was necessary. 'She'll be here shortly...'

But it was another twenty-five minutes before the doorbell went. Ellie dashed out while Luca waited in the kitchen, intensely curious to see what the sea had decided to wash up.

He had a rough idea of what to expect and he wasn't disappointed.

'Luca, this is my sister, Lily.'

Ellie watched the interplay with eagle eyes and, to Luca's credit, if he was impressed then he wasn't showing it.

She felt an uncharitable spurt of satisfaction because Lily, just his type, was even more stunning after months spent in the Californian sunshine.

She had been toasted golden-brown and her long white-blonde hair fell in a glossy curtain down her back. She was dressed in next to nothing—a little crop top that rose to reveal her firm belly and the tattoo of a swallow just below her belly button, low-slung ripped jeans that seemed designed to show off legs that went on for ever, and flip-flops.

Plus she was in full flirtatious mode, talking quickly with lots of engaging hand gestures, and using her body language to suggest that what he could see was only the tip of the iceberg.

Ellie had seen her sister in action a thousand times but her heart was still thudding painfully because this was the first time she was really sickened at what might happen if she weaved her magic charm and sucked Luca in with those big, blue eyes.

'You'd take to life over there like a duck to water,'

she was trilling as she tossed her blonde mane over one shoulder and made herself at home at the kitchen table. 'It's full of movers and shakers in the media world and you'd really fit in. Have you ever thought about making a movie? I have a lot of connections...not that you'd need any!' She dimpled a smile, batted her lashes and pouted. 'I know you've gone out with a number of celebs.'

'Not my thing,' Luca responded politely.

'You could even be an actor.' Lily tilted her head to one side and looked at Luca narrowly while, standing to the side, Ellie gritted her teeth. 'You have just the sort of dashing, dark looks. Such a catch, Els!' She winked, making sure that Luca saw that wink, making sure he knew that she knew that it was all an act.

'I'm going to catch up on some work.' Luca was making for the door. 'Give you two time to catch up.'

Ellie hovered, but in the end didn't say anything, because she was too busy agonising over her thoughts. She'd just agreed to his proposal but was already beginning to see the holes in it. Here in Spain, in this bubble, it was easy to forget the outside world. Lily had wafted through the door, bringing that outside world in with her, and Ellie questioned whether, once they were back in London, Luca would be able to resist the charm offensive of all those beautiful Lily lookalikes who flocked around him. Playing happy families because of his godson might begin to look a little less alluring.

'He is *gorgeous.*'

Startled out of her introspection, Ellie moved to top up her sister's glass and asked politely, 'Have you eaten, Lily? I could fix you something.'

'Ever the home maker. No thanks. Dieting.' She patted her stomach. 'You wouldn't believe the competition out there.'

'But it's going well? You've barely mentioned what you've been up to.' *Too busy flirting with Luca.*

Lily brushed aside the show of interest and strolled through the kitchen, taking everything in. 'Course it's going well. Why wouldn't it be? Anyway, I would have helped out with Dad, you know that, but it was a bad time financially for me just then. You have to invest to create and just then I'd sunk quite a bit into portfolios and the like. You know how it is.'

Ellie had no idea.

'But, doesn't matter now anyway! Tell me all about the hunk. I know you're just here for the kid but you two must, you know, socialise now and again… Fill me in.'

Ellie began opening cupboards, fetching stuff from the fridge, ignoring her sister and the avid curiosity etched on her lovely face.

Lily hadn't come to make sure everything was okay. She had come because curiosity had got the better of her. How had the sister who had always faded into the background suddenly found herself in a position where she was being written about in a gossip column? Was there any truth behind that engagement story? Surely not?

'When was the last time you ate?' She knew that she was clinging to her composure by a thread, fighting against habits of a lifetime which compelled her to fade into the background.

Because she *had* accepted Luca's proposal, hadn't she? She really *was* going to have a ring on her finger, wasn't she?

Admittedly, it wasn't actually there yet, and would probably not materialise now that Luca had been given a tantalising glimpse of the sort of thing he'd been missing out on ever since he had become a hermit living in a villa in the middle of nowhere, but still...

In a flash, Ellie knew that Lily would make a pass at Luca without a second's thought.

Just as she had done with Paul.

Lily would make a pass at Luca because he was the sort of man she had spent her entire adult life trying to get. He was rich, he was powerful, he was good-looking. He was the kind of man that other people hung around, looked up to and tried to be friends with.

He was, in short, the ultimate catch.

'I told you, Ellie, I'm not hungry. Stop fussing and sit and tell me about Luca. Is he single? I mean, really? Or is there some celeb stashed away somewhere waiting in the wings until this whole stupid engagement nonsense blows over?'

'Why do you ask?' Ellie's voice was tight as she sat in front of an unappetising omelette and dug into it, making sure not to look at Lily.

'Okay, tell me if you're all right with this—and I'm sure you will be—but if he isn't taken then I might, you know...'

'No, explain.'

'Well, he's pretty fabulous, and I'm not going out with anyone at the moment. So many gays out there, you wouldn't believe, and most of the guys I meet are a lot more into themselves than they are into me. None of them can walk past a mirror without crashing into it.'

'I'm sorry to hear that,' Ellie said with genuine sympathy because, like a plant needed nutrients, Lily needed the adoration of men to thrive.

This was the first chink in that coat of armour her self-confident sister always presented to the world.

Which didn't mean that Ellie was going to let herself fall right back into the status quo, fading into the background and accepting that her sister would always get what she wanted because of how she looked.

'Well.' She sighed and pushed her plate away from her. She linked her fingers on the table, then looked gravely yet kindly at her sister. 'I hate to be the bearer of bad tidings, Lily, but as matter of fact Luca is most definitely taken.'

'Is he?' Lily narrowed her eyes and Ellie could see her mentally working out how she could trump the opposition.

'He is. By me.'

'You're having a laugh, Els.'

'I'm not. The fact is…we're engaged. For real.' Empowered, she sat back and cocked her head to the side, as though deciding how much to tell and how much to withhold. Her heart was hammering inside her chest. Her skin was clammy at the enormous leap into the unknown she was taking. 'Okay, I admit when that story first broke about us seeing one another it was all a load of bunkum. Luca had taken me to a country pub to discuss Jake, and his ex had shown up and seen us together and then decided to wreak a little havoc.'

'I can't believe this.' Lily was flabbergasted. Ellie could have told her that the sky was falling in and she wouldn't have received a more stunned reaction.

'And then there was that business in the tabloids about an engagement. By then—and this is just between the two of us—Luca and I were…well…*you know…*'

'Sleeping together?'

'Falling in love. Truly, madly and deeply. I don't know how it happened, but I tell you what, it's the most wonderful thing I've ever felt in my life.' She could feel herself welling up. Lily might think she was welling up with tears of joy. Ellie knew that she was welling up because the picture she was painting was half-true and she wished that it was all true.

'He's terrific, Lily. He comes across as arrogant at first, but as soon as you get to know him you see that there's so much more to him than meets the eye. He's smart, funny, thoughtful, and incredibly frustrating sometimes, but I don't think I could love anyone as much as I love Luca.'

'And he feels the same way about you?'

'Why else would he have asked me to marry him?' Ellie neatly evaded a direct answer to that question.

'I don't see a ring on your finger.'

'That's because he wants to take me to his jeweller's in London when we get back. Don't forget, this wasn't planned. I mean, it's taken both of us by surprise. But, when love strikes, what can a person do?'

She laughed gaily, stood up to take her dishes to the sink, simultaneously avoiding her sister's sharp, probing eyes, and heard a deep, dark, velvety and very familiar drawl behind her.

'What indeed?'

Ellie swung round, almost dropping the plate and glass because her hands were suddenly as slippery as if they were coated in oil.

Her mouth fell open and colour rushed to her cheeks in a tidal wave of bright red.

'Luca!'

'My darling.' Luca looked at Lily whilst strolling

across to wrap his arms around Ellie, before dipping to kiss her on the side of her mouth. 'I'm very glad you listened to me and told your sister about us.'

He turned and pulled Ellie towards him so that he was standing with his back to the kitchen counter with Ellie in front, her back against his stomach, his hands draped loosely over her shoulders.

'She wanted to break it to her dad at the same time, put paid to all those pesky rumours doing the rounds. Yes, it may have been a piece of malice on the part of my ex coming up with that story, but how was she to know that the engagement she'd fabricated would turn out to be the real deal?'

Lily made a strangled sound and rose to her feet, suddenly looking very young and vulnerable in her confusion.

'So, just for the record,' Luca said without batting an eye, 'I'm not up for grabs.'

'I… Well, of course…'

'And I know you wouldn't be so tactless as to make a pass at the man your sister intends to marry, but if you do you should know that I wouldn't take to it kindly.'

'I wouldn't dream of… No… Well, congratulations to both of you. I'll… I'm off to sleep and I'll leave first thing in the morning!'

'I'll make sure there's a taxi waiting for you. You can have full use of my private jet. Say eight-thirty tomorrow morning?'

The silence that settled as Lily shut the door behind her could have been cut with a knife.

Luca slowly turned Ellie round to face him.

'Well, well, well…'

CHAPTER TEN

ELLIE CATAPULTED HERSELF out of his arms and spun round to face him, arms folded defiantly, eyes blazing.

'How long have you been standing outside that kitchen door *eavesdropping*? Do you think that listening to other people's conversations is *acceptable*? Because *I don't*!'

'Totally unacceptable,' Luca conceded smoothly. 'But I couldn't resist once your sister started asking whether I was open territory. I was curious to see where the conversation was going to go.'

'Lily's always thought that she could do what she wanted when it came to guys,' Ellie gritted stiffly. 'I was just being *human* when I decided to show her that there were limits!'

Luca poured himself a long glass of water then pulled up a kitchen chair and sat down. 'Let's talk.'

'Let's not.'

'Forget about those declarations of love for a minute. I want to ask you about your sister.'

'Why?'

'Ellie, stop inching towards the door. We either talk here or we talk in the bedroom but we're going to talk.'

'Isn't that a bit dangerous, Luca?' Ellie threw back at him. She was frantically trying to work out what, exactly, she had said. Lots of incriminating stuff. She'd poured her heart out to Lily, blissfully unaware that the wretched man was lurking outside the door with a glass pressed against it, hearing every word.

'What do you mean?'

'*Talking*. Isn't *talking* dangerous for someone who likes keeping it superficial? For someone who gets into a panic if there's a woman in the kitchen with a frying pan in her hand and a recipe book on the counter? Isn't that why this *arrangement* of ours is so convenient for you, because it bypasses all that nasty domestic stuff you feel trapped by?'

'If we get married, then I'm assuming you'll have a frying pan in your hand and a recipe book on the counter from time to time. Did you think that your sister was my type because of the way she looked? And for God's sake, stop hovering! Sit down.'

'Stop yelling at me,' Ellie muttered, shifting to sit, mostly because her legs were beginning to feel wobbly.

He was tying her in knots. He didn't do love and he didn't do domestic. What he did was *business arrangement; no emotional ties, thanks very much*. So why wasn't he peeved at the thought of her doing something such as cooking for him? Wasn't he suspicious that that might be the start of something unfortunate?

She looked at him in defiant silence.

'Answer my question.'

'Of course I thought that! She's blonde and beautiful and she's not backward at coming forward!'

'I'm surprised you didn't give her the green light to strut her stuff for me,' Luca said drily, and Ellie reddened. 'It crossed your mind, didn't it?' He looked at her narrowly, his dark eyes cooling by several degrees, and she shook her head.

She felt drained. So what was she going to do now? How was she going to handle this situation? Lie? Pretend? She was fed up pretending.

If he was so keen for them to talk, then talk she would, and she was going to tell him the truth—how she felt, when she'd started feeling what she felt, what she really wanted out of any relationship with him.

If he didn't like it, then he would be free to walk away.

She'd been stupid to buy into the notion that marrying him was going to be the better option because she would be able to indulge her love for him and then maybe, just maybe, he might start returning some of that love.

This arrangement had been formulated with Jake in mind. If Luca had any feelings for her at all, then they largely revolved around feeling *turned on* because he fancied her, and that didn't count.

Okay, so maybe he liked her well enough, but that wasn't love, was it?

Was she really going to be satisfied with him *liking her well enough*?

Wouldn't it be better for her, in the long term, to walk away and hope that one day she might meet a guy who could love and cherish her the way she deserved to be loved and cherished?

Yes!

'No,' Ellie told him truthfully. 'It really didn't occur to me. Or if it did, I barely registered that. Thing is… I had a boyfriend once. His name was Paul and I thought that it was the real deal. That was a couple of years ago. He was a good, solid guy. Really nice. Very caring.'

'Sounds deadly.'

Ellie frowned and realised that Paul, whilst ticking quite a few boxes, hadn't been a riveting match, especially when she compared him to Luca.

'He wasn't at all Lily's type,' Ellie mused, gazing off into the distance. 'Lily always went for good-looking, solvent and hunky. But she turned her attention to Paul. I don't know if she did that to be mean, or if she did it unconsciously because flirting with guys just came as second nature to her. Anyway, whatever. He fell for her hook, line and sinker. One minute, he was talking about holidays and a life together with me. The next minute, he was drooling after my sister. So was I tempted to tell her to have a go with you, if that was what she wanted? No.'

'In fact, you decided to do just the opposite,' Luca murmured, expression veiled, and Ellie shrugged and looked away.

She now expected him gently but firmly to set her straight on what he had overheard. Probably tell her ruefully that there was no way he could fulfil the arrangement because he wasn't looking for what she wanted.

'I'm only human.'

'Has it always been like that?'

'Like what?'

'Living in your sister's shadow.'

'Pretty much. She had the looks and my mother cultivated that. She wanted Lily to succeed where she thought she had failed. My mother was a disappointed woman. She was very beautiful, and I think she thought that she deserved more in life than to be married to my dad, who was just an ordinary guy.'

'An unhappy marriage,' Luca murmured. 'And yet you still have all those romantic notions about love and marriage.'

'What's wrong with that? Because my parents didn't have a good marriage, doesn't mean that good marriages don't exist.'

'Did you get a kick out of telling your sister that the engagement was for real?'

Ellie blushed and said grudgingly, 'Huge.'

'Bigger question coming here. Did you mean any of it?'

Ellie looked at him. This was it. Crossroads time. She had a choice. The truth would free her, whatever the outcome, whether he fled the scene in terror or not. But a little white lie was so much more compelling...

She would be able to clear off with her pride intact and her head held high. She could laugh gaily and tell him that *of course, she hadn't meant a word of it!* He'd laid down the rules of the game and he would be relieved that she had stuck to them.

'All of it.' Her eyes were clear and steady, and she took a deep breath and forced herself not to look away. 'Every last word. I'm sorry. You warned me enough times about keeping emotions out of this, and I wish I could have done that, but I couldn't.'

Ellie wished he would say something. Anything, really. But he just sat there, very, very still, his dark eyes revealing nothing. Which meant that she had to play a guessing game, and she hated that.

However, now that she had started, she felt compelled to carry on and lay herself bare.

'I'm in love with you. I know you never signed up for that, and I know I probably shouldn't be telling you this because you're the guy who's locked his heart away somewhere and thrown away the key, but there you go. I'm in love with you. I don't know why or how or when

I fell in love with you. I wish I could be noble and say that I agreed to the whole engagement thing because I thought Jake would benefit from having both of us on the scene, and I suppose there was a bit of me that was persuaded by that argument, but truthfully? I wanted to do something out of the box just for once in my life and I also thought that, if we did end up together, I might stand a chance of somehow getting under your skin.'

'I have never let any woman get under my skin.'

Ellie cringed, even though he wasn't exactly saying anything she didn't already know.

'I know, but you've never been engaged to anyone before, have you?' she threw at him. 'Or have you?'

'Never been stupid enough.'

'Why are you so cold?' She looked away. Her skin was prickling, her heart was beating so hard she felt in danger of passing out, her mouth was dry and her head was throbbing.

'Practical.'

'No, it's not *practical*, Luca! Packing sunblock when you go on holiday to a hot country is *practical*! Being ice-cold and having no emotions…' She gazed at him helplessly.

'I saw what my mother's death did to my father,' Luca grated. 'I think I've told you this already.'

'Doesn't mean I agree with you!'

'He never recovered. You'd have to be a fool to let yourself feel so strongly for another human being that you end up losing your way if something happens to them! And after she died? Let's not forget that I witnessed first-hand how callous and greedy women could be when it came to money. Hell, I was just a teenager at the time, but there were some who didn't think twice about trying it on with me when their advances hit a dead end with my father!'

'You'd rather spend the rest of your life being lonely than take a chance?' Ellie was pleading. She could hear it in her voice and it shamed her.

'I've never been lonely in my life.'

'I'm not talking about having a woman in your bed! I'm talking about having a woman in your heart!'

'I'll take my chances on being just fine without that complication.'

'Right.' She leapt to her feet. Tears were stinging the back of her eyes but there was no way that she was going to let him see her break down in front of him. 'I think it's a good time for me to head upstairs.'

'Ellie...'

'Don't say anything else, Luca.' She spun round on her heels and headed straight for the kitchen door. No way was she going to get up early tomorrow to bid a fond fare-well to her sister. She'd be seeing her soon enough, and how Lily was going to have a bit of fun at her expense.

Strangely, Ellie didn't care.

She couldn't hurt worse than she was hurting right now.

She had become accustomed to sleeping with Luca. She almost went to his bedroom through force of habit. Instead, she swerved and quietly let herself into her own bedroom.

Her suitcase was stuffed in the wardrobe and she pulled it out and opened it. When she had packed to come over, she had been filled with excitement and trepi-dation. It had felt like the greatest adventure of her life.

Now, she looked at that suitcase and knew that this

time, when she was packing it, she would be filled with misery.

She had no idea how long she'd been stuffing clothes into the case, but the knock on the door carried the impact of a hand grenade because she knew who it was going to be. Lily might have scuttled out of the kitchen when faced with Luca, but her curiosity would be boundless, and Ellie knew that she probably would have heard her coming up the stairs.

She hurriedly flung the suitcase into the wardrobe and composed herself into the image of a woman in love who, mysteriously, was not sharing a bedroom with the guy she was supposedly all set to marry.

She was smiling as she pulled open the door. It was a rictus smile but it was the best she could muster given the circumstances.

She expected Lily with a list of questions.

She got Luca.

She didn't budge.

'Let me in, Ellie.'

'Go away.'

'What are you doing?' He peered around her and Ellie followed his gaze to the half-open wardrobe.

'Packing.'

'Let me in.' Luca shifted uneasily, raked his fingers through his hair. 'Please. I... I've been a fool, Ellie.'

'Really?' Her voice was the temperature of ice. 'I thought that was my terrain.'

'I was a fool,' Luca muttered with low urgency, 'to think that I could live without you.'

Their eyes tangled and Ellie glared at him.

'Right. And I'm supposed to believe that?'

'I don't want to have this conversation with you out

here.' He shuffled when she didn't say anything. 'I've never begged for anything in my life. I'm not sure I'd know how but, if you don't let me in, then I'm going to have to give it a go.'

Ellie stood aside with visible reluctance and, as soon as he was in the bedroom and the door was shut, she removed herself to the broad window sill and perched against it with her arms folded, staring at him.

Undeterred, Luca positioned himself right next to her. 'You told me you loved me.'

'I don't want to be reminded of that,' Ellie muttered viciously.

'You told me that you loved me and I did what came naturally to me. I turned away. It's the way I've been programmed. My life was as placid as a lake until you swept in like a whirlwind, breathing brimstone and fire. You didn't care what I thought. You said whatever you wanted to say and I had no idea how addictive that would become.'

'If you're saying all that to butter me up into re-considering the engagement thing for Jake's sake, then forget it.'

'If I were terrified of being with a woman who loved me, then there's no way I would be considering any engagement, Jake or no Jake.'

'Just say what you have to say, Luca.' Hope was beginning to send out alarming tendrils and, before they became too profuse, Ellie wanted him to spit it out.

'I thought that there was strength in building an ivory tower around myself,' he said quietly. 'I was protected and no one had ever been able to breach my ramparts. And then along you came and you managed to find a way through within seconds. I asked you to come out here because I needed you to be here for Jake—but where I would have been cautious about having any woman around, sharing my space for that length of time and in that capacity, with you I felt…comfortable.'

'Comfortable.' Why did that word sound so…*dull and boring*?

Luca laughed. 'It's a compliment, Ellie. It's also something that should have alerted me to the fact that you weren't just different from the women I've known. It should have alerted me to the fact that I was falling for you.'

'Falling for me…? Is that why you listened to me pour my heart out and then sent me on my way?'

'Like I said, I responded on cue. A lifetime of telling myself that love was the one thing I didn't do swung into action. I'd say I was shocked by what you said, but in fact I wasn't. I'd say I felt trapped, but no, that would be a lie as well. As soon as you walked out of the kitchen, I felt sick.'

'But you never let on…'

'I didn't have it in me and, anyway, I didn't recognise the signposts because I'd never walked down that road before and I'd never wanted to. Honestly, I didn't get the appeal,' he confessed with wrenching honesty. 'You were nothing like what I was used to and, to start with, I just figured that you were different, that you were a tonic for my jaded palate, but then we slept together and you blew me away.'

'You blew me away, too.' Ellie rested her hand on his chest and felt the fast beating of his heart. 'I guess I was as rigid in what I wanted as you were. I guess some of that was down to my own insecurities. If I didn't punch above my weight then I would never be let down. Lily is the one who gets the good-looking guys, and I told myself that that was fine because I wasn't attracted to that sort anyway. When I met you, you were the last person I thought I could ever have a connection with.'

'I'll bet.' Luca smiled crookedly. He covered her hand with his, lifted it to his lips and dropped a kiss on her palm. 'We didn't exactly meet in circumstances that cast a glowing halo around me, did we? I can only imagine what you were thinking. Arrogant bastard, too much money, runaway kid...'

'But I still couldn't take my eyes off you, Luca. You mesmerised me and I hated it. It's like I wasn't really alive until you came along and then, boom, life was Technicolor-bright.' She sighed. 'You made me face all the old insecurities and come to terms with them, and finally you made me overcome them.'

'And you, my darling, made me realise that life isn't worth living unless you're prepared to take chances.' He swept her off her feet, carried her to the bed and gently deposited her as though she was as fragile as porcelain. Then he stood back and looked at her for long minutes before sliding into bed next to her and immediately curving her towards him so that their bodies were pressed against one another.

'So...can I ask you that question once again?'

'What question?' As if she didn't know. Ellie squirmed against him, fingers itching to rip his clothes off.

'Will you marry me? For real? Because I can't contemplate a life without you. I want you to be there for me, for Jake and for all the kids we're going to have together. I love you, *querida*, now and for ever...'

'How,' Ellie laughed, 'is a girl supposed to say no to a proposal like that?'

* * *

It was a fairy-tale story for avid reporters and, for the first time in his life, Luca actually gave them what they wanted because he was just so proud to show off the woman who was going to be his wife.

They were married without fanfare in the local church in the village where Ellie had grown up although several days later, and before they departed on their honeymoon to the Maldives, they threw a bash worthy of any A-lister to celebrate their union.

And not only were her father and all her friends in attendance, but so was her sister.

She and Lily had had a long talk when they had finally met up back in the UK and Ellie had been startled to learn that for every insecurity she had had, her sister likewise had her own.

'You were so bright,' Lily had admitted. 'I could never get higher than a C but you were a straight-A student and sometimes it felt as though Dad only had eyes for you. I could slog my guts out and I knew I'd still never be able to make it to university. It was easier in the end to just let Mum have her way and, you know... I got accustomed to making the most of my looks. But your brains will last for ever. My looks won't and I know that.'

Then it had all come out in an outpouring of emotion that had left Ellie feeling closer to her sister than she had in a very long time.

Lily had gone to seek fame and fortune but instead she had just joined the quagmire of hopefuls all out there looking for the same thing. She'd become just one of many pretty faces trying to clamber up the same tree.

'I ran out of money,' she'd admitted. 'That's why I couldn't send any over for Dad. I had none. I was waitressing by night and then going round and round, looking for agents, trying to get hold of connections. Everyone was doing the same thing. You wouldn't believe what it's like...'

The steps Jake had made in forming a bond with Luca had been quite remarkable. The memories of his parents would never leave him; Ellie knew that. But he was no longer the lost child who had felt the need to run as fast and as far as he could from a place he didn't like.

And the Maldives...

Ellie looked at the wedding band on her finger and smiled. Sitting out here, with an orange sunset dropping over sea that was as calm as a lake, she almost had to pinch herself that she wasn't playing the lead role in a dream, one from which she would cruelly awaken at any minute.

Back in England, Jake was with her father and her sister, who had given up dreams of stardom and was slowly realising that there was a lot to be said for ordinary.

Here... She swivelled around and absorbed the stunning scenery. Rich foliage was bathed in a mellow light cast by strings of lanterns that zip-lined through the trees and shivered and twinkled in the lazy evening breeze. The sound of invisible insects was a background orchestra of soothing sounds. Ahead, the dark sea was as flat as glass. It was hard to believe that, as soon as dawn broke, that black body of smooth water would become turquoise and alive with colourful fish.

The place was paradise but what made it really special was the fact that she was here with her husband.

She heard Luca behind her and turned around, smiling and already tingling because he never failed to impress her. He was just so spectacular, prowling with the grace and strength of a panther. And hers! She felt a hot flare of possessiveness.

Their two-bedroom cabin was the height of luxury and so secluded that they could practically walk around naked without fear of being seen. But right now, fresh from a shower, he had a towel slung low on his lean hips.

His hair was still damp and he raked his fingers through it then stood behind her before inclining to slip his hands underneath the silk strappy dress, finding her bare breasts and gently massaging them.

Ellie squirmed and twisted round then knelt on the chair so that she could hold his face in her hands and kiss him.

'Sometimes I can't believe it's possible to be so happy,' she murmured and Luca smiled.

'Nor can I,' he admitted. He sauntered round to sit next to her on the padded two-seater on the wooden deck of their cabin.

'You were the man who felt claustrophobic at the thought of a woman cooking for you,' she teased, holding his hand and linking her fingers through his. 'Remember?'

'How could I forget when you got me an apron saying "domesticated and proud of it" to show me the error of my ways?'

'You never wear that apron.' She sighed, smiling.

'I wouldn't want to invade your territory. I know you like cooking for me so why spoil your fun?'

Ellie burst out laughing. He didn't wear the apron but he could cook a mean steak.

'I look back at the man I used to be, afraid of letting go in case I got hurt, and I marvel that I could ever have been so short-sighted. Although, maybe I was just waiting for the right woman to come along and show me the error of my ways...' He pulled her towards him and kissed the tip of her nose, then covered her mouth with his, stroking her rib cage and firing her up so that she just wanted to haul him back into the cabin so that she could have her wicked way with him.

'And now that we're married,' he continued with a smile in his voice, 'maybe it's time we took this to the next level...'

'Next level?'

'I think it's time for Jake to have a sibling, don't you?' He chuckled and then swung round the chair so that he could hoist her into his arms, caveman style, carry her back into the cabin and into the bedroom with its four-poster bed. 'And why put off for tomorrow what can be done today?' His grin was wicked as she began stripping off the slip of a dress under which she was completely naked.

'Just today?' she teased.

'Today,' Luca said with tenderness, 'tomorrow and every day for the rest our lives.'

* * * * *

MILLS & BOON

Coming next month

CLAIMING MY UNTOUCHED MISTRESS
Heidi Rice

'Your sister told me exactly how deep your financial troubles go,' I said. 'I have a possible solution.'

'What is it?' Edie said, desperation plain on her face.

'Would you consider working for me?' I asked.

'You're... You're offering me a job?'

She sounded so surprised, I found my lips curving in amusement again.

'As it happens, I am hosting an event at my new estate near Nice at the end of the month. I could use your skills as part of the team I'm putting together.'

'What exactly do you need me to do?' she said, her eagerness a sop to my ego.

'The guests I am inviting are some of the world's most powerful businessmen and women.' I outlined the job. 'They have all shown an interest in investing in the expansion of the Allegri brand. The event is a way of assessing their suitability as investors. As part of the week, I will be offering some recreational poker events. These people are highly competitive and they enjoy games of chance. What they don't know is that how they play poker tells me a great deal more about their personalities and their business acumen—and whether we will be compatible—than a simple profit and loss portfolio of their companies. But I find that successful people, no matter how competitive they are, are also smart enough to know that they cannot best me at a poker table. So I need someone who does not intimidate them, but who can observe how they play and make those assessments for me.' I kept my eyes on her reaction, surprised myself by how much I wanted her to say yes.

My attraction to her might be unexpected, but I had spent a lifetime living by my wits and never doubting my instincts. When I had originally considered giving her a hosting position I'd been aware of the possible fringe benefits for both of us and I didn't see why that should change. She had made it very clear she was more than happy to blur the lines between employer and lover, and all her responses made it equally clear she desired me as much as I desired her.

'I'll pay you four thousand euros for the fortnight,' I said, to make her position clear. This was a genuine job, and a job she would be very good at. 'Joe can brief you on each of the participants—and what I need to know about them. If you do a good enough job, and your skills prove as useful as I'm expecting them to be, I would consider offering you a probationary position.'

She blinked several times, her skin now flushed a dark pink. But didn't say anything.

'So do you want the job?' I asked, letting my impatience show, annoyed by the strange feeling of anticipation. Why should it matter to me if she declined my offer?

'Yes, yes,' she said. 'I'll take the job.'

Continue reading
CLAIMING MY UNTOUCHED MISTRESS
Heidi Rice

Available next month
www.millsandboon.co.uk

LET'S TALK
Romance

For exclusive extracts, competitions
and special offers, find us online:

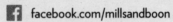 facebook.com/millsandboon

@MillsandBoon

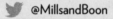 @MillsandBoonUK

Get in touch on 01413 063232

For all the latest titles coming soon, visit
millsandboon.co.uk/nextmonth

COMING SOON!

We really hope you enjoyed reading this book. If you're looking for more romance, be sure to head to the shops when new books are available on

Thursday 7th March

To see which titles are coming soon, please visit

millsandboon.co.uk/nextmonth